Ring Truth

By Michael Patterson and available from
Crescent Books Publishing:

Playing at Murder
Deadly Retribution
Ring of Truth

Ring of Truth

Michael Patterson

Crescent books

Copyright © 2015 Mike Patterson

All rights reserved. No part of this publication may be reproduced or transmitted in any form or by any means, electronic or mechanical including photocopying, recording or any information storage or retrieval system, without prior permission in writing from the publisher.

First published in the United Kingdom in 2015 by
Crescent Books Publishing

ISBN 978-0-9569798-4-1

Produced by
The Choir Press, Gloucester

For my wife Anji, daughter Holly and son Sam.

Chapter 1

'I imagine, sir, you are really pleased that you didn't actually retire,' said Milner.

'I'm not sure I understand what you're saying,' replied DCI Tom Stone.

Acting Detective Sergeant Milner had worked with DCI Stone long enough to recognise, just by the tone of his voice, when he was slightly annoyed, and so, not for the first time, an alarm bell suddenly started to ring in his head. But, having learnt through his past mistakes, Milner adjusted his next comment accordingly. So in as matter-of-fact a way as possible he said, 'What I meant was, if you had decided to take retirement you would not have been involved in everything which has happened over the past year.'

Tom didn't immediately reply. Instead he took a sip of his red wine, and there followed what seemed to Milner, at least, an uncomfortably long silence. This simply reinforced his earlier concern. Just as Milner was about to break the silence, Tom spoke.

'Milner, first of all, I didn't realise that you were privy to my personal plans.' He paused momentarily before adding, 'What's more, I certainly don't remember discussing any impending retirement or, in fact, anything to do with my personal life with you. Or am I getting so senile, in my old age, that I just can't remember any more?'

'Sorry, sir. I thought that you had mentioned it to me. I must have been mistaken,' replied Milner, somewhat defensively, although, rather wisely, not adding that DCI Stone's impending retirement had once been the talk of the station.

DCI Stone, now getting into his stride, continued. 'And there are a couple of other things. To begin with, if I had retired Pauline Jones would almost certainly not now be dead and, secondly, I would not have been accused of her murder. Being accused of deliberately killing another human being is not something I would recommend. Retired or not retired.'

For the second time within a couple of minutes, Milner felt a bit foolish. Tom, sensing this, realised, not for the first time in his dealings with Milner, that he had been a touch too hostile in his reply, and so felt a small pang of guilt. When he next spoke his tone was much more conciliatory. 'I apologise for that. I know you just meant you were pleased for me. It's just that sometimes you have to see things from all sides, not just the most obvious one.'

Milner couldn't look directly at Tom. Instead he took a sip of his drink, although in his case it was mineral water. There remained an uneasy silence.

'Look,' continued Tom. 'This is supposed to be a party. Let's try and enjoy ourselves tonight. No talking shop.' He paused for a while and then added, 'Agreed?'

'Agreed,' answered Milner, although not with any great enthusiasm.

This wasn't lost on Tom and, just as he was about to say something else, he was interrupted.

'So, how's the birthday boy? Have you recovered yet from the shock of your surprise party?' said Mary. They had been in a relationship for just under a year now and it was she who had arranged his surprise party. Tom wasn't a party type of person, and he definitely didn't like surprises. Clearly, there were many things which she still had to learn about him.

She was the more outgoing of the two. Not surprising really, given that amateur dramatics was one of the great passions in her life. Whilst his natural default position was to err on the let's-get-on-with-this-conversation side of life, she, by comparison, was naturally easier with the lighter, more expressive and social side of life. This was exemplified by her long-standing membership of the North-West Surrey Players Amateur Dramatic Society. Whilst Tom would not normally have any great enthusiasm for this, to his great surprise, he had found himself taking a much keener interest since he had met her and had even attended one of her productions.

She was a couple of years younger than him, and had been widowed now for over five years. She had two grown-up sons, Greg and Aaron, and he was about to meet them tonight for the first time. So, yet another surprise for him to look forward to!

'Well,' replied Tom, trying, not too convincingly, to make his words seem as enthusiastic as possible, 'you certainly managed to keep it a secret. It must have taken you a long time to get it all organised.'

'Not really,' replied Mary, turning her head to look directly at Milner. 'David here did most of the work. Well, at least when it came to liaising with your colleagues. Anyway, a birthday, at your age, is worth a party.'

'Thanks very much for reminding me,' Tom answered, before adding, more to himself than to anyone in particular, 'Just what I wanted to hear.' He then turned to face Milner. 'So you were involved in this, were you, *Milner?*' he asked, deliberately emphasising his surname.

Milner knew that this could now go one of two ways. Either DCI Stone would be impressed that he had been able to make the arrangements without him knowing about it, or, and his experience told him this was the more likely outcome, he would be annoyed that all of this had been done without his knowledge. Actually, without his realising it, there was a third potential outcome. In this particular case, Tom's aversion to surprises was compounded by the fact that his well-developed antennae had clearly not been working, otherwise he would have realised that something was happening. For Tom, this was possibly the most worrying scenario.

Milner considered saying how it was Mary who had asked him to do it and, therefore, he didn't feel as though he could refuse. After all, Mary was his boss and mentor's partner. But that wasn't his natural style and so, on the basis that attack sometimes is the best form of defence, and feeling slightly emboldened by Mary's earlier introduction, he simply said, 'That's right. I thought, given everything which you had been through recently, it was the least I could do.'

His strategy appeared, on the surface at least, to have worked as Tom replied, 'Thank you. It was very good of you. And thoughtful.' He then added, 'And, incidentally, congratulations for keeping it so secret. Very impressive.'

Milner didn't respond, although his face did suddenly develop a slightly quizzical expression. He still wasn't used to compliments from DCI Stone, who had a reputation, well-deserved and honed over many years, for being very economical with his compliments.

'I hope you two weren't discussing police business,' said Mary, echoing Tom's earlier comment. 'I'm sure that can wait a bit longer.' Now looking at Tom, she added, with obvious enthusiasm, 'Greg and Aaron have just arrived. I can't wait to introduce you to them. They are really looking forward to meeting you.' With that, she grabbed hold of his hand and led him towards her two sons, who were standing together in a corner of the room.

'Tom,' she said, 'this is Greg and this is Aaron. I've told them so much about you.'

Tom held his hand out towards Greg, and having shaken his hand repeated the process with Aaron. 'Great to meet you both at last. Mary has told me about both of you as well. Anyway, thank you for coming tonight. I know that you have both travelled quite a distance to get here.'

It was Aaron who replied. 'That's not a problem. When Mum told us that you were having a party, and that we should come, we felt as though we couldn't say no.'

'I know what you mean,' answered Tom. 'I also always do what she tells me to do.'

This seemed to relax everyone as they all started to laugh.

Now it was Greg's turn to speak. 'Mum mentioned that you are a serving policeman but it seems that, since you two met, you've been very busy. I read about you in one of the nationals.' This was a reference to two very high-profile cases which had attracted extensive national media coverage, and in which Tom had been involved. 'Is police work always that exciting?'

Tom looked at Mary. 'Not really. It's a bit like buses. You can go for years without anything interesting and then a few come along at the same time.'

'From what I read, and what Mum has told me, there were a few dangerous moments,' added Aaron, slightly more seriously.

'A few,' replied Tom, 'but most police work is mainly investigative. Don't think what you see on television is normal.'

'I'm sure you are just being modest. It seemed quite dangerous to me,' he answered.

Suddenly a bit of tension had returned.

'Anyway, I think it's time for you to cut your cake,' said Mary, wanting to steer the conversation away from this particular topic.

Tom's heart sank when he heard this, although he tried very hard not to let his voice, or body language, betray his views on all cutting-of-the-cake ceremonies. 'I'll be there in a minute. I just want to get myself another drink,' he said, without adding something to the effect of how it might help him to get through the ordeal.

'Okay,' answered Mary, 'I'll see you over there.' She moved off towards the cake.

'Good to meet you both,' Tom said, once again shaking both of their hands. 'I'm sure we'll get the opportunity to speak again later in the evening.' He then added with a quiet laugh, 'I think I might need this drink.'

As he was refreshing his glass, Milner appeared alongside him.

'Milner, how long have we worked together?' Before Milner could reply, Tom answered his own question. 'Long enough for you to know how much I dislike surprises. Springing surprises is the prerogative of the senior officer. And the last time I checked I was still your senior.' He then spotted Mary beckoning to him to join her. To no one in particular, and with just a hint of foreboding in his voice, he said, 'Right, let's go and get this cake cut. I'm sure everyone here has been waiting for their piece of cake.'

With that he headed towards where Mary was standing. She already had the cake knife in her right hand. Tom suddenly thought that everyone would be expecting him to make a speech. As he was deciding what he should say, Mary suddenly spoke. 'Ladies and gentlemen, thank you very much for coming along tonight to Tom's birthday party. And thank you for keeping it such a surprise for him. I'm sure you know how much Tom loves surprises.' Everyone, but particularly his colleagues, immediately started to laugh. She then went on, 'It's great for me to be able to meet so many of his friends and colleagues here tonight.' She picked up the knife and handed it to Tom. 'Tom, if you could do the honours.'

As he started to cut the cake someone started to clap and, before long, the whole room had joined in. Whilst mildly embarrassing it also came as a welcome distraction. He decided not to make a speech.

Chapter 2

'I really enjoyed Saturday night,' said Milner. 'And it was also good to see Mary again.' It was the Monday morning after the birthday party, and Milner was standing in DCI Stone's office, a file under his arm and a plastic cup in each hand. 'I've brought you a cup of coffee,' he said, before placing it on Tom's desk. 'I'm afraid it's from the machine, but at least it's hot.'

Tom was still thinking about Milner's reference to Mary. He instinctively didn't like this recent overfamiliarity. He was from the old school. Business and pleasure should be kept, wherever possible, at arm's length. He had wanted to mention this to Mary, after she kept using Milner's Christian name, but had decided against it. He probably should have done the same with Milner but, instead, found himself saying, 'Milner, Saturday night was a one-off. I'm glad you had a good time and enjoyed yourself. But we are now back at work.' He took a sip of his coffee. The expression on his face immediately betrayed his thoughts on the quality. 'Okay. Let's make a start. What's been happening whilst we were all partying and eating birthday cake?'

There was a chair opposite Tom and so Milner, having placed his own cup on the table immediately in front of him, sat down and opened his file. 'Well, it looks like it was quite a busy weekend. The usual late-night fights. A few people arrested for dealing drugs, a few cars stolen and a couple of domestic burglaries. Oh, and I took a call from the pathologist, a Dr Panton. He asked if you could call him back regarding a post-mortem which he's just carried out.' He handed Tom a piece of paper. 'Here's his number.' He hesitated, giving DCI Stone the opportunity to ask any questions, or pass any comment, relating to anything he had just said. When none came, he continued. 'The most serious incident, however, and you might have seen this on television, as it was on all of the news programmes, was the recovery of a man's body from a house which had been ablaze. It looks like the house was being used to grow cannabis plants and either there was some sort of problem with the electrics, which caused the fire, or it was started deliberately. The fire investigation team are already on the case.'

Tom had indeed seen this on the news, although there had been no mention of the cannabis plants.

'Do we know who the dead man was?' he asked, forgetfully taking another sip of his coffee. He once again recoiled at the taste and then pushed his cup away. 'Does anyone check to see if there is actually any coffee at all in these drinks?'

Milner took this as a rhetorical question and so carried on by answering DCI Stone's first question. 'Not yet, I'm afraid, and, anyway, the body was pretty badly burned. Uniform have already started their enquiries. Initial reports suggest that quite a few men were seen visiting the house over the past few weeks. It was a rented property and so we are trying to find out who the landlord is. Hopefully, we'll have more definite leads after uniform have finished their house-to-house enquiries. Forensics are also there, of course, and so we'll also have to wait to see if they find anything.'

'What about CCTV? That might help to identify any of the visitors to the house,' suggested Tom.

'We are on to it already, although I wouldn't hold out any great hopes as the house is in a fairly run-down area.'

'Well, check anyway,' replied Tom. 'Anything that would suggest foul play?'

'Not yet,' answered Milner. 'The post-mortem is being carried out this morning. So we should get some feedback, hopefully, later today.'

'What's the evidence to suggest that there were cannabis plants in the house?'

Milner referred back to his file. 'Apparently there was also extensive water damage. The fire people say that it was consistent with extremely high levels of heat and humidity. Plus the fact they found, undamaged, a small quantity of cannabis plants in one of the rooms. It looked as though it might have been grown on quite an industrial scale.'

'Okay. Let me know when you hear about the PM results and forensics.'

Milner stood up and headed towards the door. But, rather than leaving, he suddenly turned back to face DCI Stone.

Tom, sensing Milner's indecision, looked up. 'Was there something else which you wanted to discuss?'

Milner seemed to take a deep breath before saying, with just a hint of nervousness now in his voice, 'Actually there was, sir.'

He then hesitated just long enough for Tom to interject. 'Go on, then. What is it?'

'I'd intended to mention this on Saturday evening but, somehow, it didn't seem appropriate.' A second deep breath was immediately followed by, 'I wanted to let you know I'm thinking of applying for a DS position in the Brighton area.'

Milner had worked with Tom for just over a year and had originally been assigned to him during a period, in Tom's career, when his personal and professional stock was at an all-time low and the expectation, amongst his colleagues, was that he would soon be taking early retirement – either voluntary or 'encouraged'. But a series of events had conspired to dramatically change the situation when they had both found themselves involved in some of the most high-profile cases of recent times. In fact, right now, Tom's reputation and standing was probably as high as it had ever been during the twenty-five years or so he had been a police officer.

During the relatively short period they had worked together Tom had seen how Milner had developed from, initially, an idealistic and often naive young detective into someone who could be a force for good within the Metropolitan Police. Tom, recognising this, had been the person who had recommended his promotion to his current position of Acting Detective Sergeant. What's more, he had come to like Milner. In fact Mary had, on more than one occasion, suggested how Milner, in the absence of Tom's own son Paul, had, perhaps, become something of a surrogate son. At first Tom had refuted this but, as they continued to work together, he'd begun to admit to himself that, perhaps, there was something in what Mary had said. He hadn't seen Paul since Paul's mother, Tom's former wife Anne, had emigrated to Australia many years previously. Just recently, though, he had begun to think more and more about Paul. What was he doing? Did he have his own family? Did he ever think about Tom? Maybe Mary was right after all. Meeting her sons, Greg and Aaron, had simply reinforced those feelings.

With all of these thoughts now in his mind he found himself genuinely shocked by what Milner had just told him, although, when he spoke, his tone didn't betray his feelings.

'Milner, that's the second surprise you've sprung on me within a couple of days.' He continued, 'So, why do you think you have to leave?'

Milner had anticipated this question. In fact it was a question which he had been thinking about ever since he'd heard about the opportunity. 'I just feel that I'm now ready to take on the extra responsibility.' He carried on but this time a bit more defensively, 'It wasn't something I was particularly looking for. It's just that it suddenly became available.'

Tom continued to look directly at Milner, who, to his credit, remained silent. Eventually it was Tom who spoke next. 'Have you actually applied for it yet?'

'No. Not yet. I felt as though I should let you know first.'

'That's very considerate of you,' replied Tom.

Whilst Milner was trying to understand the exact meaning of this, Tom continued, 'I thought you were happy working at the station here?' He couldn't quite bring himself to add 'with me'.

'I am, sir,' Milner replied, now starting to get into his stride. 'As I said earlier, it's just that it's a position which is currently available. Also, it's an opportunity to move to a new area and start a new life. I've lived around here all of my life. To be honest I don't still want to be here when I retire.'

Milner's facial expression suddenly betrayed the realisation of what he'd said and how, possibly, this could be seen as a criticism of DCI Stone's own circumstances. Tom, recognising this, attempted to reassure him. 'Don't worry, Milner. I know you probably had me in mind. Actually, I don't blame you. I would always recommend that a young detective officer gains as much experience as possible and, more often than not, that involves moving location.'

Milner didn't respond.

'But you haven't actually applied yet, though?' asked Tom, for clarification.

'No. Not yet. As I said, I wanted to speak with you first.'

This time Tom's reply was unambiguous and genuine. 'I appreciate that.' There was another brief pause. 'Promise me one thing, though,' he said. 'If you are offered the job, speak to me first, before you accept.'

'I promise I'll do that, sir.'

Chapter 3

Tom spent the rest of the morning catching up on various admin issues although, in truth, he couldn't help thinking about his earlier conversation with Milner. The more he thought about it, the more concerned he found himself becoming. Whilst he sincerely believed Milner would, one day, make a fine detective sergeant, he did not think that time was right now. In his opinion, Milner hadn't gained enough experience. In fact, in terms of running a team, he had no experience and, whilst Tom didn't believe in the 'dead men's shoes' school of promotion, he strongly believed there was no substitute for putting in the hard miles. And that could only be done by putting in the time.

There was also the danger that too much might be expected of Milner. With case successes there inevitably followed an almost exponential increase in expectations. To date, all Milner had experienced was success. It was often not how you reacted to success but how you handled failure which was more important. It was a bit of a cliché but Tom knew, through long experience, some of it personal, that there was a great deal of truth in this and he worried how Milner would react to these inevitable failures, especially if there wasn't someone more experienced around at the time.

His thoughts were still on this when his phone rang. Tom picked it up. 'DCI Stone.'

'Tom, this is DCS Small. Is now a convenient time to speak?' Small was Tom's nominal boss. The previous head of the station, Superintendent Peters, had resigned as a result of his indirect involvement in a previous crime case, which Tom had been involved in, and had yet to be replaced.

'Now's okay,' replied Tom, relieved to be distracted from the Milner situation.

'Good. Could you come over to see me later today? I'd like to discuss a position which you might be interested in.'

'Position? What sort of position?'

'Well, that's why I'd like you to come over. I'd rather we discussed it face-to-face than over the phone,' replied DCS Small, clearly leaving no room for discussion.

Although Tom was naturally intrigued, his opinion of the top brass was generally less than complimentary. Face-to-face meetings with them usually meant trouble. He had yet to be called to see them to be told he was doing a good job.

'Okay. I've got a couple of outstanding things to clear first. How about 3pm?'

There was a brief pause and Tom could hear a faint rustling as if pages were being turned.

'Three is fine. I've got a couple of things either side but I'll make sure it's kept free for our meeting. That's settled, then. I'll see you later.'

With that he was gone, leaving Tom with his phone still to his ear.

'Today is full of surprises,' he muttered as he replaced the phone. 'I wonder what that's all about?'

As he did this he noticed the piece of paper that Milner had handed to him earlier, containing Dr Panton's number. As someone who liked to get things out of the way as quickly as possible, he picked it up and dialled the number.

Almost immediately the phone was answered. 'Panton.' The voice was clear and crisp, suggesting to Tom someone who used no more than the absolute minimum number of words.

'Good morning. It's DCI Stone here. I understand you were trying to get hold of me earlier.'

'Ah. DCI Stone. Yes, thank you for calling back,' he replied, although this time in a much friendlier manner. Perhaps Tom had misjudged him after all. Panton continued, 'I understand you are the man to contact when things are a bit suspicious.'

'Well, I'm not sure about that,' he answered, unclear if his comment was meant to be a compliment. 'Anyway, how can I help?'

'I suppose I had better introduce myself first. I'm Dr Panton, the new pathologist. I've just taken over from Dr Green.'

'Yes, I had heard he'd retired,' replied Tom.

'Anyway, let me get straight to the point,' said Dr Panton, in a business-like manner which suggested that the formal introductions were now over. 'I've just finished the post-mortem on an elderly man. A Mr Wilson. The cause of death is quite clear. It was a heart attack. But that's not why I called you. What was also clear was that his arms had been restrained just before death. In addition there were bruises on other parts of his body. His wrists, for example, but specifically both of his shoulders. It looks as though he had been held down.'

'What makes you think he had been held down? Couldn't the bruises be natural or have been caused some other way? After all, you did say Mr Wilson was an elderly man.'

'That's a very good question,' replied Dr Panton, in a slightly patronising tone. 'I think, though, that even you could spot the finger imprints on each shoulder. Unless he was some type of contortionist, and could suddenly increase the length of his fingers, I think I'll stick with my earlier diagnosis.'

Tom hesitated whilst he thought through what Dr Panton had just told him but particularly the tone in which he had said it. He decided that, perhaps, a more assertive approach was what was now needed. 'Look, Dr Panton. I'm clearly not as forensically qualified as you are, but I have been a police officer all of my working life. So there might just be one or two areas where my expertise is just marginally ahead of yours. Don't forget that you made the first call. If you want to discuss this with any other officer then I'm not going to get upset. I'm long past the time of being precious about those types of things. In fact, if you wish, I can give you the names of two or three other good officers who you can call.'

There was an extended silence before Dr Panton responded. 'You are quite right. It was not my intention to cause offence but, if I did, then I apologise.'

Tom was slightly taken aback by Panton's sudden contrition.

'I guess both of our jobs make us say and do things which, sometimes, we regret,' answered Tom, in his most conciliatory tone. He didn't give Dr Panton the opportunity to respond. Instead he simply asked, 'Would the finger impressions suggest a lot of force was applied?'

It was almost as though their early, testy, conversation had been forgotten as Dr Panton replied, comfortable that he was now in more familiar territory, 'Well, that could be the case, but not, I think, in this particular instance. Mr Wilson was being treated for acute angina. In fact, just a year ago he'd had a mini-stroke and his GP had prescribed blood-thinning medication. One of the side effects of this particular drug is that the patient tends to bruise very easily. Just inadvertently bumping into something can often leave an angry-looking bruise. So, knowing this, there would normally be nothing suspicious about Mr Wilson having some bruises. What is suspicious, however, is where the bruises were located and, of course, the clear finger marks.'

'But the cause of death was a heart attack. Is that correct?' asked Tom, for clarification.

'Absolutely. One hundred percent,' answered Dr Panton. 'Incidentally, his GP also mentioned to me how Mr Wilson had been displaying symptoms associated with the early stages of Alzheimer's.'

'I assume you took photographs of the bruises. If you could let me have copies, that would be useful.'

'Of course I took photographs,' replied Dr Panton, a little tetchily. When he next spoke, however, his sudden curtness had disappeared. 'Anyway, that's not a problem. I will make sure you have a set.'

There was another brief silence whilst Tom decided what to do next. 'Thank you, Dr Panton. I think there's enough here for us to at least take a look.' He hesitated before adding, 'One final question. It's not mandatory to carry out post-mortems, particularly where elderly people are concerned. So why did you?'

'I knew Mr Wilson. Well, not personally but via a neighbour of his. Mrs Bishop is in my bridge group. We try and play every week. Apparently she had been worried, for some time, about the care which Mr Wilson was receiving at home. When he died she voiced her concerns to me.'

Tom interrupted. 'Are you saying you carried out the post-mortem because your bridge partner had asked you to?'

'Well, yes. I suppose I did.'

'Okay. Thanks again for the information, Dr Panton. I'll be back in touch with you shortly.'

Chapter 4

DCS Small personally invited Tom into his office. It wasn't as large as Tom had imagined and was fairly minimalist in its furnishing, although the view from the one window was spectacular. A large rectangular table was located in one corner of the office with six functional chairs placed around it. An impressive-looking coffee pot, milk jug and sugar bowl had already been placed on the table. Tom immediately noticed there were three china cups alongside the coffee pot.

'Are we expecting someone else?' asked Tom, pointing at the three cups on the table.

'You see, Tom, that's why you are such a good copper,' replied DCS Small, with a slight laugh.

At that very moment the door opened and a tall, impressive-looking man entered. He was immaculately attired in a dark blue uniform, white shirt and black tie, all of which contrasted perfectly with his immaculately coiffured silver hair. Tom had met Commander Jenkins a few times over the years and knew he was only a couple of years younger than Tom himself. He was a little alarmed to admit, however, how Commander Jenkins seemed to have aged appreciably better than him and could realistically pass for someone ten years younger. He quickly decided, for his own self-esteem, that it was probably best not to dwell on this too much.

'Tom. *Very* nice to see you again. It's been a while,' Commander Jenkins said, in a crisp and clear tone, suggesting an easy and confident charm. He extended his right hand towards Tom. 'I was trying to recall when we last had a conversation. I seem to think it must have been quite a few years ago.'

Tom extricated his hand from Commander Jenkins' firm grip. 'Yes, it must have been,' he answered, determined not to get too involved in all of this sudden bonhomie, at least until he knew the reason why he had been invited.

It was DCS Small who next spoke. 'Can I pour you a coffee? Milk with no sugar, isn't it? Or would you prefer cream?'

Tom thought back to the watery drink which had tried to pass for coffee earlier in the day. 'Is there a choice? At the station it's whatever comes out of the machine. And I'm charged 20p each time for the privilege.'

DCS Small looked directly at Tom; the expression on his face suggested he didn't fully appreciate Tom's comment. When he next spoke, though, a slight smile had reappeared. 'A perk, I suppose, of being one of the top brass.'

Tom chose not to respond in kind. Instead, he simply said, 'Milk would be fine.'

Once everyone had their own drink, DCS Small gestured to Tom to take a seat.

'Sorry to sound so secretive earlier but, as I said, I felt it best if we had this discussion face-to-face. Anyway, let me get straight to the point. We' – as he said this he looked towards Commander Jenkins – 'would like you to take on Tony's …' He hesitated momentarily and continued, 'Superintendent Peters' role, *pro tem*, until we appoint a replacement.'

Of all of the possible scenarios as to why he had been asked to attend this meeting, this had not been anywhere on his radar. This must have registered on his face because Commander Jenkins said, 'You look mildly surprised. Why did you think that DCS Small had asked to see you?'

'Well, I must admit, I wasn't too sure. Perhaps you felt, again, this was a good time for me to retire. And anyway, I thought I was only seeing DCS Small.'

His reference to retirement, but particularly the emphasis on 'again', seemed to touch a nerve. It related to the time, not too long ago, when retirement was a strong possibility and one that, at that time at least, seemed to have the enthusiastic support of both DCS Small and Commander Jenkins.

'Well, yes,' answered a hesitant DCS Small, 'that was a while ago and the situation has clearly changed since then.'

The resulting silence was broken by Commander Jenkins. 'You are probably thinking that you are not cut out for a position such as this. A desk job, lots of reports and paperwork, and then, of course, there's all of the politics that comes with this position.' Tom didn't know whether or not Commander Jenkins was trying to be funny. He quickly got his answer when he continued, 'But there is, of course, the compensation of having the choice between milk and cream with your coffee.'

Tom could see that they were both going out of their way to be uncharacteristically friendly. He decided that overfamiliarity could be a double-edged sword and so chose not to respond along similar lines. 'You said *pro tem*. Exactly how *pro tem* do you have in mind?'

This time it was DCS Small's turn to speak. 'Hopefully not too long. What's important, though, is that there is some leadership at the station. I've seen before the way in which a station can quickly become rudderless without clear leadership. The longer the time this goes on, the more difficult it is for the station to become effective again. And, frankly, in today's environment, with all of the pressure on results and possible cost reductions, that is something which we are determined to avoid.'

'Isn't this a bit irregular?' Tom asked. 'That is, a DCI taking on a Super's role.'

It was Commander Jenkins who answered. 'Well, yes, I suppose it is, but there have been precedents. Anyway, it's only until we find a ...' Commander Jenkins hesitated briefly and, for a moment, Tom thought he was about to say 'better'. In the event he said, 'Well, a more appropriate candidate.'

Tom, still thinking about the exact meaning of Commander Jenkins' comment, asked, 'Is there no one else who could take on the role? There must be someone, from another station, or even from here, who could do the job.'

'To be perfectly frank,' answered Commander Jenkins, 'there probably is, but we want to move fast. Besides, in lots of ways, you are the obvious person, particularly given your recent, how shall we say, increased profile. You have the necessary experience. You know all of the officers and staff. But, most importantly, you have the respect of the entire station and, may I add, both myself and DCS Small.'

Tom couldn't help himself smiling. Well, inwardly at least. It was only just over a year ago that he had been considered to be almost a pariah within the very same station. Fellow officers would go out of their way to distance themselves from him. He wasn't being 'invited' to participate in operations and the general feeling was that he was well past his sell-by date and just treading water before he retired. What's more, it was a view shared, almost certainly at the time, by both DCS Small and Commander Jenkins. Although, to be fair to them, Tom admitted, at that particular time, he had also felt exactly the same.

'Do I have to make a decision right now?'

'No, not right now, although, as Commander Jenkins said, we do want to move fast. Take a couple of days to think about it. Let's aim to have another conversation on Wednesday.'

With that Commander Jenkins stood up and, once again, offered his right hand to Tom. Tom found himself also standing up.

'Would you please excuse me? I have another meeting to attend. There's a bit of a security flap on at the moment.' Commander Jenkins hesitated slightly, almost as if he wanted his comment to have a particular effect. 'Tom, it was a pleasure meeting with you again. I hope you are able to take on the position. If there is anything you would like to discuss with me, please don't hesitate to give me a call.'

After Commander Jenkins had left the room, and with Tom still standing, DCS Small offered his own hand. 'Tom. Thanks for coming in. Let's speak again on Wednesday.'

Tom found himself stuck in the rush-hour traffic, heading west out of London. He had agreed to have dinner with Mary and so thought he would drive straight back home, to Staines, before meeting up with her later that evening. The drive home also provided him with plenty of time to consider his meeting with Commander Jenkins and DCS Small. His thoughts, though, were interrupted when a call from Milner came through on his hands-free set.

'Yes, Milner. Do you have some information for me?' he enquired.

'I do, sir,' he answered. 'I've just received the initial PM results for our dead man. The pathologist's report confirms that the man was already dead before the fire started. He had quite severe internal injuries, most probably the result of being attacked with some sort of blunt instrument, either an iron bar or something like a baseball bat. It seems the fire was then deliberately started, after he had been killed, probably to try and cover up the cause of death.'

'Do we know who the deceased was?' asked Tom.

'Not yet,' replied Milner. 'Hopefully we will have more information when the full report is available. I've spoken with the pathologist about this and he's promised to get back to me as soon as he's finished it.'

'What about the landlord? Any news?'

'I'm afraid not, sir. But I'm on the case.'

'Okay,' answered Tom. 'It looks like we have a murder on our hands. I'll see you back at the station in about forty-five minutes.'

His romantic dinner out with Mary would have to wait for another day.

Chapter 5

When Tom arrived back at the station he was met by Milner, standing just outside his office. Milner had a plastic cup in his right hand and the ubiquitous file in his left. Tom immediately noticed the one cup. 'Did you forget mine?' he asked, looking directly at the cup.

'I thought you didn't like the coffee from the machine,' answered Milner, not adding how it was a bit rich that he was being criticised for spending his own money.

'I'll give it another go,' replied Tom, choosing to ignore the slight confrontational tone in Milner's voice. 'Anyway, it looks as though I might need it as we are now investigating a murder.'

Milner placed the cup, and then his file, on the table, turned around and headed back towards the coffee machine.

Tom and Milner spent the next couple of hours reviewing what they knew and deciding what course the investigation should take. The immediate priority was to establish a formal murder investigation. They would also quickly have to organise wider house-to-house enquiries, in order to obtain as much information as possible about who had been living at the house and whether there had been any suspicious activity or comings and goings recently. Then there was the issue of the victim's identity. It was vital that they find a name which they could put into the public domain. That way they might then be able to establish links with other people.

Finally, there was the issue of what resources they would need to effectively run the investigation. This last question was one which was clearly causing Milner concern. 'Sir, who are you thinking of including in the investigation team?'

'Why? Do you have anyone in mind?' asked Tom, genuinely interested to see if Milner did indeed have a suggestion.

If he did then he was not willing, or able, to give it. 'No. Not really. I'm just interested to know your thoughts.'

In truth, Tom had, until now, not really given it any thought. But now one person immediately sprang to mind. Tom had known DC Gary Bennett for many years and had always considered him to be a thorough and totally dependable copper. He had lately, though, been through a tough time, both professionally and personally, and had only just returned to work.

'Don't worry. When I decide I'll make sure you are the first to know,' replied Tom, somewhat abruptly. Recognising this he quickly followed up with, 'But, whoever joins the team, you will be my DS.'

Milner seemed to be reassured despite saying, 'I didn't mean that, sir. I was just interested.'

'I know you were, Milner,' answered Tom, in his most reassuring voice. 'You shouldn't get too defensive. Right, I think that's enough for now. I'll see you tomorrow bright and early. Have you got anything planned for tonight?' he asked, trying to show interest in Milner's private life.

'Well, not now, anyway,' Milner answered, looking at his watch.

Tom looked at his own watch and saw that it was gone 8 pm. It was then he realised he'd completely forgotten to call Mary and cancel their dinner appointment.

Although Tom was looking directly at Milner as he spoke, his words were directed as much at himself as towards Milner. 'It's difficult to maintain a normal life when you work for the Met.'

After Milner had left, Tom picked up his phone and called Mary.

It was answered almost immediately. 'Hi, Tom. Where are you?'

Tom took a deep breath. 'I'm still at the station.'

There was a brief silence and Tom thought about adding an explanation, but Mary then said, 'I suppose that means we are not going out for dinner tonight after all.'

'I know. We were, but something has cropped up here which I had to get involved in. I'm really sorry. I was looking forward to it.' He paused briefly and then continued. 'I should have called you. I could say I just never had the time, but the truth is I got distracted and forgot. I'm sorry.'

There was another silence before Mary answered. 'Don't worry. You don't need to keep apologising. I'm sure, whatever the reason was, it must have been important.'

When Tom heard this he couldn't help thinking how, sometimes, Mary was just a little too understanding.

She continued, 'How about coming here? I can make you dinner.' She then added, with exaggerated temptation, 'Then you can stay with me tonight.'

Tom felt as though, even without the added attraction, he couldn't refuse Mary's offer, and answered, as enthusiastically as possible, 'That's a great idea. How could I refuse a promise like that? I'm only human, after all.' He could hear her let out an almost schoolgirl chuckle. He continued, 'I'm just about to leave and so I'll see you soon.'

Chapter 6

Tom had met Mary via a dating website about a year previously and, to his great surprise, had found himself being instantly attracted to her. Tom was not, by any stretch of the imagination, normally a dating agency type of person, but, against even his own better judgement, he had gone ahead and spent the required £200 to register on the 'You're Never Too Late For Love' website. Even now he couldn't quite understand what had actually motivated him to submit his details. Perhaps, subconsciously, he was trying to prepare himself for what seemed at the time inevitable retirement.

Whilst he had dated a few women over the years since his wife Anne had left him, the frequency had diminished appreciably as the years had gone by. What had really surprised him, however, was just how quickly his physical needs had returned since meeting Mary. What was even stranger was how his professional fortunes had changed – and significantly for the better – almost from the day he had first met her. He was certainly not a superstitious man and had never believed that fate was inexorable. Notwithstanding this, however, he was struggling to remember a time when, both professionally and personally, he had been as content and fulfilled as he was right now.

Since being widowed, Mary had owned and run a small florist's in Bagshot, close to where she lived. Tom himself lived just a few miles further east, along the A30, in Staines. So far this appeared to suit their relationship perfectly. They were not so far away from each other that the distance presented practical problems for the relationship but were just far enough away to provide each of them with their own private space. In retrospect it was probably the best £200 that he had ever spent.

Tom was lying alongside Mary in her bed. Although it was still early he had been awake for some time. He had never been a great sleeper, particularly if there was something playing on his mind. He was also not the type of person who could leave his work outside his front door.

Although the Milner situation did worry him a little, it was his conversation with Commander Jenkins and DCS Small which had kept him awake. Whilst it was certainly true that he'd never held any great aspirations to become part of the 'top brass', he could, nonetheless, see the sense in being asked to do the job. This was especially as it was clearly only on an interim basis. It was equally true that a station without leadership would, inevitably, suffer operationally. He also felt that he now did in fact have the respect of, at least, most of the officers. Those who knew him would realise it was just not his style to use this as an opportunity to position himself for further promotion. That said, he was a 'hands-on' copper, who was happiest when he was fully involved in all of the day-to-day issues associated with operations.

As he was going over all of these things Mary spoke. 'Good morning. Have you been awake long?'

Tom turned to face her. 'I've just woken up,' he replied a little disingenuously.

'I'm not surprised that you needed your sleep after last night,' she said, with a slight laugh. She then leant over and kissed him.

'What's that for?' asked Tom.

'As I've said to you before, a woman can kiss her man, can't she?'

Even now, Tom still couldn't quite come to terms with the fact that Mary saw him as her man. 'I suppose so,' he answered. 'I was just about to get up and make you a cup of tea.'

Mary leant closer and kissed him again, although this time a little longer. Tom could feel her warm body pressing on his. 'On second thoughts I think the tea can wait,' he said, gently pulling Mary towards him. She didn't resist.

Chapter 7

A while later they were both sitting at the table in Mary's kitchen. Tom had a couple of slices of toast in front of him whilst Mary was feeding the new tortoiseshell kitten she had recently acquired. 'Are you sure it's such a good idea having a kitten?' asked Tom, himself not a great lover of any particular pet. 'After all, you are out at work quite a lot. I thought pets needed company.'

'Cats are different. They don't need as much care as dogs,' she explained. 'I told you how one of my customers asked me to put an advert in the shop window, looking for people who could give a home to a litter of kittens. All of the others found homes except this one,' she said, stroking it as it ate its own breakfast, 'and I just couldn't let it go off to an animal sanctuary.'

Tom, resisting the temptation to say 'as long as you don't expect me to look after it', resumed eating his toast.

'What are you doing today?' Mary asked. 'Are you working on any more exciting crimes? Yesterday you mentioned something having cropped up.'

Tom made a point of trying not to involve Mary in his work. Any problems he would rather keep to himself. 'Something is always cropping up where police work is concerned,' he answered. 'Anyway, as you asked, there was a house fire in Hounslow, over the weekend, in which a man's body was found. It looks as though the person could have been killed before the fire started.'

'Killed? Do you mean murdered?' asked Mary.

Tom now wished that he hadn't mentioned the body, but he was now committed. 'We think so, but it's still early days yet,' he replied, trying to downplay it as much as possible.

But Mary wasn't going to drop the subject and seemed genuinely interested when she next spoke. 'So, how was he murdered?'

'Well, we are not sure,' he answered truthfully. 'Hopefully, that's something the post-mortem will be able to tell us.'

'What will you do next?'

'There's a standard protocol for this early stage of the investigation: house-to-house enquiries, statements from neighbours, forensic search of the house etc. At the moment it's mainly about accumulating as much information as possible.'

Either that had satisfied Mary or she had sensed Tom's reluctance to discuss specific details. 'Well, you just make sure you look after yourself. I wouldn't want to think you are going to get yourself into the same situation as last time.' This was a reference to Tom's last major case, which had, indeed, involved both him and Milner being placed in personal danger.

'Mary. Please don't worry. These things happen all of the time,' he said, not adding, 'I wish I hadn't mentioned it now.'

A combination of the morning's unexpected 'distraction' and unusually heavy traffic meant Tom didn't arrive at the station until almost 9.30.

As he approached his office Milner suddenly appeared. 'Morning, sir,' he said in his usual slightly overenthusiastic tone. 'I thought I must have got the time wrong.'

Tom wondered if this was Milner's way of making a point about their supposed 'bright and early' start. If that was the case then he decided not to respond in kind. 'Yes. Sorry, Milner. It's me who is late. I had a bit of a late start this morning.' This seemed to satisfy Milner and so Tom continued, 'Any news yet as to who our dead person is?'

Both Tom and Milner were now seated in Tom's office.

'I'm afraid not. The pathologist called me a little earlier with a summary of his full findings and confirmed the earlier cause of death. He was, though, able to estimate the age of the man at between twenty-five and thirty-five. By using the latest DNA matching and profiling techniques, he could also confirm the man had almost certainly originated from Eastern Europe.'

'Well, that's something, I suppose,' Tom replied. 'What's the situation with the landlord? We ought at least to be able to shed some light on who he is.'

'It seems the landlord, a Mr Grace, is away on holiday at the moment. He has, though, been informed and is apparently returning to the UK. He should be back within the next day or so.'

Tom remained silent for a while. Suddenly there was a knock on his door and a man immediately entered.

'Gary,' said Tom, 'glad you were able to join us.' He nodded his head towards Milner. 'You already know DS Milner.' He now faced Milner and added an explanation for Gary's unexpected appearance. 'DC Bennett has accepted my invitation to become part of the investigative team.'

DC Bennett was over fifteen years older than Milner, having spent all of his adult life in the police force. During the past few years, though, lack of ambition, and circumstances which had conspired against him, had meant any opportunity for promotion had passed him by.

Tom could sense Milner's concern. 'DC Bennett will report directly to you during this investigation. I've already discussed this with him and he's perfectly okay with this arrangement. Isn't that right, Gary?'

Now it was DC Bennett's turn to look directly towards Milner. 'I've heard so many good things about you from DCI Stone, as well as from some of the other officers in the station, particularly about your involvement in the Fuller case. I'm really looking forward to working with you. And, just for clarification, I do not have any issue with you as my superior officer.' He hesitated briefly before adding, 'To be honest, I'm just glad to be back working on a murder case.'

Milner was still trying to take on board the fact that DCI Stone had apparently said good things about him when his thoughts were interrupted by Tom. 'Right. Now that all of the formalities have been dispensed with, perhaps you two can make a start on trying to solve this murder.'

Chapter 8

Tom had been ushered into a small office at the pathology laboratory, and was staring out of the side window at the sweep of West London immediately in front of him. He had left Milner and Bennett to review what limited evidence was available and progress the immediate follow-up enquiries whilst he had gone to visit Dr Panton. He was so engrossed he didn't hear Dr Panton enter the office.

Dr Panton cleared his throat and this had the desired effect as Tom immediately turned around. In front of him was a short, slightly overweight man in his early fifties, with his glasses resting on the end of his nose. He was still wearing his pathologist's apron.

'DCI Stone. It's good to meet you. I wasn't expecting you to follow up on our recent conversation quite so quickly, so please excuse my attire, but I've just been working. Can I offer you something to drink? Tea, perhaps?'

'I'd love a coffee if that's possible,' replied Tom, joining in with the ongoing civility.

'I'm sure that would be possible,' answered Dr Panton, as though coffee was not something which normally would be available. 'How do you take your coffee?'

'White, no sugar would be perfect.'

Whilst Dr Panton was out of the office Tom took the opportunity to look at the framed photographs which were on the wall immediately opposite the window. They were photos of groups of mostly men, but some women, taken as either formal team photos or more informal social ones.

Once again Tom didn't hear Dr Panton return. 'Ah, I see you are interested in my collection of photographs. They were taken over a number of years. When I was at university or attending medical conferences. That type of thing. A bit of a double-edged sword, I'm afraid, as they increasingly remind me of my younger, more energetic days.'

'Well,' answered Tom, 'I suppose that could apply to all of us.' Tom had never been one for keeping, let alone displaying, photographs. Perhaps that was the reason why.

Dr Panton had placed Tom's coffee on the table. Tom was disappointed to see that it was in a polystyrene cup. He also noted that Dr Panton had declined to have one himself.

Tom spoke again. 'If you don't mind, I'd just like to recap our conversation.' He took out his notebook and, without giving Dr Panton the opportunity to reply, he immediately continued. 'You recently carried out a post-mortem on a Mr Wilson. As a result of the PM you were able to confirm that he had, in fact, died from a heart attack. However, during the PM you found unexplained severe bruising on other parts of the deceased's body, specifically his shoulders, arms and wrists. In your opinion, and despite your acknowledgement that Mr Wilson's medication could have been a contributory factor to the severity of the bruising, this was still consistent with, at some time reasonably prior to his death, Mr Wilson being forcibly held down.' Tom closed his notebook and, looking straight at Dr Panton, he then added, 'And all of this you were able to determine from an unapproved post-mortem, which you performed as a result of a concern that originated from your bridge partner, Mrs Bishop. Would that be an accurate summary?'

'Well, yes. Factually, that is an accurate summary.' There was a tense silence before Dr Panton spoke again, although this time in a quieter and more conciliatory tone. 'DCI Stone, I accept my carrying out the post-mortem was unusual, but there are lots of precedents where they have been undertaken without one hundred percent, pre-obtained, approval. Suspicious circumstances surrounding a death would be, as you no doubt know, a legitimate reason. In this particular instance it was my judgement there was such an element of suspicion. Where I do, however, fully accept your implied criticism is that this suspicion originated from my friend, Mrs Bishop. This, I can now see, could be construed as being somewhat unusual.'

This time it was Tom's turn to be conciliatory. 'Although it certainly is unusual, I'm sure you did it with the best of intentions.' This seemed to ease the earlier tension and Tom continued, 'So, you are sure Mr Wilson had been forcibly held down not long prior to his death.'

Dr Panton was now far more enthusiastic when he answered. 'That is what all of the evidence suggests. What's more, I've also now been able to identify other similar, but less recent, bruises on his body. Although they are somewhat faded they are, nonetheless, there.' After he had said this he opened a drawer and took out a large brown envelope. 'These are the photographs you asked for,' he said, placing the photographs on the table for Tom to view. He remained silent whilst Tom looked more closely at them.

'I'm not an expert,' said Tom, 'but even I can see there are clear finger marks on the body.'

'If you look closely,' said Dr Panton, pointing to the bruises on Mr Wilson's shoulders, 'you might be able to see that the ones on his right shoulder are more pronounced than the ones on his left one.'

'Yes, I can just about make that out,' said Tom, peering more closely at the photograph. 'Is there any particular reason for that?'

'Well, there could be a number of reasons but the most plausible is that whoever held him down was left-handed, as it doesn't look like he was held face-down. I've seen this before. When you are holding something, or someone, down you naturally press a little more firmly with your strong hand. Normally this wouldn't be obvious, but, as Mr Wilson was taking blood-thinning medication, this would have made the effect more apparent.'

As Tom continued to examine the photographs, Dr Panton said, 'So, you can see why I felt I had to contact you. It's my professional opinion Mr Wilson was subjected to some form of physical abuse or, at least, quite aggressive physical restraint.'

Tom looked up from his notebook. 'When do you think Mr Wilson would have incurred those bruises?'

'Some, I would say, only a day or so before he died. The others, possibly about a week earlier.'

'If you don't mind I'd like you now to let me have a more detailed summary of the specific bruising,' Tom said, before adding, 'in terms which even I can understand.'

Tom and Dr Panton then spent the next half-hour or so listing all of the identified bruises, together with the related pathology analysis and the photographs. Tom also took contact details for both Mr Wilson and Mrs Bishop. He left promising to keep Dr Panton informed of the progress of his enquiries.

Tom arrived back at the station by mid-afternoon and as he walked towards his office he immediately noticed that Milner and Bennett, with their backs towards him, unaware of his presence, were deep in conversation.

'Anything important?' he asked.

They both looked up, clearly surprised to see him almost standing over them.

'We've—' Milner suddenly stopped and, looking away from Tom and towards DC Bennett, said, 'Well, actually, it was DC Bennett who obtained them. They're the details relating to the landlord. Anyway, Gary, why don't you tell DCI Stone what you've found out?'

Tom was impressed Milner was already willing to let DC Bennett pass on any potential good news.

Without any preamble, DC Bennett, referring to his notes, started to explain. 'The landlord of the house is a Mr James Grace. According to the registry records he currently owns three houses in this area, all of which he lets out. Two, including where the fire was, are in Hounslow. The other one, coincidentally, is not far from where I live, in Feltham. He himself lives in Chelmsford, with his wife and one of his two sons, together with his daughter-in-law and grandson.'

He looked up from his notes. When Tom remained silent, DC Bennett took it as a signal to continue. 'What's really interesting, though, is Mr Grace and his eldest son, Brendan, both have criminal records. In James Grace's case, when he was growing up, he was always in trouble with the police. Theft, burglary, drug use. You know, the standard stuff for any self-respecting young criminal growing up in those days. After that he would appear to have got himself involved with some of the more professional gangs in Essex. There was some evidence to suggest he was involved in the drugs trade, which was rife then in the clubs and pubs of Essex, but it was mainly circumstantial and so nothing ever came of it.

'Then in 1987 he was sentenced to fifteen years, but was released in 1997. He had been part of a violent and nasty Essex gang which had carried out a series of armed robberies. His son, Brendan, has also done time. He received a two-year sentence in 2010 for beating someone up. According to his file it was quite brutal.

'Anyway, all was quiet then until about a year ago when there was a complaint of intimidation made against the Graces, from one of his tenants.' DC Bennett then looked down and referred to his notes. He continued, 'A Mr Darren Allen originally complained they were trying to unlawfully evict him from where he lived: the property where the fire broke out, in fact. In his statement he claimed that the intimidation had gradually escalated and eventually included the threat of physical violence against both him and his girlfriend. But Mr Allen subsequently withdrew his complaint and no further action was taken against the Graces.'

When Tom replied it was with heavy sarcasm. 'The Graces seem a really nice family. Just the type of people you'd like to have next door.' He then continued, 'Do we know where Mr Allen now lives?'

'That's the interesting thing,' replied DC Bennett. 'I checked that, whilst you were out, and it appears that Mr Allen left almost immediately after he withdrew his complaint. We are trying to find out where he moved to.'

Milner now spoke. 'We are also chasing the list of tenants who live at his other properties, although we might need to wait for Grace to get back from holiday for that information. In the meantime uniform have started widening their house-to-house enquiries.' Just as he had finished he suddenly remembered something. 'And, incidentally, I've checked on any CCTV coverage and, unfortunately, it's as I suspected.'

'Well, at least we don't have to spend hours looking at people walking along a street. Anyway, it looks as though you've got everything in hand,' replied Tom.

'There is one other thing, though,' added Milner, a little hesitantly. 'We just took a call from one of the daily papers. They have got wind of the fact that it wasn't a straightforward house fire. They wanted us to confirm their story. It seems like they have some of the basic information correct but, for the rest, I'm sure they are just fishing. It might, though, be worth considering a news conference. At least, that way, we can regain control of the investigation.'

Milner knew that DCI Stone was never comfortable with live news conferences and this seemed to be confirmed when

Tom said, 'I wonder how they found out about this. Someone must have leaked it to them. Anyway, there is not a lot we can do now.' He then continued, although this time quite aggressively, 'And what makes you think that we are *not* in control of this investigation?'

Milner chose to make the assumption that the question was rhetorical. 'Surely sometimes it works to our advantage to brief the press.'

Tom looked directly at Milner. 'I agree, but only when it truly is to the benefit of the case, and not the individual involved and then only after all other avenues have been tried. If you start using the press too often they will quickly start to see it as their right to be informed. In the meantime, let's try and get the information which we've asked for.' He continued to look at Milner. 'When we have this, we might then decide to have your news conference.'

Chapter 9

Tom was standing on the pavement outside a small bungalow in Ruislip. He opened the slightly rusting wrought-iron gate, made sure that he then closed it behind him, walked up the path towards the front door and rang the bell. Almost immediately, the door opened slightly and a woman's face peered around the side of the door.

'Good evening, Mrs Bishop. I'm Detective Chief Inspector Stone, from West London Police. We spoke on the phone earlier. I'm sorry it's a bit late in the day.'

Mrs Bishop remained silent for a while before saying, in a clear and slightly refined accent, 'May I see your identification?'

Tom removed his warrant card and held it up towards Mrs Bishop, who had obviously come prepared as she immediately put on her spectacles. After a while she said, 'After what happened to poor Mr Wilson, you can't be overly careful.' She pointed at a small mat which was inside the front door. 'Would you mind just wiping your feet before you come through to the front room?'

Tom did as he was instructed and, when Mrs Bishop was happy that his shoes met the required standard, he followed her into the front room. Although it was quite small, it was neat, tidy and spotlessly clean. There was a television in one corner of the room immediately opposite a single armchair. Against the wall was a small settee. There were crocheted, white lace coverings over the arms and the backs of both the armchair and the settee. Three porcelain figures of dogs sat proudly where the fireplace would have been and another two were on each side of the main windowsill. In the middle of the windowsill was a framed, slightly faded, black-and-white photograph of a young couple, outside a church, on their wedding day.

Alongside the chair was a small mahogany table on which

sat a bowl full of unnaturally shiny wax apples and pears. Next to this was a silver tray containing two china cups and saucers, a matching teapot and sugar bowl, and a tea strainer perched on top of its own small bowl. A silver teaspoon lay on each saucer. Mrs Bishop indicated that Tom should sit in the armchair nearest to the small table.

'Now, how do you like your tea?' she asked, already pouring the tea through the tea strainer into one of the cups.

'With milk would be fine, thank you,' he answered.

She handed him his tea, poured herself one and then sat down herself. After he had taken a sip he placed the cup on the table and took out his notebook, which contained the notes he had made during his meeting with Dr Panton.

'I understand you are the bridge partner of Dr Panton,' he said.

Mrs Bishop stood up and placed her own cup on the table. 'No, I'm not. I play bridge with Dr Panton but my regular playing partner is Mr Simmons.'

'Apologies for that,' answered Tom, making sure that Mrs Bishop saw him amending his notes. 'How often do you play bridge?'

'Why are you asking me about bridge? I thought you had come here to discuss Mr Wilson,' she said, forcibly.

'We always like to have a full background. I've learnt, over the years, never to discount the slightest seemingly irrelevant detail. Sometimes it can make all the difference.'

Apparently satisfied with his explanation, she answered Tom's question. 'I play twice a week, once on a Monday afternoon, although Dr Panton does not join us for this, and again on a Thursday evening. It's on the Thursday evening when I play with Dr Panton.'

'Thank you. How long have you known Mr Wilson?'

'Mr Wilson lives . . .' She then corrected herself. 'Mr Wilson lived two houses away from here, opposite the school, at number eleven. We were neighbours for over twenty years.'

'So you knew him quite well, then?'

'We've known each other most of that time but I only really got to know him after his wife died, about five years ago. Since then his health had deteriorated, though. He had a heart problem but was also starting to get more and more confused and forgetful. He even recently started to think that I was his wife. He would often call me Jean. In the end I didn't bother correcting him as it seemed to give him some comfort. It was, though, still very sad to see him in that condition and so I used to pop in each day just to have a chat and make him a cup of tea. It was just a bit of company more than anything else. He has no family, so he really didn't have anyone. He should really have been in a care home, but he refused. I could see he was getting more and more lonely. A few years ago I did try to persuade him to join our bridge group but he didn't want to, and then, as he got worse, it was just too late.'

'I understand it was you who found him dead. That must have been very traumatic,' Tom said as gently as possible.

Notwithstanding this, Mrs Bishop suddenly became visibly upset. Tom looked around for a tissue to give to her. Failing to see anything he handed his own, fortunately clean, handkerchief to her. She took it from him and wiped her eyes. She then handed it back to Tom.

'Thank you,' she said quietly. 'It's just so upsetting. Yes, I went to see him late that morning. He'd given me a key so I could let myself in. When I went in and saw him I just thought he was asleep in his chair. He often had a nap during the day. So I went into the kitchen to make us a cup of tea, as I usually did, and when I came back he was still in the same position. It was then I started to get concerned. I shook him gently to try and wake him, and it was then I realised that he wasn't asleep.' She suddenly started to cry again. Tom handed her his handkerchief and, once again, she wiped her eyes with it and then carried on. 'He slumped forward and I could see he wasn't breathing. I then phoned for an ambulance.'

Tom allowed time for Mrs Bishop to regain her composure. 'Thank you for that. As I said, it must have been very upsetting for you.' He then continued, 'Dr Panton mentioned how Mr Wilson was receiving daily care help. Did you ever meet any of his carers?'

Mrs Bishop's tone suddenly hardened. 'Yes, I did, and I have to tell you that I didn't like them.'

'Why was that?' asked Tom, leaning forward slightly.

'Some of them just didn't seem to care. On a couple of occasions I heard one get quite cross with him because he had knocked over his dinner and made a bit of a mess. They came twice a day to help with personal hygiene issues as well as to make his breakfast and, later, his dinner. A few times, when I went to see him, he was wearing dirty, stained clothes. Mr Wilson always used to dress immaculately and always wore a clean shirt and tie, even when he wasn't going anywhere. Some of them also smoked in his house. I could always smell the cigarette smoke after they had left. I mentioned all of this to one of his carers, including the cigarette smoke in the house, but she didn't seem that interested and just wanted to do her work and leave as quickly as possible. Apparently, they were supposed to spend thirty minutes with him in the morning and again in the evening. One day, I timed how long the lady was there, from the moment she arrived to the time she left. It was just over twenty minutes. It was also clear they didn't like it if I was there when they arrived. I found it very upsetting and so, eventually, made sure I would call in when I knew they wouldn't be there.'

'You said "they". How many people came to look after Mr Wilson?'

'That was part of the problem. It seemed as though there was a different one each day. I'm not surprised he got so confused.'

'Did Mr Wilson ever complain about the care he was receiving from them?'

Mrs Bishop considered the question carefully before answering. 'Not a complaint as such. He did, though, get quite upset a few times when he couldn't find things. Family mementoes, a few ornaments. That sort of thing. In fact, he even accused me, a few times, of taking one of his ornaments. It was one of his favourites, a figure of a black-and-white border collie. He'd obviously had it a long time, as there was an old photograph of him and his wife, when they were much younger, with it in the background. He knew I collected them.' As she said this she looked in the direction of her own collection and added, 'As you can see.' She shook her head. 'The funny thing was he had often offered it to me anyway but I had always refused.' She then added, almost as an afterthought, 'Well, it wouldn't be right, would it? Particularly as it was in the photograph.' She was silent momentarily before saying, with a hint of sadness in her voice, 'But, as I say, he was starting to get very confused.'

'One final question, if you don't mind. Why did you mention your concerns to Dr Panton?'

Mrs Bishop had now regained her previous assurance. 'One morning, a few days before he died, I noticed he had bruises on both of his wrists as well as one on his left arm. When I asked how he had got them he suddenly got very agitated but said he couldn't remember. I could see, though, he was quite frightened when I mentioned them. Anyway, a few days later I found him dead. I knew that Dr Panton was a pathologist and so I mentioned all of this to him. He said he would take a look.' She paused. 'Although I didn't expect the police to get involved.'

'Thank you very much for your time, Mrs Bishop. You have been extremely helpful. I will ensure that you are kept informed regarding any developments.' Tom drank the rest of his tea. 'Thank you very much for the tea. It was very kind of you.' He then passed a small card to her, saying, 'Here are my contact details. If you do remember anything else, please don't hesitate to call me.'

After visiting Mrs Bishop, Tom drove straight back to his own house in Staines. Although he wasn't, by any stretch of the imagination, a good cook, Mary had, since they'd met, continually encouraged him to try and be a bit more adventurous with his cooking. So that was why he now found himself attempting to cook something involving chicken, a red onion, some mushrooms and a yellow pepper, together with some boiled rice.

Mary had bought him a 'cooking for beginners' book, as an additional incentive, and, as he stood in his kitchen reading the instructions, he once again thought about just how much Mary had changed his life. Before Mary came on the scene he couldn't even remember the last time he had opened a cookbook, let alone read any of the recipes in detail. He'd had a limited number of well-practised meals which he could prepare and, frankly, given the unsocial hours associated with his job, he'd always found that to be sufficient. Anyway, he had never been a great one for reading manuals. Even when he had been married to Anne it had always been her who'd had the patience to read them.

He had called Milner on the way back from his meeting

with Mrs Bishop in order to get an update regarding the mystery dead man. There was some good news. Milner had been able to tell him they now had an address for Mr Allen, the man who had made allegations against the landlord, and were planning to go and see him early the following morning. Tom had then taken the opportunity to ask Milner to find out the contact details of the company which had been providing the care service to Mr Wilson. Tom could sense Milner was a bit puzzled by this, but Milner had, by now, become used to this type of unusual request from DCI Stone and so had simply said he would get on to it immediately.

Not that he needed any additional confirmation, but this simply reinforced Tom's view as to how he felt about the possibility of Milner leaving. It often took a while before this type of association could develop into an effective working relationship. The danger now was that, just as this was happening, it could suddenly all be lost. But it was more than that. Tom had come to like Milner. He liked his naivety as well as appreciating his enthusiasm and loyalty.

But, as he continued to prepare his dinner, he had other things to think about. He was shortly expected to inform DCS Small about whether he would be taking on the temporary role at the station. In truth he had hoped a sudden flash of inspiration, or insight, would have made the decision for him. But, unfortunately, it hadn't.

Normally, over the course of his career, he'd never had a problem with making decisions. Sometimes this had resulted in a wrong decision, but, as he liked to think, most of the time he'd made the correct one.

He had discussed it with Mary last night. Perhaps not surprisingly, she saw the offer as recognition for everything he had achieved in his career and had encouraged him to take it up. She was probably right, but there was still a doubt which continued to nag away in his head. Anyway, he would sleep on it and hope that in the morning he would have the answer.

Chapter 10

'Right, when are you planning to go and visit Mr Allen?' It was the following morning and Tom, together with Milner and DC Bennett, was in his office.
'Shortly. DC Bennett has already called him to fix a time,' answered Milner. 'We were just about to leave.'
'What was his reaction to your call?' asked Tom.
'Very nervous,' replied DC Bennett. 'I got the distinct impression he would rather not have to meet with us.'
'I bet you did,' said Tom, before adding, 'Do you want me to come along?'
It was Milner who answered. 'I think DC Bennett and I can handle it, sir. Anyway, three police officers would probably make him even more nervous.'
Tom had realised how Allen, potentially, could be one of the keys to all of this and so, under normal circumstances, he would probably have insisted on attending. But these were not normal circumstances and, anyway, it was the right time to give Milner his head. 'That's probably true. Anyway, I'm sure you and DC Bennett can, as you say, handle it.'
Milner and DC Bennett took that as their cue to leave.
Thirty minutes later they were standing outside a small terraced house in Hayes. The small front garden had been paved over, although grass and weeds were starting to cover large parts of it. Immediately to the side of the front door were two bins, on which the number 19 had been written large in white paint. Most of the other houses also had their bins out, some of which were seriously overflowing or with accompanying black plastic bags alongside.
'Looks like it's bin collection day,' said DC Bennett.
'Not before time,' said Milner, as he knocked on the door. There was no immediate answer and so he knocked again, although this time a little harder. From somewhere in the house they suddenly heard a baby start to cry.

Eventually the door opened and a woman, in her mid-twenties, appeared holding a baby. 'Did you have to knock so hard?' she asked. 'I was just getting Lilli May off to sleep and now she's awake and crying again.'

'I'm sorry,' replied a somewhat contrite Milner. 'We didn't realise.'

'Anyway, who are you and what do you want? If you are trying to sell anything then you're wasting your time.'

Just then a man appeared alongside the woman. 'Are you from the police?' he asked. He looked a little older than the woman, possibly in his early thirties, but this could have been down to his somewhat unkempt appearance. He was wearing a pair of seriously faded blue jeans and white trainers. His T-shirt had what looked like food stains down the front. His slightly dishevelled appearance was compounded by his unshaven face and receding hair.

'Yes, we are,' answered Milner, holding out his identification warrant. 'I'm DS Milner and this is DC Bennett. I assume you are Darren Allen and it was you who I spoke to earlier.'

'Yes,' he answered, 'but, as I told you then, I won't be able to help you.'

'How do you know?' asked DC Bennett. 'We haven't asked you anything yet.' They were still standing outside the house. 'Do you mind if we come in? We'll try to be as quick as possible.'

Darren stepped to one side and said, 'Okay, but there's nothing to tell.'

They stepped through the door and followed him down the short hallway and into the living room. The woman had followed them and when they were all in the living room she said, 'What's this all about, Darren? You didn't tell me they were coming.'

He ignored her and simply said, 'What is it you want to know?'

The woman had managed to stop her baby crying, by gently rocking it to and fro, and was now seated on the small settee, her baby cradled in her arms. There was only one other chair in the room and, as that had the baby's various paraphernalia covering the seat, all of the men remained standing.

Milner decided that, in the circumstances, he would get straight to the point. 'We understand, up to about a year ago, you lived at 11 Merrow Road, in Hounslow. Is that correct?'

The woman immediately turned towards him, a look of concern on her face, whilst continuing to gently rock her baby.

'Yes. So what?' Darren answered, almost defiantly.

It was DC Bennett who next spoke. 'Why did you leave?'

There was a brief uneasy silence before Darren answered. 'It wasn't big enough for us. Paula was expecting and we needed a bigger place for when Lilli May was born.'

'Was that the only reason?' DC Bennett asked.

'What do you mean?'

'Well, according to our records, you made a formal complaint against the landlord, Mr Grace. You claimed, in your statement, that he was threatening you with violence unless you vacated the house. That would seem a pretty good reason to leave.'

There was another brief silence before Darren answered. 'I've told you, we needed a bigger place.'

This time it was Milner who spoke. 'Did you see on the news there was a fire at the house where you used to live, and a man was found dead inside?'

'So? That didn't have anything to do with us,' he replied, defensively.

'No one said it did. But it's just that we have reason to believe the man who was found was murdered, and so, as this is now a murder investigation, we are investigating all potential leads.'

The mention of this clearly hit a nerve with Paula. 'That bastard Grace threatened to hurt Darren unless we left.'

Allen interrupted her. 'Paula. Be quiet. I told you it's none of our business.'

Paula, now even angrier, said, 'If it wasn't for him we wouldn't be living here and having to bring up Lilli May in this dump.' Her anger suddenly dissipated and, instead, she started to sob quietly.

As Darren made no move to comfort her, Milner took it upon himself to ease the tension in the room and, in his most comforting voice, quietly said, 'I'm sorry. I didn't mean to upset you. If you would like we can come back later.'

Still sobbing, but without looking up, she simply said, 'Tell him.'

Both Milner and DC Bennett redirected their attention towards Darren, who remained silent, almost as though he was deciding how much he should say. He cleared a few of the baby things from the chair and sat down. Finally, he spoke. 'We had lived there for six months when the place was sold and bought by Grace. At first he seemed okay. But a few weeks after he bought it he started to mention to us that we would have to leave. He said, as a new landlord, he was allowed to give us notice to leave. I asked somebody who I knew about this and he told me he couldn't do that. It wasn't legal. When I mentioned this to Grace he suddenly got really angry. That's when all of the real threats started.'

'What sort of threats?' asked DC Bennett.

Darren seemed to hesitate. Paula, sensing this, took over. 'He said if we didn't move out then Darren would get hurt.'

'Can you remember exactly what the threat was?' asked DC Bennett.

'Not exactly, but it was something about Darren having an accident one night. Anyway, we got the message. That's when we decided to go the police.'

Darren now took up the story. 'Waste of time, that was. All you lot did was ask us to write down what had happened. We didn't hear anything for weeks. Grace must have found out about us going to the police because, one night, his son turned up and started shouting at us, calling us grasses.' He was silent for a while, before adding, 'He said if we didn't withdraw our complaint then something might happen to Paula. At the time I believed he would do it. We were really scared.' Another brief pause followed. 'Anyway, we decided we couldn't take the chance. Especially as you lot had still done naff-all. So, next day we went to the police and told them we wanted to withdraw our complaint.' He looked directly at Milner. 'They weren't even that bothered. It was as if we had just been wasting their time. A week later we had moved out and into this place. It was all we could find at the time, what with Paula expecting.'

'Did Grace say why he wanted you to leave?' asked Milner.

'Not really. We heard he wanted to turn it into flats. Although it was only a bit bigger than this place, I suppose he could have got at least two flats out of it. He could then charge more money.'

'So you don't know who moved in after you,' said DC Bennett.

'Are you joking?' replied Paula, her earlier anger having now returned. 'After what happened to us, all we wanted to do was to get as far away from there as possible.'

Milner closed his notebook and said, 'Thank you for your time. You have been very helpful.' He took out a card from his pocket and handed it to Darren. 'If you do remember anything else then give me a call on this number.'

Milner thought for one moment that Darren was about to throw it down. Instead he simply put it into the back pocket of his jeans.

Chapter 11

When they arrived back at the station Tom was waiting for them. 'How did it go? Did you find out anything revealing?' he asked, as they entered the room.

'Only that, as if we didn't know already, the Graces are a nasty piece of work,' replied Milner, who then recounted their conversation with Paula and Darren.

Tom then added some new information of his own. 'Whilst you two were out I made a phone call to an old colleague of mine. DS Smith was one of the officers who worked on the case which put James Grace away. As you said, he was part of an Essex gang back in the eighties. They hijacked a security van which was on its way back to the secure depot after collecting cash from a number of banks. There were three in the gang and the van was rammed and the driver and his colleague dragged out. Although they were knocked about they wouldn't tell them the key numbers to open the back doors. That's when the real rough stuff started. They forced the mate to watch as they really laid about the driver with a baseball bat, breaking both his legs, as well as causing serious damage to his internal organs. They then told him he was next. Not surprising he gave them what they wanted and they were able to get away with over half a million. Grace was one of those carrying out the attack. But, unfortunately, at least for them, one of the gang dropped a roll of tape which he was carrying – although I'm not quite sure what he intended to do with it. What they didn't know was that there was a set of fingerprints on it. Also another member of the gang had stupidly spoken; he shouted, "Get the boot open," presumably to the driver so that they could put the money there. Anyway, that, together with some information from one of their informants, led the investigative team eventually towards James Grace and the rest of the gang. Of course, they denied having anything to do with it, but eventually their alibis were broken and they were found guilty and given their sentences.'

'What happened to the money?' asked Milner.

'It was never recovered,' Tom replied. 'One of the original gang is now dead – he died of a drug overdose not long after he was released. The other one has been back in prison since 2001. He was found guilty of murder. So Grace is the only one left on the outside. Anyway, I think that a trip to Essex is in order. It's about time we went and spoke with our Mr Grace. First, though, I have to make a couple of calls. So why don't you both get something to eat first and we'll set off immediately afterwards?'

As Milner was leaving he suddenly remembered a phone call he had received whilst on his way back to the station. He turned around to face DCI Stone. 'I have the contact details of the care company which you asked for.' He then handed over a small piece of paper. Tom took it and saw the name *Redbreast Home Care Services* in bold type, together with a contact name and number.

As Milner and DC Bennett left the office, DC Bennett said, 'I meant to ask you. What was all that about? Was it linked to this case?'

'No idea,' replied Milner, shrugging his shoulders. 'Probably one of DCI Stone's personal crusades. I've learnt not to ask. If he wants you to know, he'll tell you.'

Whilst the two of them were having lunch Tom thought about the phone calls he had to make. He decided to make the easiest one first and called the number on the piece of paper which Milner had just handed to him. Eventually he had to say that he was from the police before he was finally put through to Mr Alan Wood, the managing director. After a brief conversation he agreed to meet with Mr Wood the following day.

His next call would be to DCS Small. Considering how, as he had got older, he had become a habitually poor sleeper, he had in fact slept very well last night and had woken having decided to take up DCS Small's offer. In fact, in the end, it had been a fairly easy decision to make. So, as he called DCS Small's number, he was reasonably relaxed about the situation.

The phone was answered by his PA and he was immediately put through to DCS Small, who, when he answered, got straight to the point. 'Tom. I've been waiting for your call. What have you decided?'

Tom actually appreciated that there was no attempt to precede the discussion with any false pleasantries. It also suited him as he replied, 'I've decided I would like to take up your offer.'

DCS Small seemed genuinely delighted when he responded. 'That's wonderful news. I was hoping you would say that. When do you think you will be able to start? As you know, we are keen to get you started as quickly as possible.'

Tom now played his own cards. 'Before we agree to that, though, I do have a few caveats.'

There was just a hint of concern in DCS Small's voice when he answered. 'Caveats? Okay, what are they?'

'Well, firstly, the position should be as temporary as possible and certainly no longer than three months. That should give you enough time to find a more *suitable* replacement. Secondly, I should be allowed to continue to work on my current cases, although I accept that any new cases should be handled by another officer. And thirdly that Acting DS Milner should be confirmed as full DS.'

DCS Small actually seemed relieved that Tom's 'caveats' were not more demanding. 'I think I can agree to all of those. So when do you think you could start?'

Tom had anticipated this question. 'I will need a few days to tie up a few loose ends. How about next Monday?' He then added, 'The sooner I start, the sooner the clock starts ticking.'

'Excellent,' replied DCS Small. 'I'll get a memo out to everyone at the station confirming your appointment.'

'Temporary appointment,' said Tom.

Chapter 12

Tom, Milner and DC Bennett were standing in a large, garishly furnished room in James Grace's house in Chelmsford.

Tom showed Grace his ID warrant. 'I'm DCI Stone from the West London Regional Force and' – now turning towards Milner and Bennett – 'this is DS Milner and DC Bennett.' Tom noted how Grace didn't even look at his warrant card. 'We're here to talk to you about the body which was found in your property in Hounslow.'

The house itself seemed to reflect Grace's personality: big and brash. It was a large, mock-Georgian structure, set back from a leafy main road and standing at the end of a long paved drive. Access was through a set of impressive, electronically controlled, wrought-iron gates. At one side of the gates was an entry panel whilst above it was a top-of-the range surveillance camera. Running from both sides of the gates, facing the main road, was a high brick wall. Where the perimeter of the property turned inwards, at right angles, the wall was replaced by a wooden fence with each individual fence panel slotted into a concrete upright.

Separate from the main house was a large double garage, on top of which was an extensive additional storey. Each of the buildings had surveillance cameras fitted. Immediately outside the garage an expensive-looking silver Mercedes saloon was parked and, alongside it, a black Audi A4 Quattro. In direct contrast there was a large and slightly battered white van parked outside the front door of the house.

Tom had rung the bell and the door had been opened by James Grace himself. He was in his mid-fifties and slightly above average height, although his broad shoulders and thick forearms suggested physical work at some time in his past. Although his face was well-lined it was also tanned, probably the result of his recent holiday. His thinning hair had been swept back and dyed dark brown. He was wearing a brightly patterned, short-sleeved shirt. The top two buttons were undone, revealing a heavy gold chain which disappeared under his shirt. A chunky bracelet hung from his right wrist and both hands had more than their fair share of assorted rings. On his left wrist there was a very expensive-looking watch. His trousers were a pair of brown slacks matched by the pair of brown deck shoes he was wearing. All of this gave him the appearance of someone who was still on holiday.

Standing alongside him was his eldest son Brendan. He was quite a bit taller than his father, and even more muscular, but the resemblance was obvious. He had short-cropped dark hair and, although he was not dressed in quite the same overstated way as his father, Tom noticed that his watch was the same expensive brand. So far he had not said anything and, as he stood alongside his father, he exuded a hint of menace.

Before Tom could say anything else Grace said, in his broad Essex accent, 'Now, gents, what can I get you to drink? Scotch? Vodka? Or would you prefer just a beer?'

'We're here to discuss the death of one of your tenants,' replied Tom, making it clear that this was not a social call.

'Well. You don't mind if I have one myself, do you?' he said, already pouring himself a generous measure of what looked like whisky. 'Less than a couple of days ago we were all in Spain, at our villa, celebrating me and the missus's thirty-fifth wedding anniversary. So I'm still in a bit of a holiday mood.'

'When did you find out your tenant had been murdered?' asked Milner, in the same business-like tone as Tom.

Grace stared at Milner for a little while longer than normal. 'You're the youngest detective sergeant I've ever met. Shouldn't you still be at school?'

Brendan let out a slight laugh and spoke for the first time. 'Nice one.'

Suddenly there was an air of tension in the room. Eventually Grace himself broke the silence. 'Looks like I hit a nerve there. Anyway, to answer your question, *Detective Sergeant*,' he said, with exaggerated emphasis on his title, 'I found out when we arrived back here and the local plod arrived and told me. I thought he had just died accidentally in the fire. As I said, it was only when your local lot came calling that I was told he had been murdered.'

'From your tone I get the impression you don't have much time for the police,' said Tom.

Momentarily, Grace looked as though he was about to get angry. But it was only fleeting because when he spoke his smile had returned. 'What's your name again? Stone or Stow, isn't it? Whatever it is, I can tell you I've been questioned by much better coppers than someone like you, or' – he looked directly at Milner – 'the Milkybar Kid there. So just get on with what you've got to say.'

'Yes, I suppose that's because of your family's long association with crime.' Tom immediately carried on, not allowing Grace to respond, 'What is the name of the person who was murdered in your property?'

'No idea,' he answered, quickly and with an air of indifference.

'What? Are you really saying you know nothing about the person found murdered in a property which you own?' asked Tom, giving the impression of undisguised incredulity.

'How am I expected to know the name of everyone who works for me?' He then turned to face his son. 'Brendan, did you know his name?'

'No idea,' he answered, repeating his father's earlier words.

'So, how did you recruit him?' asked Tom, trying a different approach.

'I employ lots of people as temporary labour. They know if they turn up there might be some work for them.'

'Did you know that the DNA profiling suggested that the dead man originally came from Eastern Europe?'

Tom thought he noticed a fleeting look of concern on Grace's face but, if he did, it quickly disappeared and was replaced by a hint of anger when he spoke. 'Look, I keep telling you I've no idea who he was. If he had come from the Moon, I still wouldn't have known who he was.'

Tom thought about following up on this particular line of questioning. Instead, though, he simply said, 'Did you know that cannabis plants were being grown in the house?'

'Course I didn't,' he replied indignantly. 'I'm a respectable businessman. Do you think I would throw all of this away,' he said, looking around the room, 'for a bit of weed?'

Milner spoke. 'It was more than "a bit of weed". Even though the fire had damaged a large part of the house, we still recovered, from just one room, fifteen individual cannabis plants together with plant pots, ventilation pipes, fans, cabling and soil.'

'Look, *Detective Sergeant* Milner, the bloke was living there whilst he was carrying out some work on the house for me. I was turning the house into a couple of flats. How was I to know he was also doing a bit of freelancing on the side? Anyway, cannabis will likely be made legal soon,' he answered, showing little obvious concern for the death of one of his employees.

'Is that why you wanted to get rid of Mr Allen, the existing tenant? So you could convert the house into flats?'

Grace shrugged. 'They had broken the terms of their agreement. They had caused quite a bit of damage to the house and fixtures and fittings. That's why they left.'

'That's not the way they saw it,' replied Milner. 'They complained that you and your son' – at this point Milner nodded in the direction of Brendan – 'had used threats and intimidation to get them to leave.'

'Don't start with that. I seem to remember they dropped all of the charges against us,' Grace said confidently. He took another sip of his drink, before adding in an almost taunting manner, 'Unless, of course, you have any other evidence.' He paused for a while and then continued, 'Do you actually have any evidence?'

Tom chose not to answer his question. Instead he simply asked, 'I understand you own other properties which you rent. Are you also converting these to flats?'

'I'm not, as it happens,' he replied, surprisingly helpfully, before adding, 'Not that it's got anything to do with you. I can do what I like with them.'

'I'm sure you are correct,' replied Tom. 'So, in that case, you won't mind giving us the details of your current tenants.'

For a moment Tom thought Grace was about to respond aggressively to his request. To his surprise, however, he simply turned to his son and said, 'Brendan. Get the details for these gentlemen.'

'Why do you think the man was murdered?' asked Tom, moving on to one of the key questions.

'Haven't got a clue,' answered Grace. 'You said yourself that he was growing some weed. Maybe he'd crossed someone. There are some nasty people out there, Detective Chief Inspector. Anyway, I thought that's why we pay our taxes: so that the police can employ intelligent people like you to find out.' His undisguised sarcasm prompted another snigger from Brendan.

Once again Tom ignored his comment. 'So, I'm assuming you will be able to provide us with full employment details on him, together with the rest of your employees.'

Grace smiled. 'Detective Chief Inspector Stone.' Tom couldn't help noticing how Grace had, this time, suddenly remembered his correct name. 'I run a building company. It's a competitive business and there are a lot of cowboy builders out there. So we have to keep our costs as low as possible. I've told you already that we employ lots of casual labour. They are employed as and when we get work, and we slip them a few quid. How can I be expected to know the ins and outs of every person who does some work for us? Paperwork is not top of our priority list. I'll hold my hands up to that. I'm sure there are some people, sitting in their offices, who are employed just to check up on companies such as ours. I'll wait for the slap on the wrist.'

'How many people do you employ?' Tom asked.

'Five? Ten? I can't remember. It depends how good business is,' he replied. 'When we get a big job we pass the word round and people just turn up.'

Now it was Tom's turn to look around the room. 'It must be quite a few, as you seem to be doing very well for yourself. Is business good at the moment?'

Grace suddenly did become angry, in fact the angriest he had been during their time with him. 'Just because you probably live in a poxy little place you think everybody else should. Let me tell you something, Detective Chief Inspector Stone. Everything I've achieved has been because of these hands and *this*,' he said, pointing towards his head. 'I was born into a family which had nothing. I didn't go to a fancy school or university like you lot. If you think that you and Pinky and Perky there can come into my home and start making threats against me and my family then you have seriously underestimated me.' He then added, somewhat menacingly, 'No one takes liberties with my family and I'll do whatever it takes to protect them.'

There was another brief silence before Tom spoke again. 'Mr Grace. First of all, I can't remember any threats being made against you or your family. Secondly, all of the questions we have asked have been concerned with the murder of one of your employees and in a house which you own. And finally, just so that we are all one hundred percent clear, please be under no doubt that we will continue with our investigation, however long it takes and wherever the evidence takes us. I'm sure we will be speaking with you again.' Looking directly at Grace, he then added, 'And soon.'

Chapter 13

Tom was seated in the small reception area at the offices of Redbreast Home Care Services, having arrived a little ahead of their agreed time. The journey from his home in Staines to their offices in Farnham had taken less time than he had planned. The traffic was heavy heading towards London but, in comparison, very light in the direction he was heading. The one-way system leading into Farnham town centre had threatened to delay him but, eventually, more by chance than good navigational skill, he had found their offices.

On the table immediately in front of him were a number of impressive-looking glossy brochures. He picked one up. The front cover was dominated by the company name and logo. At the centre was a photograph of a robin perched on an outside windowsill looking through the window into a room where a couple of clearly happy and contented elderly people were seated, each drinking a cup of tea. Underneath it was the name *Redbreast Home Care Services* and the strapline: *We help make a house into a home.*

He turned the page. On the inside front cover was a photograph of the person he had come to see. Alan Wood was the managing director of Redbreast Home Care Services, and below his photograph and title was a quote:

> *Redbreast Home Care Services' mission is to provide a caring and always considerate at-home service. We treat all of our clients as individuals and the care package which we provide is tailored to their individual needs. All of our carers have undergone extensive and thorough training and their aim is to ensure they build a relationship such that our customers almost think of them as part of the family.*
>
> *Lots of other care companies are able to provide help with dressing, cleaning or preparing meals, but at Redbreast Home Care Services we pride ourselves on always doing a little bit*

more for our customers. That's why we're the ones who help make a house into a home!

As Tom was reading this the main office door opened and a tall man emerged. He was younger than Tom, probably in his mid-forties. His hair was dark brown and swept back. There were, however, traces of grey showing just above and alongside his ears, whilst his blue eyes were magnified by the large-framed glasses he was wearing. He wore a dark blue suit over a striped blue shirt, and his golden tie was perfectly colour-coordinated with his gold cufflinks. All of this, together with his very upright and erect posture, combined to exaggerate his natural presence.

Tom stood up as the man approached him. 'Mr Wood?' He held out his hand.

'That's correct. I assume that you are Detective Inspector Stone,' he said, shaking Tom's hand.

Tom corrected him. 'Detective Chief Inspector, actually.'

'Apologies for that. I never was any good at remembering titles,' he said. 'Strange, really, given that I was an army officer for nearly fifteen years.'

'Don't worry. Lots of people make the same mistake,' replied Tom, suddenly remembering his meeting with James Grace.

'Please come into my office,' said Mr Wood, already walking towards it. 'It's a bit more comfortable in here.'

As he entered, the first thing Tom noticed was just how neat and tidy it was. A flat-screen computer sat in the centre of a desk, with a printer alongside it. The only other thing on the desk was a photograph of a woman and two teenage boys. On the other side of the office there was a small circular table with four comfortable-looking chairs. Framed photographs of snow-capped mountains were on two of the walls, against one of which rested a wooden filing cabinet.

'Please take a seat,' said Wood, pointing towards one of the chairs around the table. 'Can I get you something to drink?'

'No, thank you,' replied Tom, who was keen to get started.

When they were both seated, Wood said, 'You mentioned on the phone you wanted to discuss one of our clients. So, how may I help you?'

Tom had given some thought as to how he would explain

the reason for the meeting. 'One of your clients – Mr Wilson – recently died and the post-mortem revealed a number of unexplained bruises on his body. We are trying to determine exactly what caused these bruises.'

Wood looked genuinely shocked. 'Are you suggesting he may have been murdered?'

'No. Not at all. The cause of his death was a heart attack. Of that there is no doubt,' he said reassuringly. He paused momentarily before continuing, 'However, as I mentioned, there was bruising on his body, which had occurred fairly recently, and was consistent with him being forcibly restrained.'

The full implication of what Tom had just said suddenly dawned on Wood and, when he next spoke, this was reflected in the increased aggression in his voice. 'I hope you are not suggesting any of my staff had anything to do with that.'

'I'm certainly not, but, as I'm sure you can appreciate, we do have a duty to fully investigate when this type of unexplained event occurs. As part of those investigations it would be useful, therefore, if you could let me have a list of all of your staff who visited Mr Wilson in, say, the four weeks prior to his death.'

Wood's earlier aggression had now disappeared, probably as a result of him realising the seriousness of this enquiry. 'Of course. I'll get it to you as soon as possible.'

'Thank you,' answered Tom, 'although I was hoping to be able to take it away with me today.'

'I'll see what I can do, but that might be difficult. If you could let me have the dates I'll go and find out what can be done.'

Tom provided Wood with the dates he was interested in, together with Mr Wilson's address details. Wood then stood up, opened his door and walked out into the outer office. Tom was expecting an extended wait but within five minutes or so Wood returned to his office, a couple of printed copies of A4 paper in his hand. He handed them over to Tom. 'Here's the information you need.'

Tom spent a few moments looking at the list. Eventually, he looked up. 'There seem to be a lot of different names on the list. Is that normal?'

Tom noticed how Wood suddenly looked slightly uncomfortable, but, when he spoke, his natural confidence had returned. 'Yes, that's quite normal. We employ lots of domiciliary carers and so it really depends on who is available at the time.'

'It says in your brochure that one of your aims is to ensure that your staff can be thought of as being part of the family. How can you achieve this if, as in Mr Wilson's case, for example, your clients are visited by twelve different carers over a four-week period?'

Once again Wood looked uncomfortable. 'That is definitely our aim but, due to staffing or short-notice rota difficulties, it is not always possible. Our main priority then is to ensure our clients receive the standard basic care. We make sure that they are properly dressed, clean and fed.'

'So, in those circumstances, there is no time to develop a relationship with your customers. Is that what you are saying?'

'As I said, we sometimes have to adopt a more pragmatic approach.'

'Is it your normal policy for all of your employees to be thoroughly briefed on any particular medical condition which your clients might be suffering from?'

'I'm not sure that I fully understand,' replied Wood.

'Well, in Mr Wilson's case he was being treated for acute angina and high blood pressure. In addition he had recently been diagnosed as suffering from the early stages of Alzheimer's disease. Would all of the twelve people who visited him in the four weeks prior to his death have been aware of his changed condition?'

The way the conversation had suddenly developed had clearly worried Wood and he could not disguise this increasing concern when he replied. 'They should have been. It's a key part of the client's individual care profile.'

Tom was determined to press home the point, however uncomfortable it was proving for Wood. 'Is "should have been" the same as "definitely were"? After all, in your glossy brochure you state' – at this stage Tom started to read from the brochure – '*We treat all of our clients as individuals and the care package which we provide is tailored to their individual needs.*' He placed the brochure on the table and looked directly at Wood, waiting for an answer.

As he'd done previously, Wood quickly regained his composure. 'What I meant was that I, personally, do not know. I'm sure all of Mr Wilson's medical details are on his file and that Mrs Staunton would have briefed the individual carers.'

'Who is Mrs Staunton?'

'Barbara Staunton is my care manager. She is the person who is responsible for all of the day-to-day operational issues: recruitment, arranging the work rotas as well as briefing the individual carers.'

'As I'm here, would it be possible to speak with Mrs Staunton?'

'I'm afraid she's not here at the moment. She's currently with a client.'

Tom, once again, looked at the list of names in front of him. After a while he looked back towards Wood and said, 'I will also need contact details for all of the people on this list. It's likely we will need to speak to them.'

'What? Interview them?' asked Wood, his recently acquired composure having suddenly deserted him.

'Well, I wouldn't call it an interview,' replied Tom. 'I was thinking of something a little less formal than that. Anyway, I'd appreciate it if you could provide me with their details.'

'When do you need them by?' asked Wood.

'Tomorrow morning would be fine.' He stood up and offered his hand to Wood. 'Thank you for your time. You have been very helpful. Here's a card with all of my contact details, including my email address. Don't hesitate to call me if there is anything you remember which you might think is important with regard to Mr Wilson.'

Wood took the card from Tom.

'Would you mind if I took one of your brochures?' asked Tom.

Wood didn't respond, other than to simply shrug his shoulders.

Chapter 14

Whilst Tom had been visiting Redbreast Home Care Services, Milner and DC Bennett had spent most of the morning following up on the names of the other tenants which Grace had seemed so reluctant to give to them. From the information they had it appeared, at least at first glance, that the occupants were genuine tenants. Nonetheless, Milner had asked DC Bennett to visit the other two properties, in Hounslow and Feltham, to interview the tenants. Whilst he was doing this Milner started to check Grace's business operation.

As Milner was working his way through this information his computer 'pinged' to let him know an email had come through. What immediately focused his attention was the title of this particular email. The email was from Detective Chief Superintendent Small and titled *DCI Stone appointed Interim Superintendent*. He clicked on the title and opened it and started to read with increasing surprise.

From: DCS Small, Regional Headquarters
To: All officers and staff at West London Regional Station

This is to confirm, effective next Monday, the appointment of DCI Stone as Interim Superintendent, West London Regional Station. DCI Stone will assume full responsibility for all operational matters until such time as a permanent appointment is announced.

I'm sure that I and DCI Stone can count on your continued support.

As he tried to absorb the full implications of this announcement, as much for himself as for DCI Stone, his mobile started to ring. It was one of his colleagues who had also just read the email and wanted to talk to him about it. This pattern continued for the next hour or so as people would either call or come to see him to discuss it. He also noticed how small groups of officers had suddenly formed in various parts of the station, no doubt discussing the very same thing. DCI Stone himself had often said how the tittle-tattle and intrigue that occurred in a police station could sometimes be a good match for any Westminster politician.

Milner did think he could see it as a sort of compliment that officers were seeking his input. On the other hand, though, the fact that DCI Stone had not mentioned it to him, particularly after he himself had brought up his own plans to apply for the position in Brighton, slightly undermined this feeling. Of course, knowing DCI Stone and how he was the type of person who always kept his cards very close to his chest, there was no logical reason why he should have discussed it with him.

After the initial excitement of the announcement had died down, Milner resumed his work on Grace's business operation. Just as he was finishing, DC Bennett appeared.

'I guess you've heard the news about DCI Stone. Crafty old sod kept that quiet,' he said to Milner.

'He certainly did,' answered Milner, once again thinking about his own career discussion with DCI Stone. He then added with considered understatement, 'It was a bit of a surprise.'

'So you didn't know.'

'Not at all,' replied Milner, suddenly reviving his earlier feeling of disappointment.

'I have to say I thought that it was a wind-up when DC Johnson told me. I've known DCI Stone for quite a long time now and I can't think of anyone less suited to an office job,' said DC Bennett, summarising exactly Milner's own thoughts.

'Well, I imagine he has his reasons,' answered Milner diplomatically. 'Anyway, it did say that it was an interim appointment.'

'I know, but ... what's the expression? "Possession is nine tenths of the law."' He started to laugh when he realised what he had just said. 'Quite appropriate, don't you think? Anyway, these interim appointments have a habit of becoming permanent. It's a bit like a football manager.'

'What do you mean?' asked Milner, who was not a keen football supporter.

'Well, let's say a team has a bad run of results. The manager comes under pressure and, unless there is an immediate improvement in the team's results, usually then gets sacked. Someone from inside the club – the assistant manager or even, occasionally, the youth team coach – is asked to take over on an interim basis, or, as they like to describe it, on a caretaker basis. Even he then says how he's not interested in the job on a permanent basis. Suddenly, though, the team start playing out of their skin and win a few matches. There is pressure then on the board, often from the fans themselves, to offer the caretaker manager the job permanently, which, more often than not, they do. He is flattered by the offer and, probably against his better judgement, decides to accept.'

'What normally happens after that?' asked Milner, suddenly interested in this football comparison.

'Almost invariably, the team soon start losing badly again and the new manager gets the sack and then they are back to square one.' It was clear to Milner that DC Bennett had quite enjoyed expanding on his analogy.

'If I were you,' replied Milner, 'I wouldn't recount that particular story when DCI Stone is around. I'm not sure he would appreciate the analogy – especially the ending.' He paused for a while. 'Anyway, what did you find out about the other two tenants?'

'Well, there didn't seem to be anything untoward. I spoke to both tenants. I told them we were simply conducting enquiries relating to the death in Grace's other property. They both appeared perfectly normal. They had been renting their properties for over a year and had never even seen James Grace. They did say, though, that someone would come round for the rent every month. They would pay it and then not see anyone until the following month.'

'Pay in cash?' asked Milner.

'Yes, that is a bit strange, but that's the way Grace wanted it.'

'I'll bet he did,' said Milner.

Just then they were disturbed by what sounded like singing coming from one of the other offices. They both stepped out of their office and into the corridor. There was a line of officers who were shouting and cheering. In their midst stood DCI Stone. Finally, the cheering died down and a visibly embarrassed DCI Stone held up both hands, as if in surrender.

'I'm assuming you have all now heard. All I can say is this

was as much a surprise to me, when I was asked, as it clearly is to you now. It's just a temporary placement until they find someone better than me.'

'Shouldn't take too long, then,' someone shouted. That prompted some more heckling: 'When are you getting measured for your uniform?' followed by, 'I suppose that means you don't have to buy your own coffee now.'

'He never did anyway,' someone else shouted. This resulted in widespread laughter.

'Very funny,' shouted Tom, trying to be heard. 'If I hear you say that again, after Monday you might find yourself walking the beat again on Friday nights. Actually,' he added, looking around at everyone, 'there are a few more here who might be joining you.'

Once again, everyone laughed, which had the effect of easing Tom's embarrassment.

'Seriously, though, I've worked with most of you for a few years now and so you know me well enough to know that I'm not a desk copper. So don't expect me to disappear into the office on the fifth floor and just sit there writing reports. I will still be the same person, sticking my nose into where it's not wanted.' He then went on, 'Right. Here's my first order – a bit early, I know, but I need to practise. The fun for the day is over, so everybody now get back to work.'

As he finished saying this a few people started to applaud and it wasn't long before all of the others joined in. Tom, not normally one for showing any outward emotion, suddenly felt the hairs standing up on the back of his neck but, at least outwardly, maintained a calm composure as he walked towards his own office, followed by Milner and DC Bennett.

When they were there Tom turned towards them and said, 'I suppose I owe you two an apology. I did mean to tell you both first but hadn't expected DCS Small to beat me to it. Anyway, I am really sorry about that.' Before anyone could answer he continued, 'I'm sure you both have lots of questions but the main thing is that we, that's the three of us, carry on with the house-fire murder. I won't be involved in any new cases, though. At least, that is, until I've finished my temporary stint as Acting Superintendent. So I'll soon be back.'

At this point Milner suddenly remembered DC Bennett's football manager story.

Chapter 15

All three were seated around the small table in Tom's office. He looked towards Milner. 'So, do we have any new information?'

Milner then opened a file and began to summarise what he'd been able to find out. As Grace had implied, his business – JG Building Services Ltd – specialised in renovating older houses and building extensions. Milner had managed to obtain a record of the company accounts which showed, for the latest year, it had a declared turnover of £195,000 and a net profit of £25,000. When he'd originally read this he had been surprised by just how modest the amount of profit that the business generated was when compared to Grace's conspicuous lifestyle. Grace's sons, Brendan and William, were registered as company directors whilst James Grace was shown as being the managing director. Milner had also been able to confirm that the family home, which they had purchased almost fifteen years ago, was, in fact, legally owned by James Grace's wife, Angie, together with all of the other properties.

'Hmm. It all seems to be very precise,' Tom reflected, before adding, 'and convenient.' He appeared, though, to have put this, mentally at least, to one side when he next spoke. 'Were you able to find out anything regarding his other employees?'

'I'm afraid not, sir,' replied Milner, clearly disappointed with his own answer. 'But I'm still checking. I've asked for any National Insurance numbers associated with their business.'

'I wouldn't hold your breath,' Tom said to no one in particular. 'So we don't know where they are at the moment?'

'No, sir, but I'd like to bet that James Grace does,' replied Milner.

There was silence whilst Tom considered everything he'd just been told. 'Okay, it's clear that we need to track these men down as soon as possible. I have a feeling they will help us to solve this. So here's what I want you to do.'

As Milner and DC Bennett were preparing to leave his office

Tom suddenly said, 'DS Milner, can I have a quick word with you before you go?'

Milner now knew DCI Stone well enough to know never to make assumptions as to the reason for such a request. Nonetheless, he couldn't help feeling a bit concerned.

After DC Bennett had left Tom said, 'Please sit down. There's something I'd like to discuss with you.'

Now with an increasing sense of concern, Milner sat opposite Tom.

'Don't look so worried,' said Tom as reassuringly as he could. 'It's basically good news.' He paused and then added, 'Well, *I* think it's good news. When you've heard what I have to say I hope you will as well.'

Milner didn't respond and so Tom continued. 'I've been thinking about what you said, when you told me about your plans to apply for a DS position in Brighton. Anyway, I'll get straight to the point. I have an alternative suggestion to make. What if your current Acting DS position was made permanent?'

Milner was momentarily lost for words. Eventually, though, he got his thoughts together. 'What, here, at this station?'

'Yes, here,' answered Tom, tempted to add 'where else?' Instead he carried on. 'Whilst I'm carrying out my new duties, I need you here to look after things. I've agreed, therefore, with DCS Small, that you should be made up to full DS.'

'When would that be, sir?'

'Well, how about from Monday onwards? It seems quite a popular day,' replied Tom, thinking of his own situation.

'Can I think about it, sir?' he asked.

Milner's reply took Tom by surprise and this was apparent when he answered. 'Well, yes, of course. But, as I said, I was hoping to confirm your appointment on Monday.'

'I appreciate that, sir,' he replied. 'It's just that this has come as a bit of a surprise and, to be honest, I had sort of mentally got myself excited about the possibility of the Brighton position. Can I let you know before then?'

'Of course you can,' answered a still-disappointed Tom. 'Just don't leave it too late.'

Milner stood up and, as he walked out of the office, thought how today had been a day full of surprises. First, there was the announcement of DCI Stone's appointment as Superintendent, and now this.

Chapter 16

It was seven o'clock the following morning, and they were back in DCI Stone's office.

'Are you all set?' asked Tom.

'Yes, sir,' replied Milner. 'Both of us have a pair of binoculars and a camera.' Before they had left last night they had all agreed just how important it was to find out where Grace's employees were living. It certainly wasn't the best plan they had ever developed but, unless Grace himself suddenly decided to show them where they lived, this was probably the best alternative.

It was agreed Milner and DC Bennett would spend the day discreetly tailing the Graces. Milner would take James Grace and DC Bennett would follow Brendan Grace.

'Good,' replied Tom. 'But don't get too close and,' he said with increased emphasis, 'do not get involved in any confrontation. If you think you may have been spotted, break away immediately. I have a feeling there's likely to be plenty of opportunities for heroics later on. But today is not one of them. Understand?'

'Yes, sir,' they both answered simultaneously.

'Let's aim to meet again, here, at five o'clock – unless, of course, one of you finds out something earlier, in which case make sure you let the other one know straight away, and then get back here as soon as possible.'

They both stood up to leave. Tom looked at them. 'And good luck.'

After they had left, Tom thought he would spend the rest of the morning sorting out some of the administrative jobs which he had been putting off. Monday suddenly didn't seem that far off and he wanted to start his new role with a clear desk. Although he didn't know exactly what to expect, he did think some paper pushing and report writing might be involved.

His wastebasket was almost overflowing with discarded

paper when he decided to check his emails. It always amazed him just how many pointless emails he received. Most of them were where he had simply been copied in 'for information'. To him this usually meant that the sender was covering their back just in case any blame needed, subsequently, to be thrown around. In the 'old days' people would come and talk to you face-to-face if they felt you needed to know something. And, anyway, how was he supposed to read every single email that he received, just in case it did contain something important? Over the years, he had developed an extra sense which usually told him, after a quick glance at the first part of an email, that he could safely delete it. Of course, occasionally, he did accidentally delete an email which turned out to be important, but, in his opinion, it was a risk worth taking.

As he worked his way through the emails, taking an increasingly perverse satisfaction in pressing the 'delete' button, he spotted one which grabbed his attention. It was from Alan Wood, the managing director of Redbreast Home Care Services. He clicked his mouse and opened it.

From: Alan Wood
To: DCI Stone
Subject: Contact details

Following on from yesterday's meeting please find attached contact details for all of those of our staff who were on the list which I provided for you yesterday.

If you need any additional information don't hesitate to contact me.

Regards,
Alan Wood,
Managing Director,
Redbreast Home Care Services

At least it was succinct and to the point, Tom thought. He clicked on the attachment and a list of names appeared. Alongside each name was an address and contact telephone number. After he had printed them off he compared them to the twelve names which Wood had provided him with yesterday. He was reassured to see that all of them were on the new list, together with the care manager, Mrs Staunton. He decided it would make sense if he began by speaking with her and so he called the number which was alongside her name.

After just a couple of rings his call was answered in a professional, upbeat manner. 'Redbreast Home Care Services. Barbara Staunton speaking. How may I help you?'

'Good morning, Mrs Staunton. My name is DCI Stone from the West London Regional Police and I was given your name by Mr Wood. I was hoping you would be able to help me.'

When Mrs Staunton next spoke her earlier enthusiastic tone had almost completely disappeared, to be replaced by a clearly more nervous one. 'Mr Wood told me you had been to see him about the death of Mr Wilson and might need to speak to me. I wasn't, though, expecting it to be so soon.'

Tom thought it might be best if he tried to set her at ease. 'In the police force it's often best to follow up on things quickly. You never know when something else might come along.' He paused and then said, 'Anyway, it won't take too long. I have just a few questions to ask.' When she didn't reply he carried on. 'Did you personally know Mr Wilson?'

'Not really,' she answered. 'I wasn't with Redbreast when he first became a client of ours. I have, though, been to visit him when one of the staff couldn't make it and we couldn't find a replacement in time.'

'Does that happen often?' asked Tom.

'What? That I fill in or some staff can't make their appointment?'

'Well, I suppose both,' answered Tom.

'To be honest, it's quite common that we have staff problems. All of our staff work on zero-hour contracts and so things can often change at the last minute. When that happens we are usually able to call in other staff members. But, sometimes, particularly when things happen at short notice, this isn't possible. It's such instances as these when I'll visit in their place.'

'I noticed, from your daily contact sheets, how Mr Wilson had been visited by twelve different people for the four weeks immediately prior to his death. Would that be normal?'

When she didn't reply Tom said, 'Mrs Staunton, are you still there?'

'Yes, I'm still here,' she replied.

It was now his turn to remain quiet and he let the increasingly uneasy silence do its work.

Eventually, Mrs Staunton answered his question. 'Twelve is on the high side but it's likely that a number of different carers would visit our clients over a period of a few weeks.'

'So the situation with Mr Wilson was not that unusual?' he asked for clarification.

Another momentary silence followed before she replied. 'Well, I wouldn't normally expect so many different carers but, yes, it does happen.'

'And what did they specifically have to do, with regard to Mr Wilson?' asked Tom.

It was clear, when she answered, that she had anticipated this question. 'Mr Wilson's local authority had contracted for thirty minutes in the morning and another thirty minutes in the evening. In the morning, for example, our carers would make sure that he was washed and dressed, as well as making his breakfast. In the evening they would make dinner and get him ready for bed.'

'How are your carers monitored to ensure that they always, say, spend the contracted thirty minutes with him?'

This time it appeared that Mrs Staunton had not anticipated this particular question and, when she answered, it was lacking her earlier confidence. 'Well, they have to sign their work sheet to confirm that they have been there.'

'So it's possible they could sign for thirty minutes even though they actually might have been there for less than thirty minutes.'

A tense silence followed before she finally answered. 'I suppose it's possible but I don't think it's likely.'

'As I understand it, your carers are not paid for the time they spend travelling between clients. Is that correct?'

'Yes, that's correct. It's fairly standard practice within the domiciliary care sector.'

'That might then provide a reason why, sometimes, carers don't spend the contracted time with their clients. Because they need to make up time.' Before she could respond Tom then asked, 'How much are your carers paid, Mrs Staunton?'

'It varies slightly from person to person,' she answered before adding, rather defensively, 'although I know it is above the minimum wage level.'

It was again Tom's turn to remain silent as he considered pursuing this line of questioning. He finally decided that he had all of the information he needed and so opened up a new one. 'Are all of your carers properly trained to carry out their tasks, before they make their visits?'

Her immediate reply suggested she felt more confident with this particular question. 'Yes,' she answered assertively. 'All of our staff *have* to be properly trained before they are allowed to visit clients. That's standard and is one of the most important requirements when running any home care service. We also, by the way, have to carry out police checks before we employ any of our staff.'

'I see,' he said. 'Does that training also include being briefed on any particular medical condition which your client is being treated for?'

'I'm not sure what you mean,' she replied.

'Well, take Mr Wilson for example. He suffered from high blood pressure and severe angina. In addition, he had been diagnosed with early signs of Alzheimer's disease. Would all of those twelve carers who came to visit him have been made aware of his condition?'

'Yes, certainly his high blood pressure. That would have been included on his personal file. Apart from the file, which we hold in the office, each of our clients also has a summary of their particular condition – medical, dietary etc. And this has to be prominently displayed within the client's house.'

'Isn't it the correct protocol to also report anything which is out of the ordinary?'

'It is,' answered Mrs Staunton a little hesitantly, evidently wondering where this was about to lead.

'Mr Wood, no doubt, has informed you about the bruises on Mr Wilson's body. So why were these bruises not reported?'

'I'm afraid I don't know. Perhaps they were not that easy to spot.'

Both remained silent. Finally Tom spoke. 'And what about his Alzheimer's condition?'

'I'm not sure about that,' she replied quietly. 'It depends when he was diagnosed with it. I would have to check.'

'Could you, please? I'd also be grateful if you could email me a copy of Mr Wilson's personal care file. Mr Wood already has my email address,' he said. 'Thank you for your time, Mrs Staunton; you have been very helpful. I may, though, have to speak with you again.'

Chapter 17

Although Milner and DC Bennett had travelled in separate cars they had managed to coordinate it so they both arrived, close to Grace's house, within a few minutes of each other. The drive clockwise along the M25 motorway had, for a Friday morning, been surprisingly trouble-free and they were both in place before 9 am, each with binoculars and cameras close to hand.

They didn't have to wait long before the front door opened and Brendan Grace appeared with what looked like a mobile phone in his left hand. He immediately started walking purposefully towards the same white van that they had seen when they had last been there.

Grace appeared to have some trouble opening the van door. As DC Bennett was taking a few photographs he could see the reason for Grace's difficulty: there was a large dent on the driver's side of the van. Eventually, with a bit of brute force, the door opened and Grace got in and started the engine. It looked like he was making a phone call, on his mobile, and this was confirmed when his van emerged from the gates and turned left down the main road. DC Bennett also noticed how Grace had not bothered to wear his seatbelt and, as he started to follow, said to himself, 'That's a good start. Two offences already and he's only just come out of the house.'

Taking care to keep his distance, he followed the van for a couple of miles along a main road and then a further mile or so along a minor one until Grace suddenly turned left. DC Bennett continued straight on but, as he drove past the opening, he caught a quick glimpse of Grace's van disappearing down a narrow path. He drove on until he came to a mini-roundabout, turned around and headed back until he passed the path which Grace had driven down. A little further along the road he could see a narrow lay-by and so he indicated left and pulled in. As agreed, he then called Milner and explained what had happened.

'What do you want me to do next, sir?' he asked. 'Wait for him to come back or take a nosey around?'

'How open is it?' asked Milner.

'I've just checked the maps app on my phone. It looks as though the path turns to the right and then, after about half a mile, the trees on either side give way to open fields. Over the fields there's what looks like a farm and outbuildings.'

There was no immediate reply as Milner was deciding what to do next. If it was him he would try and get a bit closer, but, of course, now that DC Bennett reported to him he suddenly had other things to consider. On the other hand, now was a good time to have faith in DC Bennett.

Finally he answered. 'Okay. Go and see what you can find out. But don't get too close, and stay under cover of the trees. Remember what DCI Stone said to us about no heroics.'

'I will. Don't worry. I've got no intentions of trying to become an instant hero. I'll just see what's going on there.'

'Call me when you've finished.'

'Roger that,' he replied.

Picking up his binoculars and camera, DC Bennett got out of his car, locked it and started to walk back towards the path. When he got there he could immediately see that, although the path was initially quite straight, it did, as his app showed, take quite a severe turn to the right after about a hundred yards. He took Milner's advice and resisted the temptation to walk straight along the path. Instead he made sure he kept well within the left-side line of trees.

When he got to the point where the path turned right, he stopped and hid behind a large bush and picked up his binoculars. He could see that, after another hundred yards or so, the trees on either side of the path started to thin out, and they disappeared entirely after another few hundred yards, to be replaced by open fields.

Having considered his next move, DC Bennett decided he could, provided he didn't get too close to the point where the trees thinned out, safely move a bit nearer. So, with his binoculars around his neck and camera in hand, he started to move closer. Eventually he realised that to go any closer would simply be to invite trouble and so, having found another large bush, set well back from the path but with a relatively unimpeded view of the farmhouse, he knelt down and picked up his binoculars again.

He was reassured by the fact that he could clearly make out Grace's van, which was parked directly outside the farmhouse. Alongside it were a white van and a large, red pickup truck. Considering these worthy of a few photographs, he picked up his camera and took a few shots. As he was doing this the door of the farmhouse opened and Grace, now carrying a small parcel, emerged from it, immediately followed by another man and then a couple of dogs. The man was tall and well-built, probably in his early fifties, with short-cropped grey hair. DC Bennett switched the focus of his camera over to them. As soon as he was happy he had some good photographs he returned to his binoculars.

Grace and the other man, followed by the two dogs, walked towards one of the outbuildings. When they got there the stranger took out a key, placed it in the lock and opened the large door, and men and dogs disappeared inside. DC Bennett still had his binoculars focused on the door when the two men emerged, once again followed by the dogs. What surprised him, though, was that another five men also emerged. He quickly grabbed his camera and tried to focus it on the newcomers as they all walked towards Grace's van.

When Grace reached the van he opened the back doors and all five of the men from the building climbed into the back. Once they were all in, Grace closed the door and walked towards the driver's door. Before he got in he shook hands with the older man and then pulled hard on the door handle. This time it opened fairly easily and he climbed in and started the engine, swung the van around and made back towards the path.

DC Bennett had been focused on continuing to take as many photographs as possible and so he was slightly taken aback to suddenly realise that the van was heading back towards him. Fortunately he still had enough time to ensure he was well-hidden behind the bush. Nonetheless, he decided to get down as low as possible whilst still being able to take photographs. He was positioned on the van's right, and as it came past him he could clearly make out Grace in the driver's seat. As the van made its way down the path and towards the road, he kept taking photographs. After a few minutes he considered it safe to make his own way back towards his car.

When he was back in his car, as instructed, he phoned Milner and explained what had happened.

'Should I get back to the station or go and have another snoop around the farm?' he asked.

'Don't push your luck. Just get back to the station and I'll see you there,' answered Milner. 'It's all been quiet here. Grace hasn't come out of the house and no one has visited him. Not even the postman. I'll hang around for a bit longer, though, but, if nothing happens, I'll then make my way back to the station. When you arrive back, get those photos printed so we can take a closer look.'

It was just after lunchtime when DC Bennett arrived back. He immediately went to see the photo lab boys and explained how he needed the photographs urgently.

As he was heading towards the office he shared with Milner, he spotted DCI Stone walking towards him.

'You're back early. No trouble, I hope,' said Tom. Before DC Bennett could reply, Tom carried on, 'Why don't you get us both a coffee from the machine, and then you can fill me in?'

DC Bennett had been in the force for a long time and so knew there was a clear protocol which said you should always brief your immediate boss first. He had, therefore, been hoping that he could do this when Milner got back, but now felt as though he had no choice but to break that protocol. This was not a good start in his relationship with DS Milner.

Chapter 18

Due to an accident, anti-clockwise along the M25, which caused a long tailback, it was after 4pm before all three were once again together. Even though DC Bennett had already briefed him, Tom recognised it was important for Milner to feel as though he was part of the updated briefing.

Looking directly at DC Bennett, Tom said, 'Okay, now that we are all back again, why don't you tell DS Milner and me what you saw?'

Although DC Bennett didn't show it, he was relieved that DCI Stone had not indicated that he knew already what had happened.

DC Bennett spent the next few minutes recounting what had happened and what he had seen. When he had finished he opened an A4 buff file, revealing a selection of oversize photographs. He started to lay them out on the table. 'These are the photos I took. A few of them aren't quite up to a professional standard, but it's not easy taking the perfect photo when you are squatting behind a bush.'

Tom pulled out one of the less clear ones. 'Don't ever try and get a job as one of the paparazzi,' he said as he put it to one side.

They spent the next few minutes reviewing all of the photos in order to select those which most clearly showed all of the men. After they had done this, they stood back to consider what was in front of them.

'Apart from "young Mr Grace", do either of you recognise any of them?' Tom's attempt at a little levity clearly wasn't recognised by either Milner or DC Bennett.

'I certainly don't,' replied Milner.

'What about you, DC Bennett? You've been around for a while.'

'No, I can't say that I do either,' he answered.

Tom, still looking directly at DC Bennett, said, 'Any idea where they were heading after they left the farm?'

'None at all. Sorry. By the time I got to the main road they were long gone.'

'Okay,' said Tom. 'Any ideas?'

Milner replied first. 'What we do have suggests these are the men who Grace uses for his building work. Of course, I might be wrong, but there's just too much circumstantial evidence. So we could stop them the next time they try to leave the farm. As an alternative, I suppose we could follow them to where they are working and then grab them.'

'DC Bennett, any ideas?'

'I agree with DS Milner's suggestions. My preference, though, would be to nick them at the farm. If we try and do it in a public place then you just never know what might happen. It might all get a bit emotional.'

Tom considered what they had both said. After a while he had clearly made up his mind. 'Let's get them at the farm. At least that way we have them in a fairly open place and, as DC Bennett meant, more under our control.' He carried on, 'Milner, I want you and DC Bennett to put a plan together. The resources we will need, what back-up, what paperwork needs to be completed. You know the routine by now. When you have finished, call me so that we can finally agree it.'

'When should we do it?' asked Milner.

'As soon as possible,' replied Tom, a little sharply. 'Why wait? The sooner, the better, as far as I'm concerned. This is a murder investigation.' He then, almost as an afterthought, added, 'Plus there's the fact I've taken an instant dislike to James Grace.'

After Milner and DC Bennett had left to work on the plan, Tom took out the list of carers which Wood had provided him with. He could see that for the four weeks immediately prior to his death, Mr Wilson had fifty-six individual visits: two each day. Of the twelve different carers who had visited, three of them had visited more than the others. He made a separate note of their names and contact details, together with the actual dates they had visited.

The person who had made the most visits, presumably because she was his main carer, was Ruth Brown. She had attended to Mr Wilson a total of twelve times, the last time being just three days before he died. Joanne Stawling was next, in terms of visits, with ten, although none of those were within a week of his death. The final person on his revised list was Diane Filton. She had been to Mr Wilson's home a total of eight times, all of them within his final two weeks, and, in fact, had been the person who had visited on the morning he had died. Tom decided there was little more he could do today and so put the new list in the file with the other one.

By now it was after 7pm and, before he left the station, he called Mary. She answered almost immediately.

'That's really strange. I was just thinking about giving you a call when my mobile rang,' she said, with an almost schoolgirl enthusiasm. 'Perhaps it means we have started to subconsciously read each other's minds.'

'Or maybe it's because I knew you would be back at home now and you knew I would probably be back or, at least, on my way home,' he replied.

'That's what I love about you, Tom Stone. You are such a romantic person.' She laughed. 'Why couldn't you have just humoured me by agreeing?'

'Sorry,' he answered, slightly sheepishly. 'I'll try and remember next time.' Before she could carry on this line of conversation he said, 'Anyway, what sort of day have you had? Busy?'

'Friday and Saturday are our two busiest days,' she answered. She was referring to the flower business she had owned ever since her husband had died. 'Are we still on for our date tomorrow night?'

Earlier in the week they had agreed that Mary would come over to Tom's house on Saturday evening, when he would make dinner for them both. Whilst he had not completely forgotten about this, and indeed was looking forward to seeing her again, nonetheless he had to admit the day's events had somehow managed to get in the way of this commitment.

'We certainly are,' he answered as enthusiastically as possible. 'I've already started thinking about what I will cook.'

'Really?' said a genuinely surprised Mary. 'You really are becoming quite the modern man.'

Tom didn't know whether he should take this as a compliment or an insult. Despite Mary's best intentions and nurturing, the many years he had spent alone seemed to be winning the battle against him ever becoming a modern man.

'Yes, I suppose I am,' he replied. 'Anyway, I hope that you are also planning to stay over.'

'Why, what do you have in mind?' she said teasingly.

'Well, I thought that we could carry on where we left off the other morning.'

Mary laughed. 'It's almost as though you're a teenager again. I hope you will still be this passionate when I'm old and grey.'

'I'm sure I will,' he answered diplomatically. 'Anyway, I can't help fancying you. I'm only human. What time do you think you'll get to my place?'

'By the time I've closed the shop and collected a few things from home, I should be with you between seven and seven thirty. I was hoping that we could spend most of Sunday together as well. Perhaps we could go for a walk.'

'Yes, that's a good idea,' he said. 'But let's see what the weather is like first,' he added, somewhat less enthusiastically. 'Anyway, I'll see you tomorrow evening.'

'Love you,' she replied, but Tom had already gone.

Chapter 19

It was Saturday afternoon and Tom was just starting to think about the evening's dinner when his phone rang. It was Milner.

'Hello, Milner. I'm assuming you have some news.'

'Not news as such, sir, only that DC Bennett and myself have now finalised the operational plan and, as you said you wanted us to get back to you straight away, I thought I'd give you a call to say we are ready to discuss it with you.'

'When are you suggesting that it take place?'

'We could do it early Monday morning,' answered Milner, clearly quite proud of the fact that they had been able to pull it together so quickly. 'You did say you'd like it to happen as quickly as possible. We've agreed the resources and, in fact, I've taken the liberty of putting them on standby for Monday. All it needs now is a senior officer's OK.' He paused and then added, with some obvious satisfaction, 'And as you, from Monday, will be the most senior officer, I was hoping you could sign it off today.'

On the one hand, Tom was highly impressed that Milner had been able to organise this operation in such a short period of time. On the other, however, it had now presented him with a bit of a dilemma, personally as well as professionally.

'Yes, I suppose I could sign it off,' he eventually said. 'But I want to see the plan first. We are only going to get one chance to do this. I've seen too many similar operations go off half-cocked due to sloppy planning.' He paused for a while, as he thought through the various options available to him. 'Right. I'll be with you in about half an hour.'

When he arrived at the station he found Milner and DC Bennett examining a sheet of paper. 'What's that?' he asked as he entered the office.

They both looked up. 'It's the final list of officers who we would like allocated to the operation,' said Milner.

'It looks a long list,' said Tom.

'Well, you did say you didn't want it to go off half-cocked. We are just making sure it doesn't do that simply because we didn't have enough officers there.'

Tom chose not to reply. They spent the next hour or so reviewing the plan and, where necessary, making a few changes and it was just after 5pm by the time they had a final plan which they were all happy with.

'All we need now is for the targets to be at this farm when we come calling,' said Tom. 'I will look a bit silly if, after getting this team together, there's no one there. Particularly as it's the first day in my new role.'

Milner, perhaps because it was his plan, seemed far more positive. 'Where else are they likely to be, sir?' There was a slight hesitation before he added, 'I suppose we could go and have another look tomorrow just to make sure.'

'What do you think, DC Bennett?' asked Tom. 'After all, you're the one person who has actually seen them there.'

When he answered there was no hesitation. 'I agree with DS Milner. It looked to me as though that's where they were permanently based. But, if you want me to go back and take another look, then I'm happy to do it.'

Tom considered what they had just said before replying. 'No, let's not take the chance of tipping them off. I agree with both of you that all of the available evidence suggests they will still be there.' He then continued, albeit in a quieter tone and as much for his own consumption as Milner's or Bennett's, 'Anyway, the worst that could happen is I get fired before I've even started.' He stood up. 'Okay. As agreed, make sure all of the team are here Monday morning, 4am sharp, for the final briefing. Call me if anything else, in the meantime, develops, and keep thinking through the plan. There's always something which could be improved.' He looked at both of them. 'And remember the old saying: "Hope for the best but always plan for the worst." Have a nice evening.'

Milner turned to DC Bennett after they had left his office. 'Have you heard him say that before?'

'Only about a thousand times over the past fifteen years.'

As Tom drove home he continued, in his mind, to run through the plan. Like most coppers he had always found operations, such as the one planned for Monday morning, to be exciting and a real adrenaline rush. As he had got older, though, the potential for rough stuff had started to concern him, and his recent experience as lead officer in a raid on a local scrap dealer, when things had got a bit rough, had simply underlined this feeling. It was also true what he had said to Milner and DC Bennett about the strong likelihood of unexpected developments. The secret was to try to, where possible, identify, and then have contingency plans for, as many different scenarios as possible. The main restriction, however, in achieving all of this was available resources, and their station, like other stations, always wanted more. Milner was correct in what he had said about the number of officers he would need and, despite what Tom himself had said at the time, it was always better to have too many than too few. But they just had to work with what was available to them.

All of this had clearly occupied his mind because, almost before he knew it, he was pulling into his drive. He now had another thing to worry about. What should he cook for dinner?

Chapter 20

It was Sunday morning and Tom and Mary, hand in hand, were walking in the local park. As they were doing this, and not for the first time, Tom couldn't help being amazed by just how much his life had changed.

His adult life seemed to have developed into three distinct phases. The first phase was when he was married to Anne. Initially, of course, this had been very exciting and satisfying, especially when Paul was born, but, as the years went by, it increasingly had become a barrier to his career. In retrospect it wasn't something he was proud of and he had, anyway, paid the ultimate price by losing all contact with his son Paul.

The next phase had also begun very positively but, just as with his marriage, had ended in disillusion. Although, over the years, he had regularly been promoted, to reach his current permanent position of Detective Chief Inspector, the past few years had been some of the most depressing career years he had ever experienced. He had increasingly found that his enthusiasm for the job, together with his personal motivation, had all but disappeared, and he just felt as though he was wishing his years away until he could take retirement. What made this even worse was that this situation was not lost on his colleagues, particularly the younger ones who were full of the energy and enthusiasm that he had once had.

And then he had met Mary. Since then his life had turned around almost 180 degrees and he seemed to have rediscovered that missing energy and motivation once again. Notwithstanding all of this positivity, he still couldn't get out of his mind the thought that those earlier phases had also started like this. And look how they had finished.

'So, tomorrow is your big day,' said Mary, as they walked down the path alongside a small lake. 'Are you nervous?'

For a moment Tom thought she was referring to the operation at the farm, but, as he had not told her about this, he quickly realised she was referring to his new role as Acting Superintendent.

'I think I would be if it was permanent, but it's only likely to be for a few weeks, so I don't think I'll have the time to get nervous. Anyway, I'll continue to handle my current investigations, so that should help to pass the time until I get my old job back.'

Mary stopped walking and turned to face him. 'I'm proud of you. Don't you see that? But every time I've mentioned it you have given the impression you'd rather not have been offered it. Don't you see it as a compliment that you have been asked to do it?'

'Well, I don't think there was anyone else available,' he said.

Tom had rarely seen Mary become angry. She just wasn't that sort of person. But now she was very definitely angry. 'You are always putting yourself down. Why don't you, just for once, see it as what it is? It's not that there was no one else available. It was that you were the best person available. Don't you see the difference?'

She moved away from him, leaving him standing alone, but only moments later turned around to face him once again. By now, though, her usual equilibrium had returned and she said in a calm tone, 'I'm sorry, but sometimes you really do annoy me. I can understand how you don't always want to discuss your work with me. I can even accept being stood up occasionally due to your work commitments, but what I find difficult to accept is your inability to accept anything that is even mildly complimentary.' She then added, a little worryingly, 'I thought we were a couple. If I can't say nice things about you, then what hope is there for us?'

They restarted their walk along the path in silence with a gap between them. After a couple of minutes Tom reached out and took hold of her hand. This time it was his turn to move towards her. 'Mary, I'm the one who should be saying sorry, not you, but I can't help being the person I am. We are different. You're the one who finds it easier to express their true feelings. I can't, and it's unlikely I could change now, even if I wanted to. I promise, though, I do value your opinion even if I don't always show it.'

As they continued to walk alongside the lake they could see a group of about half a dozen teenagers up ahead of them, alongside one of the benches which were sited at regular intervals directly in front of the lake. Even though there was a litter bin within an arm's reach of the bench, there were still a lot of discarded cans, crisp packets and fast-food cartons on the ground next to the bench.

Just as Tom and Mary were passing them, one of the boys threw an empty drinks can into the bushes behind the path.

Tom stopped. 'I suggest you go and get that back and put it in this bin,' he said, pointing at the one next to the bench. He carried on, now switching his gaze to all of the discarded debris just in front of him. 'And while you're at it you can put all of these in as well.'

There was suddenly a discernible increase in tension and Mary, recognising this, moved even closer to him.

'Yeah, and what are you going to do about it, Granddad, if I don't?' replied the first boy. Some of the others started to laugh.

'Come on, Tom, let's just go,' said Mary, trying to pull him away.

The boy heard this and, with increasing confidence, swore at Tom. 'Yeah, do as she tells you.'

'What did you say?' asked Tom, now walking directly towards the boy.

'You heard,' he answered.

'Do you have to swear?' asked Tom.

'What's it to do with you if I swear? Just because *you* don't. And anyway, you can't stop me,' he said defiantly, now clearly playing up for the others.

Tom stood in front of him. The boy was slightly taller than Tom, but Tom kept his gaze fixed on the boy's face. He then said, 'You might be surprised to know that I do swear. Most of us coppers do, but there's a difference, you see. Boys, like you, know *how* to swear, but men, like me, know *when* to swear.' He then took out his ID warrant and held it close to the boy's face so the boy could see his photograph. 'What does that say?' he asked.

The boy did not say anything.

'Well, let me help you out. It says *Detective Chief Inspector Stone*,' he said with exaggerated emphasis. 'By the way, tomorrow I'm being promoted to Superintendent. So I think that I can make you do it, don't you?'

The boy didn't reply, so Tom helped him out, raising his voice slightly so the others could also hear. 'I said this means I can make you do it. Don't you agree?'

Still there was no reply. Tom stood his ground. 'I'm staying right here until I get an answer from you. So, once again, do you think I can make you do it?'

Finally, the boy appeared to concede defeat in this battle of wills with Tom. 'I suppose so,' he said quietly.

Tom fixed his gaze on him. 'Not the most convincing agreement I've ever heard, but it'll have to do. Now go in there,' he said, pointing towards the bush, 'and pick up the can you threw in and put it in this,' now pointing at the bin. He turned towards the others. 'And you lot pick up all of the rubbish which you've thrown down, and put it in the same bin.'

Reluctantly, they began to do as Tom had suggested and, after a short while, the ground was clear of their various items of litter.

'Thank you,' said Tom. 'That wasn't too difficult, was it?'

He took Mary's hand and they resumed their walk along the path. She suddenly began to laugh.

'What's so funny?' he asked.

'Granddad?' she replied.

Chapter 21

'Good morning, everyone,' said Tom. 'It's a very early start, I know, so thanks for getting here on time.'

They were assembled in the briefing room at the station. Tom was standing at the front, with Milner and DC Bennett alongside him. Most of the officers directly in front of him were in uniform and most of those had a cup of the station's coffee or tea in their hand. A few others had had the good sense to stop at an all-night fast-food place or coffee house on their way in and invest in a different brand of hot drink. Although most of the officers were known to each other there were a group of six people, standing together at the rear of the room, who were not from the station.

'You have already been briefed on why we are travelling to Essex this morning. We believe,' he said, now looking towards Milner and DC Bennett, 'that today's operation is crucial to finding out who killed our mystery man, who was murdered last weekend. Shortly DS Milner and DC Bennett will take you through the operational plan, and it's important all of you are one hundred percent sure of what your role is.' He moved his eyes to scan everyone. 'If you aren't sure, then ask.

'Most of you here today have been involved in operations like this many times before. So you know how things can go wrong, how unexpected developments can suddenly put the entire operation in danger. That isn't going to happen today. We need to sweep all of these people up with the minimum of fuss. Also, I'll remind you we will be in another region's patch. I don't want West London to become a laughing stock amongst the Essex force. And there's another reason why we can't foul up.' Tom looked at his watch. He then continued, 'As of four hours and ten minutes ago I have taken up my position as Acting Superintendent. How's it going to look if I make a complete balls-up on my very first operation as the station's Super? So I'm relying on you all to make sure I still have a job this time tomorrow.' This seemed to lighten the mood and everyone started to laugh.

'Okay, the fun's over,' he said as they started to quieten down. 'DS Milner and DC Bennett will now take you through the final briefing.'

Milner and DC Bennett spent the next ten minutes briefing the team. 'Any questions?' asked Milner after they had finished.

'What are the chances of any physical stuff?' asked one of the uniformed officers.

'Not sure, to be honest, but we have to assume there's likely to be some resistance. That's why we have special back-up on standby.'

Someone else then said, 'DC Bennett mentioned there were dogs there. How are we going to handle them if they get aggressive?'

'Essex are providing a couple of specially trained handlers in case that happens. They will be meeting us outside the property. We'll also have our own sniffer dogs, again courtesy of Essex.'

One of the female officers said, 'If, as we think, some of the men are foreign, how are we going to communicate to let them know what we are doing?'

'This might be a good time to introduce Dave Clare and his team.' Milner pointed in the direction of the small group of men and women at the back of the room. 'They are from the UK Border Force and, once we have secured the premises, they will be responsible for the handling, and subsequent questioning, of any foreigners who might be there. They have a lot of experience in this type of situation and, between them, should be able to communicate effectively. As I said, though, our job is to firstly make sure we have everyone and then make sure that there is no danger to anyone.'

Tom could sense most of the officers were keen to get going and so he said, 'Right, it's just after four twenty-five. I suggest we all now start to head off. It's a bit of a journey, and we need to be in place in plenty of time. Good luck.'

They all came out of the briefing room and made their way to their allotted transport, and by five o'clock they were on the M25 and heading east towards Essex. Given the time of day it was no real surprise that the journey was a trouble-free one and eventually all of the vehicles were positioned, behind each other, down the narrow path leading to the farmhouse.

Tom had stressed to Milner and DC Bennett the importance of keeping their plan as simple as possible on the basis that the more complex it was, the more things there would be to go wrong. They had both taken his advice on board and, as a consequence, their plan was as uncomplicated as they could make it.

The operation was to commence at 6.30am. There would be no surreptitiously creeping up to the farm. Instead, all of the vehicles would simply drive down the path and then directly into the field immediately in front of the farm. Two vehicles would make straight for the farmhouse. One would take up position at the back and the other one at the front. The same procedure would happen with regard to the large outbuilding from which DC Bennett had earlier seen the five men emerge. Two other vehicles, one carrying the team of special officers and the other one with the dog-handling team, would be held in reserve, whilst the Border Agency team would be held back, at the end of the path leading into the field, until the situation was secure. Tom and Milner would then make contact with the farmhouse's resident and present the search warrant, whilst DC Bennett would position himself with the team at the door of the outbuilding.

'Okay,' Tom said, over the phone. 'Unless anyone says "hold" we will go in thirty seconds' time.' Despite having been involved in quite a few of these raids over the years, he still found himself getting the same adrenaline rush as he had the very first time. 'Remember, everything by the book. Good luck.'

In the absence of 'hold' from any of the officers, Tom started, in his head, to count down the seconds on his watch. As the time got closer, he said so everyone could hear, 'Five, four, three, two, one. Let's go.'

All of the vehicles, one after the other, started their engines and began to move down the path, then around the right-hand bend in the path and into the open field. At this point they broke away from their single-file procession and headed towards their allocated positions. Tom and Milner pulled up outside the farmhouse, got out of the car and walked towards the front door. All of this had taken not much more than a minute.

Milner knocked hard on the front door and then immediately repeated the exercise. Almost immediately they could hear the sound of dogs barking from inside the farmhouse.

Tom turned to Milner. 'I hope the dogs are not as aggressive as they sound.' His concern was well-placed and based upon a few unpleasant experiences with dogs on past operations. 'Give it another knock.'

Milner duly obliged, although this time with even greater force. All this did, though, was make the dogs bark even louder.

Just as Milner was about to once again knock on the door, a man's voice shouted, 'Who is it? If I have to, I'll set the dogs on you.'

This simply heightened Tom's worst fears about dogs. Notwithstanding this he said, equally loudly, 'We are the police. Please open the door. We have a warrant to search your premises.' He then added, 'You also need to make sure your dogs are under control.'

'How do I know it's the police?' the man asked.

'Just look out of your window and you will see,' replied Tom. 'Please get your dogs under control and then open the door or we will be forced to break it down.'

This seemed to focus the man's attention as Tom and Milner heard him say, 'Come here before I give you what-for.' Surprisingly the dogs then stopped barking and the door was hesitantly opened to reveal the grey-haired man who DC Bennett had photographed.

Both Tom and Milner held out their ID cards in front of the man. 'I'm Detective Chief Inspector Stone, from West London Regional Police Force, and this is Detective Sergeant Milner.' Tom then put away his warrant card and replaced it with an official-looking piece of paper. 'And this is authorisation for us to search your premises.'

The man didn't bother to examine the piece of paper. Instead he said, 'What you looking for?'

Milner answered. 'We have reason to believe there are illegal immigrants being kept here.'

'They are not illegal,' he immediately replied. 'All of 'em have proper passports.'

'So you are confirming they are here?' asked Milner, slightly unnerved by his quick admission.

'Course they're here. They live in that building there,' he said, pointing towards the large outbuilding.

'Do you know what nationality they are?'

'Bulgarian? Romanian? Foreign, anyway,' he answered, matter-of-factly.

'So you wouldn't mind opening the doors, then?'

'If you want me to. Wait there a minute and I'll go and get the key,' he replied.

'We'll come in with you, if you don't mind,' said Tom, fearful that the man might try and make a run for it, and so they followed him into the farmhouse.

As they stepped inside the house they heard the dogs start to bark once more. 'What have you done with your dogs?' asked Tom.

'Locked 'em in that room,' he said, pointing towards an adjacent room.

Relieved to hear this, they walked further into the house and were met by a scene of utter filth. There were dirty cups and plates on the floor, some with half-eaten food still on them, as well as more dirty plates on most of the available surfaces. The house also reeked of the unmistakeable smell of animal faeces and urine.

The man made his way towards a cracked and stained ceramic sink, which was also overflowing with dirty plates. To the right of the sink was a wooden board which had a few nails knocked into it. On most of the nails there were hung various keys. The man selected one set and turned around and headed back towards the door.

'What's your name,' asked Tom.

'William Green,' he answered.

'Do you live here alone, Mr Green?'

'Yes, alone,' he replied.

'How long have you lived here?' Milner asked.

'About a year. I lived in Colchester before that.'

By now they were outside the house and making their way towards the outbuilding. As they got closer they were met by DC Bennett. 'Is everything okay?' he asked.

'So far, so good,' answered Milner. 'This is Mr Green. He is just about to open the doors. How are things here?'

'There's a bit of movement inside, as we can clearly hear voices, but nothing too aggressive.'

'Good,' said Tom. 'But let's not take any chances. Make sure all of the officers are aware of what is happening.' He then turned to face Green. 'Is there a rear exit to this building?'

'There's no door, just a window high up,' he replied.

'DC Bennett, get someone to check that and then send the search team and the sniffer dogs into the farmhouse.' As Bennett walked away Tom shouted to him, 'And make sure everyone is gloved up.' He pointed to the officers in front of the farmhouse. 'Milner, get those officers over here. Let's not take any chances.'

It didn't take too long for this to be sorted out and, when everyone was in place, Tom said, 'Right, Mr Green, if you could open the doors now.'

The doors, exactly as DC Bennett had described, were tall, solid wooden ones. In addition to the key lock there was a large, impressive-looking padlock keeping them secured.

'What would happen if there was a fire in here?' asked Milner. 'How would they get out?'

Green simply shrugged and carried on with the task of unlocking the doors and then the padlock. After he had done this he pulled back the right-hand door. As light flooded into the building Tom could just about make out a group of five men standing together at the back. The inside of the building was quite large with bits of old farm machinery strewn around the place. One side, however, was clear of machinery and it was here where a number of individual camp-style beds had been set up. At the very end was a metal trough above which was a single rusty dripping tap.

Tom entered the building and approached the men. He then stopped and held up his ID card. 'We are the police,' he said slowly and deliberately. 'Does anyone speak English?'

There was no answer and so he repeated what he had just said but, once again, there was silence. He then turned to Milner. 'Right. Get Dave Clare and his team here.' He looked towards the men. 'I don't think they look as though they are in any mood to get aggressive.'

A minute or so later the Border Force team arrived and Tom quickly explained the situation. 'Over to you,' he said.

Dave Clare began to say something to the men and immediately one of them answered. Dave turned towards Tom. 'It would seem they are Romanian.' He then said something else, which elicited a longer reply from the same person.

'I asked them what they were doing here. He said they have been here for a few months doing building work. They're collected most days, taken to various places to work and then brought back here after they have finished.'

As Tom and Milner were considering this, they saw DC Bennett striding purposefully towards them. 'Sir, you might want to see this,' he said, a hint of excitement in his voice.

Not giving them the opportunity to ask any questions he immediately turned around and started walking, briskly, back towards the farmhouse, with Tom and Milner in tow. When he arrived there he headed straight up the stairs and then into the first room on the left.

'Impressive, isn't it?' he said, making room for Tom and Milner to enter the room.

It looked as though it might have been one of the bedrooms, but now bore no resemblance at all to its original purpose. All the furniture had been removed and replaced with a carpet of green plants, surrounded by a network of twisting metal ducts and cabling. The room was also very humid, which immediately resulted in beads of sweat breaking out on their foreheads.

As they were taking this in, DC Bennett said, 'And there's more in the next room.' Once again he led the way and exactly the same scene awaited them when they entered the room.

'You can see, over there,' said DC Bennett, pointing towards the left side of the room, 'how part of the wall has been knocked through for the pipes.'

'What's that in the corner giving off the humming noise?' asked Milner.

'Looks like a small generator,' answered DC Bennett.

'And why is that plant so much taller than the others?' asked Tom, pointing towards a tall plant in the centre of the room.

'No idea,' answered DC Bennett, equally puzzled.

'Anything else?' asked Tom, expectantly.

'Not that we can see, but we've only had a quick nosey around so far,' answered DC Bennett.

Tom considered what he had just seen and then said firmly, 'Okay. Get everything recorded and make sure that the house is thoroughly searched. And get our dogs in to have a sniff around.'

Suddenly there was a shout from the bottom of the stairs. 'Sir,' called one of the officers, 'the guy from the Border Force team is here and wants to speak to you.'

Tom and Milner made their way, carefully, down the stairs and then out of the front door. Dave Clare was standing outside.

'I thought you would want to know this. I've just been speaking with one of the other Romanians. He said his younger brother came over with them, at the same time, but he hasn't seen him for a few weeks.'

Chapter 22

It was Monday afternoon and they were back at the station. Tom had stood down most of the operation after the five men had been taken away by the Border Force officers, just leaving the search team to carry on with their own investigation. Green was currently in one of the station's interview rooms being questioned by DC Bennett.

'It all went very well, sir. Don't you think?' asked a clearly delighted Milner.

'This time it did, but don't expect it to be so easy next time. It might have been very different if they hadn't been so compliant.' He then added, almost as an afterthought, 'In fact, I think some of our lads were a bit disappointed there wasn't any trouble.'

'The Romanians seemed almost relieved we showed up,' Milner said.

'I'm sure that is the case. Before they travelled to the UK I can't believe they would have expected to have to work all day and then be locked up, like prisoners, all night in an old outbuilding. Anyway, hopefully, we'll have more information after Dave has interviewed them.'

'What about Green?' Milner asked. 'What do you think his involvement is in all of this?'

'Having now spoken to him I can't think he's exactly the brains behind all of this, but let's wait and see what comes out of his chat with DC Bennett. In the meantime, start writing up the report. I want all the t's crossed and the i's dotted on this one.'

As Milner stood up to leave, Tom said, 'Have you decided yet about the position here as DS? I didn't want to mention it earlier because of today's operation.'

Before Milner had even started to answer Tom could see some anxiety developing in his demeanour. 'I have, sir,' he replied, a little nervously.

Tom was expecting him to then elaborate, but when nothing was immediately forthcoming he said, with a hint of impatience in his voice, 'Well, what is it, then?'

Milner looked directly at Tom and replied, but now with renewed confidence, 'I've decided to go ahead and apply for the position in Brighton.' Before Tom could say anything Milner carried straight on. 'As I said to you the other day, I do appreciate what you have done for me whilst I've been here. I've learnt so much from you, but it's just that, well ...' He was clearly now finding it difficult to explain but then, with some obvious effort, continued, 'I think if I stayed here I would always be in your shadow and simply be seen as your run-around.'

Both remained silent as they took on board the implications of what he had just said. Eventually Milner went on, 'I do appreciate your offer, although—'

But before he could continue Tom cut in. 'Milner, you don't have to justify your decision to me. You have clearly made up your mind. I can't lie and say I'm not disappointed, because I am, and, personally, I do think it's the wrong decision, particularly at this stage of your career. Nonetheless, if you need me to provide a reference I hope you know, despite my disappointment, I would provide it.'

'Thank you, sir,' answered Milner. There was another silence before he said, 'Do you mind if I ask you something, sir?'

'Of course not,' he replied. 'What is it?'

'You just said how it was the wrong decision at this stage of my career. How is it any different being a DS in Brighton than it is here in West London?'

Tom considered conceding Milner's point, if only to finish their conversation. But, as he thought he might only get the one chance to make the point, he said instead, 'As you know, I'm fifty-four now. You made a comment at my party about me retiring, do you remember?' He then carried straight on, not giving Milner the opportunity to reply. 'It's likely I will retire within the next couple of years and I was hoping we could work together during that time, with you as my DS. I'd like to think there are still things which you could learn from me.' He paused at that point and then said, 'Both good and bad.' He went on, 'Anyway, whatever they are, you are likely to be a better cop for the experience.'

Milner felt quite embarrassed to be the reason for DCI Stone's sudden bout of uncharacteristic openness. He had never heard him speak quite in this way before and so he knew it would have taken a real effort on his part. Nonetheless, he had made up his mind and if he was now, based upon DCI Stone's warm words, to change his mind and stay after all, then his die would be cast. And there was another thing. He would hate it if, later on, regretting having not even tried for the position, he started to resent the job and, more importantly, DCI Stone.

'It's not been an easy decision, sir, but I've made up my mind. There's no guarantee, of course, that I will get the job, but, even if I don't, I'll continue to look around until another DS position becomes available within another force.'

'Okay,' said Tom, 'you've clearly made your choice and I have to respect that decision.' By now they had both realised there was nothing else to be said on this particular subject.

Milner turned away from Tom and walked out of the office.

Tom was still thinking about all of this when his mobile rang. When he looked at the screen, he could see it was DCS Small. For one moment he thought about ignoring it, but his inquisitive nature got the better of him and he accepted the call.

'Afternoon, sir,' he said, a little less enthusiastically than, perhaps, he should have. 'What can I do for you?'

When DCS Small replied it was immediately obvious he shared Tom's lack of enthusiasm.

'I understand you have been running an operation today. I was rather hoping you might have informed me about it first. I've had Commander Jenkins on the phone wanting to know what has been going on, as he took a call from a DCS from the Essex region. Why didn't you tell me what you were doing?' he asked.

'I'm sorry, sir, but I didn't have any time to let you know. Some information we received meant we had to move fast. That's why it took place this morning.' Tom fell silent, hoping his brief explanation would have placated DCS Small. When the DCS answered, however, it was clear his strategy had failed.

'Who authorised it, then? It would appear most of the West London force, as well as a good proportion of Essex's, were involved,' he said. 'Have you any idea how much this little adventure will have cost?'

Tom decided to try and ignore his first question. 'I've no idea how much it cost, sir. What's important is that it was successful and no one was injured. I would call that a good use of our resources.'

But DCS Small was not about to be fobbed off quite so easily. 'You still haven't told me who authorised it.'

'Well, *I* did, sir,' he answered.

Tom instantly realised the silence which followed betrayed DCS Small's irritation, and when he did speak any possibility Tom may have been wrong quickly vanished. 'That was *highly* irregular. As you personally were involved in the operation, it should have been signed off by your immediate superior. In case you don't know who that is, I'd like to remind you that person happens to be me.'

'I'm sorry, sir, but, as I've told you already, there just wasn't time for that. It was my judgement that, unless we moved fast, we might not have had the same opportunity again.'

DCS Small chose not to respond; instead, he simply continued in the same vein, reflecting his increasing annoyance with Tom's behaviour. 'And when do you propose to move into Superintendent Peters' old office, on the fifth floor? Now you've taken the role, albeit on an interim basis, you need to locate yourself there, otherwise what's the point of you accepting the role? Your officers need to know you are taking this seriously.'

'I did intend to move in today but events overtook me. I'll make sure I'm there tomorrow,' he answered contritely.

The previous annoyance in DCS Small's voice had almost disappeared when he next spoke. 'All right. Just make sure, next time, you do things by the book.'

'I'll certainly try, sir,' replied Tom to himself, as DCS Small had already gone.

As Tom sat there he suddenly realised that DCS Small had not even asked about the reason for the operation. Nonetheless, he began to smile as he realised that he had been in his new role for less than a full day yet, already, had been reprimanded by his boss.

Chapter 23

Tom took DCS Small's 'advice' and moved into his new office on the fifth floor early the following morning. He had visited the office a few times in the past and so knew what to expect. As he didn't have too many things to physically move, the office appeared almost cavernous compared to his old one on the third floor.

The first thing he did, when he entered the office, was head towards the large window. As he looked out he could see the entire West London skyline in front of him. Although it was a partly cloudy morning he could still easily make out the Shard and, beyond that, Canary Wharf. As he was taking in this view he became aware of someone else behind him and when he turned around he was greeted by a tall, well-dressed young woman, probably in her late twenties, standing in the doorway of the office.

'Hello, sir, I'm Jenny. You must be Superintendent Stone,' she said. 'I'm sorry I wasn't here when you arrived, but I was told not to expect you until after nine o'clock.'

Tom held his hand out, assuming it must have been DCS Small who had told her. 'Very nice to meet you. Yes, I suppose I am a bit early,' he said. 'I don't think we have met before.'

'No, we haven't. Yesterday was my first full day. I was expecting to meet you then but, I understand, you had other commitments.' For further explanation she then added, 'I have been recruited from an agency as your PA. I was told my appointment would last for about three months until someone permanent is recruited.'

'Yes, I apologise for yesterday.' Without any further explanation he said, 'I'm sorry I can't show you where everything is as it's all new to me as well.'

'Don't worry. I actually had a half-day's induction last Friday. One of the other secretaries kindly gave me a brief tour of the station and then showed me where most of the things are kept.' She paused and then said cheerfully, 'As I now know where the tea and coffee-making facilities are, could I get you something to drink?'

'That's very kind of you. I'll have a coffee, please, white with no sugar.'

As Jenny left his office he suddenly thought how, at least, that was a good start to his day. A few minutes later Jenny returned, carrying a tray on which there was an impressive pot of coffee alongside a matching china cup, saucer and cream jug.

'I'm sorry,' she said, 'but there doesn't appear to be any milk in the fridge. There was only cream. I hope you don't mind.' She placed the tray on his desk.

'I understand,' he replied, 'although I'm not used to this type of coffee pot. I never know how far to push down the plunger.'

'I'm sure you will get used to it.' Without giving him the opportunity to respond she asked, 'Is there anything else?'

'Not at the moment,' he replied, 'but I'm sure I'll need your help again soon.'

After she had left he picked up his coffee and resumed looking out of his window. He could see a line of planes as they started their final descent into Heathrow. From where he was it looked as though they were almost nose-to-tail, one after another, in the sky. He had read somewhere that, at peak time, they were landing every two minutes. As someone who lived near to the flight path he was unconvinced about the need for a new runway. Anyway, did they actually need any more planes landing?

Just as he was pondering this great issue of the day, whilst taking another sip of his drink, the buzzer on his desk suddenly made a sound, making him jump and almost spill his coffee. Placing his cup on his desk he walked around to where his chair was and could see, slightly to the right, a flashing light. He pressed the button immediately under it and almost instantly he could hear Jenny's voice.

'Superintendent Stone, I have Detective Sergeant Milner with me. He wonders if he could see you for a few minutes.'

'Send him in,' he answered.

He was still fiddling with the buttons on the intercom when Jenny and Milner appeared. Without looking up, he said,

'Jenny, you must show me how this thing works. I can't seem to turn the flashing light off.'

Jenny walked around to where he was sitting. 'You just have to press that to call me,' she said, pointing at one of the buttons, 'and that one to receive a call.' She turned to face Milner. 'Could I get you something to drink, Detective Sergeant Milner?'

'Thank you,' he replied politely. 'A tea would be good.'

Tom looked directly at Milner. 'I thought you only needed to see me for a few minutes.'

'I do, sir.' He looked at the impressive drinks tray on his desk. 'But perhaps you might need some more help with the buzzer,' he said, a thin smile appearing on his face.

Jenny interjected. 'That's not a problem. It won't take me long to make it.' With that she left the office, leaving Tom and Milner alone.

'Take a seat,' Tom said, pointing towards one of the chairs which were placed all around the large table. When they were both seated Tom asked, 'So, what is it?' secretly hoping Milner might have changed his mind about the Brighton vacancy and, therefore, giving him a bit of slack about his earlier 'buzzer' comment. Not for the first time recently, with regard to this particular subject, he was soon feeling disappointed.

'We know who the dead man was,' Milner answered, matter-of-factly.

Tom suddenly forgot about their little heart-to-heart yesterday. 'Was he the brother?' he asked hesitantly.

'Yes, he was. His name was Bogdan Inanescu, the younger brother of Ilie Inanescu, who we saw at the farm.'

'How did we find out?'

'The search team found six passports hidden in a box at the farm. Five of them belonged to the ones we took into custody. The other one belonged to Bogdan. It seems there is no doubt he was the dead man found at the house in Hounslow.'

Tom was silent as he considered what Milner had just told him. Milner took this as his cue to continue. 'We've also had a report back from Dave Clare, from the Border Agency Force. It seems that all six travelled to the UK from Romania, together, about four months ago. They travelled by coach all the way from Bucharest and arrived at Victoria coach station, where, apparently, they were met by a fellow Romanian national, who then drove them to the farm in Essex. They had actually paid to come to the UK, on the back of a promise of a well-paid job, working on building sites. After they'd earned enough they were hoping to return home. That was the plan, anyway,' he said, 'but, when they arrived at the farm, their passports and mobile phones were immediately taken away from them and it was then they started to realise that something was wrong.'

'Do we have any idea who this other Romanian was?' Tom asked.

'Not yet. They only knew him as Florin. Anyway, we are working on it.' He then added, 'But it wasn't just passports which were found at the farmhouse. They also discovered a large quantity of processed cannabis and cocaine. The lab boys are still carrying out tests on it all.'

'Hmm,' replied Tom. 'Seems like it was a real Aladdin's cave of criminality.'

'Yes,' answered Milner. 'We got lucky.'

Hearing this, Tom immediately looked at Milner. 'Well, sometimes you have to make your own luck. I can't remember who said it, but there's a lot of truth in the saying ... what is it? "Luck is when you prepare to meet the opportunity."'

For the second time in as many minutes, a thin smile appeared on Milner's face. 'Actually, sir, that particular saying is usually attributed to the first-century Roman philosopher Seneca, and the correct quote is, "Luck is when preparation meets opportunity." Anyway, I get your point.'

Tom, inwardly at least, smiled to himself. Perhaps Milner was ready, after all, to enter the big, bad world all by himself. 'Well, I suppose that's what a private education does for you,' he simply replied. After a brief moment he continued, 'And what about our friend William Green? What was his role in all of this?'

'You were right about him,' replied Milner. 'He would cook their meals, that sort of thing. But it would appear another of his jobs was to act as a babysitter, making sure, after work, they all kept well out of sight.'

'What about the cannabis plants? Has he admitted to that?' asked Tom.

'Well, he could hardly deny knowing about them,' he answered with a slight laugh. 'It turns out that cultivating cannabis plants was another of his duties.'

'And the cocaine?'

'He says he didn't know it was there,' answered Milner.

'So who employed *him?*' asked Tom, suspecting he already knew the answer.

'It took a while before DC Bennett got an answer to that particular question, and it was only when he mentioned the murdered man that Green started to talk. Surprise, surprise, it turns out it was James Grace. DC Bennett said how the first time he showed any concern was when Grace's name was mentioned, and he was even less happy when he heard about the murdered Romanian man being found in one of Grace's properties. Apparently he and Grace came from the same part of Essex and, back in the eighties, Green had done some work for him.' He paused before adding, 'Probably most of it illegal. Anyway, Grace paid him to look after the plants and to make sure the Romanians were ready for work when Brendan Grace came to collect them.'

Tom considered this before saying reflectively, 'And they said slavery had been abolished. Do any of them know why Bogdan Inanescu was actually at the house in Hounslow?'

'All they knew was that Brendan Grace needed someone to do a special job and, apparently, he volunteered.'

Just then Jenny knocked on the door. 'Come in,' Tom answered.

Jenny entered with another tray, this time containing a teapot, cup, saucer and milk jug. Tom noticed that the design matched his coffee cup and saucer.

'I'm not sure if you take sugar, Detective Sergeant Milner, but I've brought some anyway.' She smiled at Milner. 'Can I get you some biscuits?'

Before Milner could reply Tom answered, 'Thank you, Jenny, but that's not necessary. Anyway, we wouldn't want to spoil DS Milner.'

After she had left, and just as Milner started to pour his tea, Tom said, 'I think Jenny has taken a shine to you.'

Milner blushed slightly before saying, 'I've only just met her.'

There then followed an uneasy silence, as both, once again, recalled yesterday's conversation. Eventually it was Tom who broke the silence.

'Look, Milner, let's try and forget, for the moment, about

what happened yesterday. As I said, I'm disappointed but I respect your decision. In the meantime, we have a murder to solve, so let's get on with that.'

This seemed to ease the tension and, when Milner spoke, it was with his normal enthusiasm. 'I agree, sir. What do you think we should do next?'

'I think another trip to visit our Mr Grace might be in order. Let's see what he has to say about all of this,' he said. 'It would help, though, if we knew who owned the farmhouse. Can you see what you can find out?'

Milner made a note and placed it in his file. He took another sip of his tea and, leaving the rest, stood up. 'When should we go and see Grace?'

'Well, by now, he'll know about our raid on the farm and that Green and all of the Romanians are currently in custody. So let's go and see him first thing tomorrow. This time, though, let's turn up unannounced. It will be good to catch him off-guard.'

Chapter 24

It hadn't taken Tom long to move his things into his new office on the fifth floor, mainly because he didn't have many things to move. As he had packed his most important items into a box he had suddenly realised just how little he actually had to show for over thirty years working in the force. He'd already arranged, with one of the techies, for his computer and printer to be set up on his desk.

Behind and to the right of his new desk were two sturdy, four-drawer, metal filing cabinets. He pulled on one of the drawers and, finding it locked, tried the other cabinet, with the same result. So, tentatively, he pressed the 'call' button on the intercom. It was immediately answered and, feeling pleased with himself for having come to grips with this advanced technology, he heard Jenny's voice coming through loud and clear.

'Yes, Superintendent, how can I help you?'

It was very strange, after many years as a DCI, to be addressed with his new, albeit temporary, title. He'd asked most of his colleagues to refer to him by his old one.

'Hello, Jenny. Could you please come in for a moment?' he answered.

Almost instantly Jenny entered the office.

'Do you have the keys for these filing cabinets?' he asked, pointing towards them.

'I don't, but I know what happened to them. When I had my induction they said the keys had been taken away for security reasons after the previous PA left.'

This was no great surprise as the 'previous PA' had been involved in a major crime which had had potentially life-threatening implications for Tom personally as well as, unknowingly, involving Tom's immediate predecessor. Nonetheless, he couldn't help thinking that it was a case of the stable door being closed after the horse had bolted. 'Can you please find out who has them now?'

'Certainly, sir,' she answered, seemingly pleased that she had been given a specific task to undertake. She then added, 'Perhaps we could sit down together this afternoon and go through your diary. There's a meeting in your diary already and I was wondering what else you might have arranged.'

This came as a surprise to Tom, and it showed in his voice when he replied. 'Really? I wasn't aware of any meeting. Who is it with?'

'Tomorrow, at 10am, at Regional HQ, you have a meeting with Detective Chief Superintendent Small. Apparently this meeting always takes place on a Wednesday morning.'

'Sounds exciting,' he replied unconvincingly.

'I was just about to get some lunch,' she said. 'Can I get anything for you whilst I'm there?'

This suddenly presented him with a bit of a dilemma. Should he go down to the canteen himself, as he would normally do, for lunch, or have something to eat here, in his office? After a little consideration he replied, 'If you could get me a couple of ham and cheese rolls, that would be great,' and handed over a £5 note to her.

After Jenny had gone, leaving him alone in his big new office, he suddenly felt quite lonely. It was far quieter than the workspace he had been used to. Over the years he had learnt almost to shut out all the different sounds and noises, raised voices and the constant ringing of phones, associated with a working office. But this was a different sort of quiet and one which he was already finding quite unsettling. So he thought he would give Mary a call.

After a few rings it went to voicemail. *'I'm sorry I'm not available to take your call at the moment. Please leave your contact number and I'll call you back as soon as possible.'*

He decided not to leave a message. Perhaps he should have gone to the canteen after all.

Chapter 25

'How was lunch?' Tom asked. Jenny had just brought him his two ham and cheese rolls. 'You weren't long.'

'Lunch was fine. I saw Detective Sergeant Milner there, so I sat with him and his colleague Detective Constable Bennett. They both seem really friendly people,' she said.

Tom thought it best if he didn't respond to that. Instead he said, 'Thank you for the rolls.' He wondered if he should ask about any change from his £5 note, but decided it might send the wrong message.

'Can I top up your coffee pot whilst you are eating your lunch?' she asked.

Even Tom, who liked his coffee, was already starting to think that you could have too much of a good thing. 'No, thanks. I think I've had enough for one day as it is.'

'If you need me for anything, just give me a buzz.'

Tom stood up and, whilst eating one of the rolls, walked towards the large window. As he looked towards the omnipresent lined-up aeroplanes, his thoughts returned to his enquiries relating to Mr Wilson. Whilst there was clearly something unprofessional regarding Redbreast's care procedures and protocol, he wasn't sure this constituted outright negligence, even though there remained a nagging doubt in his mind. He had, however, promised Dr Panton and, more especially, Mrs Bishop that he would investigate. So he walked to the stand where his coat was hanging and, from the inside pocket, took out the list he had made previously, containing the details of those three Redbreast employees who had visited Mr Wilson in the days prior to his death.

Ruth Brown was Mr Wilson's main carer and so she would be a good place to start. Although Joanne Stawling had visited ten times, none of those visits were within a week of his death, whilst Diane Filton had been there on the morning of his death. So she would be the next person he would contact.

He sat down at his desk and dialled Ruth Brown's contact number and, almost immediately, it was answered. She was understandably nervous after he explained who he was and the reason for his call. Nonetheless, they agreed a time, for Thursday morning, when he could visit her at her home in Aldershot. When he called Diane Filton's number it was answered by a man who explained she was currently at work, and so Tom left his number for her to call back.

By this time he'd had enough of being stuck in his office and so decided he ought to go and show his face around the station. Wherever he had worked, officers always seemed to complain, justified or not, about how they rarely saw any of the 'top brass' around the station, although they also seemed to complain if they did see any. It would be easy to become deskbound in his office on the fifth floor, and so he was determined this wouldn't happen to him, even though everyone knew his was only a temporary appointment.

As he made his way through the station he was, inevitably, met by many less-than-deferential comments and a few which would, in a court of law, give him a more-than-winnable chance if he decided to bring any slander actions. Nonetheless, by the time he returned to his office, he was glad he had done it and decided he would try to repeat it as often as possible.

Tom was, yet again, suddenly startled when his office buzzer came to life. 'Yes, Jenny?' he said, still pleased with himself for having now mastered the technology.

'I have DS Milner and DC Bennett here. They would like to see you.'

As he heard Jenny say this he thought how quickly she had begun to use their abbreviated titles. 'That's okay,' he answered.

After they had both entered his office, Jenny closed the door.

'Jenny seems very nice, sir,' remarked DC Bennett.

'That's funny because, earlier, she said the same about you two, after you'd all had your cosy lunch together,' he replied, with a slight laugh. 'Seems like a bit of a mutual love-in to me.'

Although DC Bennett laughed, Tom noticed how Milner, as he had done earlier, flushed slightly.

Once they were all seated at the circular table, Tom said, 'I assume this is about tomorrow's visit to see Grace.'

'It is, sir,' answered Milner, placing his file in front of him and speaking his first words since he had entered the office. 'We thought you'd want to have an update and summary on what we know.'

'I certainly do,' he replied. 'I suspect tomorrow's meeting might be a lot more difficult than last time, and so it's important we have a clear idea of what we want to achieve. It's no good just showing up with no plan.' He immediately carried on, 'And there's another thing. Let's not underestimate James Grace. He might have a few rough edges, but he wouldn't have got where he is now without being a smart operator. So, Milner, why don't you summarise what we know?'

Milner took out a piece of A4 paper from his file. Tom could see it contained about half a dozen numbered points, which Milner used as a summary during the briefing. After he had finished, Tom asked DC Bennett if he would like to add anything.

'Only that when I interviewed William Green he said his job was just to babysit the Romanians and look after the plants. He insisted he didn't know who owned the farm. This afternoon, though, I had confirmation that the farmhouse was actually rented in his name. According to the agency he's been renting it for about eleven months now. A full year's rent was paid in advance and in cash. They've promised to email a copy of the agreement to me.'

'You mentioned arriving unannounced. So is this a formal raid?' asked Milner.

'No. Not tomorrow. We would need a lot more time, compared to the last one, to plan it. Somehow, I can't see any raid on *Chez Grace* being as trouble-free as the one on the farm. Can you?' Before either of them could answer he added, 'And, besides, we don't have any hard evidence, or at least evidence which would stand up in court, against James Grace. What we do have is mostly circumstantial. A good defence lawyer would tear it to shreds.' He went on, although this time more reflectively, 'No. Tomorrow is about trying to flush him out in the hope he will make a mistake and give us that evidence we need.'

Chapter 26

DC Bennett pressed the buzzer on the intercom attached to the gates outside Grace's house.

'Give it a few more long presses. Let's let them know we are here and mean business,' said Tom.

It seemed to have the desired effect because a few moments later a woman's voice said, 'Who is it?'

'It's DCI Stone, from West London Police. Could you please let us in? We'd like to speak with James Grace.'

'Hang on a minute,' the woman replied.

A little while later the gate clicked and started to open. They waited for it to be fully open and then drove down the drive and stopped behind a line of cars already there. In addition to the two cars that had been outside last time, there was also the latest registration black BMW four-by-four parked in front of the house.

'Do you have your camera with you?' Tom asked, directing his question at DC Bennett.

'Not the big one, but I've got my phone. Why?'

'Take a couple of photos of those cars and make sure you get the front of the house in the background,' he answered.

After DC Bennett had taken the photographs they all got out of the car just in time to see the front door opening and James Grace appearing, immediately followed by his son Brendan, and then by another slightly younger man. As they stood there, outside their front door, they presented an intimidating and formidable barrier.

Inevitably it was James Grace who spoke first, although his tone was far from friendly. 'You again. What is it you want now?'

'Would it be possible to go inside?' asked Tom.

Grace briefly hesitated before he answered. 'I suppose so, but it can't be for long 'cause we're going out soon.'

They followed Grace and Brendan, together with the third

man, into the same large room as previously. This time, though, it was clear there would be no offer of welcoming drinks.

'Look, I've already told you everything I know, so what is it this time?'

It was Milner who answered. They had agreed how important it was for all three of them to be involved in any conversation and fully control the agenda this time. 'We thought you'd be interested to know who the man was, found murdered in your property in Hounslow.' As there was no immediate interest, Milner, taking out his notebook, carried on. 'His name was Bogdan Inanescu, a twenty-four-year-old Romanian. He, along with his brother and four other Romanian nationals, was living at Long Lane Farm, just a few miles from here.' He looked up and, staring directly at James Grace, said, 'They are all currently in the custody of the UK Border Force.'

'Illegal immigrants, were they?' asked James Grace.

'Actually, Mr Grace, they were in the UK perfectly legally. They are being held in custody as witnesses. We believe they were the victims of people trafficking. Anyway, as I said, they are currently being very helpful to us. In the farmhouse there were bedrooms which had been converted so that cannabis plants could be grown there.' He paused momentarily and then said, 'Just like your place in Hounslow.' He went on, 'We also found a large amount of ready-to-sell cannabis and cocaine,' and then, quite provocatively, 'It must have been very valuable to someone.'

When there was no response from Grace, it was Tom who took over. 'Have you or any of your sons ever been to Long Lane Farm?'

'Why do you want to know? Are you trying to pin all of this on us?' Grace asked aggressively.

'I'm asking if you or any of your sons have ever been to Long Lane Farm, that's all.'

'No, we haven't,' he finally replied. 'Why should we?'

'DC Bennett,' Tom said, turning to face him, 'perhaps you could show Mr Grace your photographs.'

DC Bennett took, from a file he was carrying, a selection of the photographs he had taken at the farm. One by one he laid them neatly on a large coffee table in the middle of the room.

'This one shows your son Brendan speaking with a Mr William Green outside the front door of Long Lane Farm, and this one,' he said, placing it alongside the first one, 'shows your son exiting the farmhouse, whilst this one is a good photograph of Brendan standing next to the five Romanians.' After he had placed the three photographs on the table he stood aside, allowing everyone, if they wanted, to take a closer look. No one did.

Tom now turned to face Brendan Grace. 'What were you doing at Long Lane Farm?'

But before he could reply, his father interrupted. 'Brendan, don't say nothing.' He pointed at the photographs, his face now betraying his increasing anger. 'Where did you get those from?'

'It's normal, in situations like this, for the police to ask all of the questions,' Tom said.

Grace's anger suddenly boiled over. 'Don't get smart with me, copper. If that's all you've got then get out.'

'Well, let's just see what we do have. Firstly, a man was found murdered in your property in which there was a cannabis farm. Secondly, the murdered man and five other Romanians were being held, probably against their will, at a place where more cannabis plants were found, along with large amounts of processed cannabis and cocaine. Next, the place was being run by a known associate of yours, William Green, who, incidentally, is also currently being very helpful. Finally, your son Brendan was photographed, at the farm, with both Green and the five Romanians.' Whilst saying this Tom hadn't taken his eyes off James Grace. But he hadn't finished. 'It doesn't look good for you, does it?'

Just then a middle-aged woman entered the room. She had long blonde hair and a deep tan. 'What's going on, Jimmy?' she asked.

'Nothing. These gentlemen are just leaving.' He turned to face Tom. 'Get out and don't come back unless you've got some real evidence, not just a few holiday snaps.'

DC Bennett picked up the photographs from the table and followed Tom and Milner out of the room. As they emerged from the house Grace calmly said, 'I've warned you before, I won't let anything, or anybody, hurt my family.'

Chapter 27

It was early afternoon and Tom had just walked into his office when Jenny came almost running after him, even though she was carrying what seemed like a large number of files. 'DCS Small has been in touch. In fact, he's called a few times to find out where you are. You were meant to have your weekly review with him at ten this morning,' she said with genuine concern. She then added, a bit more defensively, 'I'm sure I mentioned it to you.'

Tom, sensing her unease, said, 'You did. In fact, I have it in my own diary. I had to drive over to Essex to interview someone as part of an ongoing murder investigation,' he added as explanation.

She handed him the files she had been carrying. 'These are your daily files. Some are just for your reference but the others need your input and signature.'

Although his earlier comments had seemed to reassure, just as she was leaving, she turned around. 'Just to let you know, DCS Small did sound a bit cross.'

'Don't worry,' he replied. 'I'll give him a call straight away.'

After Jenny had left, he placed the files on his desk and, as he waited for his computer to power up, he reflected on their earlier meeting with James Grace. Although Tom was sure they had rattled him, Grace was correct when he said they didn't have any rock-solid evidence or, at least, any which would stand up in court. Nonetheless, Tom was still happy with the way they had handled the meeting, even though they still had no real idea who actually had murdered Bogdan Inanescu. They needed a breakthrough, although a little bit of Seneca's luck would also be welcome.

His emails included the usual number 'for information', together with reports full of police jargon. He often wondered if the titles of various committees and exercises, which the force's hierarchy loved, had been specifically contrived so that an impressive-sounding acronym could be devised.

A short while later, with Tom once again feeling good with himself for having been able to significantly reduce the number of unopened emails by the simple process of deleting them, a text came through on his mobile. He could see that it was from Mary and so he immediately opened it.

Hi Tom. Can we switch our get-together to tomorrow night? An extra rehearsal for the play has been arranged for tonight. Call me when you get the chance. Love you. xxxxx

Their 'get-together' had been for him to stay over at Mary's tonight, whilst the 'rehearsal' comment referred to her involvement with the North-West Surrey Players Amateur Dramatics Society. They would, in a few weeks' time, be performing *Hamlet* at Camberley Theatre, and Mary was playing the role of Gertrude. He immediately replied to her text.

I see. You've dumped me for a play about a ghost. I suppose I'll just have to wait another day. See you on Thursday. xxx

As his attention returned to his emails he noticed one from Barbara Staunton and clicked his mouse to open it.

From: Barbara Staunton, Care Manager, Redbreast Home Care Services
To: DCI Stone
cc: Alan Wood
Subject: Mr Wilson

Attached is a copy of Mr Wilson's care plan. When I checked, unfortunately, it had not been updated to include Mr Wilson's recently diagnosed Alzheimer's condition. We have, however, now introduced a system to ensure that all of our clients' changed medical conditions are included on their personal care plans as soon as we are notified.

Regards,
Barbara Staunton
Care Manager

Tom clicked on the attachment and pressed the 'print' button. Picking up the printed A4 sheet he quickly read it and then placed it in the file on his desk, along with the other information he had already collected with regard to Mr Wilson. Given everything else which he was now involved in, he was beginning to question the wisdom of agreeing to investigate the circumstances of Mr Wilson's death. But he had given his word to both Dr Panton and Mrs Bishop and so was determined to now see it through to the end.

This suddenly reminded him how he still had not been able to make contact with Diane Filton. He reopened the file, looked up her contact details and then dialled the number. This time it was answered by a woman.

'Good afternoon, this is Detective Chief Inspector Stone from the West London Regional Police Force. Who am I speaking to?'

Clearly concerned, the woman replied, 'The police? What do you want?'

'Apologies,' he replied, 'I didn't mean to cause any anxiety but I would like to speak to Diane Filton.' He paused. 'Are you Diane?'

'Yes,' she answered, the nervousness in her voice still apparent. 'What is it you want?'

'I understand you work for Redbreast Home Care Services and one of your clients was Mr Wilson. Is that correct?'

'Well, I did visit him a few times but I wasn't his main carer.'

'Yes, I understand that. Anyway, would it be possible to come and see you, as there are a few things I'd like to discuss with you? We are speaking with all of Mr Wilson's carers.'

'Like what?'

'Well, I think they would be better discussed face-to-face.'

'Well, when?'

'I was hoping we could do it tomorrow,' he replied patiently. 'I understand you live in Farnborough. I'm seeing your colleague, Ruth Brown, tomorrow morning. As she lives near you, in Aldershot, it would help if I could see you after I've seen her.'

'I suppose so,' she answered, 'but I'm not sure there's anything I can tell you.'

'Thank you very much, I appreciate your help. How about 11am?'

'Okay,' she simply replied.

*

As he was taking his daily walk around the station, he met Milner. 'Any news yet on the whereabouts of Florin?' he asked.

'We have a number of possible suspects,' Milner answered, 'although Florin is quite a popular Romanian name. Anyway, based upon the age profile that we got from the other Romanians, we have been able to whittle the list down to about twelve. We've sent their passport details over to Dave Clare for him to show them. Hopefully, something will come out of that.'

'Good work,' said Tom. 'If we can just get hold of him then it might give us the break we need.' Before he resumed his 'rounds', he added, 'Let me know if anything happens.'

When he got back to his office, Jenny, a look of concern once again on her face, was waiting for him. With a degree of foreboding, she said, 'DCS Small has been on the phone again. I told him you were busy at the moment but would get back to him as soon as you were free.' She then added, 'I'm not sure he believed me.'

'Sorry, Jenny,' he answered contritely, 'I got a bit distracted. Don't worry. I'll call him right now.'

When he was seated at his desk he picked up the phone and dialled DCS Small's direct line number. After just a couple of rings it was answered. 'DCS Small here,' the voice said.

'Sir, it's DCI Stone. I understand you have been trying to get hold of me.'

'Yes, I have,' he replied with great emphasis. 'You do know, don't you, we were supposed to have had our weekly review meeting this morning?'

'Yes, sir, I was aware, but I am involved in a murder investigation and we were interviewing a potential suspect this morning over in Essex.'

'Essex again?' he asked nervously. 'What's going on out there?'

Tom gave him a brief summary of the main developments and then said, 'I felt that, given the potential for some sensationalist press reporting, you would want us to get this resolved as quickly as possible.'

There was a momentary silence before DCS Small spoke again. 'I suppose so but, in future, you must keep me informed if you can't make any of our meetings. I have to say, DCI

Stone, that the start to your new appointment has not been the most propitious.'

Noticing how DCS Small no longer used his Christian name, Tom remained silent.

DCS Small then continued, 'Please try and make our next planned appointment.'

'I'll certainly try, sir,' he replied.

It was now almost five o'clock and, based upon his planned date with Mary, he would, by now, have been thinking about leaving. But without that prospect he decided to catch up by reading some of the reports which Jenny had left with him, thus removing, hopefully, one potential source of DCS Small's future displeasure.

He quickly realised most were requests for additional resources or funding, as part of new or ongoing operations, and all apparently required his signature. If he recognised the name of the officer making the request and trusted that officer's judgement, then he simply signed. A request from someone who he didn't recognise he put to one side. He doubted that his particular strategy in deciding how resources should be allocated was likely to be in any management textbooks. Nonetheless, as he looked at the respective piles, he took satisfaction from seeing that the pile of officers he knew was considerably higher than the other one.

Along with the various reports there was a single A4 sheet of paper titled *Update: Jimmy Griffiths killed in prison.*

The list of officers who had received this update was quite extensive. It included all of the senior officers who had been involved, directly or indirectly, with the Jimmy Griffiths case, and so included his predecessor Superintendent Peters, along with DCS Small and Commander Jenkins. Tom guessed the reason he had received it was because someone had forgotten to remove Peters' name from the list.

Tom quickly read the update. It referred to the death of Jimmy Griffiths. He had been in Belmarsh Prison, where he had been serving a fifteen-year sentence for the murder of a fifty-three-year-old woman who had been killed two years previously. Griffiths had died as the result of a fight with another inmate.

Although Tom hadn't worked on the case, he remembered it well, not least because it was at a time when he seemed to be deliberately excluded from handling such cases. The murdered woman, Susan Chambers, was a lifelong prostitute, drug user and occasional dealer. Her body had been found by her flatmate, Shelley Ripley. Although there had been quite severe bruising around her neck, the post-mortem had confirmed the cause of death had been head trauma.

It hadn't taken long for the finger of suspicion to point in Griffiths' direction. Some witnesses had seen him outside the victim's rented flat in Shepherd's Bush, earlier in the evening of the murder. He was a known small-time criminal with a long record which included theft, burglary, drug use and dealing. Despite his denials that he had ever been in the flat, it subsequently became apparent that, up to a few months earlier, he had in fact been Chambers' occasional boyfriend. But it was the DNA evidence which convinced the jury he had committed the murder. The post-mortem had revealed that Susan Chambers had been involved in sexual activity a few hours prior to her death. The DNA found on her body, and on the butt of a cannabis joint discovered in the flat, perfectly matched that of Griffiths. In addition, numerous fingerprints, also discovered in the flat, clearly matched his own.

After reading the report, Tom put it with the others and placed them all in one of the desk's drawers. Although there was now no great urgency to leave he suddenly felt a bit weary. Perhaps it was not such a bad thing, after all, that he was not seeing Mary tonight.

Chapter 28

Tom was sitting in Ruth Brown's lounge in Aldershot. 'Thank you for agreeing to see me,' he said, notebook to hand. 'As you were Mr Wilson's main carer I just wanted to ask you a few questions about the days leading up to the time he died. From the client contact sheets I see you last visited him three days before his death. Can you remember how he was?'

'He seemed okay to me. That particular day I was there from about 5pm to about five thirty. I gave him his dinner and then, afterwards, made him a cup of tea.' She suddenly became more agitated and said, 'What is this all about? I thought Mr Wilson had a heart attack and that's what killed him. Are you trying to say that I was the cause of this?'

'Not at all,' he replied, trying to reassure her. 'There's no doubt Mr Wilson died from a heart attack.' He paused before saying, 'Let me be frank with you, Mrs Brown. There were various bruises, on his body, which suggested he might have been forcibly restrained in the days leading to his death.'

'And you think I caused them, do you?' she replied, the anger rising in her voice.

Tom chose not to answer her question. 'Did you notice any bruises, for example, when you were helping him to get dressed?'

She had calmed down a little when she replied. 'Not really. Mr Wilson was a proud man and would mostly be dressed when I arrived in the morning. Sometimes, though, I did help him to get dressed if he couldn't manage.'

'You said "not really". Does that mean there might have been some bruising?'

This time it was her turn to pause before saying quietly, 'Well, I did notice a couple of bruises, on his wrists, when I was helping him to put on his jacket one morning.'

'Didn't that worry you?'

'Not at the time. I have a number of other elderly clients and most of them have bruising of one sort or another.'

'Were you aware that Mr Wilson had been diagnosed with Alzheimer's?'

'Not then, but I have found out since he ... died. He was, though, definitely becoming more and more confused and would often forget who I was and why I was there.'

As she clearly didn't have anything else to add, Tom closed his notebook and put it back into the inside pocket of his jacket and then stood up. 'Thank you very much, Mrs Brown. You have been very helpful.'

He walked towards the front door. Just as he was leaving he turned to face Mrs Brown. 'One final question. Do you mind me asking if you smoke?'

Mrs Brown, with a slightly puzzled expression on her face, simply said, 'No, I don't. I did when I was younger but haven't done for years now.'

His meeting with Mrs Brown hadn't taken as long as he'd expected and, therefore, after driving the short distance from Aldershot to Farnborough, he found himself outside Diane Filton's house well before 11am. Rather than wait, he decided to see if it was possible to meet earlier. He knocked on the door and, almost immediately, it was opened by a man in his mid-to-late forties.

Tom, ID warrant card already in his hand, said, 'Good morning. I'm Detective Chief Inspector Stone from the West London Regional Police Force. I phoned yesterday and spoke with Diane Filton. We arranged for me to see her at eleven o'clock. I know I'm a bit early, but I was wondering if it would be possible to see her now.'

'What is it you want?' the man asked.

'Who are you?' Tom asked.

'I'm Pete Hepworth, her partner. So, what is it you want her for?'

'If I could come in, I can then explain.' Tom could hear a dog barking somewhere in the house.

'Come in, then,' he answered.

Tom was led into a small lounge. There was an ashtray, balancing precariously on an armchair, half-full of smoked cigarettes, resulting in an unmistakeable stale smell of cigarette smoke. Already seated in one of the armchairs was a dark-haired, slender woman in her late thirties.

As they entered the room her partner said, 'Di, there's that copper to see you.' He then lit up a cigarette.

'Thank you very much for seeing me. I'm DCI Stone. We spoke yesterday.'

As she showed no sign of responding to Tom's introduction he continued, 'As I said yesterday, I'd like to ask you a few questions about your client Mr Wilson.' Tom then explained, just as he had done earlier at Mrs Brown's, the purpose of his visit, particularly with regard to the bruises on Mr Wilson. After he had finished he said, 'I understand you visited him on the morning of his death. How did he seem to you?'

'What do you mean?' she asked.

'Well, did he seem to be unwell or any different from the previous days when you were there?'

'He just seemed the same to me,' she answered.

'Did you notice any bruises at all?' he asked.

'No. I didn't see any.'

Tom, sensing her reluctance to answer any of his questions in any detail, tried a different approach. 'What did you do for Mr Wilson on the morning he died?'

Suddenly, her partner, who up to that point had remained silent, said, 'What are you trying to say? That she was involved in his death?'

'Not at all,' he answered calmly. 'Mr Wilson died later that day, of a heart attack. He had a history of high blood pressure and angina. It was the heart attack which killed him. There's absolutely no doubt about that.'

This didn't appear to satisfy him. 'So why are you asking all of these questions about bruises?'

'I've already mentioned that we need to find out how they were caused.' He turned his attention back to Diane Filton. 'I'd really appreciate it if you could tell me what you did.'

'What I always did,' she replied quietly. 'I made him some breakfast and then did a bit of cleaning. After that I left.'

Tom stood up. 'Thank you, Miss Filton. You have been very helpful.'

'Is that it?' she asked, surprised but, nonetheless, clearly relieved that it had ended.

'Yes, that's it,' he said. 'Although I may need to speak to you again.'

*

He was well on his way back to the station when his phone rang.

'Morning, Milner.'

'Morning, sir,' Milner replied. By now Tom had come to recognise the different nuances in Milner's voice and had become quite adept at predicting whether the call was of a general nature or, as in this case, more informative. 'Will you be in the station today? There's been another development in the Inanescu case.'

'Well, what is it, then?' Tom answered, a touch tersely.

'Last night there was a fire at another house in Hounslow. Fortunately no one was hurt this time as the occupants were able to get out before the fire really took hold.'

Milner then paused, either to allow Tom to ask a question or, perhaps, simply because he wanted to build up the tension. Whatever his motive, it appeared to work as it was Tom who spoke next.

'And what was the connection to the Inanescu case?' he asked, his impatience on the increase.

'When the fire people examined the house they found indications that it had been started deliberately, as there was evidence that an accelerant had been used. But it's what they found next that links it to Inanescu.'

By now Tom had to work hard to resist the temptation to tell Milner to get on with it. Instead he made do with, 'So, what's the connection?'

'One of the bedrooms had a number of cannabis plants growing in it.'

Chapter 29

'Do we know who lived at the house in Hounslow?' Tom asked. He was back in his old office on the third floor, together with Milner and DC Bennett.
'All we know is that the house was owned by a Terry Birkett.'
'Terry Birkett?' repeated Tom. 'Why does that name ring a bell?'
It was DC Bennett who provided the answer. 'Perhaps it's because we put him away about ten years ago. Don't you remember? He ran that drugs and protection racket based around the airport.'
'That's right. A really nasty character, if I remember correctly. I didn't even know he was out,' said Tom.
'He's been out for about a year now. Apparently his sentence was reduced for good behaviour.'
'Good behaviour? That's a joke. People like him don't change their spots,' Tom said. 'So, he's back to his old tricks, eh? I would have thought, though, that cannabis harvesting was small beer for him.'
'You'd be surprised,' Milner said. 'I've been doing a bit of research into this. It's actually a very clever move. Did you know that each plant has a street value of around £1,000? Also, do you remember that we noticed a much taller plant at the farm? Well, that, apparently, was the mother plant used for propagation. If Birkett has one of those, it's quite easy to grow more plants. What's more, there's been a trend towards Class A drug dealers, like Birkett, muscling their way into this area. In the past, apparently, cannabis growing was dominated by Asian criminals. Even though cannabis is officially a Class B drug, skunk, a higher-strength variant, is becoming more and more popular, and that means more lucrative for the growers and dealers.' He paused, letting Tom take in everything he had said, before continuing. 'What's

interesting for us, and potentially brings us right back to Grace, is that there's evidence that competition amongst the growers has resulted in increased gang violence as they have fought to set up and protect their patches.'

It was DC Bennett who articulated what they were all thinking. 'So, Birkett sets up his own operation after he gets out. A bit later Grace starts to muscle in on his territory. Birkett finds out and reacts, in the only way he knows, by setting fire to Grace's operation, who, in true eye-for-an-eye style, then torches Birkett's place.'

'I think that sums it up succinctly,' said Tom. 'Mind you, proving it is something else.'

'What I don't understand, though,' said Milner, 'is that it's one thing to be growing and selling drugs, but it's a big leap to then start murdering people.'

'Well, we still don't know the full circumstances of Inanescu's death and, until we do, this is the best scenario we have to work on,' answered Tom. 'Check with forensics to see if they are able to give us any clue as to who might have started the fire. Also, check to see if there are any CCTV cameras in the area. You never know, we might get lucky. And we need to go and speak with Birkett, so find out where he's living.' He stood up.

Tom was walking away from them when he suddenly stopped and, taking out a small piece of paper from his pocket, turned around to face Milner. 'Whilst you are doing the CCTV check, see if there are any CCTV cameras sited on this address. Also, look into this name for me. I'd like to see if he's known to us.' He handed the details to Milner, who, having quickly glanced at them, was just about to ask if they had anything to do with this particular case, when he thought better of it and simply placed the paper in his file.

When Tom arrived outside his own office, he was met by Jenny with the now-regular look of concern on her face. Almost reluctantly she said, 'DCS Small would like to speak with you as soon as possible. It's something to do with a James Grace.'

'Thank you, Jenny. Is there any chance of a cup of your wonderful coffee?'

This seemed to cheer her up and she said, suddenly with enthusiasm, 'Of course, sir.'

As soon as Tom was seated he called DCS Small.

'I thought you should know this,' DCS Small said, without any preamble. 'James Grace's lawyer has registered an official complaint against you, alleging harassment and intimidation.'

'Intimidation?' repeated Tom. 'On what basis?'

'Apparently you and your team threatened him, and his family, after you had been invited into his home. Is that correct?'

'Of course it's not correct,' he answered, his voice betraying his annoyance. 'Well, the intimidation bit, at least.'

'What do you mean?'

'We have been to Grace's house twice now and it's true, on both occasions, we were allowed into his house. But there was no harassment, other than presenting the facts to him, and certainly no intimidation. If you've ever met James Grace you will know he's not an easy man to intimidate.'

DCS Small seemed to consider what Tom had just said before he spoke again. Finally, he replied. 'I think it's about time you fully briefed me on this case. To be frank, I get the feeling that it's all starting to spin out of control. I want you over here, first thing in the morning. And I don't want to hear any excuses as to why you can't be here.'

His friendly meeting with DCS Small and Commander Jenkins, when they had offered him the position, suddenly seemed a long time ago.

Chapter 30

Tom was sitting with Mary on her sofa. 'I'm sure he'll turn up,' he said. 'He's probably just exploring. Isn't that what cats are supposed to do?'

Mary didn't look convinced. 'I just put her out, last night, for a few minutes, like I do every night before I go to bed. They don't usually stray far when they're kittens. And anyway, she's not a "he", she's a "she". I'd feel awful if something had happened to her.'

'I'm sure you are worrying unnecessarily and he ... sorry, she will be back soon.' Then, in an attempt to take her mind off the kitten, he said, 'How was the rehearsal last night?'

This appeared to have the desired effect and, when she replied, it was preceded by a light laugh. 'It was quite funny. Do you remember Tony? I think I introduced you to him on the night when you came to see us perform *Macbeth*.'

'How could I forget?' he answered. 'It was also the night when we first slept together.'

'That's right,' she replied, with a laugh, 'that was when you sweet-talked me into bed.'

'Actually, if I remember correctly, it was you who did the sweet-talking.'

Mary leant forward and kissed him. 'I don't remember you putting up much resistance. Anyway, are you complaining?' she asked.

'Do I look as though I'm complaining?' he said, returning her kiss. 'But, before we get too distracted, you were going to tell me about Tony.'

'Oh, that's true. You see what effect you have on me. Yes, anyway, Tony is playing the part of Claudius and, whilst he was playing a scene with me, he started to recite some of his lines from *Macbeth* instead of from *Hamlet*. Everyone knew what he was doing except Joe, our director.'

'Sounds hilarious,' said Tom, his voice heavy with sarcasm.

'Well, I wouldn't expect a philistine like you to see the joke. I suppose you had to be there.'

Attempting to redeem himself, he said, 'Yes, I suppose you did. Anyway, that aside, how are the rehearsals going?'

'At the moment it seems there's no way we will be ready for our first performance. But it's always like this. I'm sure we will be ready on time.'

'Talking of being ready,' he said, once again kissing her, 'are you ready for bed?'

Mary looked at the clock on the cupboard. 'But it's only ten o'clock. Are you that keen?'

'Well, I don't get to see you that often, particularly now you are rehearsing regularly, and so I have to use every opportunity.'

She pulled away from him. 'Use every opportunity? Is that how you see it?'

'Sorry,' he said contritely, 'that didn't come out right, did it? Anyway, you know what I mean.'

'I know what you mean, Tom Stone,' she said, taking hold of his hand. 'Come on then, before the opportunity is gone.'

It was early the next morning, and as soon as Mary had dressed, she had gone downstairs and opened the back door. As she stepped out into the small back garden, Tom could hear her calling the kitten's name. By the time he had showered, shaved and dressed, Mary was back in the kitchen.

'Any luck?' he asked, knowing, already, by the look on her face, the answer.

'I can't think where she might have got to. Perhaps she's wandered into another house and they are feeding her?'

'Yes, that's probably what has happened,' he said encouragingly. 'Why don't you put out some of those small laminated posters that you see when a cat or dog goes missing? Do you have a photo?'

'Yes, I do,' she replied, suddenly a bit more positive. 'I think I might start by placing one in the shop window,' referring to her own florist's shop.

Having agreed to meet again on Saturday evening at his house in Staines, Tom set out to meet DCS Small. Although the meeting wasn't until 10am he had given himself plenty of time to get there. In view of their various discussions so far this week, he thought it might be pushing his luck a bit too much to arrive late.

Whilst he was in the car he took the opportunity to call Milner, who, as usual, seemed to be well on top of all the outstanding action points. He was still waiting for forensics to get back with their final report, but the early indications were that, unfortunately, there was no clear evidence regarding who started the fire. Similarly, Milner was still waiting to hear back on the CCTV footage. He did, though, now have an address for Birkett, and there was some other good news: they also had details of where Florin lived. From the photographs that Dave Clare had shown to the Romanians, they had quickly been able to identify him. His full name was Florin Constantin and, according to his work permit documents, he lived in Isleworth, West London.

Tom and Milner agreed that Milner should visit the address with DC Bennett and 'invite' Constantin back to the station so they could question him in more detail about his involvement with the Romanians. Tom also asked Milner to start pulling the paperwork together, as a contingency, in case they needed to carry out a subsequent search of his premises.

Tom was sitting in the same chair as when he had first met with DCS Small and Commander Jenkins. This time, though, there was no offer of coffee with cream and served in china cups. DCS Small, dispensing with any pleasantries, said, 'Now, what's going on with James Grace?'

Tom spent the next few minutes outlining the situation and what, so far, they knew about Grace's connection with Inanescu.

After Tom had finished, DCS Small stood up and walked towards the window. Tom couldn't help noticing how the view from this office was even better than from his own, on the fifth floor, back at the station, and wondered if Commander Jenkins' view was better still. He was, however, soon awakened from his brief daydream.

'From what I've heard, most of what you have is purely circumstantial. Okay, I accept there might be a link between Grace and the Romanians. But, although he might be employing a few illegal immigrants, we have no evidence to think he might actually have been involved in the murder.'

Tom could feel the tension rising in his body. He took a deep breath and said, 'Actually, they are not illegal immigrants and, with respect, sir, I believe being party to human trafficking is still illegal in this country.'

DCS Small gave Tom a steely look but, when he spoke, his voice was calm. 'My point is this. You started all of this, and particularly the enquiries involving Grace, as a murder investigation, not an investigation into human trafficking. If you are not careful you run the risk of not being successful with either of them.' When Tom didn't immediately reply, DCS Small continued in his previous measured tone. 'What are you proposing to do next?'

A very good question, thought Tom. 'We are planning to bring in Florin today, so that might open up a rich vein of information. Then, of course, there's Terry Birkett. Although I can't, somehow, see him going out of his way to help us, you never know. When criminals start these tit-for-tat scenarios, that's when they are likely to get careless and make mistakes.'

'Well, let's hope so,' DCS Small said without any real conviction, before adding, 'What else are you working on at the moment?'

Tom was reluctant to mention his involvement with Mr Wilson's death. Instead, he simply said, 'Not too much. Just tying up a few loose ends, here and there. That's all.'

'Good. I don't want you going off on any wild goose chases. Your main priority, until we make a permanent appointment, is to make sure your station runs smoothly and efficiently.'

Tom felt quite depressed as he drove back to the station. He wasn't sure if this was due to his rather tetchy meeting with DCS Small. More likely, however, it was because DCS Small was probably right.

Chapter 31

'Did he come quietly?' asked Tom, referring to Milner's visit to the address they had for Constantin.

'Well, he wasn't happy,' replied Milner. 'It was only when we mentioned how it would be better for him if he came voluntarily, rather than being forcibly taken into custody, that he had a change of heart.'

'Has he said anything yet which links him with Grace?'

'Not yet; he's still at the "I don't know what you are talking about" stage. Anyway, DC Bennett is with him at the moment, so, hopefully, we'll have a better idea when he's finished.'

'Hmm,' said Tom, clearly not sharing Milner's confidence. 'Did you get the search warrant organised just in case?'

'All prepared,' replied Milner. 'It just needs a magistrate's signature for it to become active.'

'Good work,' Tom said. 'Let me know when DC Bennett has finished. I'll be in my office.'

Just as he was about to leave Milner suddenly said, 'Sir, before you go, I have the other information you asked me to chase up for you. Here's the report on Pete Hepworth. Seems like an interesting character,' he added, handing Tom a single A4 piece of paper. As Tom quickly glanced at it, Milner continued, 'I also found out about Holy Cross Primary School. They do have a few CCTV cameras sited on various parts of their building.'

Milner waited until Tom had finished reading and then asked, 'Do you want me to do anything else?'

Tom, after taking a moment to consider Milner's question, suddenly said, 'Yes, there is,' and then outlined what he would like Milner to do.

When Tom arrived back at his office, Jenny was sitting behind her desk doing something on her computer.

'Hello, sir,' she said cheerfully.

'Hello,' he answered in a similar vein. 'Any more calls from DCS Small while I've been out?' he added, a little mischievously.

Her positive mood suddenly disappeared. 'None at all,' she answered, in such a way Tom couldn't quite work out whether she was relieved or worried. The nervous tone of her next question removed any doubt. 'Why? Are you expecting him to call again?'

'I'm not. Anyway, I think I've had more than my quota of calls from him this week, don't you?' he answered, with a laugh. 'More importantly, how has your first week been? Have you enjoyed working here?'

Tom noticed her slight hesitation before she replied. 'It's been very good, so far.'

'Is it what you expected?' he asked, sensing that she might be trying to be diplomatic.

'Well, it's not ...' She again hesitated before continuing, 'Well, it's not as exciting as I imagined it to be. Also, as I'm here by myself, most of the day, it sometimes gets a bit lonely. I'm used to working in an office where there are more people.'

'If it's any consolation, I also sometimes get a bit lonely here. Is there anything I can do to help?' he asked with genuine consideration.

Almost immediately she said, 'It would help if I knew where you were, or at least where you were planning to be. To be honest, I feel uncomfortable when I tell people I've got no idea where you are. It makes me seem, well ... a bit unprofessional.'

'I take your point,' he answered. 'In future, I'll try and let you know. And we'll see if we can make it a bit more exciting for you. In the meantime, how about a cup of coffee?'

Once again, and for some unknown reason, this seemed to cheer her a little. 'The usual?' she replied.

'The usual, please.'

Tom was sitting at his desk when Jenny came in with the coffee and placed the tray just in front of him. 'I forgot to mention. I've found the keys for the filing cabinets,' she said, placing one small, rather unimpressive key for each of the two cabinets on his desk.

'Thank you,' he replied, 'and thanks also for the coffee.'

After she had left he reread the information regarding Diane

Filton's partner. As Milner had suggested, Pete Hepworth was indeed an 'interesting' character, one who had a whole series of mainly low-level crimes against his name, ranging from petty theft to selling stolen goods. What caught Tom's eye, however, was a conviction for aggravated burglary, for which he had served a three-year prison sentence. After he had considered the implications of this he placed the paper in his ever-expanding file relating to Mr Wilson.

Picking up the keys which Jenny had left, he stood up and walked towards the filing cabinets. He put the first key in the cabinet nearest to him and, when he could see that it fitted, turned it. One by one he pulled out each of the four drawers and quickly flicked through the contents. He could immediately see that each case had its own cardboard file holding background notes, suspended on a thin metal track inside the drawer. The files could be identified by a small plastic holder fixed onto the top of each file, each with a typed case name slotted in.

As Tom continued to flick through each file heading he could see how they had all been filed in alphabetical order, and it was then he remembered the updated note referring to the death of Jimmy Griffiths. Having retrieved the note from his desk drawer, he once again flicked through the files until he found one headed *Susan Chambers murder* and then removed it from the filing cabinet. He placed the update in the file and was just about to put it back into the cabinet when he suddenly changed his mind. If he got the chance it would be interesting to read the case notes. He hadn't been personally involved in the case, but he knew colleagues who had, and it was always useful to see how other officers went about their work. So he placed the file on his desk, with a view to reading it later, and then continued flicking through the other files, some which immediately brought back vivid memories of old cases.

As he did this he suddenly found himself smiling. It would be very interesting to read the notes contained in the files for cases in which he had been involved, if only to see if there was anything he could have done better. Or if there was any comment by senior officers on his performance. But that would have to wait for another day.

Chapter 32

It was Sunday evening and Tom was alone in his kitchen. Mary had left an hour or so earlier and he was pouring himself a glass of red wine. He was starting to find it more and more difficult when, after spending time together, one of them had to leave. He was sure she felt the same, but he just couldn't bring himself to discuss it with her. Perhaps he was afraid of the consequences of any likely escalation in his commitment to their relationship. He certainly had no doubts about how he now felt about Mary. The doubts he had, though, related to whether or not he was temperamentally suited to a more permanent relationship, and this concern seemed to be clouding his judgement. Was it an example of his 'glass half-empty' personality?

They had shared an enjoyable weekend together, but Tom could sense that she was still concerned about her missing kitten. As previously he had tried to reassure her that it would be found but, deep down, he knew the time was rapidly approaching when she would have to accept that this wasn't going to happen.

'Was Constantin able to tell us anything useful?' asked Tom. It was the next morning and he was standing, along with Milner and DC Bennett, in his old office. When he had arrived at the station he had started working his way from floor to floor, making sure he kept up his visible profile amongst all of the officers. Understandably, however, given the situation, he had stayed a little longer when he came to Milner and DC Bennett.

It was DC Bennett who replied, a hint of nervousness in his voice. 'Nothing we didn't already know. When it came to any questions about Inanescu or Grace, he just stonewalled or stuck to his line that he didn't know either of them. So, without any further evidence, we had to release him on Saturday afternoon.'

'Saturday afternoon?' repeated Tom, his tone betraying his surprise, now bordering on anger. 'Why didn't you call me to let me know? I told you if we couldn't get anything out of him then we would need to quickly follow up with a search of his premises. Now he's had over a day's start on us.'

DC Bennett looked at Milner, seeking help.

'Sorry, sir,' answered Milner. 'I should have told you. It was my mistake. When I realised this I immediately took steps to get the search warrant signed off.' He paused, providing Tom with the opportunity to respond. When no response came he carried on. 'Anyway, we are good to go. I have a team on standby. We were just waiting for you to arrive at the station.'

Tom, his initial anger now having subsided, and inwardly impressed with Milner's *mea culpa*, finally answered, 'Well, we can't turn back the clock. Let's just hope Constantin is not as familiar with our police procedures as, perhaps, we are giving him credit for. Just make sure that everything is done by the book and the premises are searched thoroughly. Any problem due to a technical foul-up is the last thing we need right now.'

'Aren't you coming with us?' asked Milner.

'I don't think you need me there. You two are more than capable of handling this,' he replied.

After DC Bennett had left, to organise the search team, Tom and Milner were left alone together.

'Tell me, Milner,' Tom suddenly said, looking directly at him. 'When did you really find out that Constantin had been released?'

Milner returned Tom's gaze. 'Saturday, sir.'

'Hmm,' said Tom, clearly not totally convinced. 'You wouldn't be covering for DC Bennett, would you?'

'Sir, I'm the senior officer and it was my fault.'

'Okay,' he answered, in his previous tone. 'Just let me know if you find anything. And don't forget we also need to call on Birkett.'

As Tom was about to walk away, Milner suddenly said, 'Sir, I've reviewed Holy Cross's CCTV footage as you asked. The camera facing the road does show some footage of a man and a woman entering the premises you asked me to look out for. It's not the best in the world, but you are able to pick out some details of the man and woman. Anyway, I've set it up to show the first time they arrived together and timed when they came back again. The timings and numbers are here.' He handed Tom a piece of paper which contained various numbers, times and dates.

'Thank you, Milner. When did you do all of this?'

'Yesterday, sir,' he answered. 'I was here anyway and had a bit of time to kill.'

Tom was tempted to say something. Instead he simply made do with, 'Good luck with the search.'

Tom then continued his 'walk' through the station and it was just before 10am when he finally arrived at his office on the fifth floor. 'Morning, Jenny,' he said, seeing Jenny at her desk. 'Did you have a good weekend?'

'It was okay,' she replied, in a way which suggested possibly the opposite.

'Only okay?' he asked. 'Didn't you do anything exciting?'

'Not really. I had something planned but it was cancelled.'

'That's a shame,' he said with obvious sympathy, immediately discounting the thought of asking her for more details. He then continued. 'Just to let you know, I'm planning to be around all day. There is a chance, though, I might have to go out later with DS Milner, but, if I do, I'll make sure I keep you informed.'

'Thank you,' she answered before handing him a stack of files. 'I'm afraid these need your attention.'

'Perhaps there's something in here which will generate the excitement you mentioned,' he said, referring to her comment of last week.

'Can I get you some coffee?' she asked.

'Why not?' he replied.

He then spent the next couple of hours reading through the batch of files, reports and miscellaneous requests which Jenny had given him. Most, as before, were easily dealt with, although others required some form of follow-up or action on his part. Usually this was either a phone call or an email requesting additional information. A few, however, required a face-to-face meeting, and he tried to hold these as soon as possible.

By lunchtime he had, more or less, done as much as he could. As he sat back in his chair, looking at the various files strewn over his desk, it just confirmed to him, once again, how he was not cut out for this type of police work. He was, nonetheless, starting to develop a grudging respect for those senior officers who were confronted with this on a daily basis. As a DCI, most of his previous experiences with senior offices had usually involved him asking them for additional resources, or authorisation, to run an operation. At the time, to him at least, this was the most important priority and, therefore, required immediate action. Although he had always known, of course, that he was not the only officer requesting such approval, it was only when he had seen the sheer volume of similar requests he had realised just how difficult, and time-consuming, this task could be. It was physically impossible to agree to everything and so, inevitably, some officers would come away disappointed. Those who were fortunate enough to have their request approved simply thought that it had been a straightforward 'no-brainer'. He knew that because often *he* had been that officer. Still, another couple of months and it would be someone else's problem.

As he was thinking about all of this he was suddenly jolted back to reality when the intercom buzzed.

Tom pressed the 'accept' button and Jenny's voice came through the speaker loud and clear. 'I have DS Milner here and he would like to see you.'

'Okay. Ask him to come straight in,' he answered.

The office door opened and Milner appeared, followed by Jenny. Tom stood up from behind his desk and walked towards the larger meeting one. 'Sit down, Milner,' he said, indicating which chair to use.

'Would you like a drink?' asked Jenny, looking directly at Milner. 'I'll top up your coffee at the same time,' she added to Tom.

'Thanks,' replied Milner. 'That would be nice.'

After Jenny had left, Tom got straight to the point. 'Well? How did it go?'

Milner resisted the urge to smile too much or, worse, look smug. 'Really well. DC Bennett and the team are still there, but I knew you'd want to hear this as soon as possible. Fortunately,' he said, with a degree of relief in his voice not missed by Tom, 'Constantin hadn't been expecting us. When we got there, to begin with, he put up some resistance after we told him about the search, and a couple of the lads had to restrain him. Anyway, it wasn't long before we started to find a few things, including a whole batch of unused foreign passports, mostly Romanian but also a few from other Eastern European countries.'

'Are they genuine?' asked Tom.

'They certainly look it to me, but we are getting them checked. We also found a large amount of cash – mainly sterling but also some foreign currency – as well a number of credit cards.' Sensing how Tom was beginning to show some signs of frustration, as none of this directly linked Constantin with Grace, he then continued, 'We also found, hidden at the back of a drawer, a handgun and twelve rounds of ammunition, and, in another drawer, a written ledger, which showed itemised payments made to Constantin, going back over twelve months, alongside which was the signature of James Grace.'

Chapter 33

DC Bennett had now joined Tom and Milner. 'We didn't find anything else after you left, although we've left his computer with the techies. So there might be something else on there.' After a slight pause he asked, 'Do you think we've got enough to charge Grace?'

'With what?' answered Tom, an edge to his voice, and clearly not entirely sharing Milner's earlier enthusiasm.

'What about the signed ledger?' asked DC Bennett.

'Somehow I don't think that will stand up in court. All he has to do is say that someone has forged his signature, and that would probably be enough to muddy the waters and so introduce some doubt. Any doubt is the very last thing we need when we do finally take Grace to court.'

'So, sir, what do you suggest we do next?' asked a now slightly crestfallen Milner.

'I think we need to sweat Constantin. The gun should provide us with that opportunity. I suspect, though, the most we can hope for is a signed statement from him implicating the Graces in the trafficking. Other than that we need some help from your friend Seneca.'

'Seneca?' asked DC Bennett. 'Who's he?'

'I'll tell you later,' replied Milner, who then faced Tom. 'I'll get started on Constantin right away, sir,' and, together with DC Bennett, he started to walk towards the door.

Before he got there, however, Tom said, 'Milner, could you stay for a moment?'

After DC Bennett had left, Tom continued, 'Sit down. You are probably disappointed we didn't find any real incriminating evidence but, in truth, there was only ever likely to be a slim chance we would. Nonetheless, what we did find is important. It all adds to the case against him. I suspect, in the absence of finding Grace at the actual scene when a crime is being committed, we will need to build up, piece by piece, a whole catalogue of incremental evidence. We are only likely to get one chance to do any serious damage to him, so we can't afford to move too quickly. The last thing we need, because we moved too quickly, is for him to receive a minimal sentence or, worse, a suspended sentence. You know, and I know, that he's a nasty piece of work. So let's be patient.'

Tom's little pep talk appeared, at least initially, to have had the desired result. Eventually Milner spoke. 'I know you are right, sir. It's just that people like Grace believe they are above the law. In fact, it's worse because they treat the law with contempt.' His little outburst over, he fell silent.

A few times now, since they had started working together, Tom had heard this type of moral outrage from Milner. In fact, it was one of Milner's characteristics which appealed to him most and, in truth, was another reason why he didn't want Milner to leave. 'Don't worry, Milner. We all feel like that sometimes. Even me. It's what differentiates the good guys from the bad guys. If we were all the same, and there wasn't any greed or criminality in the world, then you and I would be out of a job.' He then went on, 'Speaking of jobs. I have another one for you.'

Milner looked up. 'What is it you want me to do?' he asked.

'I want you to show me how the CCTV playback machine works.'

A short while later Tom and Milner were in a side room, with Tom sitting in front of a console which housed an impressive number of buttons, dials and counters. Immediately above the console was a large monitor.

'Why don't you let me get the footage?' asked Milner, becoming frustrated with Tom's inability to press the correct buttons at the correct time.

'Did you have to go on a course to learn how to use this?' asked Tom, having now given up trying to make it work and with his annoyance level quickly rising.

'No. It's pretty—'

Before Milner could finish Tom interjected. 'Please don't tell me it's pretty easy to use.'

'If you've ever used a PlayStation or Xbox then this type of machine isn't as difficult to use as it looks.'

'Milner, do I look as though I've ever used a PlayStation or Xbox?' he asked rhetorically. 'Just get it to the point where the man first goes into the house.' He stood up and allowed Milner to take his seat in front of the console.

Milner pressed a button and then immediately started to turn a dial. Above the dial was a counter. When Milner was satisfied he had reached the appropriate position he said, 'If you press that button,' pointing at a small rectangular plastic button, 'the footage will start. If you want to see it again, just turn this dial anticlockwise until the counter reaches one hundred and forty-five. If you want to move the footage forward then turn the dial clockwise. The piece of paper that I gave you has the start numbers for when he next came to the house. Do you want me to stay here?' he asked, still in the dark as to what all this was about.

'You might as well. Just in case.'

Tom followed Milner's instructions and pressed the button. He spent the next forty-five minutes reviewing all of the footage showing the two people entering the house. There was also a facility to print copies of any particular frame from the footage, and this, helpfully, also highlighted the time and date. Eventually, when he had finished, Tom had about a dozen printed photographs in front of him.

'Thank you, Milner. That wasn't as difficult as I thought it would be,' he said, clearly quite satisfied with his sudden mastery of the technology.

Milner, no longer able to suppress his natural inquisitiveness, although still without any great expectation that he would get an answer, said, 'Sir? Do you mind telling me what this is all about?'

To his great surprise Tom answered, 'I suppose, after everything you have done, I owe you an explanation.' He then briefly summarised what it was about and why he was interested in the CCTV footage.

'Is there anything else you would like me to do?' asked Milner.

'No, thanks. Not with this, anyway. I want you to focus on finding out who killed Bogdan Inanescu.' He then added, 'I can handle this.'

Chapter 34

Tom was standing outside Diane Filton's house in Farnborough, a brown cardboard file in his hand. When he rang the bell he could hear a dog inside immediately start to bark, and this was followed by a man's raised voice telling the dog to be quiet. The dog ignored the man and continued to bark. Eventually the door was opened by Pete Hepworth. 'Oh, it's you again. What do you want this time?'
'Is it possible to come in? I'd like to speak with you and your partner.'
'Di's just about to leave for work, so you won't be able to talk to her,' he answered.
'What I have to say won't take long.' As he was still standing outside, he then asked again if he could come in.
'I suppose so,' replied a still-reluctant Hepworth, who then led Tom through to the same room as last time. As he entered, he saw Diane Filton standing by the window.
'I've just told him you are on your way to work,' said Hepworth, reinforcing his earlier comment.
'Then let me get straight to the point,' Tom said firmly. 'Last time I was here, I told you how we suspected that Mr Wilson had been forcibly held down, or physically restrained, at some point in the days immediately prior to his death. We now believe we know who did this.'
He paused, allowing the significance of what he had just said to sink in. Whilst Hepworth remained standing, Diane Filton suddenly sat down.
'Well, it wasn't us,' answered Hepworth, and, to reinforce his point, he added, 'and she had nothing to do with it.'
'Did you, Mr Hepworth, ever visit Mr Wilson's house?'
'I might have once or twice,' he replied, a hint of nervousness now in his voice. 'But that was to drive Di there. I never went in.'

'But you were seen entering and leaving Mr Wilson's house on three occasions in the days just before his death.'

'That's crap,' he said, now raising his voice. 'You are just trying to pin this on us because Di was the last person to see the old man. Anyway, what proof do you have?'

'Well, I'll get to that shortly,' he answered. 'On Mr Wilson's body there were clear impressions of someone's fingers, made when he was held down. I believe they were your fingers, Mr Hepworth. Anyway, it shouldn't be too difficult to prove they match. The person who held down Mr Wilson was also left-handed.' Continuing to look directly at Hepworth, Tom added, 'I believe you are left-handed.' He paused for a short while, deliberately allowing the tension to rise. 'You asked earlier what evidence we have which proves you entered Mr Wilson's house. Well, we have CCTV footage which clearly shows you arriving, entering and then leaving his house. Not just once, but, as I said earlier, on three separate occasions.' Tom then opened the file he had been holding and took out a series of photographs, all of which showed Hepworth, together with Diane Filton, entering and leaving Mr Wilson's house. One of the photographs showed Hepworth leaving with a plastic supermarket bag in his hand.

'I notice neither of you had a bag in your hand when you went into the house. What was in the bag, Miss Filton?' To date she had not said a single word and Tom was keen to now get her involved in the conversation.

'What's that got to do with anything?' Hepworth answered before she could say anything.

'Actually, I was asking Miss Filton. If you could please let her answer for herself, I'd appreciate it.'

But Hepworth, determined not to be silenced, said, 'Don't say nothing, Di. He can't make you.'

Tom decided to adopt a different approach. 'Okay. Let me try to help you, then. We also believe that some of Mr Wilson's personal possessions were stolen. Would you know anything about that?' he asked, redirecting his attention back towards Hepworth.

'I've told you, we don't know nothing,' he answered, this now becoming his stock reply.

'What about that china dog?' Tom said, pointing towards a

porcelain figure of a border collie, which had been placed on the windowsill. 'Is that yours?'

'Of course it's ours,' he answered aggressively. 'Whose do you think it is?'

'I happen to think that it belonged to Mr Wilson and you stole it.'

Hepworth didn't reply immediately, but when he finally did he simply said, 'He gave it to Di. People are always offering her things. It's not a crime.'

'Well, actually, Mr Hepworth, I think, in this particular instance, it is a crime and it was you and Miss Filton who committed that crime.' Once again he paused, expecting a response from Hepworth. Surprised when none came, he carried on. 'Are there any other items in the house which Mr Wilson "gave" you?' Still without any response, Tom then said, 'So you won't mind if we carry out a search, then?'

This time there was an immediate response. 'Don't try that with me. I know my rights. You can't search anywhere without a proper search warrant. Have you got one?'

'I'm sure you do know your rights, Mr Hepworth. After all, you've had lots of practice.' He took out his notebook and started to read out loud. 'Theft; selling stolen goods; aggravated burglary, for which you received a prison sentence. Quite a record you have, Mr Hepworth.' He replaced the notebook in his pocket. 'Do you think with your record, and the evidence we have, a jury is going to believe your story? I don't have a search warrant, but I could be back here in less than an hour with one. But it would be much better for both of you if you told the truth. The courts don't like it when people waste their time, and the taxpayers' money, by continuously lying.'

Finally Diane Filton spoke. 'He thought I was his wife and kept offering me things,' she said. 'Mr Wilson, I mean.'

Suddenly Hepworth became very aggressive and grabbed hold of her. 'Shut up. He's just trying to scare you. He can't prove nothing.'

'Can you please move away from her?' Tom said, now concerned for her safety.

Hepworth released her but then walked towards him. 'Why? What are you going to do, old man?' He pushed Tom, who, taken by surprise, fell awkwardly backwards, hit something and then found himself lying, on his back, on the floor, staring up at Hepworth.

'Do you want some more or are you too scared to get up?' he said, standing over Tom.

With some difficulty Tom struggled to his feet and said, albeit without any great confidence, 'You are only making it worse for yourself. I suggest you calm down. There are other police officers outside.' Tom had taken the precaution of asking a couple of uniformed officers to come along with him just in case, given Hepworth's record of violence, something such as this happened.

By now Diane Filton was sobbing quietly. 'I told you not to do it but you wouldn't listen,' she said between sobs.

'Shut up!' Hepworth shouted, his anger now having increased another notch.

Tom had walked back towards the front door and, after opening it, had gestured for the two officers to come in. As soon as they were alongside him, Tom said, 'Peter Hepworth, I'm arresting you for the assault of a police officer,' after which he read him his rights.

As Hepworth was being led away, he turned around and said, 'Don't say nothing.'

After he had gone, Tom gingerly sat down opposite Diane Filton and said, 'I'd appreciate it if you would come back to the station.'

'Am I being arrested?' she immediately replied, clearly frightened.

'No, you are not being arrested. All you need to do is to tell the truth,' he answered, as reassuringly as he could. 'If there are other items in the house which you took from Mr Wilson, or anyone else, then it will be better for you if you tell me where they are.'

'He made me do it,' she suddenly said. 'At first, when he offered, I wouldn't take anything from Mr Wilson, but he kept offering and so I took a few things. When I told Pete he suddenly said he wanted to come along. I tried to stop him, but he kept saying that Mr Wilson was gaga anyway and wouldn't remember. That's when he started to take other things.'

'What about your other clients?' he asked. 'Have you taken things from them as well?'

'A few,' she answered, not able to look directly at him, before quickly adding, 'I wasn't the only one. I know a few of the others have also taken stuff. No one ever checked. They didn't even check to make sure we were there for the time we were supposed to be. We just got the clients to sign to say we had done our job. Most of them didn't even know what they were signing.'

'What about the bruises on Mr Wilson's body?' he asked gently.

She hesitated briefly before answering. 'Pete had smoked some weed and he was still a bit high when we got there. He kept asking Mr Wilson where his money was but the old man just kept saying he didn't have any. Pete didn't believe him, and that's when he grabbed hold and started to shake him.' She started to cry again.

'Was that on the morning he died?' asked Tom.

'Yes,' she replied quietly, after which her sobs became almost uncontrollable. Tom waited for her to stop and, after a while, she was able to continue. 'I tried to stop him but he just kept shaking him. What's going to happen to me?' she suddenly asked.

'I don't know,' Tom replied. 'That will be for the courts to decide. But if you tell them what you've just told me, then I'm sure they are likely to be more lenient.'

When they were back at the station, Tom took a statement from Diane Filton, who separately, as far as she could remember, listed the items they had stolen from Mr Wilson and the others. He then arranged for her to be taken home, although Hepworth was still being held in custody.

'Are you okay?' asked Jenny, when he arrived back at the fifth floor. He was walking slowly and with obvious difficulty towards her. 'What happened?' she asked with genuine concern.

'I fell over,' he answered, factually correct but not telling the full story.

'Have you been to the hospital to have it looked at?'

'I don't think it's that bad,' he said. 'I'm sure it will be much better tomorrow.'

Jenny looked as though she was not totally convinced but, before she could say anything else, Tom asked, 'Anything important happened?'

'Not that I'm aware of,' she replied, clearly disappointed. 'There are more reports and files for your attention. I've left them on your desk.'

Tom walked carefully into his office and, with some difficulty, sat down. Initially the pain had been mostly in his back. Now, though, it was his right side which was giving him the most pain and discomfort.

There was a knock on his door and then Jenny appeared carrying a tray containing coffee and milk. 'I thought you might need this,' she said. She placed the tray immediately in front of him. 'Are you sure you are all right?'

'I'll be fine, thanks,' he answered as positively as he could.

After Jenny had left and he had poured himself a cup of coffee, he began the daily ritual of reading through all of the reports. It was, however, very uncomfortable, as every time he moved, even slightly, he felt a sharp pain in his right side. Just as he was thinking about, perhaps, going home, the intercom buzzed.

'Sorry to disturb you, but I have DS Milner here. He says it's important he sees you as soon as possible.'

'You'd better let him in, then,' he replied.

Almost immediately the door opened and Milner appeared, the ubiquitous folder in his hand. Tom could see instantly, from Milner's body language, he was eager to share some information with Tom.

'Sit down, Milner,' Tom said, pointing at the table. 'But excuse me if I don't join you.'

'I'm okay standing, sir,' he replied.

'Well, what is it?' asked Tom, a touch impatiently. 'You're obviously keen to tell me something.'

'I thought you would want to know this, sir,' he said. 'Our friend Seneca has just made an appearance.'

Chapter 35

'Seneca's appeared?' Tom echoed, suddenly understanding the meaning of Milner's comment. 'Well, let's hope so. We need as much help as we can get with this case. So far, all we seem to be doing is gathering mainly circumstantial evidence.'

'This, I think, is more than circumstantial,' answered Milner. 'We have identified someone who looks suspiciously like Brendan Grace, outside Terry Birkett's house, on the night it was set alight.' Before Tom could ask anything, he quickly added, as an explanation, 'I checked all of the CCTV in the area and, fortunately, Birkett's house is almost directly opposite a courier delivery depot. They've had a few break-ins over the past year and so have had CCTV installed recently. Anyway, I received the tapes this morning and, when I rolled through to the night of the fire, there he was, petrol can in hand.'

'Thank goodness for CCTV,' Tom said, more to himself than to Milner, and thinking back to the situation with Pete Hepworth. With a bit more concern in his voice, however, he then asked, 'Are you sure it's Brendan Grace?'

Milner opened the file he was holding and took out a series of photographs which he had printed from the CCTV footage. 'Take a look yourself,' he said, arranging them on Tom's desk.

Tom looked at them for a while and then said, with a hint of disappointment, 'Well, they certainly look like him but they are not one hundred percent conclusive. The hood he's wearing is, unfortunately, partly obscuring his face.' Tom looked up at Milner. 'You and I know it's Brendan Grace, but I'm not sure a jury would.'

Milner, having anticipated this response, said, 'We do, though, have some other evidence linking him to the scene of the crime.'

'Really?' asked Tom, with some hope now back in his voice.

Milner pulled out another two photographs and placed

these alongside the first ones. 'As you can see, this one,' he said, pointing at one of the photographs, 'shows the same man – let's call him Brendan Grace – getting out of a white van. The van had been parked just around the corner from Birkett's house, but the CCTV camera on that side of the depot picked it up. You may remember there was a similar white van parked at Grace's place when we first went to see him.'

'That's right. A *similar* white van,' Tom said, stressing the word 'similar'. 'Similar doesn't mean it is his van. It could be yet another coincidence. As you know, in this business I'm not a great believer in coincidences, but, unfortunately, most lawyers don't share my view.'

A thin smile appeared on Milner's face, before he took out yet more photographs from his file. 'These,' he said, placing another three photographs on the desk, 'were taken by DC Bennett, when he followed Brendan Grace to Long Lane Farm. This one clearly shows Grace getting into the driver's seat. You can also see the registration. It's the same registration as on the van near to Birkett's. This next one, again, shows Grace, but this time driving the van, and *this* one,' he said, with some flourish, 'shows the large dent on the driver's door. Again, if you look closely you can see it matches exactly the dent on the van on the night of the fire.'

Tom sat back in his chair, momentarily forgetting about the pain in his side. Finally, he spoke. 'Maybe I was too hasty about DC Bennett's prowess with a camera. I'm still worried, however, that Grace will just say the man in the photos is not him. But let's cross that particular bridge later. In the meantime, I think we have enough now to, at least, bring him in for questioning. Pull together all of the evidence we have against him, and let's go and visit him tomorrow morning and invite him back here.'

'What about Birkett? Should we pull him in as well?' asked Milner.

Whilst it was the obvious thing to do, it was clear Tom was still not totally convinced, and this was confirmed when he answered, 'We have even less evidence linking him to the death of Inanescu than we have on the Graces. Let's wait until we've had our discussion with Brendan Grace. We don't want to show our hand too quickly.'

Milner picked up all of the photographs and put them back

into his file. Tom, his mind on the case, stood up, and a sudden sharp shooting pain instantly reminded him about his current incapacity.

'Are you okay, sir?' asked Milner, a slightly puzzled expression on his face.

'Yes, I'm fine,' he answered. 'I had a little fall this morning, that's all.'

'Have you had it checked out? You never know with falls. Sometimes the pain gets worse later on.'

'Thank you, Milner. When I need your diagnosis, I'll ask for it.'

Milner metaphorically shrugged his shoulders and, file in hand, walked out of the office.

Chapter 36

Tom had spent a long and uncomfortable night trying to sleep. Even though he had eventually given in and taken a few painkillers, the searing pain in his right side had instantly returned every time he had moved. His strategy was, therefore, to sleep on his back, not daring to move at all.

Eventually he must have fallen asleep, and when his alarm clock woke him it was with some initial trepidation he got himself out of bed. The prospect of taking a shower and, worse, then getting dressed was, at that particular moment, not something he was looking forward to. Recognising this might be the case, he had given himself more time than usual to carry out these tasks. Nonetheless, by the time he arrived at the station it was later than he had planned. This morning, he thought, as he walked through the station's entrance, was not a good one to be taking his usual stroll around the various floors.

By the time he arrived at his own office, Milner, DC Bennett and Jenny were all waiting for him. It was she who, seeing the difficulty with which he was walking, asked the obvious question.

'You really don't look well, sir. Have you been to the hospital?'

'Thank you for your concern, Jenny, but I'm okay. Just a little sore, that's all.'

'Is that what they said at the hospital?' she asked.

'I haven't been to the hospital,' he replied sharply. Recognising that he may have been a little brusque, he then added, in a more considerate tone, 'Maybe I'll go after we get back from visiting Brendan Grace.'

So far, Milner had not spoken, but, having just heard this, he suddenly said, 'Do you think that's a good idea, sir? It looks as though you can hardly walk. What if there's a bit of rough stuff?'

'I'm sure there won't be any rough stuff, Milner,' he answered confidently.

'Sir, with respect, you just don't know that.'

'Milner, "with respect" usually means that the speaker doesn't agree. Is that what you mean?'

'It is, sir,' he replied, without hesitation. 'DC Bennett and myself, as you've said yourself, are more than capable of handling it. And anyway, if there is any aggression we have a few uniformed officers with us.'

Tom remained silent as he thought about what Milner had said. Eventually common sense prevailed. 'Okay, but let me know as soon as you've done it, and don't forget to—'

'Make sure we do everything by the book?' interrupted Milner.

Tom gave Milner a steely stare but then, suddenly, a hint of a smile appeared on his face. 'Yesterday you were diagnosing medical conditions and today you're a mind reader. I think you might be wasted in the police force.'

As Milner and DC Bennett both turned away, Tom couldn't resist a final comment. 'Good luck,' he said, as they were exiting the office.

'Are they going somewhere dangerous?' asked a suddenly concerned Jenny.

'It shouldn't be,' answered Tom, 'but you never can really tell, particularly when it involves people who have a volatile nature. Anyway, I'm sure they will be okay.'

As Tom walked slowly into his own office, Jenny, once again, raised her favourite subject. 'About the hospital, I really do think you should go and get yourself checked. You look a lot worse than yesterday.'

Either Jenny's constant nagging or a dose of common sense finally seemed to have had an effect. 'I think I will,' he answered. 'I'll go tomorrow.'

'That's not very wise, sir,' she said. 'You really should go today. Why don't you let me take you?'

'That's very kind of you, but I think I can take myself there.' He then added, with a slightly forced laugh, 'Okay, you win. I'll go now. But I'll drive myself. I just need to make a couple of phone calls and then I'll go. I promise.'

One of the phone calls he was referring to was to DCS Small. He had promised he would keep him fully informed about any new developments in the Grace case. So, as soon as he was seated at his desk, he made the call.

'Sir, it's DCI Stone. I just wanted to let you know what the situation is regarding Grace.' He then proceeded to update him, specifically informing him about the current operation involving Milner and DC Bennett.

'Is there any reason why you are not involved?' DCS Small asked. 'I would have thought you would want to be there.'

'Normally, I would, sir. But I've had a slight accident and am just about to go to the hospital.'

'Accident? What sort of accident?' he asked, suddenly concerned.

Tom told him about his current predicament.

'And you did it when you fell over?' asked DCS Small.

'Yes, that's right. Stupid, really, but just one of those things, I suppose,' replied Tom, doing his best to make light of it.

'Hmm. Okay. Let me know how Milner gets on with Grace, though.'

'Will do, sir,' he answered, noting how he hadn't asked how he was feeling.

The other call was to Alan Wood, the managing director of Redbreast Home Care Services. After Tom had been put through he spent a few minutes informing Mr Wood about the Pete Hepworth and Diane Filton situation.

'That's unbelievable,' Wood replied, clearly stunned by what Tom had told him. 'What's going to happen to them?'

Tom gave his stock answer. 'That's for the courts to decide. All we can do is present the evidence.'

There was a brief silence before Wood spoke. 'Will Redbreast's name be mentioned?'

Tom could feel himself becoming quite angry. 'Is that what you would prefer, Mr Wood?' But, not allowing Wood to answer, he then carried on. 'One of your employees has committed a series of thefts, as well as being an accessory to an assault on an elderly, vulnerable person at a time when he was supposed to be receiving consideration and care from your company. I would have thought not only is it inevitable that your company's name will be mentioned but, frankly, it's also necessary.'

This seemed to increase his earlier concern almost exponentially, and when he next spoke it was in a quiet and almost defeated tone. 'What will happen next?'

'Hepworth and Filton will be charged and then due process

will take its course. As far as you are concerned, I'm afraid I have a duty to pass all of the details to the relevant authorities. I understand the Care Quality Commission is the main watchdog authority within your industry, so I would expect a visit from them shortly. As there has also been an allegation of more widespread theft involving your staff, there will also be a separate police investigation.' Tom paused momentarily, allowing Wood the time to fully understand the seriousness of the situation. As there was no response he then added, 'I'm afraid, Mr Wood, Redbreast Home Care Services is likely to be in for a difficult time.'

Chapter 37

Tom had spent the rest of the afternoon and early evening in the A&E department of his local hospital. For someone whose patience levels were not especially high even at the best of times, the seemingly interminable waiting around was so frustrating that, on a couple of occasions, he had seriously considered just walking out. Eventually, though, he managed to survive the long process of being seen by a triage nurse, then a doctor, followed by a radiographer and then, finally, the same doctor again, who confirmed he had cracked a couple of ribs. He was prescribed more powerful painkillers and told to rest for a few days.

When he eventually got out of the hospital, he immediately switched on his phone and could see he'd had a few missed calls. One was from Mary and the others from Milner.

His general mood wasn't helped by having to pay what he considered to be extortionate car park charges, and by the time he retrieved his car it was almost 6pm, just in time to hit all of the homebound traffic. As he edged his way into it he thought to himself that he'd certainly had better days! He decided to call Mary first.

'Hello,' she said, answering his call. 'I've been trying to get hold of you all afternoon. We will be finishing rehearsals a bit earlier tonight, and I wondered whether I could tempt you to come round and stay here.'

'I'd love to, but I'm afraid I'm slightly incapacitated,' he replied.

'Why?' she asked, and then, with an almost discernible increase of foreboding in her voice, 'What's wrong?'

'Don't worry, it's nothing serious. It's just that I fell over yesterday and hurt my back. I was hoping it would have eased by today, but as it hadn't I decided I'd better have it checked out and so I went to the hospital. In fact, I've only just got out and am currently on my way home.'

'Fell over?' she repeated. 'What happened?'

'I tripped and landed awkwardly. It's nothing too serious, just a couple of cracked ribs.' Mary didn't reply immediately and so Tom continued, 'Anyway, thanks for the offer but I don't think I'll be much use to you tonight.'

Still trying to get more details from him she said, 'You said you tripped. How did that happen?'

'I stepped back without looking. A sign of old age, I'm afraid,' he answered, not wanting to tell her what had actually happened.

'Knowing how much you dislike hospitals, I can only assume you must have been in pain to actually go to one.'

'It wasn't too bad, but I was bullied into it by Milner and Jenny.'

'Good for them.' Suddenly having a thought, she added, 'Why don't I come to you tonight? I could look after you.'

'Mary, I really don't need to be looked after. They gave me some painkillers and told me to rest. I'm sure I'll be fit enough for us to meet up again at the weekend.'

'Well, if you need anything, promise me you'll call.'

'I promise,' he answered. Just as he said this his phone buzzed and he could see it was Milner again. 'Mary,' he said, 'can I call you back later? Milner has been trying to get hold of me all afternoon and he's just trying again.'

'Okay,' she replied. 'But don't forget to rest, like the doctor told you.'

After Mary had gone he called Milner, who answered his phone immediately.

'Milner, it's me,' said Tom. 'I see you've left a few messages for me to call. How did it go?'

'That's why I've been trying to get hold of you,' Milner said. 'Not very well, I'm afraid. Brendan Grace wasn't there and we've not been able to track him down.'

'Was James Grace there?' asked Tom.

'James Grace was there, all right,' he replied, with a slight laugh. 'As you can imagine, he wasn't exactly thrilled to see us again.' He paused before adding, almost as an afterthought, 'He did ask where you were, but not, I have to say, with any great affection. Of course, he wanted to know why we needed to see Brendan.'

'And what did you say?'

'Well, it was pretty obvious, with the other uniformed officers in attendance, that it wasn't a purely social call. So I had to come clean and say we needed to speak with his son in connection with the arson attack on Birkett's house and that it would be in his best interests if he handed himself in at the station.'

Tom remained silent whilst he considered what Milner had just told him. 'Okay, I guess you couldn't really say anything else. Was that it, then?'

'More or less, although it was intermingled with quite a bit of profanity, together with a few threats.'

'Threats?' Tom repeated. 'What sort of threats?'

'How he wasn't going to let us get away with this constant intimidation against his family. How we didn't have a shred of evidence to link the family with any crime. How you were conducting a personal vendetta. That type of thing.'

'Me?'

'Yes. Apparently, and this is according to him, sir, you've taken a liking to all of the publicity that you received after the recent cases and are just trying to get more personal coverage for yourself.' Before Tom could respond, Milner added, 'He said we should expect his lawyer to be in touch soon. He then said something quite strange.'

'What did he say, then?' asked Tom.

'He said to tell you he knew all about you.'

Chapter 38

It was the following morning and Tom, as instructed, was resting at home. This hadn't, however, prevented him from phoning Jenny to see if anything important had come across his desk. She, not knowing anyway what was important or just routine, had politely, but firmly, reminded him that it was not a good idea to keep calling, as he was supposed to be resting. He was beginning to like Jenny. Unbeknown to her he had also phoned Milner a couple of times already, to see if there was any news on Brendan Grace. Despite Milner's assurance that he would contact him as soon as he knew anything, Tom still had to make a conscious effort not to call him again.

Mary had phoned before she had left for work, mainly to see how he was but partly, he suspected, to make sure that he was actually at home and not back at the station. He'd never been the type of person who liked pottering around the house or garden. For the same reason, he'd also never been keen on beach-type holidays. In truth, he found the time spent on holiday slightly boring, and generally viewed holidays as a waste of valuable time, rather than simply an opportunity to relax and recharge the batteries. His cracked ribs also, of course, restricted the opportunities open to him in terms of using his unexpected downtime.

By mid-morning, not having heard from Milner, he found himself becoming more and more frustrated, feeling that he really should be doing something more productive.

He made himself a cup of coffee, and then sat down at his kitchen table and opened the Susan Chambers file he had found in the filing cabinet. At the time the feeling had been that the case was very straightforward. There was DNA, and plenty of other evidence, placing Griffiths at the scene of the crime when Chambers was killed. What's more, he was an ex-boyfriend of the deceased, and both had a history of drug-taking and lived a fairly chaotic and dysfunctional lifestyle. So all of the criminal holy trinity boxes could be ticked. He had the means, the motive and the opportunity. For these reasons, Griffiths' arrest, trial and subsequent sentencing were concluded quickly and without any undue complications.

Tom began by flicking through the headings on all of the files, and most of them were as he would have expected: individual notes from the officers involved, general reports, a few photographs of the deceased, other photographs of the evidence as well as copies of witness statements. What was a little unusual, however, was just how widely some of the reports had been circulated, particularly for such a straightforward enquiry. He decided, rather than picking out individual reports, he would read the case notes in chronological order and, within a short while, found himself fully engrossed in the case, especially as he personally knew most of the officers involved.

After a while he decided to take a break, but the real reason was that he could no longer resist the urge to phone Milner for an update.

'Yes, sir?' Milner said, in a resigned manner, as he recognised who the caller was.

'I was just wondering if Brendan Grace has appeared yet.'

'Not yet, sir,' he answered. 'I did say I would call you immediately once we had tracked him down.'

Tom ignored Milner's terse comment. 'I have a little job for you.'

Milner's heart sank. Somehow, whenever DCI Stone used those words, it ended up involving him in anything but a 'little job'.

'Can you find out where the man who was involved with James Grace in that security van hijacking currently is? If I remember correctly, a few years after he was released, he was sentenced for murder. Anyway, it shouldn't be too difficult to find the name of the prison where he's serving his sentence.'

'Any particular reason?' asked Milner.

'I just feel it would be useful to gather as much information as possible on Grace. Someone like him, who has, no doubt, been involved in many shady situations throughout his life, must have made a few enemies along the way. So let's see if we can find some of those enemies.'

'I'll find out where he is and get back to you.' Changing the subject, he then said, 'Anyway, sir, how are your ribs today? Still as painful?'

'A bit better, thank you, Milner, but just because I've got a couple of cracked ribs doesn't mean my mind has gone. Anyway, don't worry, I'll soon be back.'

With that thought still in his mind, Milner said, 'That's something we can all look forward to, sir.'

'Just don't forget to call me the moment you find Brendan Grace,' replied Tom.

Although it was only just past midday, he suddenly found himself hungry. With everything which had gone on yesterday, by the time he'd arrived home, he hadn't felt like cooking anything. Instead, he had reverted to his old default position and had poured himself a bowl of cornflakes. He still wasn't motivated enough to cook anything substantial, and so made do with a couple of toasted cheese sandwiches and a cup of coffee.

After he had finished his lunch he resumed reading the file notes, and it was then he noticed a reference to a name he recognised very well. His and Pete Duffy's careers had, more or less, run in parallel after they had both become detectives. They had, though, lost contact for a number of years when Pete had transferred to another force within the London region. About five years ago he had returned to West London, to take up another DCI position, where he had stayed until his retirement a few years later. In fact, Tom could still clearly recall attending Pete's retirement party, not least because quite a few of the top brass were also there.

Although Tom had not had a busy case load, it was Pete who had been chosen to be the lead officer on this particular investigation. It wasn't really surprising Tom had not been chosen as it had coincided with his own 'dark' period, when he was convinced that there was a campaign to deliberately exclude him from all operational matters. That period now seemed, however, as though it was almost a lifetime ago.

He was still reflecting on all of this when his mobile phone began ringing. As he picked it up he was hoping it would be Milner. Instead, a number he didn't recognise was displayed on the screen.

'Tom Stone,' he answered.

'Is that the famous Detective Chief Inspector Tom Stone?' asked the vaguely recognisable voice in a tone heavy with sarcasm.

'Who is this?' he asked.

'Don't you recognise me?' the voice replied. 'It's your old friend James Grace.'

Chapter 39

'How did you get my number?' asked Tom, clearly not interested in any pleasantries.
'That's no way to talk to someone who has gone to the trouble to call you, is it?'
'I asked you where you got my number from.'
'You're not the only copper I know.' He was silent, for a while, but then went on. 'I've been doing my homework on you. Seems you are a bit of a celebrity these days.' When he next spoke, the initial friendly tone had disappeared and had been replaced by a much harder one. 'I had a visit from your two monkeys yesterday. Looks like you sent them to do your dirty work. Too scared to come yourself, were you? They said they'd come to take Brendan in. I've warned you before, I won't let anyone harm me or my family, and that includes you, Detective Chief Inspector Stone.'
'Are you threatening me?' Tom asked.
'Do I sound as though I'm making threats?' Grace answered, his voice suddenly calm and controlled. 'All I'm doing is reminding you that I'm a family man. Families are the most important thing. Always remember that. You should respect yours as well.' Before Tom could reply, he added, 'By the way, how's that lovely girlfriend of yours? Mary, isn't it? Lives in Bagshot. Has she found her lost kitten yet? She must be really worried.'
A sudden shiver travelled up and down Tom's spine at the mention of Mary's name and, momentarily, he was lost for a response.
Before he could gather his thoughts Grace continued. 'We all need our families and friends, don't we, Tom?' The use of his Christian name was almost as sinister as the earlier reference to Mary, and, as a last comment before he hung up, Grace said, 'It might be good for you if you remembered that.'
Tom's mind was racing as he tried to recall everything

which Grace had said. There were so many questions. How had Grace got his mobile number? Did Grace also know where he lived? Why go to the trouble of finding out about his recent career? Most worrying of all, of course, were the not-too-subtle references to Mary, and, as unlikely as it seemed, his mention of Mary's missing kitten. It was these which, no doubt, were the reason why Tom had suddenly developed a sickening feeling in the pit of his stomach. Despite Grace's well-chosen words there was little doubt in Tom's mind that they were meant as a threat. The meaning was clear: stay away from my family and I'll stay away from yours. More worryingly, the opposite was equally true.

Ever since he had met Mary his main worry had been about the conflict which would, at some point, inevitably occur between his commitment to his job and his relationship with her. He had never, however, considered that this conflict would involve a possible threat to her personal safety. The likelihood, of course, was that Grace was simply using her as a form of leverage against him, but, given his previous liberal use of violence, this was not something he was willing to rely on.

His mind was in turmoil as he tried to organise all of these thoughts. In the past, when he had been trying to make sense of difficult or conflicting issues, he had found that walking away from them, even for a short while, often helped, and so he decided that maybe the distraction of boiling the kettle and making himself a cup of coffee might do something to calm his thoughts. By the time he had done it he quickly realised, unfortunately, that this wasn't one of those occasions. If anything he was even more anxious, unable to see any clear way through this.

As he was sitting at the kitchen table, drinking his coffee, he ran through all of the options which were available to him. Firstly, of course, he could simply treat the words as hollow threats, as yet another confirmation of Grace's guilt. As he ran this scenario through his mind he suddenly realised how this still carried very real dangers with it. If Grace felt the net was closing in on him and his family, then it was possible those threats would be converted into violence.

Another possibility, and one which raised his anxiety to the highest possible level, was that these were the actions of a desperate man. In fact, a man who was not averse to dispensing violence in order to achieve his aims. If this was the true situation then, perhaps, he would have no choice but to back off the case and let someone else handle it. But, in that case, the question would be who? Milner? DC Bennett, or another officer entirely? If this was what he did decide then he would have to discuss it with DCS Small first, but he had little doubt that, if he did, DCS Small would have no choice but to agree to it. There had been similar examples over the years, albeit very few in number, which Tom was aware of. As far as he could remember, however, they had mostly been due to some form of incapacitation, either physical or mental, which had affected the lead officer. And anyway, wouldn't Grace simply redirect his threats towards whoever took on the case?

Perhaps he could quietly drop the case. After all, he had had the real impression, when he had first spoken with DCS Small about it, that Small didn't seem to have any real enthusiasm for pursuing it. But then how would he square this off with Milner and DC Bennett, let alone his own conscience? Somehow, this seemed the least appealing of all the options.

So far, he had, consciously, tried to think through the different courses of action available to him without considering Mary's position and the possible consequences for her. The reality, however, was that he couldn't just ignore his emotional attachment and, more importantly, concern for her safety.

In a further attempt to take his mind away from it he resumed his reading of the Susan Chambers case file. As he read through the various notes he noticed a reference to a statement Pete had taken from Chambers' flatmate, Shelley Ripley. Tom quickly flicked through everything that was included in the file but couldn't find Pete's statement. He reread the original note.

See DCI Duffy's record of his interview with Ms Chambers' flatmate Shelley Ripley.

Thinking he might simply not have spotted the note he, once again, checked through the entire file, this time making sure it wasn't hidden in another part of the file. He still couldn't find it, though. It wasn't unknown for notes or, occasionally, even entire files to go missing. After all, the police could give the Civil Service a run for their money when it came to bureaucratic cock-ups. In fact, this was presumably the reason why Superintendent Peters' name had still been included on the wide distribution list for the note announcing Griffiths' death, even though he no longer worked for the police.

Tom continued to read through the file and certainly, based upon the mass of evidence contained in it, there seemed little doubt that Griffiths was the person who had murdered Susan Chambers. He closed the file and, having put it to one side, immediately found himself dwelling again on the phone call with Grace. Picking up his own phone, Tom pressed the 'recent calls' button and made a note of Grace's number, after which he called Milner.

'I was just about to call you, sir. Brendan Grace has handed himself in.'

Chapter 40

'Has he admitted anything?' asked Tom.

'What do you think, sir?'

'If I knew the answer already, I wouldn't have asked you,' he answered. Instantly regretting his tone, he immediately added, 'Sorry, Milner. I didn't mean to be so sharp with you. It must be due to all of the spare time I have on my hands.'

'That's okay, sir. I'm sure you must be frustrated, not being able to do anything.'

That wasn't quite how Tom saw it but, nonetheless, he let it go. 'So, what has he said?'

'He turned up with his lawyer. I interviewed him and showed him the evidence, including all of the photos. But he just let his lawyer do most of the talking. When he did speak he simply denied it was him outside Birkett's house. According to him, he had been at home, in Essex, at the time.'

'What about the van?'

'He said it had recently been stolen.'

'Where is he now, then?' asked Tom, already guessing what Milner's answer would be.

'I'm afraid we had to release him.'

There followed an extended period of silence. Eventually, it was Milner who broke the silence. 'Are you still there, sir?'

'Yes, I'm still here,' Tom answered calmly.

'Are you okay, sir?' asked Milner, detecting that, perhaps, DCI Stone wasn't quite his normal self.

'I'm fine, thanks. As I said, I'm just not used to all of this free time.' Before Milner could respond, he went on, 'Take another look at the CCTV footage outside Birkett's house, and see if there's a clearer image of his face. Also, I want you to get hold of Birkett's mobile number and see if he's made any calls to this number, or received any from it. Do you have a pen and paper?'

'Yes, sir,' Milner answered, it being almost second nature

for him to have these available at all times. Tom then read out James Grace's mobile number.

'Whose number is that?' asked an intrigued Milner.

Tom considered keeping the information from him but, almost instantly, discarded the thought. 'It's James Grace's,' he simply replied. Milner, just about to ask how he had acquired Grace's number, had his question answered. 'I haven't been drinking coffee all day, you know.'

If Tom could have seen Milner, he would have noticed a big smile suddenly breaking out over his face. That was more like the DCI Stone who he had come to know. He also noticed, however, he had still not revealed how he had got hold of it.

After he had finished his conversation with Milner, Tom once again picked up the Susan Chambers file. He had always known Pete as an old-school cop: diligent, thorough and meticulous. Nowadays, Tom thought, when everything was about achieving instant results, those qualities would probably be deemed as belonging to someone who lacked personal drive and came from a bygone age. He suddenly found himself smiling as he realised those very same characteristics could equally be applied to him.

But there was one other characteristic, which would never be found in any training manual or textbook. It was, arguably, even more important than how you were perceived by others, simply based upon your outward personality and actions. In his experience, all successful coppers were able to develop an additional sense or 'nose' which allowed them to instantly gauge whether something just didn't seem right, even if, at first glance, their intuition went in the face of the available evidence. Of course, this wasn't a characteristic which an individual was born with, as part of their DNA. It was something which, over the years and multiple different situations, that individual was able to develop for themselves. The longer the time period involved, the more confident the individual became in trusting those instincts, even when all of the available evidence suggested something else. Every organisation needed young, enthusiastic and even impatient people who could bring about any necessary change, but the really successful groups and teams also included a number of 'grey heads'. Both he and Pete Duffy were very definitely in the latter group.

After he had reread part of the file, he suddenly decided to put all of his theorising into practice and give Pete a call. Although he hadn't seen him for a couple of years he still had his number in his personal contact book, and it didn't take long to find it and call the number. The phone continued to ring and, after a while, the answer message cut in. Tom immediately recognised Pete's voice.

'*This is the voice message of Peter Duffy. Sorry I'm not available right now. Please leave your name and number and I'll get back to you at the earliest opportunity. Thank you for calling.*'

'Pete. This is Tom Stone. I hope you are well and enjoying your retirement. I just need to pick your memory on a case you worked on – the Susan Chambers murder. Anyway, there's no great urgency, so just call me when you get the chance.'

Tom then left his own mobile number and rang off. Almost immediately his phone started to ring. Assuming it was Pete who was calling him back, he simply pressed the 'answer' button and said, 'That was quick.'

'What was quick?' asked a familiar voice, clearly not belonging to Pete. Momentarily Tom couldn't place the voice. 'Who were you expecting?'

'Hi, Mary,' he answered, his brain now having finally caught up with his ears. 'Sorry. I just assumed it was someone else. Anyway, how are you?'

'I'm fine. More to the point, how are you? Are you feeling any better?'

'I am, actually,' he answered, although just the mention of his condition seemed to result in a sudden twinge in his side.

'You're not back at work, are you?' she asked, concern suddenly returning to her voice.

'No. I'm still at home. Anyway, I wouldn't dare go back,' he said, with a slight laugh.

'Well, that's good to hear. For one moment I thought you'd sneaked back to work.' Before Tom could respond, she went on, 'I have an idea. How about if I come around tonight and make you dinner? I feel a bit guilty about leaving you in this condition, knowing you are all alone.'

Tom suddenly remembered his earlier conversation with James Grace and, instantly, felt the sickening, tightening knot re-emerge in his stomach. When he replied, however, his voice didn't reflect his true anxiety. 'That would be nice. But don't you have any rehearsals tonight?'

'Not tonight,' she quickly answered. 'Should I bring my overnight bag?' This had somehow almost become their private code for a romantic date.

'Why don't you?' he answered enthusiastically, before adding, with a laugh, 'Although I'm not sure I'm capable of meeting your full expectations.'

'Full expectations? Whatever do you mean, Tom Stone?' Now it was her turn to laugh. 'I'll just have to try and be gentle with you.'

Chapter 41

It was mid-morning, the following day, and, as Mary had left for the shop, Tom was, once again, sitting alone at his kitchen table. It had been a really enjoyable evening, being able to spend some unexpected time together, and they had agreed she would stay over again tonight. Although the pain in his side was diminishing day by day, she had, probably correctly, felt he still needed her personal care and attention. For Tom's part, he felt much more comfortable with her being here, with him, rather than alone in her own house. He realised he couldn't keep doing this and knew he needed a more permanent solution, although he didn't, as yet, know what that solution was. What he did know, however, was that it did not include telling Mary about his conversation with Grace.

Suddenly, he was brought back to the present when his mobile rang. Although he recognised the number he couldn't immediately put a name to it.

'Is that Tom?' asked the voice on the other end of the phone.

'It is,' he replied, before finally recognising the voice. 'Pete. Thanks for calling back. How are you?' he said with genuine enthusiasm and warmth.

'I'm fine,' he answered in a very positive tone. 'In fact, couldn't be better.'

'Sounds like you're enjoying your retirement. Are you still living in the West London area?'

'No. We moved down to Devon, a few months after I retired,' he explained. 'We bought a small guest house, on the coast, and had it converted to include a restaurant. Nothing too fancy. Just enough to keep Pat and myself busy.'

'Well, you certainly sound as though you are enjoying it.'

'Tom, we love it. I just wish we had taken the plunge a few years earlier. It's only when you stop doing something you suddenly realise how much it had taken over your life. Don't get me wrong; it can get stressful here, as well, but it's a different type of stress. It's difficult to explain, but I suppose it's a more satisfying type of stress. I know Superintendent Peters is no longer in the force, but I will always be grateful that he offered me the opportunity to retire earlier than my official date. Anyway, how are you? I saw you on television, and all over the papers, a while ago with those acting murders. Congratulations, by the way. That must have been exciting.'

'You know what these things are like. The adrenaline keeps you going at the time,' he replied.

'And what about Superintendent Peters' secretary? Who would have guessed what she was up to and that she and Superintendent Peters were having an affair?' He then added, almost disappointedly, 'It all seemed to kick off just after I left.'

'Just the luck of the draw, I guess,' said Tom. 'Sometimes you can't spot the things which are closest to you.'

'That's very true,' he replied. 'I assume, from your message, you are still with the force.'

'I am but, hearing how you are enjoying your retirement so much, I wonder whether or not I should take retirement as well.'

'No disrespect, Tom, but wasn't there a time when that was a distinct possibility?'

Tom started to laugh. 'More than a distinct possibility. I think the top brass couldn't wait to get rid of me.'

Pete, no doubt wondering whether to pursue this subject, remained silent as he considered how to respond to Tom's comment. He wasn't given the opportunity, however, as Tom spoke again. 'Given all of that, you might be surprised to hear that I'm currently Acting Superintendent for the station.'

'Acting Superintendent?' repeated a clearly astonished Pete. 'Now that is a surprise.' Before Tom could answer, Pete quickly added, 'Sorry, Tom. I didn't mean it to come out like that. It's just that I would have put money on you being the last person to take on a desk job.'

'You and me both,' said Tom. 'Thankfully, it's only for a short period.' He then provided Pete with the background details as to how he had come to be in his current temporary position. 'It's actually because of this appointment that I called you.'

'Really?' he said, suddenly intrigued. 'What's it got to do with me?'

Tom then briefly told him about the note relating to the death of Jimmy Griffiths.

'Jimmy Griffiths dead?' Pete said. 'I didn't know. Not surprising, really, I suppose, as I'm now out of it.'

'So you remember the case,' said Tom.

'Yes, of course. How could I forget? It was the last murder case I was involved in before my retirement. Anyway, why are you asking? Have there been any new developments?'

'No. None, in fact, although you make it sound as though you wouldn't be surprised if there had.'

'To be honest, there were certain aspects of the case which just didn't seem right. Well, to me anyway. You know how it is. Sometimes there's a nagging doubt, at the back of your mind, which you can't get rid of. All of the evidence pointed to Griffiths having killed Susan Chambers. There was no doubt about that. But somehow it was all a bit too ...' There was suddenly a noticeable hesitation in Pete's voice. 'Well, just too convenient, I suppose.'

'What was the gist of your interview with Dale Thompson?' asked Tom.

'It's all in the file. I'm sure you've read it.'

'I have,' Tom replied, 'but I'd just like to hear it directly from you.'

'The gist of it was that Thompson was willing to testify how Griffiths was with him at the time of Susan Chambers' death. According to him they were both at his house, getting out of their heads on booze and drugs. He said they could hardly stand up, let alone drive or walk to where she lived, murder her and then get back to his place.'

'Wasn't there evidence Chambers and Griffiths had sexual contact sometime earlier?'

'Griffiths claimed he'd met up with Susan earlier in the evening. They'd done some drugs and then had sex, after which he left and went to stay with Thompson. The prosecution's case, though, was that it was only after he had killed her that he went to Thompson's. Anyway, it's all in my report.'

'So, why do you think Thompson's evidence wasn't accepted by the jury?'

'He wasn't the most convincing witness and was ripped to

bits by our prosecution lawyer.' He paused briefly, almost as though the full details of the case had suddenly started to come back to him. 'Not surprising, really, given his own criminal record. It didn't take long before he was totally discredited.'

'What was your view? Did you think he was lying?' asked Tom.

There was just the hint of hesitation before Pete answered. 'I must admit, despite his lack of credibility, I did feel there was an element of doubt. Just as there were no witnesses who saw Griffiths at Thompson's, equally there were no other witnesses who placed him at Susan's around the time she was murdered. It was just that all of the other evidence, when combined, was so overwhelming. The break-in also bothered me.'

'When did that happen?'

'I thought you said you'd read the file notes,' he answered. 'The break-in on the night Susan Chambers was murdered. Well, not a break-in as such, as there wasn't any evidence of a forced entry. The place, though, had been partly turned over, as though whoever did it was searching for something. The consensus was that Griffiths did it trying to get his hands on some of Susan's drugs after he killed her. The problem was that, although Griffiths' prints were in the flat, we couldn't find any near to where some of the drawers had been emptied.'

'Didn't that, together with Thompson's statement, start to ring a few alarm bells?'

Pete was shrewd and experienced enough to know when a line of questioning was not quite as straightforward as it might appear. When he replied it was in a much harder tone. 'Tom. Where are you going with this? You're asking me a lot of questions about a case which happened quite a while ago. Why are you asking me all of these questions when you have the file?'

Tom decided he couldn't continue trying to be clever with someone like Pete by attempting to disguise his real concerns, so he made an instant judgement call and confessed. 'I'm sorry, Pete, about all of the questions. Let me come clean with you. I should have done that right at the start. I did receive a note about Griffiths' death, but it was meant for Superintendent Peters. Apparently the bureaucratic wheels haven't turned enough yet for them to realise he is no longer with the force. Anyway, as I had a bit of time to kill, I thought I'd have a sneaky read of the full file. It was then I came across your name and a passing reference to an interview you carried out with Susan Chambers' flatmate. However, when I tried to find the full statement it wasn't in the file. What's more, until you just mentioned it, there was no reference anywhere to the lack of Griffiths' prints all around the flat.' He fell silent, waiting for Pete to respond. When there was no immediate reply he continued, 'As I said, I apologise for trying to be smart. I should have known it wouldn't work with you.'

'That's okay,' he answered. 'It takes a copper to know a copper, I suppose. So, what is it you really want from me?'

'Can you remember what was in your notes when you interviewed Shelley Ripley?'

'Tom. I came down here to get away from all of this. I'm only doing this because we've known each other for a long time.'

'I understand,' Tom answered. 'If you feel you don't want to tell me, then that's fine.'

'I'm sure you don't really mean that,' replied Pete with a slight laugh. He immediately continued, with the answer. 'She said that Susan had mentioned having something which was worth a lot of money. Apparently she was very excited about it.'

'Did Ripley know what it was?' asked Tom.

'No. Of course, she did ask, but Susan simply told her she would find out soon enough. All she knew was that Susan was very excited. Apparently she had received a bit of money already but the really big stuff was still to come. It might just have been that she was trying to show off and there wasn't anything, but it was just something which stuck in my mind at the time.'

'Did you include it in your interview notes with her?'

'Of course I did,' he answered, a little indignantly. 'You know how we were always taught to include everything, however seemingly trivial, in our reports. It's something which I always did throughout my career.'

'Thanks, Pete. I appreciate it.'

'Tom, why are you doing this? Haven't you got other, more important things to worry about?' he asked.

Despite Pete's question immediately reviving memories of his conversation with James Grace, when Tom answered it was in his most calm and controlled voice. 'I just feel there's something not quite right about this case. It's a bit of a gut instinct, really, but, like you said earlier, the evidence which was used against Griffiths was just too convenient. Also, why would the record of your interview with Shelley Ripley be missing from the file? Then there's the issue of the break-in and the lack of fingerprint evidence.'

'Put like that, it seems as though there was a gross miscarriage of justice and it was me who was responsible for it.'

'Pete, don't go down that particular route. We've all been there. Anyway, as you know, in these situations it's always better to make a decision based upon *all* of the available evidence. It was probably just another administrative cock-up. We've both seen plenty of them over the years.'

An uneasy silence followed before Tom spoke again.

'I won't keep you any longer. I'm sure you restaurateurs are always very busy. Anyway, it's been great speaking with you again. It sounds as though you are not missing the force at all. And, by the way, thanks again for letting me make use of your memory.'

When Pete replied it was in a tone discernibly different from what he had previously used. 'Tom. Do you think this is a good idea?'

'What do you mean?' asked Tom, knowing perfectly well what Pete meant.

'Digging up all of this again.'

'Probably not,' Tom replied.

Chapter 42

As he was sitting at his kitchen table, Tom thought back to his conversation with Pete. Instinctively he knew Pete was correct and that, sometimes, it was best to just let sleeping dogs lie. In any case, what was there to be gained, especially right now, given everything else he was involved in, by trying to reopen a case where the vast weight of evidence pointed towards Griffiths having been correctly sentenced?

And yet his gut instinct told him this particular case, somehow, was not as straightforward as it appeared to be on the surface. There were anomalies and discrepancies, particularly in the recording and availability of witness statements, and these, by themselves, threw up a few red flags. When, however, these anomalies were combined with even Pete's own nagging doubts and concerns about various aspects relating to the case, they became even more concerning. After all, Pete was the lead officer on the case.

Even if he eventually decided that there was sufficient doubt about Griffiths' guilt to request that the case be reopened, there was still a protocol to follow. Credible new evidence, and not just someone's gut instinct, would have to be produced in order to convince the relevant authorities that there was a strong possibility there had been a miscarriage of justice. As important, of course, was that if the original verdict was subsequently overturned, then it would mean that the real murderer remained at large. And then there was the potential damage to the force's reputation. If the original verdict was quashed then legitimate questions would be asked about the force's competence and, even more damaging, their motives for pursuing the original prosecution. A point regularly levelled at the police by their critics was that, statistically, there were far too few instances where cases were reopened, the obvious suspicion being that it was often better, at least for the police, due to their vested interests, simply to maintain the *status quo*, having already secured their conviction.

As he sat there he realised it would be far easier to simply do nothing. But he instantly rejected that option. He wasn't the type of person who would just take the easy route and, anyway, if Griffiths was not the murderer then someone else was. So he decided, at least for the time being, to carry on with his unofficial enquiries and then make a judgement as to whether or not to take his concerns to the next level.

As soon as he came to this decision he found himself in a much more positive frame of mind. It was almost as though the act of just coming to a decision – any decision – had freed his mind from all of the various options available. He knew he was only postponing the final decision day but, nonetheless, he felt much better for it and, building on this feeling, immediately picked up his phone and made a call.

The phone rang a few times before it was answered. 'DS Gilbert.'

'Jim. It's Tom Stone. How are you?'

Although Jim Gilbert now worked in a different London region, they had known one another for almost fifteen years. Whilst they would never consider themselves to be close friends they had, nonetheless, developed a mutual respect for each other during that time.

'Tom. Good to hear from you again. I can't remember the last time we spoke. Must be at least three years ago.'

'Yes, I guess it must be. Just goes to show how quickly time flies by. I haven't caught you at a bad time, have I?'

'Not really. Anyway, it's good to be able to talk again. You usually get that young DS of yours – Milner, isn't it? – to call me when you want something. So I'm thinking that, for you to call, either he's not available or you don't want him involved. Am I right?'

Some time ago Tom had given Milner Jim's contact details as the 'go-to' person whenever he needed to get hold of a phone number or address. Tom had, indeed, considered asking Milner to make this call but had almost immediately rejected the idea. Given the very unofficial nature of his investigations, it was probably best for Milner not to be involved.

'Jim, I think we know each other too well. You are right. The call is not purely social. I do have an ulterior motive.'

Jim laughed. 'I'd have been disappointed if you didn't. What can I do for you?'

'There are a couple of addresses I'd like you to get for me. I have the names, and the area where they lived about eighteen months ago, but that's about all.'

'I'll see what I can do. Just give me what you've got.'

Tom then read out the names, and last known locations, of Shelley Ripley and Dale Thompson.

'Is this an official request,' asked Jim, 'or just between the two of us?'

'Will it make a difference as to how quickly you can get me the information?'

'Not really,' answered Jim. 'I was just being nosey.'

'Well, as you've asked, I would appreciate it if it's kept just between us.'

'No problem,' he replied, having heard many similar requests from officers during his time with the police. 'When do you need them?'

'Would yesterday be too soon?' asked Tom, only slightly tongue-in-cheek.

'I'll see what I can do. Is it okay if I email them over to you?'

'That's fine,' said Tom. 'Could you send them to my home email address, though?'

There was just a brief hesitation before Jim answered. 'If that's what you want, who am I to question it?'

Tom then provided Jim with his personal email address and, after a few more pleasantries, finished the call.

It was now lunchtime and Tom thought he might make himself a sandwich. As he went to get the loaf from his bread bin his mobile rang. It was Milner.

'Hello, sir,' said Milner. From just these two words Tom could tell that Milner was excited to tell him some news.

'Hello, Milner,' he answered. 'Do you have anything new?'

'I certainly do, sir,' he replied in a way which confirmed Tom's earlier assessment regarding Milner's excitement.

'Well, tell me, then,' he said, a touch impatiently.

'It looks like we do now have some definite evidence putting Brendan Grace outside Birkett's place.'

'Were you able to get a clear shot of his face?'

'No. He had his face partly covered all of the time. But when we rechecked the CCTV footage DC Bennett spotted how the man – Grace, that is – threw away a cigarette after he got out of the van. He threw it under some bushes rather than into the road. Fortunately for us, it hasn't rained since then.'

'Have you been able to retrieve it?' asked Tom expectantly.

'DC Bennett went there this morning and found it. It's currently with the lab boys for testing. They've already said, though, that it shouldn't be too difficult getting some DNA from it. As you know, Brendan Grace did some time a few years ago and so we already have his DNA on file.'

'That's good,' said a relieved Tom. 'When will they know for sure?'

'I've asked for it to be a priority and so, hopefully, we might have something back tomorrow.' Before Tom could respond, Milner continued, in the same excited manner, 'But that's not all. You also asked me to check for any calls between Birkett and James Grace's mobile phones. Well, surprise, surprise, the record shows that Birkett called Grace a week or so before Bogdan Inanescu's murder. The phone call lasted just under five minutes. Then, after Grace returned from holiday, in fact the day after we first went to see him at his house, Grace called Birkett's number, although this time the call only lasted for about one minute. It seems what he had to say didn't take long.'

As Tom didn't immediately respond, Milner guessed he would be considering their next move. During these periods of silence he had learnt to also keep quiet. Sure enough, after a few moments, Tom did respond.

'Good work by you and DC Bennett. It seems, at last, we are getting somewhere.'

'What do you suggest our next move should be?' asked Milner.

'Let me think about that. Anyway, first, we really need confirmation that Brendan Grace's DNA is the same as on the cigarette.' He paused. 'Whatever we decide, though, I suspect James Grace isn't going to like it.'

As he put down his phone he said to himself, with a sense of foreboding, 'And you can bet on that.'

Chapter 43

It was late Friday evening and Tom and Mary, having eaten earlier, were sitting next to each other on his sofa.
'Are you sure you are fit to go back into work?' she asked.
'I'm fine,' he answered. 'The last couple of days' rest have definitely helped. I'm not in anywhere near the same pain as I was.'
Mary didn't look convinced. 'You still don't look right to me. Anyway, I thought the doctor said to take more than a couple of days off.'
'I told you, I'm fine. Please don't worry.' He reached over and held her hand.
Worrying, in fact, was something he couldn't avoid at the moment, as he continued to recall his conversation with James Grace. Whilst Mary's presence was reassuring, it also, ironically, had the effect of heightening his sense of anxiety for her personal safety. In his more rational moments he realised Grace's comments were likely designed to throw him off-balance rather than to be a direct, clear and present threat. But it was becoming increasingly difficult to think rationally where Mary's safety was concerned.
For a fleeting moment the thought had struck him how it might actually be best for his, and Mary's, personal situation if there was no match between the DNA on the cigarette butt and Brendan Grace's. But all of his instincts told him the Graces were up to their necks in all of this and, as a police officer, it was his duty to bring them to justice. To protect Mary he'd also considered trying to persuade her to go away for a few weeks, perhaps to stay with one of her sons, until all of this was over. But he knew she was unlikely to agree to this, even if he was to come clean with her, and, anyway, it would probably only make her even more worried. It was better for him alone to carry the worry. The other option, which he had also seriously considered, was to ask for police protection for

her, but that, of course, brought its own complications, not least the likelihood he might be accused of overreaction due to his relationship with her.

During all of his years with the force, he'd never experienced anything quite like this before. Of course, there had been many times when he, personally, had been threatened and even, occasionally, when he had found himself in real danger. But this was different. He now had someone else to think about. In fact, he couldn't remember thinking quite this way even when his son, Paul, had been born. He was sure he must have, but the passing of time plays strange tricks with the memory, and perhaps this was one of those times. He sincerely hoped so.

'Why is it that I don't quite believe you?' she asked. 'But at least promise me you will try and take it easy next week.' She then added, with a light laugh, 'Leave all of the chasing of criminals to David.'

'I promise,' he answered, once again feeling a little uncomfortable with her use of Milner's first name.

'How is that murder enquiry you told me about progressing?' she suddenly asked, referring to the death of Bogdan Inanescu.

Hearing this, he instantly regretted having previously mentioned it and made a mental note never to do so again. 'We are making a bit of progress but, unfortunately, are nowhere near making an arrest yet.'

Fortunately this seemed to satisfy Mary. 'Do you mind if I go to bed now?' she asked. 'As it's Saturday tomorrow I have an early start at the shop. There are two big weddings and we have to prepare all of the flowers.'

'I'll be up later,' said Tom. 'I just need to do a couple of things.'

'Okay,' she replied, 'but try not to be too late.'

After Mary had gone to bed Tom made himself a cup of coffee, went into his small study, sat down in front of his computer and then pressed the 'start' button. After a while his broadband kicked in and when all of the different icons appeared on the screen he clicked the one which opened his emails. Immediately he could see he had thirty-five new emails, including one from Jim Gilbert, and so he decided to systematically work his way through all of them, saving Jim's until last.

He began by deleting all of the ones which informed him either that he was due a refund from HMRC or that a bank account he didn't even know he had opened had been experiencing unusual activity and, therefore, had been temporarily suspended. It was amazing how many of these he regularly received. When he had first started to receive them he had opened a few of the emails but had quickly realised they were blatant scams, not least because of the very poor spelling and grammar, and always ended by asking him to provide them with his bank details. He hoped no one was taken in by this type of email fraud. The suspicion, however, given the huge number of emails of this type which were received by people, was that, unfortunately, they would persuade a few unsuspecting individuals to provide their personal financial details. Surely, he thought, it was not beyond the wit of some techie genius to come up with a way which allowed the authorities to track down these people. But, fortunately, that wasn't his problem.

Eventually, he had deleted the more obvious scams and quickly answered the messages which needed his immediate attention. Finally he clicked on Jim's email.

From: Jim Gilbert
To: Tom Stone
Subject: Contact details

Hi Tom,
Good to speak with you earlier. I've attached contact details for Shelley Ripley and Dale Thompson. Hope that they prove to be useful.
I'll wait until you need something else from me before we speak again!

Cheers,
Jim

Tom opened the single-page attachment and pressed the 'print' button. Dale Thompson's details were shown at the top of the page and Tom could immediately see that Thompson still lived at the same address in Perivale. Shelley Ripley, however, had a new address. Pete had mentioned how, when

Susan Chambers had been murdered, they had lived together in Shepherd's Bush. She now had an address in White City.

He continued to gaze at the sheet of paper for a while, as he considered what his next options were. Finally, he placed the sheet on his desk, closed down his computer, switched off the room light and went to bed.

It was Saturday morning and Mary had already left to open up her florist's shop. Before she had left, however, they had agreed she would spend the rest of the weekend with him. When he had suggested it she had jumped at the idea and, although she would need to call in at her own home to get some fresh clothes, she was clearly looking forward to spending the entire weekend together.

Tom was eating some cereal when his mobile rang.

'Morning, sir. How are you feeling today?' enquired Milner, once again in his best 'I have some exciting news to tell you' voice.

'Getting better by the day, thank you,' replied an equally enthusiastic Tom. 'In fact, I will be back at work on Monday morning. So that's something for you all to look forward to.'

His attempt at mild sarcasm was either missed by Milner or, more likely given what he was just about to say, simply ignored. 'Sir, you might want to consider coming back a bit sooner after what I'm just about to tell you.'

'Go on, then,' he replied expectantly, having already forgotten himself about his earlier failed attempt to inject a bit of humour into the conversation.

'The lab boys have confirmed it *was* Brendan Grace's DNA on the cigarette. But that's not all,' he added, the excitement in his voice now even more obvious. 'I also took a call from them yesterday evening. I'd asked them to return and take another look at the house in Hounslow, and they came back yesterday evening to say they had found some tiny specks of blood on the carpet near the front door.' He paused before adding, 'They were a bit embarrassed about missing them first time round, but at least they found them this time.'

Tom interrupted Milner's flow. 'Why didn't you tell me this last night?' he asked, in a slightly confrontational manner.

'I thought I would wait until I also had the Brendan Grace results,' he replied, his excitement momentarily disappearing.

Tom appeared to accept Milner's explanation because, when he next spoke, there was a clear sense of anticipation now in his own voice. 'Do we know whose blood it was?'
'We do, sir. It's Birkett's blood.'
For a moment nothing was said. Finally Tom spoke. 'Right, get all of the information together. I'm coming in. I'll see you in about forty-five minutes.'

Chapter 44

Tom, Milner and DC Bennett were all seated around the table in Tom's office on the fifth floor. They were interrupted by a knock on his door, which, when opened, revealed Jenny carrying a large tray on which were three sets of cups and saucers, a pot of coffee and another one containing tea, together with all the other necessary accoutrements.

'Jenny. What are you doing here?' asked Tom, clearly surprised by her presence.

'David called to tell me you were all coming in, and so I thought I'd also come in. Anyway, sir, how are you? It's good to see you again.'

Tom was touched by her genuine concern for his well-being. 'I'm much better, thank you. But you really didn't have to come in on a Saturday.'

'That's okay, sir. I didn't really have anything else to do anyway,' she answered. 'It looks like it's important and so I thought that a drink might help.' She placed the overloaded tray on the table and then added, 'If you need anything else I'll just be outside.'

After she had left, Tom turned to Milner. '"David"? Is there anything you want to tell us, Milner?' he asked mischievously. A smile appeared on DC Bennett's face.

Milner, the hint of a flush appearing on his own face, simply said, 'No, sir.'

'If you say so,' said Tom. 'Okay, let's get on to why we are all here. Milner, why don't you briefly summarise what we now know?'

Milner, clearly relieved they had now moved on to more comfortable territory, opened his file and began his summary. He started by referring to the murdered body of Bogdan Inanescu, together with the cannabis farm, found at James Grace's partly burnt-out property in Hounslow. There was evidence, albeit unproven, that the previous tenants, Darren

Allen and his partner Paula, had been subjected to threats and intimidation, by Grace and his son Brendan, to vacate the property so that they could set up the cannabis farm.

Bogdan Inanescu was one of a number of Romanians who had travelled to the UK to find work, organised by fellow countryman Florin Constantin. In reality they had effectively been trafficked by Constantin and subsequently kept locked up at a remote farm. Long Lane Farm was, ostensibly, rented by William Green, but almost certainly funded by Grace. Green and Grace had a long association, dating back to the time when they grew up together in Essex. The Romanians had found themselves working for Grace, either in his building business or, in the case of the unfortunate Bogdan, as a horticultural caretaker for the cannabis plants; Grace had installed him in Hounslow under the pretext of doing some conversion work to the property. All of the remaining Romanians were currently being held in custody and being questioned by officers from the UK Border Force.

Milner then mentioned how phone records had shown that Terry Birkett, a well-known and previously convicted drug dealer with a history for dispensing violence, had made a telephone call to James Grace a few weeks prior to the fire at Grace's property. Different phone records showed how James Grace had then called Birkett just a day or so before, coincidentally, there had been an attempt to torch Birkett's own house.

He went on to say how they now had new evidence placing Brendan Grace outside Birkett's house on the night of the fire. In addition to the CCTV footage that showed Grace's white van nearby, they now had a sample of Brendan Grace's DNA close to the house. But the real breakthrough had come last night when forensics had been able to confirm that Birkett's own DNA, contained in some tiny specks of blood, had been found in the house where Inanescu had been murdered.

He finished his summary by saying, 'We now have clear, indisputable evidence linking Birkett to Grace.'

Milner placed the file in front of him and then, looking directly at Tom, asked the obvious question. 'As I said, we have the link, but do you think we now have enough evidence to charge them?'

'A very good question, Milner,' replied Tom, slightly

evasively. 'Certainly, at least based upon the latest DNA evidence ...' Tom hesitated at this point, before saying, 'Incidentally, that was a smart move of yours, to ask forensics to go back to Grace's house in Hounslow. I'm sure they didn't exactly appreciate your request. I don't think I would have thought to do that.' As neither Milner nor DC Bennett responded, Tom carried on. 'As I was saying, based upon the latest DNA evidence, I think there's a good chance we can now get a conviction. The problem, though, is that we only have enough clear evidence to convict Birkett and Brendan Grace: Birkett for murder and, in Brendan's case, probably for, at best, attempted murder but, more likely, something less serious. His lawyers will, no doubt, claim how he hadn't intended to kill Birkett or, more likely, that he didn't think he was even in the house at the time. But, nonetheless, given his previous, I believe we still have enough to get him some sort of custodial sentence. Unfortunately, though,' he added, now with somewhat less enthusiasm, 'I still don't think we have enough to put James Grace away.' He directed his gaze towards DC Bennett. 'What have we got on James Grace?'

'Well, apart from the fact he doesn't like police officers, not a lot, I'm afraid. What we do know is that he served a long prison sentence, back in the eighties and nineties, for armed robbery. Since then he seems to have gone straight.' He then added, as an afterthought, 'Well, as straight as anyone like him could. Anyway,' he continued, 'it would appear his building business has been very successful – certainly looking at that big, fancy house of his and all of those cars we saw when we were there. We know, though, he has been involved with Florin Constantin in trafficking Romanians, so, no doubt, they could provide him with cheap labour for his building business.' He paused. 'But, as you said, apart from that, nothing which would earn him a long prison sentence.'

Now they all fell silent before Milner eventually spoke. 'Sir, we all know his business is dodgy. There's no way he could be living that lifestyle based upon his declared business profits. Perhaps there's something there we can get him on.'

'Good idea,' answered Tom. 'We should definitely pursue that. Why don't you quietly pass over the details to the fraud team? But be discreet. The last thing we want to do now is to warn him what we are doing. I'm sure they will be able to find something. The problem, though, is that this is unlikely to result in an Al Capone moment. Somehow, I doubt very much this will get him an eleven-year sentence. No, we need something else.'

'Won't Brendan's arrest prompt a reaction from him? After all, he doesn't seem the sort of person who would accept this lightly. Perhaps that will make him do something irrational.'

Milner was correct but, right now, it wasn't something Tom wanted to be reminded about. Before Tom could respond, Milner mentioned another possible scenario.

'Then there's his original conviction for armed robbery. We know the money was never found. Is it just coincidence that, just a few years after he came out of prison, he had his business up and running and was successful enough to fund his lavish lifestyle?'

'I agree,' replied Tom, clearly thinking along the same lines. 'Have you had the chance yet to find out which prison the surviving member of the original robbery gang is in?'

'I'm still working on it.'

'Okay, when you know, let's go and pay him a visit. Perhaps we might be able to stir up a bit of a reaction. In the meantime, we can't leave one potentially known killer and another would-be killer out on the streets. I'll speak with DCS Small and fill him in on what we are planning. While I'm doing that, start pulling together all of the paperwork.'

Just as they were about to leave, Milner suddenly said, 'Sir, could I have a word with you?'

'Of course,' replied Tom apprehensively.

Milner looked towards DC Bennett. 'I'll see you downstairs. I shouldn't be long.'

After DC Bennett had left the office, Tom asked Milner to sit down.

'What is it?' Tom asked.

As had happened when he had first raised this particular issue, Milner appeared to take a deep breath before he replied. 'I thought I should tell you that I have an interview for the DS position in Brighton, next week.'

For a moment nothing was said. Milner decided to continue. 'It's on Wednesday. I was wondering if I could take the time off as a holiday.'

'That's not a problem,' answered Tom quickly. 'I'm sure the

force owes you lots of days anyway.' Tom couldn't let this go without one last attempt to dissuade him. 'Are you sure this is what you want to do? Isn't it exciting enough here for you?'

'I'm sure, sir,' he answered, matter-of-factly.

'Okay. You know how I feel about this, but you've obviously made up your mind.'

Milner stood up and, as he was leaving, Tom said, although without any obvious enthusiasm, 'Good luck anyway.'

Chapter 45

Perivale wasn't that far away from the station and so Tom decided, as he was in the vicinity, to pay Dale Thompson a visit. He'd anticipated this was a possibility and so, before he'd left for the station, had picked up the printed page containing Thompson's address details and put it in his pocket.

As he drove along the A40, heading east towards London, he thought back to his meeting with Milner and DC Bennett. Somehow he felt much more relaxed now they had decided on a definite course of action. His concern about James Grace's unpredictable reaction was still there, of course, but the situation had now been taken out of his hands by the sudden availability of Brendan Grace's DNA evidence.

The traffic was fairly light and so it wasn't long before he found himself standing outside the address Jim Gilbert had provided him with. The property was typical of many of the houses built in the area after the war. It was a fairly substantial semi-detached house, one of many similar white-fronted ones which formed a long line of houses running parallel to the main A40 road. He had driven past the house a couple of times already, trying, unsuccessfully, to find somewhere to park. The street was full of parked cars and, with no obvious place to park, he'd had to drive into the next street before he had managed to find somewhere.

As he stood outside the address it looked as though, at some stage, the original wooden-framed windows had been replaced by white PVC ones, whilst the small, paved area in front was home to a slightly beaten-up red car. A digital television dish, one of many on the street's houses, dominated the front of the property. The white paint had, in places, become stained and dirty, and what looked like small plants were growing in the guttering above one of the bedroom windows. The white PVC downpipe on the right-hand side of the house had detached itself from a couple of its fixings and looked as though it was about to completely fall down at any moment. Clearly this was a house in urgent need of extensive repair and maintenance.

Three small rectangular transparent plastic name signs had been fitted to the side of the front door, with a button alongside each name and a metal intercom device immediately above. Dale Thompson's faded name could just be made out on the middle name sign. Tom pressed the button and, after a short wait, and not knowing whether or not it was working, pressed it again, this time with increased force. When there was still no answer he knocked on the door itself and was just about to knock again when he heard some faint movement inside the house.

As the noise got nearer, eventually a man's voice said, 'Just hang on. I'm coming.'

The door was then opened to reveal a tall young man in his late teens or early twenties. He had short, well-groomed dark hair with the obligatory designer stubble. He was wearing faded blue jeans and a white T-shirt. Tom could also see that he wasn't wearing any shoes or socks.

'Can I help you?' the man said politely.

'I'm looking for Dale Thompson. I understand he lives here. I did try ringing his buzzer but I'm not sure if he heard me,' replied Tom.

'Even if he was here, he wouldn't have heard you anyway. Those things,' he said, pointing at the name plates, 'haven't worked for ages. Pretty much like most of the things in this place.'

'So you live here as well, do you?'

'Only for the time being. I've been looking for somewhere else for ages but can't find anything I can afford. Not on a student loan, anyway.' He looked directly at Tom. 'As I said, if you are looking for Dale then he's not here. Saturday afternoons ...' He hesitated briefly and then continued, although this time with a slight laugh, 'Well, most afternoons, actually, he goes to the pub.'

'What time is he likely to be back?' asked Tom.

'You never know with Dale. It could be soon or, if he decides to go on a bender, he might not return for days. I think it just depends how flush he is. Do you want me to tell him that you wanted to see him?'

Tom, conveniently ignoring the question, said, 'Do you have any idea which pub he's likely to be in?'

'He usually starts in the Crown. It's about a ten-minute walk from here, over there on the other side of the A40,' he said, pointing with his right hand to somewhere vaguely in the distance. He hesitated again. 'That is, unless he's been barred again. Dale gets a bit rowdy when he's had a few. Anyway, who are you?'

'A friend of a friend, I suppose,' he answered evasively.

The young man looked at Tom with a quizzical expression, and then said, quite perceptively, 'Really? Somehow, you don't look as though you would be a friend of Dale's. With respect, all of his friends are a lot younger than you.'

Tom chose to ignore the comment about his age. 'Anyway, thanks for your time. I appreciate it.'

As Tom turned to walk away, the young man called after him, 'You didn't say what your name was.'

Tom, though, continued walking, thinking how that young man had all of the hallmarks of a good police officer.

As it was still only early afternoon, and Mary wasn't due at his place much before six thirty, he decided to try to find the Crown pub and see if Dale was there. Tom could remember seeing a photograph of Dale in the file attached to Pete's interview notes, and so had a good idea what he looked like. He began to walk in the direction which the young man had pointed towards.

After a while, and having asked a couple of people for more specific directions, he spotted the pub. Although the Crown was a small pub the owners had tried to utilise all of the available space. As he got close up he saw a sign directing customers towards their garden, although he could easily also see that by no stretch of the imagination could the tiny area be deemed to be a garden. The incongruous setting, with the noise of the A40's traffic a constant presence, did not, however, seem to have been much of a deterrent, as all of the available 'garden' tables were taken by people who were happily drinking their drinks and eating their food. In contrast the inside of the pub itself was only partly full. Clearly, he thought, he'd been far too judgemental when it came to the popularity of the pub's garden. Perhaps that was why he would never make a successful businessman.

It didn't take long to spot Dale. He and two other men were seated together on uncomfortable-looking bar stools. Tom ordered himself a small lager and then found a seat in one of the window alcoves. It was not difficult to tell that Dale and his friends had already had a few drinks. The decibel level of their conversation was on the high side, with regular loud laughs interspersed with the occasional profanity. He could also tell, simply by watching his body language, that the attendant barman was beginning to get very concerned about where their drinking would lead.

Tom knew from the file that Dale was in his early forties but, as he studied him more closely, he noted that he looked quite a bit older, not helped, no doubt, by his lifestyle. He was tall and overweight, and this combined with his completely bald head to generate an intimidating presence.

Just as Tom was considering the best way to approach, it was decided for him when he heard Dale say he was going outside for a smoke. Tom drank what was left in his glass and followed him.

'It's Dale, isn't it?' he asked, as cheerfully as possible.

Dale looked suspiciously at Tom. 'Do I know you?' he asked, not reciprocating Tom's cheerful tone.

'Not really. But I'd like to ask you a few questions about Jimmy Griffiths.'

There was a tense silence whilst Dale continued to look directly at Tom. 'You're a copper, aren't you?' he asked, the tone of his voice making it clear what he thought about police officers.

'Don't worry. I'm not here to give you any trouble. I just want to ask you a couple of questions, that's all.'

Dale continued to look suspiciously at Tom. 'Yeah, right,' he replied. 'The only reason you lot ever want to talk to me is so that you can stitch me up for something.'

Tom didn't immediately respond. 'Look,' he eventually said, 'if it's what you want, I'll go right now and leave you alone. But, believe it or not, I'm here to help. I know Jimmy's dead but, if he didn't do it, then I might be able to at least help clear his name. Anyway, it's up to you.'

'He didn't do the murder,' Dale suddenly said. 'He was with me at the time. I told this to the other copper and then in court. But nobody believed me and now Jimmy's dead. Why should you be any different?'

Tom could sense the emotion in his voice when he mentioned Jimmy's name. He waited a while before saying, 'Were you and Jimmy good mates?'

'Ever since we'd done a bit of time together.' Now it was his turn to pause. 'He was a bit of a scally, but he weren't a killer. Okay, him and Sue were always arguing but they always got back together. Why would he kill her? She was good to him.'

'Did she give him drugs?' asked Tom, prompting Dale, once again, to look at him with great suspicion. 'Don't worry. I'm not interested in the drugs. I'm just trying to understand their relationship.'

This seemed to reassure him. 'Sometimes drugs. Sometimes money. She was still on the game, so she could get her hands on money.'

'What did Jimmy think about her being a prostitute?'

'It didn't bother him. She was only doing it for the money. That's why he left her that night, 'cause she was going back to work later.'

'Can you remember what time Jimmy arrived at your place?' asked Tom, now directing the conversation towards the main reason why he wanted to talk with Dale.

'That other copper asked the same thing. I can't remember exactly. I'd already had a skinful when Jimmy showed up. I don't know. Nine o'clock? Ten o'clock? Something like that.'

'Did you then go out?'

'No. Definitely not,' he answered firmly. 'We stayed in. He'd brought some smokes and some lager cans with him, so we made a night of it. Must have been a good night 'cause we both passed out and woke up next morning where we'd been drinking.'

'Do you know where Jimmy got the lager from?'

'What do you mean?'

'Well, did he bring it from Susan's or buy it when he got here?'

'He bought it in the off-licence, just round the corner from here.'

'How do you know?'

''Cause he told me. Anyway, there were little stickers on the cans with the price and name of the shop. I chucked them all in the bin next morning when we got up. I usually get my own drink from the same place when I get my money.'

'One last question. How did Jimmy get to your place that night?'

'He got the Tube.'

For a moment nothing else was said until Tom broke the silence. 'Thanks for talking to me.' He handed Dale a card. 'If you remember anything else, just give me a call.'

Dale took the card and immediately started walking back towards the bar. Before he got there, however, he threw Tom's contact details into the bin that was sited outside the entrance.

Chapter 46

'What have you been doing today?' asked Mary. 'I hope you've been taking it easy.'
It was early Saturday evening and Mary had just arrived at Tom's house in Staines.
'Nothing much. Just catching up on a bit of paperwork. Checking my emails. That type of thing,' he answered, less than truthfully. After he had left Dale Thompson, he had located the off-licence which he'd mentioned and called in to speak with the manager. Briefly he had considered driving to the White City address where Shelley Ripley now lived, but he had quickly realised he might not then get back home in time before Mary arrived. It was important he was there when she turned up.
'How were the wedding orders? Did you manage to get everything done?' he asked.
'It was a bit of a rush at the end, but we managed it in time. I think they were happy with the selection and arrangements.'
Tom looked at her. 'You really enjoy your work, don't you?'
'I do,' she answered. 'It's sometimes a bit stressful, particularly when we get a big last-minute order, but the end result is usually worth it.' She paused and then continued, in an almost reflective tone. 'What I really like about it, though, is that it's my own business. I've set up the business and so it's down to me, no one else, to make it work. I also get to meet some really nice people. My customers always seem to be happy when they come into the shop.'
Tom, now laughing, suddenly interjected, 'I wish I could say the same about my customers.'
Mary carried on, 'To be honest, I don't know what I would do now if I didn't have the shop.'
'You'd still have your amateur dramatics. That seems to keep you busy.'

'That's true, but it's not quite the same. As I said, running my own business is different. It's my responsibility alone to make it successful.'

This seemed to trigger something in Tom's mind. 'The performance is in a few weeks' time, isn't it? Have you learnt your lines yet?'

'You are still coming, aren't you?' she suddenly asked, an element of concern appearing in her voice.

'Of course I am. You know how much I like seeing you when you are acting. I'm sure you'll put on another great performance.' Tom had, in fact, only attended one of Mary's performances but had, to his great surprise, found himself genuinely transfixed whenever she was on stage. 'Perhaps I can test you with your lines?' he added.

'Thanks, but I'm not sure that would be a good idea. Anyway, I get nervous enough without your added pressure.'

'Nervous?' he echoed. 'You don't strike me as being a nervous type of person. In fact, when I saw you, you seemed to be relishing every moment.'

'Everyone gets nervous, trust me. Many years ago I worked backstage on a West End production. The leading man was one of the biggest stars of the day. Even he had to have two large glasses of brandy every time before he went on stage.'

'Who was it?' asked Tom, genuinely interested.

'I couldn't possibly say, I'm afraid. The acting profession has its own code of silence.'

'A bit like the Mafia, then,' he replied.

'Yes. I suppose it is,' she said, before starting to laugh. 'I hadn't thought of it that way. Anyway, more importantly, what should we do tomorrow?'

'I hadn't really given it any thought,' he answered truthfully.

'Let's go out for the day.'

'Do you have anywhere in mind?' he asked.

'I haven't been to Kew Gardens for years. We used to take the children there. It would be nice to see it again.'

Tom was not, naturally, someone who would normally use his free time by visiting such places. But he could tell that Mary was very keen on the idea. 'That's a good idea,' he replied, as enthusiastically as he could manage without sounding slightly patronising. 'Actually, I can't even remember the last time I went there. Let's do that, then.'

But Mary would soon, once again, find out that making domestic plans when you are in a relationship with a police officer is a precarious business.

Chapter 47

They had got up early ahead of their day out together and were eating breakfast when Tom's mobile rang.

Mary, looking at the phone suspiciously, and with an instinctive sense of foreboding, said, 'Do you have to answer it?'

Tom picked up his phone and looked at the screen. 'It's Milner. Let me just see why he's calling.'

A degree of resignation had now crept into Mary's voice. 'I don't suppose he's calling, on a Sunday morning, simply to see how you are.'

Tom pressed the 'accept' button. 'Morning, Milner,' he said cheerfully. 'Haven't you got better things to do on a Sunday morning?'

Milner, not quite sure what to make of Tom's comment, said, 'Have I caught you at a bad time?'

'Milner, what is it?' he asked, reverting to his usual, direct style.

'Sir. We now have almost everything in place to bring in Birkett and Brendan Grace. I just wanted to see if you've had your conversation with DCS Small yet.'

The truth was Tom had planned to do this tomorrow, when he was back at the station. But, in retrospect, he should have anticipated that Milner would have managed to arrange things ahead of that schedule.

'Where are you now?' Tom asked.

'I'm just on my way in to the station. DC Bennett and I still need to tidy up a few loose ends before everything is finalised. It shouldn't take long, though. I just thought you'd want to bring them both in as soon as possible.'

'When are you proposing we bring them in?'

'We could do it today, at a push, but it's normally best to do these things early in the morning when the targets are still half-asleep.'

Tom was tempted to reply that he already knew, through years of experience, which was the best time to mount this type of operation. But he quickly realised that might be interpreted as both churlish and unfair.

So, instead, he made do with, 'Yes. That usually catches them off-guard.' He recognised that Milner was probably waiting for him to make a decision and so said, 'I'm on my way in. I'll see you both shortly.'

Now, looking directly at Mary, he simply said, 'Sorry.'

There was a tense silence before she replied. 'That's all right. I'm sure it's something important. Anyway, we can always go to Kew Gardens some other time.'

'It's the murder enquiry I told you about. We are just about to make some arrests.'

'Tom. You don't have to justify it to me. I know how important your work is. As you mentioned to me once before, crime doesn't just happen between a Monday and a Friday and then conveniently resume again after the weekend. Anyway, I suppose I'll just have to get used to it.'

He leant forward, took hold of her hand and then kissed her. 'I promise, when I get the chance, we'll go to Kew Gardens.'

Less than an hour later he was back at the station, once again seated with Milner and DC Bennett around his meeting table.

'No Jenny today?' he asked, trying not to specifically direct the question at Milner.

DC Bennett, sensing Milner's slight embarrassment, said, 'I'm sure she would have come in if I had asked her, but we'll just have to manage without her today,' before adding, 'I suppose that means I'll have to get the drinks.'

'Good idea,' replied Tom. 'I'll have my usual, please, although I don't hold out any great hopes that the quality has improved since I've moved up here.'

'Sir, I'm not too sure how you'll cope when you have to move back down to the third floor,' replied DC Bennett as he stood up to leave the room. 'I won't be long,' he added as he walked out.

After he had left there followed an uneasy silence, almost as though neither could think of anything to say. Milner's application, and now upcoming interview, for the position in

Brighton had, despite their best efforts, placed an increasing strain on their relationship. For Tom's part, he felt as though he was walking on eggshells, trying not to do or say anything which might unwittingly force Milner even faster down the Brighton path. He also sensed how Milner himself was trying even harder than usual to be as professional and diligent as possible. All of this seemed to combine to produce an unnatural tension in their relationship. It was almost as though they were both going out of their way to be as nice as possible to each other – a situation which, within the police force, would, if it lasted for an overlong period of time, be counterproductive.

It was Tom who eventually broke the silence. 'Good work, by the way, getting all of the paperwork done so quickly.'

This seemed to break the tension. 'Well, it wasn't just me. DC Bennett and Jenny also helped.'

'I'm really starting to like Jenny,' Tom said almost reflectively. 'I hope she stays after I've moved back downstairs.' As Milner didn't respond, Tom changed the subject. 'There's a little job I'd like you to do for me. It's not related to this particular case. It's something else I'm looking at.'

Tom took out from his pocket a piece of paper and handed it to Milner. Written on it was the name of the off-licence which Dale Thompson had told him about.

Milner read out the name. 'Perivale Off-Licence. What is it you want me to do, sir?'

'They have their own CCTV cameras in the shop. I'd like you to check to see if some footage is still available. The manager told me that, as it's from over a year ago, he's not sure if it is still being held. You'll have to check with this company.' Tom handed Milner a second piece of paper, this time with another company's name and contact details, together with a date, written on it. 'They are the security company which installed and operates the CCTV. The date on the paper is the day I want you to try and find.'

'All day, sir?' asked Milner, a little hesitantly.

'No. Specifically between 8pm and 11pm.'

'And what am I looking for?' he then asked, not unreasonably.

'I want you to see if you can spot someone who purchased some cans of lager.'

Milner looked at Tom, a quizzical expression on his face. 'But it's an off-licence, sir. They sell lager.'

'Good point,' answered Tom. He then added, this time with some sarcasm, 'I hadn't thought of that.' He stood up and went towards his desk. Opening the left-hand drawer he took out a buff file, opened it and then pulled out an A5-sized photograph.

He handed the photograph to Milner. 'This is who I'd like you to look out for. His name is Jimmy Griffiths. Well, it was Jimmy Griffiths because he's now dead. It's likely he was there sometime between nine and ten but, if that's not successful, check an hour either side. If you do find him then set the machine up and I'll come down and take a look for myself.'

'Is that all?' asked Milner. 'Or is there anything else I can help with?'

'Thanks for your offer, but that will do for the time being.'

At that point DC Bennett reappeared carrying a small cardboard box which contained three plastic cups. As he placed the box onto the table, Tom and Milner could see that the bottom of the box was quite wet.

'Sorry, sir. I spilt a bit of your coffee on the way up here.'

'Don't worry,' replied Tom. 'Probably not such a bad thing anyway.'

After they had each taken their drinks, Tom carried on. 'Right. How do you want to handle this?'

Milner then explained what he and DC Bennett had discussed. The plan was very straightforward. They would make the arrests concurrently at 6.30am the next morning and bring both Birkett and Brendan Grace back here, to the station, where they would be formally charged. No doubt, particularly in the case of Grace, their lawyers would soon be trying to seek bail for their clients and so they needed to be well-prepared in order to counter that.

DC Bennett took Tom through the resources which they felt they needed. Although, unlike the raid on Long Lane Farm, just two individuals were involved, albeit at two separate locations, it was prudent to plan on the basis there might be some resistance. The old adage of 'hope for the best but plan for the worst' was one which Tom had put into practice many times over the years. And, anyway, how would it look if, due to a lack of manpower, one or both of them were able to give them the slip and get away? It was for those reasons, therefore, that they were requesting such a disproportionate arrest team.

'We have the teams on standby. In fact, most of them were there when we raided Long Lane Farm. All we need now is someone's approval.'

'How likely is it they will be at home when we knock on their doors?' asked Tom.

It was DC Bennett who answered. 'Birkett, we know, has moved to a new address after the fire at his house. There's no reason why he shouldn't be there. The same with Brendan Grace, although I think the main problem with him will be getting through those security gates without warning him that we are there.'

'Can't we just disable the security?'

'I don't think it's that easy. The gates and system are both serious bits of kit. Anyway, I'm not sure we can take the chance. The easier alternative is to take down one of the fence panels at the side of the property and gain access that way.'

'And we have the necessary warrant to do that, do we?'

'Yes, sir.'

Tom came to a decision. 'Okay. I suppose, in my current position, I could, theoretically, approve this. But, after what happened last time, I'd better run it by DCS Small.'

Milner seized on Tom's comment. 'Why? What happened last time?'

'Let's just say there was a misunderstanding concerning the line of communication,' he replied, deliberately ambiguously. 'Why don't you two give me a few minutes whilst I call him?'

Milner and DC Bennett took their cue and stood up. 'We've got a few things to do anyway, sir,' said Milner, diplomatically.

After they had left Tom picked up his phone, clicked on the 'contacts' section and, when this opened, scrolled down until he came to DCS Small's private number. He called it and, after just a few seconds, it was answered.

'Yes,' said DCS Small.

'Sir, it's Tom Stone. Have I caught you at a bad time?' he asked, echoing Milner from earlier in the morning.

'Well, it is a Sunday,' answered a slightly grumpy DCS Small.

'Yes, sorry about that, sir. It's just that you did ask me to keep you posted on developments in the James Grace case.'

'Yes, I believe I did,' he answered, this time with slightly more enthusiasm. 'So, what have you got?'

Tom then briefly summarised where they were, especially stressing the new DNA evidence which they now had, and ended by outlining their plans for the following morning's arrests.

'I suppose you want me to authorise the arrests?'

'Not really, sir,' Tom replied. 'I've already done that. What I would like you to do, though, is to sign off the number of officers and back-up which we will need tomorrow.'

Tom waited for DCS Small to respond. The ensuing silence appeared to go on for an overlong period of time, although in reality it probably only lasted a few seconds. Eventually, DCS Small broke the silence.

'What is it you want?' he said grudgingly.

Tom proceeded to briefly list the resources they were asking for, after which DCS Small said, 'Do you really need all of those officers?'

Tom, declining to supply any detailed justification, simply answered, 'Yes, sir.'

'Well, it's your call. I'll email you the authorisation straight away. Just make sure nothing happens which might embarrass the region.'

With those final motivational words still in his mind, Tom put his phone into his pocket and went down to the third floor to meet up with Milner and DC Bennett.

When they saw him they immediately stopped what they were doing. Tom could see a look of concern on both of their faces. It was DC Bennett who articulated that concern. 'Did DCS Small approve it, sir?'

'He did, although, I have to say, not with any great enthusiasm. Still, I don't suppose you can blame him when, no doubt, he has to justify every pound to his superiors.'

'There was one other thing, sir, which we still have to decide,' said Milner mysteriously.

'And what is that?' Tom replied.

'Which arrest location each of us should attend.'

'Well, I'm definitely pulling rank on that one. I want to be there when we arrest Brendan Grace.'

Chapter 48

Tom had left Milner and DC Bennett to finalise the make-up of each arrest team and then to ensure that each of those officers would be at the station early on Monday morning for the final briefing. Although he had not been too specific when Mary had asked him what time he was likely to be returning home, he had said he hoped it would be no later than mid-afternoon. It was now just after noon and, at least according to his idea of what mid-afternoon meant, was still well within that time frame, thereby giving him just enough time to visit Shelley Ripley at her White City address.

Once again, the relatively light traffic worked to his advantage and he was soon making good progress. It was only when he tried to navigate around Shepherd's Bush that he ran into any heavy traffic. He had driven this way hundreds of times over the years and, almost invariably, the traffic flow had been disrupted by some combination of road repairs, new pipes being laid, accidents and, worst of all, traffic light failure. Fortunately, today, despite the large number of vehicles in the area, the traffic kept moving and it wasn't long before he was on the A219 heading north towards White City.

Shelley Ripley's address was located almost underneath the A40 Westway, not far from Wormwood Scrubs prison. The property, a small terraced house, had seen better days and, just like the house where Dale Thompson lived in Perivale, was in urgent need of some major repairs. He rang the bell and stood back, having clearly heard that it had worked. After a while, the net curtain at the window of a room on the ground floor was pulled to one side and he just caught a glimpse of a woman looking at him before the curtain was once again pulled back to its original position. The front door was then partly opened and a woman's head appeared.

'Are you Shelley Ripley?' Tom asked.

'Yes,' she answered. 'What do you want?'

Tom took out his identification card and showed it to the woman. 'I'm Detective Chief Inspector Stone. I wonder if it's possible to have a word with you. I was hoping you might be able to help me. I won't keep you too long.'

'What is it you want?' she asked again, suspiciously.

'Is it possible to come in? It would be much better if we could speak inside.'

Shelley hesitated for a moment before finally saying, 'I suppose so.'

She opened the door fully and Tom followed her into the front room. The room was a mess, with empty beer and lager cans on the floor, on the small table and even some still resting on the arm of one of the armchairs.

'Sorry about the mess. We had a bit of a party last night and I haven't had the chance to clean up yet.'

Tom had guessed she'd had a late night. Shelley, red-eyed with her hair uncombed, was still wearing her dressing gown.

She moved a few things from the other armchair. 'Do you want to sit down?'

'Thanks,' he answered, judging that it might perhaps help to win her confidence if he accepted her offer.

'Can I get you something to drink? Tea? Coffee?' she asked politely. 'I'm going to have one anyway.'

'Coffee would be great. Milk, no sugar, please.'

'I won't be a minute.' She then walked out of the room towards the kitchen.

Tom's immediate impression of Shelley was that her polite manner didn't seem to match her shambolic appearance and surroundings. It wasn't long before she returned, carrying two slightly cracked mugs.

'Do you live here alone?' Tom asked, after she had handed him his coffee.

'No. I live with Paul. He's still upstairs in bed.'

'It must have been a good party,' Tom said.

This appeared to, once again, arouse Shelley's suspicions. 'You said I might be able to help you.'

'I understand you and Susan Chambers were sharing a flat at the time she died. I just want to ask a couple of questions about Susan.'

'I told the police everything I knew at the time,' she said. 'Has something else happened?'

Tom, trying not to directly answer her perceptive question, simply said, 'In your statement, you said that Susan had mentioned how she was expecting to come into some money. Did she tell you where it was coming from?'

This seemed, at least for the time being, to placate her. 'No, she didn't. But, whatever it was, she was very excited about it.'

'Did you get the impression it was a large sum of money?'

'Possibly. Susan was always short of money; that's why she did what she did.'

'You mean being a prostitute?'

'Why do you say it like that?' she asked, quite angrily. 'Do you think she liked doing what she was doing? She did it because she had a drug and alcohol addiction and needed money to pay for them.'

'I'm sorry,' replied Tom contritely, 'I wasn't being judgemental. I'm just trying to understand why she thought she was about to come into some money.'

Once again, Tom's comment appeared to have had the desired effect. 'Although we'd been sharing the flat for a year or so I had never seen her quite that excited. So, yes, at least to her, it must have been a lot of money.'

'So she didn't give you any clue as to what she had that could make her such a large amount of money?'

Once again Shelley hesitated before answering. 'One night, when we were both drunk, I vaguely remember her saying how she knew something which, one way or another, would make her a lot of money.'

'Had something or knew something?' asked Tom.

She shook her head. 'I can't remember. She said she'd already had some money but she was expecting a lot more. But when I mentioned it to her the next day she couldn't even remember saying it. So, at the time, I thought she was just showing off.'

'So she'd had some money already?' asked Tom, surprised.

'That's what I thought she said. Something about receiving a down payment, but, as I told you, we were both drunk.'

'Did she only mention it that once?' asked Tom. 'Getting some money, that is?'

'That was the first time, about four weeks before she was killed. The next time was about two weeks later. This time she was sober. Well, she'd still had a few drinks but wasn't totally hammered. Anyway, she said something about soon being able to get herself a decent flat. That's all I know and that's what I told that other detective.'

'I understand you found Susan's body,' he said, as gently as possible.

Despite Tom's sympathetic tone, Shelley suddenly became visibly upset. Eventually, after she had regained her composure, she answered. 'I got back to the flat at about ten o'clock in the morning. I'd been staying with my boyfriend for a few days. Not Paul. I had a different one then. When I came in I could see the place was a mess. Well, even worse than usual. It was then that I saw Susan. She was lying on the floor. At first I thought she was just drunk but, after a while, I could see she was dead. It was then that I called the police.'

'Thank you for that. I know it must be distressing. A couple more questions, if you don't mind. Did Susan ever tell you who she was bringing back?'

Shelley looked at Tom with something bordering on incredulity. 'She didn't have an appointments diary, you know. She wasn't working for some fancy West End escort agency. She was walking the streets.' She paused briefly and then continued. 'Although she had a few regulars, most of the time it depended on which drunk or stoned punter she came across first.'

Tom took a sip of his coffee and then said, 'What happened to Susan's belongings after she died?'

'She didn't have much. All of the furniture in the flat belonged to the landlord. She had a few clothes which were either thrown out or given to a charity shop. The few remaining personal things she owned were, I think, given to her daughter.'

'Do you know where her daughter lives?' asked Tom.

'Somewhere up in Hendon, I think. I only met her once – at the funeral. I'm sure she said something about living there. To be honest, I didn't even know she had a daughter until I met her at the funeral.'

'What was her name? Can you remember?'

'Sharon? Shannon?' She paused before adding, 'I'm almost certain it was Sharon.'

'How old do you think she was?'

'I don't know. Mid-to-late thirties. Something like that.'

Tom stood up. 'Thank you for your time and thanks for the coffee. You have been very helpful.'

As Tom was just about to leave the room, Shelley suddenly said, 'Jimmy didn't kill her. He might have been a smackhead but he wasn't a murderer.'

Chapter 49

'I may as well go back home tonight,' said Mary.

Tom had arrived home just after three o'clock and, as he had not eaten since breakfast, they had decided to have an early dinner.

'You don't have to,' he answered.

'I know, but as you have to leave so early tomorrow morning it just seems a bit silly staying here, by myself, when I could just as easily be back in my own home.'

Earlier, he had mentioned to her how he needed to be at the station by 4am for the briefing to the two arrest teams.

'You are probably right,' he conceded. 'I'm sorry about that. It hasn't been much of a weekend, has it?'

'Well, it's not exactly what I was hoping for, but I'm sure we'll have other opportunities to spend a bit more time together.'

'I'm sure we will,' said Tom, trying to reciprocate in the same positive voice.

'You will be careful, won't you?' Mary suddenly said. 'I do worry about you when you tell me about these things.'

Tom had felt he had to tell her why he had to be back at the station so early the following morning. He had tried to keep the details as ambiguous as possible but suspected that Mary, by now, was beginning to get wise to his wordplay. Nonetheless, her comment simply reinforced his determination to tell her, in future, as little as possible about any similar operations. He would try, wherever possible, to apply the 'what you don't know can't harm you' principle. Although he didn't like doing this to Mary it was, he thought, in both of their long-term interests.

It was just before 6.30am and Tom, DC Bennett and the rest of the team were all assembled at the side of Grace's property in Chelmsford.

'Is everyone in position?' Tom asked.

'All set to go, sir,' replied DC Bennett. 'I've just had a call from DS Milner to say that they are also in place.'

'Good. Let's do it, then,' said Tom, to no one in particular.

DC Bennett nodded to two of the uniformed officers, who immediately began to pull out a fence panel which they had previously selected. It came out much more easily than Tom had imagined. They all then stepped through the open space and walked quickly, but without running, towards the house itself. A few of the officers, as previously agreed, immediately made their way around to the rear of the house, whilst a few others stayed as back-up. When everyone was in position Tom, looking directly at DC Bennett, said, 'Give it a good knock. Make sure they know we are not the postman.'

DC Bennett gave the door a few hard raps whilst simultaneously holding his finger on the bell. It wasn't long before there was movement from within the house and a minute or so later the door was opened by a bleary-eyed middle-aged woman who Tom recognised as James Grace's wife, Angie.

Turning her head around she shouted, 'Jimmy, it's the police. They're at the front door.' She then redirected her attention towards Tom and his colleagues. 'What is it you want?'

It was DC Bennett who answered. Holding up a piece of official-looking paper he said, 'This is a warrant for us to enter your property.'

'Is Brendan at home?' asked Tom.

'He's not here,' she replied, a touch too quickly. 'We haven't seen him for a few days.'

Just then James Grace appeared wearing a brown dressing gown, partly covering his light blue boxer shorts and plain white T-shirt. 'It's you again, is it? How long are you going to keep harassing me?'

'It's not you we are looking for,' Tom said, before adding, 'Well, not this time anyway. We have come to arrest Brendan.' Then, looking at DC Bennett, he said, 'DC Bennett. Please show Mr Grace the arrest warrant.'

DC Bennett also had this ready and handed it to Grace, who simply ignored it.

'Could we please come in?' asked Tom.

There was a brief stand-off as Grace considered what to do

next. Eventually, clearly having now decided, he simply said, 'Let them in, Angie.'

'Thank you,' answered Tom, who, walking through the front door, was immediately followed by DC Bennett and five other officers, whilst another two remained outside.

Just as they were about to go upstairs, Brendan Grace and his younger brother suddenly appeared at the top of the stairs. Both had managed to throw on some clothes and, judging in part by the expression on their faces, but more so by their aggressive language, were not planning to make this easy for the officers.

It was the younger brother who made the first move when he began to run down the stairs. Tom and a uniformed officer, with DC Bennett behind them, were at the bottom of the stairs and so directly blocking his path. This didn't seem to deter him because he simply launched himself at them from the second-from-bottom step. Tom and the other officer took the full force of his attack, sending both of them crashing to the floor, leaving Tom temporarily winded. DC Bennett and the other officers then grabbed the brother and forced him to the floor.

Seeing his brother being held by the officers, Brendan now ran down the stairs and joined the fight. Grabbing hold of DC Bennett, he dragged him off his brother and then started to repeat the process with one of the other officers. Just then the two officers who had remained outside appeared and began to grapple with him.

By now the sheer weight of police numbers was starting to have an impact and slowly the energy which the younger brother had shown earlier began to dissipate, allowing a couple of the officers to disentangle themselves from him and assist their two other colleagues who were trying to subdue Brendan. Tom, by now, had partly recovered from the impact of the attack and shouted to one of the officers to call for the back-up. It wasn't long before they were on the scene, although by then Brendan and his brother had, more or less, been subdued. Both of them were lying face-down with a couple of officers sitting on top of them.

During the fight Tom had heard Angie screaming obscenities at the officers and encouragement to her sons. Bizarrely, whilst all of this had been happening, James Grace had stayed out of the way and remained silent. Now, though, he finally spoke. 'Big men, ain't you? Took all you lot to stop my boys. What you going to do now? Have a go at Angie?'

This seemed to reignite Angie's vitriolic touch paper as she resumed her swearing, although this time Tom noticed how it was directed specifically at him rather than to the officers in general.

'Make sure that those cuffs are on tightly,' he said. 'DC Bennett, please read them their rights.'

Even though his ribs were now hurting again, Tom was trying hard not to let James Grace see that he was in any pain.

Nonetheless, it was Grace who had the final word. 'You and your bosses will soon be hearing from my brief. You'd better have cast-iron evidence, because if you don't I'm going to sue the arse off you.'

But it was Grace's final comment which, notwithstanding his painful ribs, caused Tom the most concern. 'If I were you, Detective Chief Inspector Tom Stone, I'd make sure that girlfriend of yours locks her doors at night.'

Chapter 50

As soon as Tom's team arrived back at the station, they were met by Milner. Noticing how Tom was walking quite deliberately, Milner, with a degree of trepidation, asked, 'How did it go, sir?'

'Fine,' replied Tom. 'We have Brendan Grace and his brother both downstairs in the cells.'

'His brother?' asked Milner. 'Did they resist?'

'You could say that,' and then, as an afterthought, 'I'm glad you asked for those extra officers. Without them, we might have been in real trouble. Just try and remember that. It's always better to have too many officers rather than too few.'

'Are you okay, sir?' asked Milner, deciding not respond to his little homily. 'You seem to be walking a bit delicately.'

'One of them crashed into me. My ribs are a bit sore again, that's all. Anyway, I hear Terry Birkett came a bit more quietly.'

'Eventually,' Milner replied. 'Initially, he put up some resistance, but we were able to easily restrain him. He's also down in the cells.'

'Okay, make sure that all of the paperwork is correct before we get a visit from their lawyers. We don't want a foul-up now, after we've gone through all of this,' he said, gingerly feeling his ribs. 'I'll be upstairs in my office if you need me.'

Tom made his way slowly towards the lift. No stairs for him today. When he got to the fifth floor Jenny was already waiting for him.

'David ... sorry, DS Milner told me you were on your way. Are you in pain again, sir?' she asked.

'Well, today's events haven't exactly helped the healing process. But I expect I'll survive.'

'I'll bring some coffee in. I'm sure you could do with one.'

'Yes, thanks. I think I could,' he answered.

He sat down at his desk, took out his mobile and made a call.

'Panton,' the familiar voice said.

'It's DCI Stone here. Is now a good time to speak?'

'DCI Stone,' repeated Dr Panton. 'Yes, of course. Good to hear from you again. Do you have any news for me? Is that why you've called?'

Tom, slightly taken aback by this burst of *bonhomie*, said, in a similarly positive tone, 'Actually, I do. I wanted to let you know what has happened.'

Tom then updated him on the developments.

'Sounds like you've been very busy,' said Dr Panton, 'and I have to admit I'm also relieved that my concerns were proven to be correct.'

'Yours and Mrs Bishop's. Sometimes, we just have to trust our instincts, although I also think luck played its part. Without the CCTV evidence it would have been much more difficult to prove Hepworth had been in Mr Wilson's house.'

'That's true but, occasionally, we make our own luck,' he said. 'What do you think will now happen to the care company?'

'My guess is that the CQC will be all over them. After that, I'm not too sure, although we will also be seeking a conviction. The assault on Mr Wilson by Hepworth is serious enough for us to pursue this. But, as far as the company is concerned, as I said, that will be for the CQC to decide.'

'This type of company makes my blood boil,' Dr Panton said, displaying a sudden burst of genuine anger. 'They profess to have their clients' interests – often very vulnerable and elderly people – at heart, when really all they are interested in is making as much profit as possible. How were they allowed to employ someone whose partner has a criminal record?' He didn't give Tom time to respond. 'They should be closed down. That would send a strong signal to all of the other care companies.'

'I'm afraid that will be for someone else to decide. I'm sure, though, there are many more totally dedicated and caring companies which, on a daily basis, provide an excellent service, often in difficult circumstances.' He paused briefly before continuing. 'Actually, Dr Panton, there is something I would like your help with.'

'Really?' asked Dr Panton, clearly surprised by Tom's request. 'Is it of a professional nature?'

'It is, actually. I wonder if you would be able to provide me with a copy of the post-mortem report which your predecessor, Dr Green, carried out on a murder victim.'

'Is this an official request?' asked Dr Panton.

'Well, let's just say it will assist with an investigation I'm currently involved with.'

'Given what you have done for me, I really don't see how I could possibly refuse,' he answered, with a slight laugh. 'If you give me the name of the deceased, together with your email address, I'll see what I can do.'

After Tom's call with Dr Panton had ended he immediately made another one. As soon as it was answered he said, 'Jim, it's Tom Stone here again. I was hoping you could help me out again.'

'I don't hear from you for ages and then I get two calls in the space of a few days. You must be a busy man. What is it you want this time?'

'Sorry, Jim. I don't want to give you any flannel. It's related to the other addresses you got for me. By the way, thanks for those. They proved to be very useful. I'm afraid I now need one other contact address. This time, though, I suspect it will not be quite as easy for you to track down.'

'If that's your attempt to tease me,' he said, now laughing, 'by questioning my abilities, then it's worked. Who is it you need to find?'

Tom then provided him with all of the limited information he knew relating to Susan Chambers' daughter, Sharon.

'Is that all you've got?' asked Jim, this time without the laughter.

'I'm afraid so.'

'I'll see what I can do but, frankly, I wouldn't hold your breath.'

Tom now made his third call since he'd returned. This one was to DCS Small.

'I was hoping you would call. How did it go?' asked DCS Small.

'Very well.' He then gave DCS Small a quick summary of the morning's events.

After Tom had finished DCS Small said, 'Did anyone get injured?'

'There was a bit of rough stuff and a few cuts and bruises

but nothing serious,' he replied, not giving a completely accurate account. 'But it was definitely the correct decision to have all of those officers there,' he added pointedly.

'Good work,' DCS Small said, before adding the sting in the tail. 'Just make sure the arrests stick. I don't want to hear they've been released because their briefs have found something wrong with your investigation.'

The reference to 'your investigation' was not lost on Tom.

Jenny knocked on the door as he hung up and, not waiting for a reply, opened it and came in, holding the obligatory tray. 'What happens now, sir? Will they go to court?' she asked.

Tom poured himself a coffee from the pot. 'We'll carry out the formal interviews. The hope is always that they confess but, somehow, in this particular case, I doubt very much that will happen. Their lawyers will try to obtain bail for them, we'll resist it and then the decision will be taken out of our hands. A trial date will be set and then it's up to the jury and the judge to decide if they are guilty and, if so, what sentence they should serve. Our job now is to make their decisions easy.'

After Jenny had left, Tom delicately began to feel his ribs. Initially they didn't seem too bad but, when he applied a bit more pressure, he felt an immediate sharp pain. The pain, he knew, would eventually go away as his ribs healed. What, however, was unlikely to go away was the confirmation, once again, that he was getting too old for all of this rough stuff. In his earlier days he would probably have anticipated the sudden attack by the younger Grace, and been able to avoid it. The truth, however, was that his reflexes were no longer as fast as they used to be.

He was shaken from these depressing thoughts when his phone rang. It was Mary.

'Hello,' he said. 'This is a nice surprise.'

'How are you?' she immediately asked, without any of her usual pleasantries.

'I'm fine,' he answered. 'Why are you asking?'

'I just wanted to make sure you were all right, that's all, and that you'd returned from this morning's operation safe and sound.'

'I'm fine,' he repeated. 'Mary, you don't need to call me after every operation.'

There was a short silence before she spoke. 'I got the impression, last night, that this morning's operation wasn't quite as straightforward as you were trying to make out.'

'Look, Mary,' he said, a little too sharply, 'I've been doing this job for over twenty-five years and managed to survive so far.'

Another silence followed. 'I was worried about you. That's all.'

'I know you were,' replied Tom, this time in a much more contrite tone. 'I'm sorry for being a bit sharp.'

'Do you want me to come around tonight?' she asked.

'You don't have to if you don't want to,' he answered, instantly recognising how the words hadn't come out quite the way he had intended them to.

His reading of the situation was immediately confirmed. 'Is that what you really think?' she asked, her voice rising, reflecting her obvious anger. 'How can you even think I wouldn't want to come round to see you?' Tom sensed how her anger had now turned into something more upsetting, and, when she spoke next, it was interlaced with the occasional sob. 'Why don't you call me when *you* think the time is right?'

As he sat at his desk he wondered how he had, with just a few ill-chosen words, managed to make Mary cry. It was clear he had totally underestimated her deep concern for him, and it was equally clear that, unless he made some fundamental changes to the way he viewed their relationship, he would lose her for good and then probably be destined to spend a lonely retirement. That particular thought suddenly held no attraction.

Tom was on his way home. It was just after six o'clock and earlier he had spent the remainder of the afternoon discussing, with Milner and DC Bennett, how they would approach tomorrow's first formal interviews with Birkett and Brendan Grace. Although they now had compiled a raft of evidence against both of them, Tom was still worried that a lot of it could be construed as simply circumstantial. Fortunately the DNA evidence indisputably put both of them at the scene of the respective crimes. Whether it would be enough, however, to prove they had committed those crimes was another matter.

Being there was one thing, but being there and committing the crime was something entirely different.

His main concern right now, though, was his relationship with Mary. It was clear they had reached a crossroads and so the choice of direction which, in particular, he next made would decide whether or not they had a future together. He was not normally the type of person who would just stand by and let a situation drift, particularly when the stakes were so high. But, somehow, this was different. He could see how things were moving inexorably towards a situation which he didn't want. He was sure Mary felt the same, but unless he did something – and he knew it was he who would have to make the change – they seemed destined to split apart.

As he came off the M25 slip road he decided to make that move. Instead of turning left, towards his house in Staines, he carried straight on, along the A30, following the signs for Camberley and Bagshot. When he arrived at Mary's he could see her car on the drive. He parked his own car behind hers and then rang the doorbell.

'Tom. What are you doing here?' she asked, clearly surprised by his presence.

He had already rehearsed, in his mind, what he would say, but now that he was there all he could say was, 'I'm sorry.' He moved towards her and held her close to him.

For a while, neither of them said anything, until Mary broke away from him and said, 'I think you had better come in, otherwise my neighbours will wonder what's going on.'

Tom followed her into the kitchen.

'I was just making myself some dinner. Have you eaten?'

'Not yet,' he answered. 'Are you offering?'

'You know I am,' she replied, before adding, 'So, why are you here?'

Although he considered himself to be a good judge of body language, so far Mary had not given any clues as to whether or not she was welcoming him or simply being polite. He suspected that the next few minutes would provide the answer.

'I've been thinking about you all afternoon and what a fool I've been. I don't want to lose you and, if I haven't made that clear, then I am now.'

Tom now got the answer he was hoping for as, this time,

she pulled him close to her. She then looked at him and said, 'If it's any consolation, I've also had a pretty miserable afternoon. I felt like one of those teenagers who had just been dumped by their boyfriend and so their whole world had collapsed.'

'Well, it's good that sometimes we can still act like teenagers,' he replied, with a slight laugh.

As they drew apart Mary noticed how Tom had winced slightly, as he felt the pain in his ribs.

'Are you still in pain?' she asked.

'A little,' he answered, without any further explanation.

'You haven't been resting, have you?' she asked reprovingly.

'It's difficult,' he simply answered.

Mary, probably not wanting to push this potential source of disagreement any further, instead said, 'Tom. I hate it when we argue. I know it's inevitable, even in the best of relationships, but let's both make sure we always make up afterwards.'

Once again, he pulled her towards him, although this time it wasn't out of politeness. He suddenly felt a real urge to be even closer and so began to kiss her and she soon responded in a similar fashion. He pulled away from her and said, 'Why don't we continue making up upstairs?'

Mary turned away from him and walked towards her cooker. Switching off the gas, on which a saucepan containing pasta was busily bubbling away, she said, 'As long as you don't mind a late dinner.'

Later, as they were lying in her bed, Mary suddenly said, 'What is it, Tom? You haven't been yourself for the last week or so. Is it me?'

'Of course it's not you,' he answered, before adding, 'Well, not in the way you probably mean.'

'What do you mean?' she asked, sitting up.

Tom took a deep breath. 'I'm a bit worried for you, that's all.' He hesitated briefly and then continued. 'Actually, I am more than a bit worried for you. For your safety, that is.'

If he hadn't before, he now had her undivided attention. 'My safety?' she repeated.

Of all of the places he had imagined telling Mary about the situation with James Grace, being together in her bed was very low down his list. He held her hand and then told her about Grace and his mounting threats. He told her how Grace knew where she worked and where she lived. He told her how his continual references to her being so close to Tom now represented a way in which he could possibly cause Tom serious harm. What he couldn't, however, bring himself to tell her was how Grace also knew about Mary's missing kitten. Somehow that just seemed a step too far.

'But I thought you had arrested him this morning,' she suddenly said.

'That was his son. Well, actually two of his sons. Although we know James Grace has been involved in other things, there is no real evidence to link him with the arson attack.'

'Can't you arrest him for making the threats?'

'Not really. They weren't direct threats as such, more like psychological ones. Anyway, it would be his word against mine.'

'So do you think he's bluffing?' she asked.

'I hope so,' he answered, 'but I'm not willing to take the chance. He seems the type of person who would try and exact some sort of personal vengeance, however irrational.'

Mary had now become silent as, no doubt, the full implications of what Tom had just told her had started to sink in.

'It's not an excuse, but, hopefully, you can see now why I have, perhaps, been a bit off with you. I suppose I was trying to protect you from knowing about all of this.'

'What do you think I should do?' she asked quietly, with real concern, for the first time, appearing in her voice.

'For now,' he answered, 'I should at least stay here with you for a few more days. I'm sure there's no danger during the day. I know, though, given my job, it wouldn't be very practical for me to stay here every night. I was going to suggest that you go and stay with one of your sons, until all of this is over.'

He waited for her response, wondering how she would react.

'I suppose I could,' she said, surprising Tom with the sudden acceptance of his suggestion, 'although I would have to try and arrange some cover for the business first.' She hesitated briefly before adding, 'But what about the play?' suddenly remembering that personal commitment. 'Rehearsals are just about to move into full swing. I can't miss those.'

Tom knew how much she was looking forward to participating in the play and, therefore, what a wrench it would be for her to miss rehearsals. 'Hopefully, it won't be for long. Do you think they could do without you for a week or so?'

Mary didn't answer Tom's question. Instead she said, 'What does your boss – DCS Small, isn't it? – think you should do?'

This, of course, was a very good question and one which he hadn't considered Mary might ask. But now that he had started he was determined to try and tell her the truth. He judged that now was a good time to put the theory into practice.

'I haven't actually told him yet. I was hoping to have a bit more hard evidence before I did so. So far, Grace's words have been mainly innuendo. Police officers receive threats all of the time. But, unfortunately, we don't have anything concrete so far.'

Mary's earlier reasonableness now turned to something verging on anger. 'So, you have to wait until he actually does something before you can arrest him.'

Tom took both of her hands. 'Mary, this is exactly why I didn't want to tell you. But please trust me. I won't let anything happen to you.'

Mary got out of bed. 'Why don't we go and have something to eat?' she said, her usual equilibrium having now returned.

As Mary dressed Tom thought about what he had told her. Somehow he couldn't help thinking that it hadn't been the cleverest thing to do, but he now couldn't undo what had been done. In a way, though, it had simply reinforced his determination to bring Grace to justice and, hopefully, before he could inflict any more damage, either psychologically or physically.

Chapter 51

Tom had stayed over at Mary's and left for the station at the same time as she had left for work. It had been a difficult night. He felt as though he had not slept at all and suspected the same had been the case for Mary. Lying beside her, he had heard her shallow breathing, but it hadn't seemed the type of breathing which suggested an uninterrupted sleep. This seemed to be confirmed in the morning, when he noticed how she had suddenly acquired the hint of dark patches under each eye. Neither of them had mentioned last night's conversation. The only oblique reference to it had been when they had agreed that Tom would stay with her for the remainder of the week, after which she would stay with one of her sons, Greg or Aaron.

As he entered the station's car park he could see that Milner's car was already there. It was parked in what was considered to be the prime parking space, suggesting he had arrived early. Tom walked slowly up the steps, into the station and towards the lift. The pain in his ribs meant he would, yet again, have to postpone his well-intentioned plans to regularly walk each of the floors.

Jenny was once again waiting for him as he walked into his office.

'Morning, sir. How are you today?' she asked in a tone which suggested genuine concern for his well-being.

'A bit stiff, to be honest, but hopefully that will soon go.'

'There's a pot of coffee on your desk already. There's also all of yesterday's reports and correspondence, as I know you didn't get the chance to look at them.'

'Thanks, Jenny. I don't know which I like least: reading those reports or having a few painful ribs,' he said with a slightly forced laugh.

'Incidentally, DS Milner would like to see you. Should I ask him to come up?'

'Why not?' he answered. 'Ask him to come up now. The reports will just have to wait a little longer.'

Tom just had time to switch on his computer and pour a cup of coffee before he could hear Milner, outside his open office door, talking with Jenny.

'Come on in, Milner,' he shouted, just loud enough for Milner to hear him. 'Let's get started.'

A few moments later Milner entered, this time holding two files.

'Morning, Milner. I noticed you were one of the first to arrive this morning.'

'I wanted to make sure that everything was in order before we started the interviews,' he answered, wondering how DCI Stone knew that.

'Okay, how do you want to do this?' asked Tom.

Milner opened the file titled *Brendan Grace*, removed a single sheet of A4 paper, which had the heading *Summary of Evidence* written on it, and then briefly took Tom through its contents. After he had completed this he repeated the process with the other file, titled *Terry Birkett*. Although Tom asked a few questions and made some minor changes, he was impressed by the way Milner had distilled all of the available evidence into something which was coherent and compelling.

'That's very impressive, Milner. Hopefully, even their briefs will have difficulty in trying to dismiss it. It must have taken you quite a while to pull it together.'

'Not really, sir,' replied Milner, modestly. 'Anyway, I did have help from DC Bennett.'

This seemed to trigger something in Tom's brain. 'I've been meaning to ask you: how are you and DC Bennett getting on together? Any problems?'

'Fine, sir,' he replied. 'No problems, as far as I'm concerned.' He hesitated. 'I must admit I was a bit worried to begin with that he might have resented the fact I'd been promoted above him. After all, there is a bit of an age difference and he's been in the force a lot longer than I have, but, if he did have a problem, then I haven't been aware of it and it hasn't affected the quality of his work. I think he's a really good bloke.'

'That's good,' said Tom. 'I'm glad you are getting on so well.' He almost added how Milner should perhaps hope for someone as good as DC Bennett when he was a DS in Brighton. Fortunately, though, on this occasion he managed to resist the temptation. Instead, he made do with, 'So, we'll interview Birkett first. I'd like to be involved in that one, if you don't mind.'

Milner, taken aback slightly by DCI Stone's sudden burst of uncharacteristic deference, simply said, 'Of course, sir. I assumed you'd want to be involved in both of them.'

'As you've done most of the prep work, I just wanted to make sure you were happy with that,' Tom said.

Milner, a little unnerved by all of this, couldn't immediately think of anything to say in response. Fortunately, Tom broke the silence. 'Good. I'll see you outside the interview room at eleven o'clock.'

'Sir?' Milner said. 'I hope you don't mind me asking, but DC Bennett mentioned to me that James Grace had threatened you or, more specifically, Mary. Is that correct?'

Tom was quite touched that Milner appeared to be genuinely concerned. 'Just him trying to unnerve me, that's all,' he replied.

Milner, not entirely convinced, said, 'If there's anything I can do, sir, you only have to ask.'

'Thank you, Milner. I'm sure that Mary would appreciate that. Rest assured that if I need your help I will ask.'

Milner stood up to leave, but before he did so he said, 'Incidentally, I've managed to find the CCTV coverage showing the man in the off-licence. It was quite easy in the end, although the security firm did say that if we'd left it a few weeks longer, then they would have wiped the tape.'

In truth, with everything else that had recently happened, Tom had temporarily forgotten about this, but, hearing what Milner had just told him, suddenly his mind was refocused.

'Really?' asked Tom, betraying his surprise.

'Yes, sir,' replied Milner. 'I've set it up on the same machine we used last time. I'll take you through it later on, if you'd like.'

'Milner, thanks for the offer, but I think I can manage. Anyway, I'll see you outside the interview room.'

After Milner had left, Tom sat back in his chair and thought back to his conversation with Dale Thompson. He knew how people who were regular users of alcohol and drugs, and especially those who used a combination of the two, often lost all sense of time. Whilst Thompson was quite sure that Griffiths had arrived at his place somewhere between 9pm and 10pm, his time frame could be wildly out, especially after an already heavy afternoon drinking session. Tom suddenly felt a real sense of apprehension, as he wondered what the footage would show.

Chapter 52

'Have you ever spoken with James Grace or any of his sons?' asked Milner, directing his question at Terry Birkett.
'No comment,' replied Birkett. So far, this had been his stock answer to every question asked of him.
'Okay, let me try and help you, Mr Birkett. Here's a record of all of the calls you've made from your mobile. The highlighted number is one you made a couple of weeks before the body of Mr Inanescu was found in Mr Grace's property in Hounslow. That number is Mr James Grace's personal mobile number.' Milner then placed another piece of paper, listing a different set of telephone numbers, in front of him. 'And the highlighted one here is a call which Mr Grace then made to you a few days after Mr Inanescu's body was found. Do you remember those conversations?'
'No comment,' he repeated.
'Why were illegal cannabis plants found in your house?'
'No comment.'
'Mr Birkett,' interrupted Tom. 'When this goes to trial – which it will – the jury will be aware of your refusal to answer any of our questions. I dare say they will draw their own conclusions from that.'
When this elicited no response, Milner continued. 'They will also be able to draw their own conclusions from the fact that DNA – your DNA – was found at the scene of the crime. As you know, we have also removed all of your clothing from your house for further testing. It's likely you thought you had got rid of everything, but you cannot be sure, can you? I think Mr Inanescu probably put up a fight before you killed him, and that's why we were able to find evidence of your blood in the house. I don't know whether you deliberately set out to murder Mr Inanescu or whether things just got out of control. All I would say is that manslaughter is a very serious offence but murder is *the* most serious offence. Either way you are

looking at a prison sentence. But you do have a choice. Cooperate with us and that sentence is likely to be less than fifteen years. Remain silent and it could be a life sentence. As I say, it's your choice. If I were you I would seriously think about that.'

As Birkett continued to be uncommunicative, Tom, once again, interjected. 'I understand your wife and two teenage daughters were in the house on the night someone deliberately tried to set it alight.' This appeared to generate a reaction from Birkett as, instead of staring directly in front, as he had done so far, he moved his gaze instead to look at Tom. 'If it hadn't been for the quick response of the fire service it's possible they could now be seriously injured or, worse, dead. How do you feel about that, Mr Birkett?' When there was no response, Tom continued. 'It's almost certain you will be spending quite a few years in prison, but the person who tried to kill you and your family is likely to stay free. I know normally there is an unwritten law that you never grass on someone, but this is hardly a normal situation.' Still with no response from Birkett, he then added, 'I expect over the next few years your daughters will be thinking about getting married and having their own children. If you receive a life sentence then there's a strong possibility you will never be able to share any of that with them. But, as DS Milner said, it's your choice.'

After the interview, Milner and Tom went back to Tom's old office, where they were joined by DC Bennett. 'How did it go?' he asked.

'Difficult to say,' replied Milner, 'especially as, apart from "no comment", he didn't utter a single word throughout the interview. What do you think, sir?'

'I thought I saw some reaction when you mentioned the likely sentence he could expect, and then again when I mentioned his daughters. But you never know with the criminal fraternity. Sometimes they would rather try to play the long game and hope for the best than cut their losses by cooperating. Anyway, we'll soon find out.' He then continued, 'I'll be in my office if you need me; otherwise, I'll see you when we interview Grace later this afternoon. Somehow, I don't think we will have any difficulty in getting him to speak.'

Chapter 53

Tom returned to his office after the Birkett interview, sat at his desk and began to scroll down his emails. He was looking for one from Jim Gilbert and one from Dr Panton. Although he couldn't see one from Jim, he was, nonetheless, in luck as he quickly spotted Dr Panton's name. He clicked and opened the message.

From: Dr Robert Panton
To: DCI Stone
Subject: Pathology report for Miss Susan Chambers

Tom,
I've attached the full report relating to the above deceased. I'm sure, as a very experienced officer, you are familiar with most of the terminology contained within the report. I have, however, taken the liberty of summarising the main points.

1. Death was caused by a severe blow to the back of her head, in my opinion probably caused by her head hitting something hard as she fell backwards. She had two distinct bruises suggesting her head first hit either a door or wall and then the floor as she fell (or was pushed) backwards.
2. There was also evidence of bruising around the neck, suggesting she had been held quite tightly.
3. There was a high level of alcohol, together with a moderate level of cocaine, in her blood.
4. There was evidence she had been engaged in sexual activity sometime earlier that day.
5. She had quite advanced liver disease, consistent with heavy drinking over a sustained period of time.
6. I would estimate the time of death as not earlier than 10pm and not later than 1am.

I do hope this is of some help to you in your investigation. If I can be of any further assistance don't hesitate to contact me.

*With best regards,
Robert*

Tom opened the attachment and clicked the 'print' button, although he suspected everything he needed to know was included in Dr Panton's summary. He was tempted to head immediately down to the video room in order to see the CCTV footage of Jimmy Griffiths. In the event, he resisted the temptation, deciding that it could wait until after the interview with Brendan Grace. Before then he spent his time dealing with the other emails and making a start on reading the ever-growing pile of reports which Jenny had placed on his desk. He must have become engrossed in his work because he was suddenly startled when the intercom buzzer sounded.

'Just to let you know, sir,' said Jenny, 'that DS Milner is downstairs in the interview room.'

Tom looked at his watch and was surprised to see that it was almost time for the planned interview. He closed the file that he'd been reading, stood up and walked out of his room.

'Do you expect to return?' asked Jenny.

'I hope so,' he answered, with a slight laugh, 'otherwise I'll never get through all of those reports you keep putting on my desk.'

Brendan Grace and his lawyer were already in the interview room when Tom and Milner entered. Once again, it was Milner who initiated the interview.

'Where were you on the night that Terry Birkett's house was set alight?'

'Who?' answered Grace with an almost contemptuous laugh. 'Never heard of him.'

'That's very odd, Mr Grace, because we have CCTV evidence showing your van parked just a short distance from his house on that particular night.'

'The person who nicked it must have left it there.'

'How about the CCTV footage which showed you outside?'

'It must have been someone who looked like me,' he replied confidently, adding the same laugh for extra effect.

'Then we have a cigarette butt, immediately outside the front door, which has your DNA on it.'

'Must have been planted there by someone trying to frame me.' He paused briefly and then added, looking directly at Tom, 'It was probably him. He has it in for my family.'

'So, what you are saying is that someone stole your van and then parked it close to the victim's house. Someone who looked like you, carrying a can of petrol, got out of the van and was then seen outside the front door. Finally, your DNA, which was found at the scene of the crime, had been planted there by someone who was trying to frame you. Is that what you are saying?'

'Got it in one,' he answered. 'You're not as stupid as you look.'

Tom, looking up from the notes in front of him, then spoke. 'Mr Grace, I see that you've already served two years in prison for attacking someone. I understand it was quite a brutal attack. During your arrest yesterday you also attacked a number of police officers. That alone is likely to get you another sentence. So, with your record, do you seriously think any jury will believe you?'

Grace, ignoring Tom's final point, said, 'How are you feeling after Billy gave you a bit of a smack yesterday?'

Tom was not willing to rise to the bait but, even if he had been, Grace's lawyer's sudden intervention would have prevented him. 'Do you have any other evidence against my client? Because all you have presented so far is pure conjecture. My client has told you that he was not there on the night in question. It's obvious someone was impersonating him. If you can't produce any real evidence then I will be requesting his immediate release.'

Grace started to laugh. 'Nice one,' he said.

Tom, Milner and DC Bennett were, once again, back in Tom's office on the fifth floor. There was a discernible air of despondency in the room.

'Will we have to release him?' asked DC Bennett.

'As his lawyer said, unless we have any new evidence, I suspect we will,' answered Tom. 'Well, on bail, that is.' He then added, mainly in an attempt to lift spirits, 'But we have a bit of time and even if he is released, I still think we have enough to bring him to court. Then, of course, it's up to the jury.'

An uncomfortable silence followed. It was DC Bennett who spoke first, articulating what was obvious to them all. 'What we need is definite evidence that it was Grace outside Birkett's house. The CCTV footage shows a man – Grace – holding a petrol can. As far as we can see, Grace is not wearing any gloves. If we could find that petrol can then we might also be able to find more of his DNA.'

'If he's smart he would have got rid of it long ago,' replied Milner, giving little hope to DC Bennett's idea.

'He might be smart,' said Tom, 'but he's also arrogant, and that is often a dangerous combination.' Suddenly his own words seemed to trigger something in his mind. 'When we first went to Grace's place in Chelmsford the van was parked on the drive outside the front of the house. Weren't there CCTV cameras on the house?'

'Yes, that's right,' answered DC Bennett. 'I remember seeing them when I staked out the place.'

'Are you suggesting they might show him with the petrol can?' asked Milner.

'Why not?' said Tom. 'In any event, the footage should make for interesting viewing. Why don't you get hold of the footage from the security company? I seem to remember their name was alongside the front electronic gate. But be discreet.'

Milner and DC Bennett, slightly cheered by the fact that at least they were doing something, walked out of Tom's office, leaving him to finish dealing with the reports still on his desk. After a while, deciding he needed a bit of a rest from them, he refreshed the emails on his computer and his eye immediately fixed on one recently sent by Jim Gilbert. He opened it and read the contents.

From: Jim Gilbert
To: Tom Stone
Subject: Sharon Storey

Tom,
Here's the information you were after.
Sharon Storey, maiden name of Chambers, age 39, married to Steve, two children, Jason and Amelia.
  Address: 63 Longton Road, Hendon.
  You owe me!

Cheers,
Jim

Tom printed the email, put it with all of the other information relating to the Susan Chambers murder and placed the file in the top drawer of his desk. He then stood up and walked out of his office.

'Jenny, I'll be downstairs in the video room if anyone needs to contact me. I have my mobile with me.'

'Will you be long, sir?' she enquired.

'I shouldn't be,' he answered, and he made his way towards the lift.

When he arrived at the video room he sat down in front of the same machine he had used previously. He pressed one of the buttons but nothing happened. He pressed it again and suddenly the machine sprang to life, with the video footage running so fast that he couldn't make out anything at all. He pressed the 'stop' button and the footage froze. Repressed the 'start' button and, once again, the footage was flying by at breakneck speed. He finally pressed the 'stop' button again, picked up his phone and made a call.

'Milner, I'm in the video room. I'm not sure what you've done to the machine but it just won't work. Can you come and sort it out?'

Within a few minutes, Milner was in the room and had reset the machine to its original position. 'Which button did you press, sir?' he asked.

'That one, like you told me to,' he answered.

'Did you press anything else, sir?'

'I may have pressed that one,' replied Tom, pointing at a

button which had three chevrons above it, all pointing to the right.

'That's the one which fast-forwards the footage,' he explained.

'I think you had better stay here for a few minutes,' Tom said, 'just in case it decides to play up again.'

Milner smiled to himself. This wasn't the first time and, no doubt, wouldn't be the last time that technology had got the better of DCI Stone.

This time Tom pressed the correct button and the screen immediately showed footage of a man buying what looked like cans of lager in an off-licence. The man was Jimmy Griffiths and the time, at the top of the screen, was 22.10.

Chapter 54

Tom had spent the night at Mary's. Although she was clearly still concerned about what might happen, the previous night's anger – at least the anger directed towards Tom – had disappeared. She had organised someone to look after the shop and had spoken with her son, Greg, and arranged to go and stay with him for a few days, beginning on Sunday. The pretext she had used was that she had the opportunity to take a few days off and so thought it would be a good idea to visit him and his wife.

Once again, Tom waited until Mary was on her way to work before he himself left for work, but instead of driving to the station in West London he was headed towards Hendon in North London. Travelling from his start point in Bagshot to his destination in Hendon was never the easiest of journeys, and as he found himself inching his way towards Hanger Lane he understood just why. The sheer volume of traffic and the seemingly interminable number of sets of traffic lights combined to make it one of his most unpleasant ever driving experiences. Fortunately, though, as he drove east along the North Circular the traffic began to thin out a bit, and eventually he found himself on the A41 and not far from his destination in Hendon.

Longton Road was one of the main roads in Hendon and so Tom had little difficulty in finding it. Soon he was standing outside number sixty-three. He rang the bell and stood back and it wasn't long before the door was opened by a woman of above-average height in her mid-to-late thirties.

'Can I help you?' she asked, politely.

Tom held out his identification card. 'I'm Detective Chief Inspector Stone from the West London Police Force. Are you Sharon Storey?'

The woman suddenly looked very worried. 'I am, yes. Oh, my God, something's happened, hasn't it? Is it Steve?'

Tom quickly reassured her. 'Please don't worry. Nothing has happened. I apologise. I should have called you earlier to let you know I wanted to speak with you.'

Tom's words appeared to have the desired effect. 'That's a relief. For one moment I thought something terrible had happened.' A slight pause was followed by, 'How can I help you?'

'Is it okay if I come in?' he asked.

'Would you mind if I had another look at your ID? You can never be too careful these days.'

Tom passed his card to her and waited while she examined it closely. Apparently now convinced that he was, in fact, who he said he was, she handed him the card and said, 'You'd better come in, then.'

She led him into the downstairs room. Whilst the room itself was quite small it was very neat and tidy, and gave the impression of being much bigger than it actually was.

'Can I get you something to drink?' she asked.

'That's kind of you, but I'm fine for the time being,' he replied.

After they were both seated, Tom said, 'If you don't mind, I'd like to speak with you about your mother, Susan.'

'My mother?' she answered, clearly surprised. 'But she died a couple of years ago.'

'Yes, I'm sorry about that,' he said sympathetically.

'To be honest, I didn't really know my mum that well. I know that sounds strange, but she had me when she was only sixteen and, because she had problems and didn't know who my father was, I was placed into care when I was about six and later with various foster parents. When I was younger I did sometimes get a birthday card from her, but even they stopped when I became a teenager. I never actually saw her again.'

'That must have been very difficult for you,' suggested Tom.

'Well, it wasn't ideal, but you sort of get used to it.' She hesitated and Tom could see she was beginning to get upset. 'Anyway, that was a long time ago. As I said, I didn't really know her and so I'm not sure how I will be able to help you.'

Tom decided that getting straight to the point would probably be the best strategy. 'After your mum died I understand you were given some of her personal possessions. Do you still have them?'

Sharon looked at Tom quizzically. 'They were just a few bits and bobs in an old shoebox. That's all. Why do you want to see them?' she asked, not unnaturally.

'I'm investigating a related case and it's possible some of your mum's possessions might be able to help.'

'Really?' she asked, dubiously.

'Do you still have them?' he asked for the second time.

Despite clearly not being totally convinced, Sharon said, 'I'll just go and see if I can find them. I won't be a minute.'

True to her word, not long after, she returned with an old, faded shoebox in her hand. 'This is all I received,' she said, handing it to Tom.

'Thank you very much,' he replied. 'Do you mind if I look through it?'

'Please go ahead,' she simply replied.

The box had been secured with string and he had a little difficulty untying the knot. Eventually he placed the string to one side and removed the lid. As Sharon had indicated, even this small shoebox was far from full. He removed a small box covered in a red velvety material. When he opened it he could see that it contained a few inexpensive-looking rings, together with a couple of necklaces and a pair of large earrings. In the shoebox was also a bundle of old black-and-white photographs, some of which were torn, whilst others were very faded.

'I think those are photos of Mum's parents,' explained Sharon. 'I can only vaguely remember them, though. That one,' she said, as Tom looked at one specific photo, 'is Mum, when she was little, with her parents, apparently on holiday in Southend.'

Tom retied the bundle and placed it back in the box.

There was a small tin box in the corner of the shoebox. As he took off the lid he could see what looked like two different locks of hair. One was dark brown and quite thick whilst the other one was blond and very sparse and wispy. The box also contained two white plastic bracelets. As he looked more closely at them he could see the words *Chambers* and *dob: 20/05/76* written on one. The other one also had the name *Chambers* on it, but this one had the date *15/02/86*.

Tom looked up. 'I assume this one,' he said, holding up the first one, 'is yours.'

'That's correct. I think the dark hair is also mine. I didn't even know she had kept all of those things until I received the box.'

'So whose is this one?' he asked, now holding up the bracelet showing the date *15/02/86*.

'I've got no idea,' she replied. 'Perhaps Mum had another baby? But, if she did, then this was the first I knew about it. As I said, apart from a few birthday cards, we never had any contact.'

Tom then picked out a piece of paper. It was folded in half and, again, quite faded. He could see it was Susan Chambers' own birth certificate, giving her date of birth as 2nd May 1960, and her place of birth as Barking, Essex.

As he fully opened the birth certificate a slightly faded Polaroid colour photograph suddenly fell out. This one showed two smiling couples together on a large sofa, with a few other people in the background. Each of the women on the sofa sat on the lap of a man, who, in turn, each had one arm resting on the shoulder of his partner. The man seated on the right-hand side of the sofa was holding a cigarette in his left hand. In front of the sofa was a small table, on which was placed an overflowing ashtray surrounded by different-sized drinks glasses.

'Is this your mum?' asked Tom, pointing towards the young woman seated on the right-hand side of the sofa.

'Yes, it is, although I don't know who the others are.' She then continued, quite wistfully, 'Actually, she looked quite pretty.'

Tom continued to look closely at the photograph, something in it clearly holding his attention. Eventually he asked, 'When do you think it was taken?'

She took the photograph from him and examined it. 'I would say sometime in the eighties. Mid-eighties probably, looking at the big hair.'

'Would you mind if I took these with me?' he asked, holding both the photograph and the small tin containing the birth bracelets and locks of hair. 'I will make sure you get them back.'

'Do you think they are important?' she asked.

'I really don't know,' he answered truthfully.

Chapter 55

It was early afternoon by the time Tom arrived back at the station. As he walked into his office, Jenny saw him and he could immediately tell, from her expression, that something was worrying her.

'Sir, just to let you know, DCS Small has called a couple of times. He wants you to call him back straight away,' she said with some urgency.

'Did he say what it was about?' he asked.

'No. He just said call him as soon as you return.'

'Could you ask DS Milner to come up?' he said.

'I'm afraid DS Milner is not in today. He has taken a day off,' she answered, before adding, almost defensively, 'I understand he did agree this with you.'

Suddenly Tom's memory sprang back into life. How could he have forgotten it was today that Milner was having his interview for the Brighton role?

'That's right, he did,' he said.

After he had settled himself in his office, it wasn't long before Jenny arrived with the usual coffee. She placed it on his desk and was just about to leave when Tom said, 'How are you now? Are you starting to enjoy working here a bit more?'

This momentarily caught her off-guard. 'Why? Is there a problem?' she asked.

'No. No problem at all. In fact, DS Milner, DC Bennett and I were all saying recently just how well you had settled in and that we would really miss you if you left.'

Tom's words appeared to reassure her. 'That's very kind of you all. I'm really starting to enjoy it. It's taken a bit longer than I expected, but I now feel as though I'm part of a team.'

'That's good,' he replied. 'As you know, my appointment is only temporary, but, if you would like me to, I would be more than happy to put in a good word for you with whoever takes over.'

'Thank you, sir,' she replied. 'I think I would like that.'

After she left he realised he could no longer put off returning DCS Small's call.

'Good afternoon, sir,' he said, attempting to sound cheerful.

DCS Small, not for the first time, dispensed with any pleasantries. 'Where have you been?'

'I had to visit someone,' he answered as vaguely as possible.

'Who?'

'It was someone who I thought might be able to help us with the Inanescu murder,' he answered, not entirely truthfully, making the judgement that now was probably not the best time to inform DCS Small about his unofficial enquiries relating to the Susan Chambers murder. 'But it proved to be a bit of a wild goose chase, I'm afraid.'

This either placated DCS Small or, more likely, took him on to the reason for his earlier calls.

'Well, whilst you've been out on your wild goose chase, I've had a call from Mr Grace's lawyer and I have to tell you it wasn't just to pass the time of day. He's threatening all sorts of legal actions unless we immediately release his client. When are you planning to release him?'

'Well, actually, sir, the idea is to keep him as long as possible, not release him,' he replied with undisguised sarcasm.

This wasn't lost on DCS Small. 'Don't get smart with me, DCI Stone. You know exactly what I meant. So you have enough to hold him longer, do you?'

Tom quickly realised he wouldn't win this particular battle. 'At the moment, the answer is "no". We are, though, currently actively pursuing a couple of other possible leads.'

'Well, I suggest you catch up with those particular leads as quickly as possible,' he said sharply, 'otherwise you might find Grace's lawyer pursuing *you*.' He then added, ensuring Tom got the point, 'If you don't have anything else by this time tomorrow, then release him.'

Although he didn't like to admit it, Tom knew DCS Small was right. The evidence they had was strong but not game-changing. It was enough to get Grace to court but not necessarily enough to get him convicted. They desperately needed another visit from Mr Seneca.

When he had hung up, Tom took out the photograph which Sharon Storey had given him. Once again he looked at it closely. He then pressed the buzzer on his intercom, and it was almost immediately answered by Jenny.

'Yes, sir,' she said. 'Do you need something?'

'Jenny, could you please come in?'

She soon appeared.

Tom passed her the photograph. 'Could you please scan this photo and then email it to me?'

'I'll do it straight away.' She walked out of his office.

It wasn't long before his computer 'pinged' and he could see the email, together with an attachment, from Jenny.

He clicked on the attachment and the image of the two couples appeared on his screen. Once again, he concentrated on the photo, and then he clicked on the 'zoom' function, now focusing his attention on both men. Suddenly he looked up, away from the screen, and sat back in his chair, staring at some point in the distance, deep in thought.

He was suddenly startled when his intercom buzzed.

'Sir, I've just spoken with DS Milner,' Jenny said. 'He's on his way back to the station.'

'Really? I thought he was on holiday.'

'I thought he was, as well. Anyway, he just wanted me to let you know.'

'Okay, thank you. Ask him to come up when he arrives.'

Although it was a fairly pointless exercise to speculate on why Milner wanted to get back to the station, Tom still couldn't help thinking that it must be related to his job interview. But he would soon find out.

In the meantime he printed a couple of copies of the photograph and, together with the original, put them into the Susan Chambers file. But not before he had removed the email from Dr Panton. As he once again read the contents he realised that his enquiries had suddenly, and quite unexpectedly, led him into potentially dangerous territory. When he'd started looking into the Susan Chambers case file it had mainly been due to professional curiosity. Yes, there had been a few anomalies, but, then again, the same could be said about most of the investigations he had been involved in over the years. But this was different. It looked as though, at least based upon the time when Susan was killed, an innocent man – Jimmy Griffiths – had been wrongly accused and, subsequently, convicted of her murder. Based upon what he had seen in the photograph, this case had now moved in a quite dangerous and much more sinister direction.

Chapter 56

'Sir, DS Milner and DC Bennett are here. Should I ask them to come in?'

'Thanks, Jenny. Yes, ask them to come in.' It was later in the afternoon and, as Tom's thoughts had kept returning to what he had seen in the photograph, he now welcomed Milner's appearance.

'I thought today was your day off,' said Tom, directing his implied question towards Milner.

'It was, sir, but when DC Bennett called me to tell me what he'd found, I had to get back.' Once again, Tom could tell by Milner's body language, as well as the way in which his speech had quickened, that he thought whatever he was just about to say was good news.

And it certainly was good news. Whilst Milner had been in Brighton, DC Bennett had spent the morning at the offices of the company which had installed the security system at James Grace's property. He had reviewed the CCTV footage for the day when the attack on Birkett's house had taken place. It hadn't been long before he had seen what they had all been hoping for. The footage clearly showed Brendan Grace putting a petrol can into the white van. But there was a bonus. On a hunch, DC Bennett had continued to run the footage. His hunch had paid off because it also showed Grace returning. Not only could he be seen putting the can in the van, but there he was again, after the arson attack on the house, returning in the same white van. The very same van which he had claimed had been stolen earlier that day.

'Do you have the footage?' asked Tom.

'Yes, sir,' answered DC Bennett. 'The tapes are downstairs.'

'Thank goodness for security cameras,' Tom said, to no one in particular. He gave a light laugh. 'Ironic, really, isn't it? The evidence which is likely to put him away was provided to us by their own security system.'

'That's true,' replied Milner, with sudden realisation. 'Although I doubt, somehow, he will appreciate the irony.'

'Okay,' said Tom. 'Let's make sure we do everything by the book. I don't want his lawyer to be able to use some fancy legal footwork in order to get him released. Inform him that we will be resuming our interview with Brendan Grace later today.' He paused briefly, before adding, 'And great work. I think there's a real danger that we might actually now have something which sticks.'

After Milner and DC Bennett had left, Tom's thoughts immediately returned to the Susan Chambers murder. He was now convinced Jimmy Griffiths had not killed her and, although he didn't know who the killer was, he was beginning to develop a few ideas as to why she had been killed. The key, he now suspected, was contained in the photograph.

He clicked on the search engine icon on his computer and typed in a name. He never failed to be impressed with just how much detailed information was included in a Wikipedia profile. As he read through the contents he made a number of notes on a separate sheet of paper. After he'd finished this he typed in a name and added the words *contemporaries at Oxford University 1983–1986*. Soon he had tracked down a fairly long list of people who had been at the university at the same time. He printed off the list. He then typed in the same name but with the title of a specific academic course. This time the list was much shorter. As he looked down it he immediately recognised a few of the names, as they all now held prominent positions in society, but there was one in particular which caught his attention. He printed this list and placed it alongside the first one, and then sat back in his chair and wondered where all of this would lead next.

Later, they were back in the interview room. Tom and DS Milner were seated at one side of the desk with Brendan Grace and his lawyer immediately across from them. Behind Tom and Milner was a uniformed police officer.

'Unless you have any additional evidence, and I mean real evidence, not the tittle-tattle you presented yesterday, you have to release my client immediately,' said Grace's lawyer, clearly believing in the principle that attack is the best form of defence.

'I understand that,' replied a subdued Milner. 'But before we have to do that I'd just like to go over a few points again, if that's all right with you and your client.'

'Please feel free,' answered his lawyer, 'but let's try and get this over with as quickly as possible.'

Milner, now turning to look at Grace, said, 'Yesterday, you said how it couldn't have been you outside Terry Birkett's home, on the night of the arson attack, because your white van had been stolen earlier that day. Is that correct?'

'I told you all of this yesterday,' replied Grace in his usual unhelpful tone.

'But, just for clarification, could you please confirm that was the case?' asked Milner.

'Yes, that's right,' he answered.

There was a short silence as Milner searched through his file, eventually retrieving a few photographs. He placed the first one on the table in front of Grace. 'So how could it be that this photograph shows you, with a petrol can, alongside your van? And how is it that this photograph,' he said, placing another one alongside the first, 'shows you in the same moment directly outside a house, which, if you look closely, you'll see is your house? Then there's this one,' he said, placing a third one with the others, 'which, in my opinion, is possibly the most interesting. As you can see, it shows you a few hours later getting out of the very same van – the one you said had been stolen earlier in the day – once again outside your house.'

There was no immediate response from Grace, who, instead, turned to look at his lawyer, presumably for some assistance.

'These photographs,' said his lawyer, pointing dismissively at the three photographs, 'are clearly fake. They are all part of the conspiracy to frame my client.'

It was now Tom's turn to speak. 'Unfortunately for your client, these are stills taken from video footage. This video footage.' He gestured to Milner, who pressed a button on the machine, and the recorded footage from the security cameras immediately started to play. It began at the point where Grace could clearly be seen with the petrol can in his hand. After this had been shown, Milner fast-forwarded to the time when Grace returned to his house.

'Incidentally, thank you, Mr Grace, for this,' Tom said. 'It's not often the arrested person provides us with the evidence.'

Tom's sarcasm was not lost on Brendan Grace. 'You bastard!' he shouted, before lunging forward in an attempt to grab hold of Tom. Fortunately the desk between them restricted his ability to get hold of Tom and the police officer standing immediately behind Tom, together with Grace's own lawyer, were able to restrain him.

'Brendan. Don't be a fool. You'll just make it worse,' his lawyer said.

After things had calmed down, Tom resumed. 'So, let's just recap on what we have. First, there is a strong suggestion that there was an ongoing vendetta between Terry Birkett and your family, probably the result of your drug incursions into his territory. Secondly, immediately before the arson attack, there is CCTV footage showing you, and your van, close to his house. Next, your DNA was found on a cigarette just outside the front door of his house. And now we have your own CCTV which shows you, petrol can in hand, just about to get into the van, and then your return a few hours later.'

Before either Grace or his lawyer could respond, Tom added, 'Mr Grace. You will shortly be formally charged with the attempted murder of Terry Birkett and his family.'

Chapter 57

'Surely we now have enough evidence to get a conviction?' asked DC Bennett. It was early evening and the three of them were now in Tom's old office.
'I would be amazed if we didn't,' answered Tom. 'The evidence is so compelling. Okay, there is some circumstantial stuff as well, but, when taken all together, especially now we have Grace's own CCTV footage, it is such a strong case. But,' he added, as a caveat, 'I've learnt not to try and second-guess what a jury decides. What we need now, though, is similar strong evidence which would also get James Grace convicted. Speaking of which, what's the current situation with him?'
It was DC Bennett who answered. 'Well, we now have the name of James Grace's fellow gang member. His name is Johnny Taylor and he's currently serving life in Belmarsh Prison. I've arranged to go and visit him tomorrow. Would you like to come along, sir?'
'Definitely, if that's okay. I don't expect we'll get anything out of him, but you never know. Make sure you bring those photos of Grace's house and cars with you.' He then faced Milner. 'Anything from the fraud people yet?'
'Nothing, sir, other than a confirmation from them that they have received my report.'
'Okay,' said Tom, looking at his watch. 'I don't think there's much else we can do tonight, so why don't you both go home? I'll see you both bright and early tomorrow morning.'
Tom was tempted to ask Milner to stay behind so that he could ask about his job interview but, on reflection, thought it was perhaps not the most sensible thing to do. Probably better to leave it to Milner to make the first move.
Tom arrived back at Mary's just as she was preparing to serve dinner. 'Just in time,' she said as he walked into her kitchen. 'I'm afraid you'll have to eat by yourself tonight. I ate

earlier as we have rehearsals tonight. You hadn't forgotten, had you?'

'No, I just got a bit delayed, that's all,' he answered, not totally truthfully. 'How are you getting there?' he suddenly asked.

'Don't worry,' she said, 'Tony is taking me and bringing me back afterwards. In fact, he should be here any minute.'

It had become clear to Tom, since their initial uncomfortable conversation, that Mary was now trying very hard to lead as normal a life as the circumstances allowed. From Tom's perspective, however, this presented him with a bit of a dilemma. On the one hand it was good that Mary was carrying on with her life, but, on the other, he also felt it was still prudent to minimise the time she spent alone.

It was the following morning, and Tom and DC Bennett were in a small interview room inside Belmarsh Prison. Facing them was Johnny Taylor, James Grace's one-time gang associate.

'What do you want to see me for?' asked Taylor.

'We'd just like to speak with you about your association with James Grace,' answered Tom.

'Jimmy?' he replied. 'That was a long time ago.'

Taylor was below average height but very solidly built. He had lost most of his hair and what remained was a steel-grey colour and shaved very short. Although he was in his mid-fifties his well-worn face suggested someone quite a bit older.

'Have you seen him lately?' asked Tom. He immediately regretted his phrasing.

Taylor looked at him with something on the border between amusement and contempt. 'I don't know whether you've noticed, but I've been banged up in here for quite a while. Maybe next time I get the day off I'll drop in and see him.'

'Yes, sorry. That was a stupid question,' said Tom. 'What I meant to say was have you been in contact? Do you know where he lives? That type of thing.'

'Why do you want to know?'

'Let me be totally honest with you. We are still looking for the money which you and Grace stole from the security van job, or, at least, would like to know what happened to it. I was hoping you might be able to help.'

'And why would I want to do that?' he asked, clearly amused.

'Well, for one thing, you are in here and Grace is outside, living the life of luxury. I just wondered how you felt about that.'

'Good luck to him. That's what I say,' he answered.

'DC Bennett, why don't you show Mr Taylor the photos?'

DC Bennett laid out a series of photos showing Grace's house as well as the assemblage of luxury cars parked outside the house.

'He's also owns a big holiday villa in Spain. In fact, the whole family have just returned from spending a holiday there.' Tom hesitated before continuing. 'Mr Taylor. I can't do anything about your sentence, but I might be able to make your time here a little more comfortable. All I'm asking in return is that you help us to find out what happened to the money. No one will find out. You have my word on that.'

'Your word?' he repeated with a contemptuous laugh. 'And what about my word?' he asked, suddenly displaying real anger. 'I've done a few naughty things in my time and usually paid the price. But I've also been fitted up, by you lot, for things I never done.'

Another uneasy silence followed before Tom spoke. 'I can't change what's gone, but I may be able to slightly change your future. That's all I'm saying.' He stood up. 'If you change your mind then just contact me,' he said, handing Taylor his card.

'Wait,' Taylor suddenly said. 'And you guarantee that no one will get to hear about this?'

'I do,' answered Tom.

'I don't want any favours for myself. I can handle it here, but I want something for my missus. She lives in a crappy little council flat. I want you to get her a better place so that the grandkids can come to see her. If you can do that then we'll talk.'

'I'll see what I can do,' answered Tom. He held out his hand.

Taylor, ignoring it, said, 'Just do that for me first.'

It was just after lunchtime when they arrived back at the station. As seemed usual these days, Milner was waiting for them. Tom briefly updated him on their conversation with Taylor.

'Are you able to do that, sir?' Milner asked, referring to Taylor's request.

'I've got no idea,' Tom answered honestly. 'I suppose it depends on how keen we all are to find out what happened to the money. But it's got to be worth a try.'

'Well, I've got some news for you,' Milner suddenly exclaimed. 'Birkett is willing to plead guilty to manslaughter.'

Chapter 58

'I think he must have reflected on what you said, sir, about not seeing his kids grow up,' Milner said. 'Anyway, whatever the reason, his lawyer says he's now willing to admit to manslaughter if we drop the murder charge.'

'Have you spoken with him?'

'Not yet, sir. I was waiting for you to return.'

'Okay,' said Tom. 'Set up the interview for this afternoon.'

When Tom arrived back at his office he immediately called DCS Small and updated him on the situation regarding Brendan Grace as well as Birkett's offer to plead guilty to manslaughter.

'I wondered where you were, yesterday, when you didn't arrive for our weekly review meeting,' said DCS Small. Tom was left trying to work out if that was intended as a rebuke or his attempt at humour. Before he had found the answer, DCS Small provided it for him. 'Well, at least, I suppose, you were doing something useful.'

Tom decided to let it go, particularly as he now needed DCS Small to do something. He then recounted this morning's visit to Belmarsh Prison to see Johnny Taylor.

'So let me get this correct,' said DCS Small. 'You are asking me to arrange for Taylor's wife to get better housing. Let me remind you that this man is a convicted murderer. How do you think that will look if the press get hold of it?'

'In my opinion, this is our best opportunity to find out what happened to the missing money. I know it was a long time ago, but think how much kudos the region would get if we were able to finally resolve this. It would also send a strong message to the public and criminal fraternity alike that we will continue our investigations, however long it takes.'

DCS Small's tone had softened when he answered, clearly having now thought about the upside rather than just the risks. 'It's most unorthodox, but I'll see what I can do.'

Tom, picking up his sudden positivity, said, 'Thank you, sir. But I think we need to move fast, otherwise Taylor might start to have second thoughts.'

'Thank you for that, DCI Stone,' he answered, a degree of sarcasm in his voice. 'I wouldn't have thought of that myself.'

Tom's next call was to his now-regular contact Jim Gilbert.

'Oh, no. Not you again,' said Jim as he answered his phone. 'What is it this time? Let me guess. I know. You want to buy me dinner. Yes, that'll be it.'

'Got it in one. I hope you've bought some lottery tickets because with your clairvoyance talents, you are sure to win.'

'If only,' he replied. 'In the meantime, though ...'

'This is a little bit off the beaten track, but I'm sure you'll still be able to do it.'

'Tom. Cut the flannel. Just tell me what you want me to do.'

And that was exactly what Tom did.

After that call, he took out a sheet of paper and began to write various names on it. Some of these he then linked together with a simple line. He'd found, over the years, that his brain seemed to work best when he had written things down and could see them in front of him. Usually it helped him to confirm the more obvious connections as well as, occasionally, to spot other, less likely, ones.

After he had finished he sat back and reviewed his work. It was amazing, he thought as he looked at it, how a simple visual name chart could be so informative. Either what he was looking at suggested something way beyond what he had originally intended or it was just a series of coincidences. And he had never believed in coincidences.

Later that afternoon Tom and Milner were back in the same interview room where Birkett's initial interview had taken place. Sitting immediately opposite them were Birkett and his lawyer.

'I understand you are now willing to admit to manslaughter in the death of Bogdan Inanescu. Is that correct?' asked Milner.

The lawyer began to read a statement. 'My client feels, given the unfortunate death of Mr Inanescu, that he would like to give you every help possible. My client feels nothing but remorse for his death and, therefore, is willing to now accept some degree of personal responsibility for that death.

Notwithstanding this, he wishes to make it absolutely clear that his death was totally unintentional.'

'I'm sure the family of Mr Inanescu will be hugely relieved to hear you describe his death as "unfortunate",' answered Tom, his sarcasm not lost on anyone in the room.

It was Milner who partly relieved the sudden increase in tension. 'Mr Birkett, please tell us what happened that night.'

His lawyer suddenly interjected. 'I have a statement from my client which covers that. I'd like to read it out.'

'Thank you, but I think it would be better for Mr Birkett if he was able to tell us in his own words what happened,' said Tom.

Birkett's lawyer turned to face his client. Birkett simply gave a shrug of his shoulders and then began to speak. 'I had been growing a few cannabis plants. That's all, and, anyway, it will soon be legal.' His words were not lost on Tom, as they almost matched what James Grace had said when they had first visited him at his house. 'There is a big demand for it and I was only giving people what they wanted.'

Tom was tempted to mention how he was selling, not giving away, the cannabis, but decided not to interrupt his flow.

'I'd heard, on the grapevine, that Grace had moved into our patch. Then he started selling stuff.'

'Just cannabis?' asked Milner.

'And other stuff,' replied Birkett. 'Crack, skunk, ecstasy.'

'How do you know that?' asked Milner.

Birkett looked at Milner with something bordering on contempt. 'Because we are there, on the streets. That's how.' After a short pause, he continued. 'So I phoned Grace to warn him off.'

'Did you threaten him?' asked Tom.

'You don't just move into someone else's patch without there being consequences.' He then added, apparently as justification, 'That's always been the way we handle things.'

'So how did he react?'

'He told me I was just small beer and that, if I was to accept his operation, then I could work for *him*. He told me how he would soon have a few more places.' He paused momentarily. 'How could I accept that? I'd be a laughing stock in my own manor.'

'Was that when you decided to do something about it?'

'I couldn't let it go, could I?' he answered, almost as though killing someone was the most logical reaction. 'I found out where he was growing his cannabis and, one night, went there to do something about it. I swear to God, though, I didn't know he had someone there. I had some weed killer and was putting the stuff on the plants when that bloke suddenly jumped on me.' He paused again. 'I didn't know he was there,' he repeated. 'He was a big bloke and was holding me down. Somehow, I managed to push him off but he just came at me again, this time, though, with a baseball bat in his hand. I hit him and then grabbed him. It was then he dropped the bat. I picked it up and...'

'You hit him with it,' said Tom.

'I had no choice. The bloke would have hit me with it if I hadn't done it first. I didn't mean to kill him. He went backwards onto the wall and then fell on the floor.'

'Did you see if he was okay?'

'Are you joking? He'd just tried to kill me. I just wanted to get out of there as quickly as possible.'

'But you still found time to start the fire. So you couldn't have been in that much of a hurry,' said Tom.

'That was stupid. I wasn't thinking straight. I'd cut my hand on one of the broken pots when we were fighting. I could see the blood on the floor. I knew if the blood was found it would soon be matched to mine. That's when I decided to torch the place to try and cover up the blood.'

'With Mr Inanescu still in it,' said Tom.

Once again there was a brief silence. 'I told you, I wasn't thinking straight.'

It was Milner who next spoke. 'What did Grace say to you when he phoned you?'

'What do you think? He threatened all sort of things. Told me how the Old Bill was now all over his place and that I'd pay.'

'Did you believe him?'

'Do you know Jimmy Grace?' he asked, once again with contempt dripping from each word. 'He's not the forgiving type. So of course I believed him.' He suddenly became quite emotional and there was a crack in his voice when he continued. 'I didn't expect him to try and torch the place when my missus and the kids were there, though.'

The lawyer cleared his throat. 'I'd like it to be a matter of record how my client has, reasonably and honestly, answered every single question which you have asked.'

'Noted,' Tom replied.

Chapter 59

They had just returned from the interview room and Tom could sense that Milner was on a bit of a high. There was nothing wrong with that. In this business, he thought, there were more failures than successes, and so it made sense to celebrate a success when it did come along. But, being a naturally cautious man, he couldn't quite bring himself yet to share Milner's elation.

Objectively they had now compiled a strong case against James Grace. They had evidence linking him to human trafficking and imprisonment. They also had evidence that he was involved in the criminal activity of growing cannabis. Birkett's claim that Grace was also selling drugs was useful but could not be definitely proven, not least because it was the statement of a self-confessed dealer, someone who also happened to have a very clear revenge motive. The phone calls between them might help, though. Tom had asked Milner to see if he could get hold of the recording of their conversations. This was never as easy as, given all of the advances in monitoring personal communications, it would appear to be, but it was worth a try.

Then there were Grace's construction business interests. Tom was sure this would prove to be fertile ground for his fraud squad colleagues. The problem here, though, was that this type of investigation was notoriously slow to bring to a conclusion.

Where he did, however, hold out some hope was in their dealings with Johnny Taylor. If they could just obtain evidence which proved that Grace had used some of the missing money, that could be a real game-changer. In the court of public opinion, someone who had funded their lifestyle of conspicuous consumption from ill-gotten gains was unlikely to win any support or sympathy. It was not as though Grace was some latter-day Robin Hood character who had used the stolen funds to help the disadvantaged. He was using them so he and his family could live the high life.

'We probably have enough,' Tom suddenly said, 'but, as I've said previously, it would be much better if we hit him with a big bazooka rather than a few rifle shots. So I think we should, for the moment, keep our powder dry.'

Milner didn't reply. Tom could see that, his probable mixed metaphors aside, Milner was also having difficulty with his military analogy.

'What I mean,' Tom clarified, 'is that we would have a much stronger case, and, more importantly, it would be far more effective, if we were able to present the court with a whole raft of evidence proving Grace's involvement in many different criminal activities.'

'Yes. I thought that was what you meant, sir,' Milner said. Before Tom could respond, he continued, 'Did you speak with DCS Small about Taylor's request?'

'I did. I'm waiting for him to get back to me. Unfortunately, I have a feeling that this type of unusual request is likely to take quite a while to move up and down the bureaucratic ladder. Anyway, in the meantime, I suggest you and DC Bennett start pulling together everything we have against Grace. Make sure that the statement from Birkett is fireproof. I don't want Grace's lawyer tearing it to shreds.'

After Milner had left, leaving Tom alone in his office, Tom's thoughts stayed with James Grace. He would definitely know by now that his son Brendan had been retained in custody and been formally charged with the attempted murder of Birkett and his family. Although his other son, Billy, had been released on bail, he too could look forward to a prison sentence as the courts didn't take too kindly to attacks on police officers. Then there was James Grace himself. Given everything which had happened to him and his family over the past few weeks, he must have realised that it was only a question of time before he was also arrested. Once he knew about Birkett's confession, that would simply reinforce his feeling. The key question, though, was how would Grace now react to all of this? Tom wouldn't have to wait long for his answer.

Chapter 60

'Sir, I have DCS Small on the line. Should I put him through?' Jenny had by now learnt, even though she had never met him, that a phone call from DCS Small was not normally something that Superintendent Stone looked forward to.

'Why not?' he replied. 'Let's get the day off to a good start.' It was the following morning and Tom, having just arrived at the station, was clearing his emails ahead of the daily task of report reading.

DCS Small got straight to business. 'Good. I'm glad that you are in. I want you over here as soon as possible. Commander Jenkins would like to see you about your request for better housing for Taylor's wife.'

Tom seemed to remember that, whilst he had made the original request, he'd got the distinct impression that, albeit grudgingly, he'd received the support of DCS Small. Still, it sounded as though there had been some progress.

'He's only available for a short while, so you'd better get over quickly.'

'Is there a problem, sir?' asked Tom, trying to determine the lie of the land.

'I'm sure, if there is, Commander Jenkins will inform you,' answered DCS Small, not very helpfully.

'I'm leaving right now,' said Tom.

Less than an hour later, Tom was seated outside Commander Jenkins' office.

'Can I get you something to drink while you're waiting?' asked his PA.

'Thank you. Coffee, white, with no sugar, please,' he answered.

'Hopefully Commander Jenkins shouldn't be too long,' she said, before adding, rather less encouragingly, 'but you never know. There's always something going on which requires his attention.'

But before she even had the chance to bring him his coffee, Commander Jenkins' door opened to reveal DCS Small, who simply said, 'You can come in now.'

Commander Jenkins was seated behind his large desk in the office and, without any preamble, said, 'So, what's all this about wanting me to get involved in the housing market?'

By now DCS Small had also sat down, leaving Tom standing in front of them.

'Do you mind, sir, if I sit down?' Tom asked. 'I feel like a schoolboy who has been asked to see the headmaster.'

Although Commander Jenkins began to laugh, Tom noted how DCS Small didn't.

'Please sit down,' said Commander Jenkins. 'Have we organised a drink for you?'

'Thank you, sir. Yes, it's all in hand.'

Almost on cue, there was a knock on the door and Commander Jenkins' PA entered, carrying a single cup of coffee.

'Thank you, Julie. I believe that is for DCI Stone.'

Julie placed the cup in front of Tom and then left.

'Now, why don't you tell me what all of this is about?' Commander Jenkins asked. 'DCS Small has already given me the outline but I'd like to hear it in your words.'

So Tom laid out the case. He told him about the death of Bogdan Inanescu in the house containing the cannabis plants. He told him about the trafficking of the Romanians. He told him about the attempted murder of Terry Birkett and the discovery of Brendan Grace's DNA as well as the incriminating video footage. Finally he told him about his conversation with Johnny Taylor.

'So you really think that there's a chance to get the money back, do you?' asked Commander Jenkins.

'I doubt very much we will get the actual money back. I suspect that was spent years ago. We might, though, get to find out what happened to the money. If we can prove that James Grace used it then there ought to be a good case for arresting him again as well as seizing his assets. In addition, of course, it would be a great boost to the Met's reputation. I'm sure the dailies will really go to town with the story.'

'And Taylor is willing to provide that evidence, is he?'

'He indicated that he would, but only if we could move his wife to better premises.'

'Do you believe him?'

'He's been a criminal all of his life, sir. So, under normal circumstances, of course I wouldn't believe him. But I had the feeling, when we spoke, that he just might have been telling the truth this time. I can't guarantee it, but sometimes you have to trust your instincts.'

Commander Jenkins was silent for a moment as he considered what he had just heard. Finally he said, 'Okay. I'll see what I can do. I'll have to run it by the Commissioner first, though.'

'Thank you, sir. I appreciate that, but will it take long? My concern, as I indicated to DCS Small, is that, if it does, then he might change his mind.'

Tom caught a glimpse of DCS Small's stern look.

'I'm afraid it will, as they say, take as long as it takes,' replied Commander Jenkins. 'DCS Small will let you know as soon as we hear back from the Commissioner.'

As that seemed to be the end of the meeting, Tom stood up to leave. This appeared to prompt another question from Commander Jenkins. 'Incidentally, how are you enjoying your new role?'

Tom had half-expected this question and so was able to give a considered answer. 'There are certain parts of the role I have found very interesting, but, and I have to be very honest with myself, I don't think I'm temperamentally suited to such a role.'

'Hmm,' said Commander Jenkins. 'Well, thank you for being so honest.' He offered his right hand to Tom. 'Good luck.'

The drive back to the station was one of those occasions when the driver found, upon arrival, that he couldn't remember anything about the journey. The reason for Tom's distraction and lack of awareness wasn't anything to do with Commander Jenkins' response to his request. In fact, if anything, he had steeled himself for his request to be declined, so the fact that Commander Jenkins had agreed to push it right to the very top was very encouraging. No, the reason why he had been so distracted was entirely unconnected.

When he finally returned to his own office he immediately switched on his computer and there, amongst the dozens of other emails, was the one he had been hoping to see. It was from Jim Gilbert. He was just about to open it when he also spotted one from the person at the Care Quality Commission to whom he had sent his report regarding Redbreast Home Care Services. Suddenly intrigued, he decided to open that one first.

It was brief and to the point, informing him that the Commission had now completed their initial investigation into the operations and procedures at Redbreast, and, based upon those findings, had, with immediate effect, withdrawn the licence that Redbreast needed in order to operate. A more detailed investigation was now under way which might possibly result in criminal proceedings against the owner Alan Wood. It finished by thanking him for bringing this matter to their attention.

Tom was genuinely stunned that such a quango, no doubt with all of the associated bureaucratic layers, could actually move so fast. Although he had expected Redbreast to be severely criticised, in truth he had not anticipated such a draconian outcome and suddenly felt genuine guilt that those loyal and hard-working staff would now, most likely, lose their jobs. But his attention was soon, once more, drawn towards the email from Jim. He opened it.

From: Jim Gilbert
To: Tom Stone
Subject: DOB: 15/02/86

Hi Tom,
Me (yet) again!
Susan Chambers gave birth to Peter John on 15th February 1986. I've attached a copy of the birth certificate (father unknown). It seems, not long after his birth, he was taken into care, as the team's judgement was that his mother would not be able to look after him. I checked to find out where he had been placed and it looks as though he's lived in various care homes during his early years. Anyway, his current address is 34 Redbridge Road, Bromley.
I hope this helps. Please don't call again for a while as I do have other work!!

Regards,
Jim

Tom took out the sheet of paper which showed all of the various names he'd previously written down, some of which he had then linked together. He now added the name *Peter John Chambers* and an additional few words under one of the other names. As he continued to look closely at his work his mind was suddenly made up. He definitely didn't believe in coincidences.

Chapter 61

It was Sunday afternoon and Tom was back at his own home. Mary had left for Greg's earlier in the day, trying to avoid the traffic.

As the last few days had passed, the earlier tension had continued to ease, possibly because neither of them had wanted to raise the subject. Mary had not asked what was happening with Grace and Tom had not volunteered any information. He had half-expected Mary to question whether her trip was necessary, but, as the week had progressed, she had seemed to become more excited about visiting her son and his family. In particular, she was really looking forward to seeing her six-year-old granddaughter, Louise, again. Living so far apart, together with her work commitments, meant she was unable to see her as often as she would have liked.

In truth, Tom was relieved that Mary was no longer around. Of course he would miss her; in fact, their extended time together had simply reinforced his feelings for her and he'd surprised himself with just how much he had looked forward to coming home to her each day. His relief was based upon the fact that she was now out of any immediate danger, however unrealistic.

He was also now beginning to recover from the pain in his ribs. Whilst he still felt the occasional, and unexpected, twinge, there were now long periods when he didn't even think about it any more.

Suddenly his phone rang to distract him from his bout of daydreaming.

'It's your friend here,' said the caller, in a voice he instantly recognised. It was James Grace. 'I just wanted to make sure you'd received my little message.'

'What message?' Tom asked, genuinely unsure as to what Grace meant.

'Have you not looked at your post yet?'

As Tom had been away for a few days there had been a pile of letters and leaflets on the hall floor when he had opened his door. He had picked all of them up and placed them on the kitchen table, thinking he would go through them later.

'I think you had better go and have a look,' Grace continued. 'You will want to see what's in it. It's the large brown envelope.'

Tom could see an envelope like the one Grace described amongst the others on the table. He walked to where it was, picked it up and, with an increasing sense of foreboding, opened it. It contained a large photograph. As he took it out, he immediately recognised Mary, who appeared to be in conversation with a young man.

'What is this?' asked Tom, now fearing the worst.

'I thought that would get your attention,' said Grace, a slight and disconcerting laugh suddenly appearing in his voice. 'I'll tell you what it is. It's your girlfriend buying some crack from a known dealer.' There was a pause. 'Who would have thought that your sweet, innocent girlfriend is an addict?'

'That's ridiculous,' said Tom, now clearly angry.

'Is it?' Grace asked, in an unnervingly calm tone. 'You of all people should know that, these days, anyone can be an addict. Anyway, the photo doesn't lie.'

There was another silence, this time a little longer than the previous one. Finally, Tom said, 'Are you trying to blackmail me?'

'I'm just saying if you scratch my back I'll scratch yours, that's all.'

'And I suppose scratching your back means letting your son go free.'

Grace laughed again. 'You're quick on the uptake, aren't you?' When he next spoke, though, the laughter had stopped and his tone had changed to one of more obvious menace. 'I told you not to do anything to hurt my family. You should have listened. When I say something, I mean it.'

Tom decided to play Grace at his own game by adopting a more assertive stance. 'And do you really think you can threaten me with something like this? It just shows how desperate you are.'

'Well, copper, let's see who is desperate when your pretty little girlfriend's picture is all over the papers. They'll have a field day. I could write the headline myself. *Famous Met detective's girlfriend is a crack user.* And there are more where that came from. Let's see what your bosses make of you then.'

'And how am I supposed to now let him go free? We've already charged him.' Tom was desperately trying to buy more time whilst he tried to consider what his options were.

'You can do it. If you contaminate some of the evidence then you'll have no choice but to let him go.' He then added, 'You've got two days. After that, look out for her photo on the front page of all of the papers. Enjoy the rest of your evening.'

Tom was stunned at this turn of events. His concerns, to date, had been focused on Mary's safety and not on something like this. Every time he thought about his conversation with Grace he felt a hollow sickness inside his stomach.

His immediate concern was whether or not he should speak with Mary about it. Of course, logically, he owed it to her to tell her what Grace was alleging. But, on the other hand, what was the point in worrying her if he could somehow get this resolved in the next couple of days?

The problem was, though, that he didn't think he could get it resolved in the next couple of days. However hard he tried, he couldn't envisage a scenario in which Grace did not or could not pass on the photo to the press. The worst possible scenario was that he didn't warn Mary and so the first she knew about it was when she saw herself in one of the dailies. And he was under no illusions that the press would, for some ethical reason, refuse to run with the photograph and accompanying copy. The story would make good reading. His recent 'fame', together with a love interest angle, would ensure that. No doubt it would be suitably worded in some form of legalese which protected the paper from any subsequent defamation or libel action. Even when Grace's claim was proven to be totally false – and he was absolutely convinced that would happen – the damage done to Mary's reputation would be almost irrevocable, whilst any subsequent apology issued by the papers would probably appear hidden away somewhere in a future edition. No, however difficult it would be, he would have to tell her. And now was as bad as any other time!

Chapter 62

'That's incredible, sir,' said Milner, after Tom had taken him and DC Bennett through the previous night's events. 'Mary must be absolutely devastated.'

It was the following morning and Tom, unsurprisingly, had slept little. He had called Mary, with the predictable result that she had become completely distraught. Initially, though, she had simply laughed when he had repeated Grace's allegation, thinking that it must be some sort of joke. It was only when she noticed that Tom wasn't joining in with her that she suddenly realised he was deadly serious. It was then that her initial laughter had first turned to anger, only to be quickly followed by fear and dread. Tom could hear her crying and it was quite a while before she had composed herself and was able to speak again. Slowly, Tom had then been able to hear her version of events.

It was a few nights ago when she and Tony had gone to rehearsals. Tony had dropped her off outside the hall where the rehearsals were taking place, whilst he found somewhere to park. Whilst waiting for him she was suddenly approached by a young man. Initially she had been a little alarmed as he seemed to have appeared from nowhere, but that concern was assuaged a little when he handed her a small white package, claiming that she must have dropped it. She had taken the package from him, quickly examined it and then handed it back, as, whatever it was, it did not belong to her. What was strange was that, suddenly, he was now holding a few £20 notes in his hand. She remembered how she had even thanked him for his consideration. He had then disappeared into the night and, a short while later, Tony had reappeared and they had both gone into the hall.

Grace had clearly set up the entire incident to effect a situation which could be photographed. Grace had mentioned how the young man was a known drug dealer. It was all very simple, really, but very effective nonetheless. Grace probably knew it would eventually be proven that it had been staged. By then, though, the damage would have been done, leaving both Mary and Tom to try to rebuild their lives, and reputations, after such a devastating event.

For once, Tom didn't mind Milner using Mary's Christian name. 'I think "devastated" hardly does it justice, if I'm honest,' he answered quietly.

'Is she staying with her son or coming home?'

'She wanted to come back but I eventually managed to persuade her to stay. Of course, I had to tell her son what had happened.'

'How did he react?' asked DC Bennett.

'Predictably, I suppose,' he answered. 'Initially he was angry. Angry at Grace and then angry at me. I don't blame him, really. Anyway, eventually, after he'd calmed down he agreed with me that Mary was in the best place.'

'That must have been difficult, sir,' said Milner.

'Not nearly as difficult as it now is for Mary and her family,' replied a now-pensive Tom.

A subdued silence followed, before Milner spoke. 'Why don't we pull Grace in? I'm sure we've got enough to hold him for a few days, anyway. That might at least give us a bit more time and delay the publication of the photo.'

'Milner,' answered Tom testily, 'I appreciate your motives, but let's try and base our arrest strategy on the evidence available rather than trying to second-guess when the photo might be published. We can't risk everything we've built up on him for this. That would be playing right into his hands.' He then immediately added, 'I'm sorry about that. I shouldn't take out my frustration on you. I know you are only trying to help.'

'That's okay, sir. I can't begin to understand what you must be going through. But there must be something we can do.'

It was DC Bennett who suddenly interjected. 'What about finding the man who gave her the package? It's quite a clear photo and so it shouldn't be too difficult. Why don't I show his photo to a few of the boys in the station?'

'Good idea,' answered Tom, in a far more positive manner. 'If he's such a well-known dealer, as Grace suggested, then someone downstairs must know him. Why don't you get on to that right away?'

'What about Mary, though? Are you happy, sir, that our officers will then know who she is?' asked Milner.

'You mean my girlfriend?'

'Well, yes. I was just thinking that, if we can arrest him quickly, then all of this might be unnecessary,' he explained, returning to his original suggestion.

Tom, touched that Milner was so obviously concerned about Mary, looked directly at him and said quietly, 'In normal circumstances I would agree with you, but, unfortunately, this is not normal. No one wants to preserve Mary's anonymity more than I do, but it's my judgement that, at this stage, we need all of the help we can get. I don't like it, but I'll have to live with the consequences.'

Suddenly, there was a real danger that the mood would now develop into some form of maudlin despair. Tom, recognising this, realised that it was his responsibility to make sure this did not happen.

'Look,' he said, in as confident a tone as possible, 'let's not allow Grace to set the agenda here. We need to stay in control of events. We know why Grace is doing this. He's simply trying to intimidate me. In some ways I'm actually quite relieved, because, at one stage, I seriously thought he would try and hurt Mary.'

Before he could continue Milner suddenly interrupted him. 'Hurt Mary? When did this happen?'

Tom, realising what he had just said, now felt as though he had little choice but to tell him and DC Bennett about Grace's threatening phone calls.

After he had finished, it was DC Bennett who asked the obvious question. 'Why didn't you tell us sooner, sir? We might have been able to do something.'

'I probably should have,' he answered, uncharacteristically contritely. 'But what could you have done? The threats were mostly veiled, nothing specific as such.'

'I remember now,' said DC Bennett, 'when we arrested his sons Grace made similar threats. At the time I just thought they were for the benefit of his wife.'

Milner, with a sudden burst of newfound confidence, now took it upon himself to articulate what they were all thinking.

'Sir, I know you are reluctant to do it, but it's *my* judgement that we can't wait. We need to pull him in now and then hit him with everything that we have.'
   So that's exactly what they did.

Chapter 63

Once they had made their decision, Milner and DC Bennett wasted little time in pulling all of the necessary paperwork together. As they were doing this, Tom called DCS Small to inform him of their plans.

Understandably, DCS Small questioned whether they had sufficient hard evidence to charge and hold Grace. Whatever doubts he may have had were increased even further when Tom told him about the photograph and, at that point, Tom thought he might be overruled. In the end, though, Tom made it almost into a point of principle. He didn't exactly use the words 'back me or sack me' but the implication was clear. Reluctantly – in fact, very reluctantly – DCS Small eventually agreed, and the following morning Grace was arrested. Predictably, the arrest was not incident-free as both Grace and, even more so, his wife Angie put up considerable physical and verbal resistance, accompanied by the occasional threat.

Tom and Milner, with a burly police sergeant also in attendance, now sat opposite James Grace and his lawyer. The lawyer was the same one who had represented Brendan Grace and, as they were in the same interview room and sat in the very same positions, the coincidence was not lost on at least three of them.

'Before we start, and for the record, I'd like to read out a statement,' said the lawyer. 'My client would like to register, in the strongest possible terms, how he and his family have been continually harassed and victimised over the past few weeks. It has become increasingly clear that, due to unknown reasons, DCI Tom Stone has been waging a personal vendetta against Mr Grace and his family. My client has now obtained evidence which will prove this.' He paused for a while, allowing what he had just said to sink in, before continuing. 'Whatever evidence is subsequently presented by DCI Stone and his officers is wholly predicated on this basis.'

'Well, let's go through that evidence, then,' replied Tom, looking directly at Grace. 'Detective Sergeant Milner. Why don't you summarise the case against Mr Grace?'

Milner opened the file in front of him and took out a single A4 sheet of paper. He seemed to examine it for a few moments before looking up and beginning to speak.

'A good place to start would be the fire at your property in Hounslow, and the death of Mr Bogdan Inanescu. Initially you denied you knew who Mr Inanescu was, but later you confirmed that he was staying at your property and at your request. You say he was there doing conversion work – although, incidentally, there was no evidence of any working tools at the property.' So far, very unusually, Grace had not uttered a single word, and so Milner continued. 'But he wasn't there to carry out conversion work. He was there to look after a large number of cannabis plants, which you were growing in the house. Unfortunately for Mr Inanescu, this had instigated a feud with another local drug dealer, who took exception to you opening your drug operation in what he considered to be "his" area. Terry Birkett is well-known to us as, amongst other things, a drug dealer. He has already admitted making a phone call to you when he threatened reprisals if you continued with your own drug operations.' Milner looked at Grace, who had his arms folded. 'We have the phone records confirming this call, as well as the one you later made to him. Incidentally, Birkett has also provided us with details of your other drug-dealing operation in the West London area.' He continued, this time with deliberate emphasis, 'Birkett has also admitted to the manslaughter of Mr Inanescu.'

Grace's lawyer suddenly interjected. 'This is all very interesting, but who is likely to accept the word of Terry Birkett, who, by your own admission, is a known criminal? You will be a laughing stock.'

Milner, not rising to the taunts, continued. 'Then we come to Mr Grace's role in another major crime, this time involving human trafficking and imprisonment. Working with Mr Florin Constantin, you' – once more he looked directly at Grace – 'ran an operation whereby you enticed Romanian nationals to come over to the UK, on the pretext of offering them legitimate work. But the reality was somewhat different, wasn't it? When they arrived in the UK you immediately took away their passports. During the day they worked for your building company, but at night you kept them under lock and key, in an outbuilding at Long Lane Farm. When we released the five Romanian nationals we also discovered more cannabis plants in the farmhouse.'

'And what evidence do you have implicating my client in any of this?' asked the lawyer.

'We have photographic evidence of Mr Grace's son, Brendan, arriving at the farm to collect them and then drive them to wherever they were working that day. Brendan Grace, incidentally, is currently in custody charged with assaulting police officers and the attempted murder of Terry Birkett and his family.'

At this point Grace unfolded his arms, leant forward menacingly and stared at Tom. 'If Brendan gets sent down I swear I'll kill you.'

Grace's lawyer quickly intervened and, pulling Grace back, said, 'My client is clearly upset and did not intend to threaten anyone.'

But Grace was not in any mood to show any contrition. Instead, he simply pushed the lawyer away from him and said, 'I mean it. I'll kill you.'

His lawyer, a look of resignation on his face, simply shrugged his shoulders and sat back.

'Let the record show that Mr James Grace has just made two serious threats against my colleague, Detective Chief Inspector Stone.' Milner referred to his notes and then continued. 'Documents were found at Mr Constantin's address which provided details of payments made by Mr Grace to Mr Constantin, relating to the illegal trafficking of these Romanians, together with other previous trafficking occasions involving Mr Grace.' He placed the A4 sheet in the folder, closed it and sat back.

'And that's it, is it?' asked a now-calm Grace. 'Growing a bit of weed and employing a few Romanians. It's hardly the Great Train Robbery.'

It was Tom who now spoke. 'Well, let's see if a jury finds your involvement in growing and dealing drugs, together with human trafficking and imprisonment, a bit more serious than you've just described.'

'And let's see what the papers make of your little girlfriend being a druggie. That should be interesting when they get the photograph,' said Grace.

'What photograph is that, Mr Grace?' asked Milner.

Once again, Grace's lawyer quickly intervened. 'My client is not aware of any photograph,' he said, rather unconvincingly.

Tom returned to his office after the interview with Grace and had only been back a few minutes when his phone rang. It was Commander Jenkins.

'I understand you now have James Grace in custody,' said Commander Jenkins.

'Actually, sir, we have James Grace and his son Brendan Grace in custody, together with Terry Birkett. The only one we had to release, on bail, was one of his other sons, Billy Grace.'

'Good work,' he replied, before adding, 'I'm the bearer of more good news. The Commissioner has approved my request to provide Mrs Taylor with alternative accommodation.'

Tom smiled to himself, as he had thought it had been his request. Notwithstanding this, he was pleasantly surprised by just how quickly Commander Jenkins had been able to obtain approval.

'We have a council house,' Commander Jenkins continued, 'which I'm reliably informed is in a very pleasant area. What's more, it's available immediately.'

Tom was now genuinely impressed. 'That's great news, sir. Would you mind emailing over the details, together with something official? I doubt very much that Taylor would simply take my word for it. He's bound to want to see something.'

'Already with you,' answered Commander Jenkins, a little smugly. 'I took the liberty of doing this before I called you.'

'Thank you again, sir,' said Tom.

'Just make sure we get some useful information from Taylor,' he replied.

Chapter 64

After Tom had read Commander Jenkins' email, he printed a copy, sat back in his chair and considered the options available to him. There was relief James Grace was now in custody and that they were now fully committed to acquiring a conviction. Based upon the evidence they had, the most important of which was his involvement in the trafficking of the Romanians, Tom was confident that Grace would eventually be sentenced. Notwithstanding this, though, he couldn't help feeling a slight sense of disappointment. Ideally, he would have preferred to also have some compelling evidence relating to his access to, and use of, the money stolen in the security van robbery – and Johnny Taylor was now the key to this.

There were also the threats which Grace had made against both him and Mary. Whilst Grace had threatened to kill him, there had been, over the years, quite a few similar threats made against him. There just seemed something different, though, about this one, and he didn't doubt that Grace was more than capable of carrying it out. Perhaps oddly, however, his main concern related to Grace's threat to publish the photo. His immediate dilemma was whether or not he had made the correct decision to, once again, warn Mary.

He had phoned her last night and had been able to sense her relief after he had told her about Grace's arrest. Of course, she had asked about the photo and he'd had to tell her about Grace's continuing threat, although he deliberately hadn't mentioned the manner in which Grace had made it. Perhaps, he now thought in retrospect, this had been a mistake on his part. Whilst he didn't want to worry her unnecessarily, equally, it was probably better if she was fully prepared for the worst. They had promised to speak again later and, somehow, he would try to make the point a bit more forcefully this time.

Then there was the issue of Susan Chambers' murder. In many ways this was now rapidly becoming his single biggest dilemma. His enquiries had reached a stage where he felt that, under normal circumstances, he would now have enough information to present all of the evidence he had accumulated. But these were definitely not normal circumstances. Although he now was in no doubt that Jimmy Griffiths did not kill her, he didn't know who had. What he did know, though, or at least strongly suspected, was why she had been killed.

As he continued to mull over all of these things, trying to decide on his next course of action, his intercom buzzer sounded.

'Sir,' said Jenny, 'I have DS Milner and DC Bennett outside. They would like to see you.'

'Thanks, Jenny. Ask them to come in.'

His ability to read Milner's body language had been receiving quite a lot of practice recently and, based upon this, he could immediately see that they were bringing good news. It didn't take long before Milner confirmed this.

'Good news, sir. We... well, DC Bennett, actually. Anyway, we've found the man who approached Mary.'

Tom had rarely seen Milner quite as animated as this and found himself quite touched by his obvious concern for Mary.

Milner continued. 'DC Bennett. Why don't you tell DCI Stone what you found?'

'I showed the photo to a few of the boys in the station, and it wasn't long before someone recognised him. Grace was correct. He is a well-known dealer. In fact, as it turned out, too well-known. His name is Ian George. He's a petty, small-time crook who has a long track record of dealing drugs.' As there were no questions, DC Bennett carried on. 'I was told where he usually hangs out and so, whilst you were interviewing Grace, I went there, just on the off-chance. I hadn't been there more than five minutes when he suddenly appeared, walking directly towards me.' He paused. 'Unbelievable, really,' he added, as though he couldn't quite believe his luck. 'So I stopped him and said that we had some new information implicating him in a big drug deal, which had occurred last night.' DC Bennett looked at Tom. 'At the time I couldn't think of anything else to say.'

'So how did he react?' asked Tom.

'All denials, of course. He said he could prove he was somewhere else at the time. Not surprisingly, he sounded very confident. Anyway, I persuaded him to come back to the station with me and make a statement to that effect. It was when we got back here that I showed him the photo.'

Tom could suddenly feel his stomach tightening. Although he almost certainly knew what the answer would be, there was still that small sense of doubt nagging away. DC Bennett quickly allayed any remaining doubt.

'He got quite upset when I told him the photo proved he was dealing drugs again. It was then he told me how he'd been approached by someone who said he'd give him fifty quid if he just walked up to the woman – Mary – and told her that the parcel was hers. He was also given some £20 notes and told to hold them so as to make it look as though they had just been given to him by the woman.'

'Was he able to give a description of the man?' asked Tom.

'Not really. It could be anyone. Late twenties. White. Average height. Wearing a hoodie so he couldn't clearly see his face.' When there was no follow-up question, DC Bennett continued. 'When he offered the package to the woman, she didn't know what it was and so didn't accept it. He then took it back to the man, handed it over, collected his fifty quid and then the man disappeared. He said it was the easiest fifty quid he'd ever made.'

The thought suddenly struck Tom that fifty quid could still ruin someone's life. As he struggled with this thought, Milner interjected, 'He's signed a statement to that effect.'

'Good work,' said Tom, trying hard not to display his relief.

'What about Grace, sir?' asked Milner. 'Should we let him know about this?'

'I don't see why not,' answered Tom. 'If he is going to send it to the papers anyway, then at least we now have the proof that it was a set-up designed to discredit me. But if it now puts him off sending it, then that's a bonus. It's probably best I'm not there when you tell him, though, otherwise he might not think rationally. Let his lawyer know that we intend to carry out another interview and then fix it up as soon as possible. Don't lead with this, though. Raise it towards the end, but don't make a big thing about it. We don't want him to think that we were worried about it.'

'We'll get on to it straight away, sir,' answered Milner.

As they were about to leave, Tom found himself saying to them, 'And thanks for your help.'

Chapter 65

It was the following morning and Tom, accompanied by DC Bennett, was once again at Belmarsh Prison and seated at a small table opposite Johnny Taylor.

'So what have you got?' asked Taylor.

'Last time we spoke, you mentioned how you might be willing to tell me what happened to the money that you and James Grace stole, in return for new accommodation for your wife. Is that still your offer?' asked Tom.

'Possibly,' answered Taylor, a little diffidently.

'Well, is it or isn't it? I don't want to waste my time if you are just playing games,' said Tom, making his impatience clear.

'Depends what you're offering,' replied Taylor.

'Okay. But before I say what I can offer, I have to tell you that this is a one-time offer. You'll see that it's signed by one of the top police officers in the Met. He will not negotiate on this. Either you accept it – today – or you don't, in which case we each go our separate ways.'

'So what is it you're offering?'

Tom placed a copy of Commander Jenkins' email on the table immediately in front of Taylor. Taylor picked it up, read it and then put it down again. 'And you can deliver this, can you?' he asked.

'I can,' Tom replied, 'provided that you sign a statement confirming whatever you tell me.'

Taylor, clearly thinking through the offer, remained silent for a while. Eventually he said, 'Okay, you've got a deal, copper.'

Tom tried hard not to betray his excitement, although it was difficult not to show it when he spoke. 'Let's start at the beginning, then. What did you do with the money after you'd stolen it?'

'After we'd nicked it we hid it in a mate's mother's loft. The plan was to leave it alone until the heat died down. We knew you lot would be watching us, so we had to play it real careful. When we felt the heat was off we were going to launder it, in small amounts. We didn't want to be seen being flash and playing Jack-the-lad with the money.' He was silent for a while and then added, with obvious disappointment, 'It would have worked, as well, except someone grassed us up.'

Tom adopted his well-tested strategy of continued silence.

'We both got nicked and served a stretch,' Taylor said.

'So did the money stay where it was whilst you were doing your time?' asked Tom, aware that they were now coming to the most interesting part of the story.

'For a few years, until we figured out what to do with it. Even though we were in different prisons it was easy to get messages to one another. Eventually we had to move it anyway. The old lady died and the council wanted the house for someone else. It was then that Jimmy came up with the idea of moving the money out of the country, to Spain. So that's what we did.'

'When was this?' asked Tom.

'Around '92, '93. Something like that. We'd keep our noses clean, get early parole and then, a bit later, move over to Spain. Happy days,' he added wistfully.

'But it didn't quite work out that way, did it? Well, at least, not for you,' said Tom.

'I was an idiot. Some mush who'd heard about me tried it on one night. I should have walked away but I'd had a few. He kept saying I was a waste of space, couldn't even get away with doing a security van. I snapped. I know I shouldn't have but I stuck him. I'd like to say that I didn't mean to kill him, but just then, at that point, I did,' he said, a crack now appearing in his voice.

Once again Tom let the ensuing silence work for him.

'And that,' said Taylor, having regained his earlier composure, 'is why I'm here and Jimmy is out there spending all my money.'

'Is that what he's doing?' Tom asked gently.

'How do you think he paid for his place in Spain or that fancy house of his?'

'The money wouldn't have paid for all of that, though,' suggested Tom.

'It was a lot more than the papers said. We couldn't count it all. There was so much that it even made my fingers sore. When Jimmy got out he told me there was only about two hundred grand left, but I heard later that he'd tried to stitch me up and that there was well over six hundred grand still sitting around in Spain.'

'What did you do? You don't seem to me to be the type of person who would take this lying down.'

'What could I do locked up in the nick doing life? He came to see me a couple of times and promised to look after my missus and the kids.' There was another brief silence after which Taylor spoke again, this time with anger in his voice. 'Do you know what he offered?' he asked rhetorically. 'He said he'd give her twenty-five grand. Twenty-five poxy grand,' he repeated for emphasis.

Tom's task was now to gently move the conversation back towards Grace and what he had done with the money. 'Did Grace buy the villa in Spain with the money?'

'That and a few other things. He found out that there was easy money to be made there by smuggling drugs. He even bought a couple of nightclubs so that he could sell direct to the punters and so make even more money.'

'Does he still have the clubs?'

'I heard that the Spanish cops started to turn up the heat on the drug scene in the clubs. There had been a few young kids dying from overdoses or from taking contaminated stuff that they bought in his clubs. Anyway, he sold up and got out.'

'Is that why he has the building business in the UK and all of the other properties which he owns?'

Johnny laughed. 'Do you really think Jimmy would be that interested in running a building company? He might do some work, but they are just legit fronts so that he can launder all of the money he gets from the drug dealing.'

'He told you all of that?' asked an astonished Milner.

'He did and, what's more, he's currently writing a statement to that effect.'

Tom had arrived back at the station, leaving DC Bennett behind to take Taylor's official statement.

Milner seemed lost for words, unable to process what Tom had just told him.

'I'm sure that I've mentioned before,' said Tom: 'don't ever underestimate the ability of criminals to provide evidence which implicates their old mates if they feel they've been stitched up. Honour amongst thieves only goes so far.'

'This is what we've really been waiting for. It opens up a whole new line of enquiry for us,' suggested Milner.

'I agree,' replied Tom, 'and not just here in the UK. I'm sure that our Spanish colleagues will be interested in all of this.'

'What should we do next, then, sir?' asked Milner, having now recovered some degree of equanimity.

'Well, first of all we should speak with the fraud squad people. It looks like this could be a real treasure chest for them. Then we need to get in touch with the Spanish authorities. To be honest, I wouldn't know where to start as there are so many lines of enquiry now available to them. Anyway, that will be for them to decide.'

'What I can't understand,' Milner suddenly said, 'is why Grace would risk all of this just to make a bit more money growing cannabis plants.'

'It's partly greed but also something a bit more intangible.'

'What do you mean by "intangible", sir?' asked a slightly puzzled Milner.

'I get the impression that James Grace has now got to the stage in his life where respect is almost as important as money. He's probably looking to establish some sort of family dynasty. Moving into another territory is a good way of demonstrating their power. Anyway, have you set up the next interview with Grace and his lawyer yet?' asked Tom.

'All set for tomorrow morning, sir. Are you sure you don't want to attend? After everything he's put you and Mary through, it might be good to see his reaction.'

'Milner,' he answered, in an almost headmasterly manner, 'I try not to confuse revenge with justice. Anyway, I have another appointment.'

Milner, having worked with DCI Stone for quite a while, knew when to remain silent.

'Just let me know when you've done it,' said Tom, making his feelings about attending crystal clear.

Chapter 66

It was the next morning and Tom was just about to leave his house. He had called Mary after he had returned home the previous evening. He hadn't told her everything, of course, just enough to reassure her. It had been a strange conversation, though. Somehow she had not sounded like her usual enthusiastic self. Polite, more than loving. Afterwards, he had thought that it had probably been him. He was still on a bit of a high after his conversation with Johnny Taylor and, perhaps, had expected Mary to be similarly excited.

Although Mary would be back in a couple of days' time, he suddenly realised how much he had missed her and how much he was looking forward to seeing her again. But in the meantime he had to try to put those personal thoughts to one side, as he had to make one of the most important decisions of his professional life. Before that, though, he had to visit someone.

Less than an hour later he was sitting in the front room of Mrs Bishop's bungalow in Ruislip.

'I just wanted to let you know what the outcome was concerning Mr Wilson,' he said, after he had placed his cup of tea on the small table at the side of the armchair. He then spent a few minutes telling Mrs Bishop about the main developments since they had last met. He omitted a few of the more graphic details but still managed to describe the events which had culminated in the suspension of Redbreast's home care operation.

'I knew there was something wrong about those people who came to look after Mr Wilson,' she said. 'I told you, didn't I?'

'You did, Mrs Bishop,' answered Tom.

'Anyway, I'm glad that they are all in prison.'

'They are not actually in prison, Mrs Bishop,' said Tom, correcting her as gently as possible, 'although it's possible one or two might end up there. But that's for the courts to decide.'

Tom's attempt at some sort of balance was clearly unsuccessful. 'If it was up to me I'd send them all to prison. That's the problem today; there's no proper law and order. People can get away with anything these days. You see it on the television all of the time.'

Tom waited until she had got this off her chest before saying, 'I'm sure you are right, but there are still a lot of people who work very hard looking after elderly people. Fortunately, not everyone is like some of those who Mr Wilson had.'

Tom could see that Mrs Bishop was not convinced and before she could make her feelings known again, he took something out of the plastic bag he had brought with him. It was a small porcelain figure of a black-and-white border collie. He handed it to Mrs Bishop.

'I'm sure Mr Wilson would have wanted you to have this. It will really look at home alongside the others which you have.'

Mrs Bishop took the figure from Tom and placed it with her existing collection. He could see that she was fighting back tears.

'Poor Mr Wilson,' she simply said.

Tom arrived at the station just before midday. As he was making his way to his office, Milner suddenly appeared.

'I've been waiting for you to arrive, sir. I thought you'd want to know how the interview with Grace went.'

'Of course I'd like to know,' answered Tom. 'Let's talk in your office. On the way, why don't you get some drinks? I'll settle up with you later.'

Milner, now smiling to himself, headed towards the drinks machine.

A short while later Tom, Milner and DC Bennett were all together in the office. Tom took a sip of his coffee and, as usual, pulled a face. 'This stuff doesn't get any better, does it? Not like the proper stuff that Jenny brings me. Milner, you should let her show you how to make good coffee.'

Tom's references to Jenny had become something of a long-running story but, for Milner, it was now wearing a bit thin and he knew his best response was simply to ignore it.

When it became obvious Milner was not about to respond, Tom asked, 'Okay, so how did he react?'

'Difficult to say, sir. His body language suggested pent-up

aggression but he didn't say a word throughout the entire interview. He just let his brief do all of the talking.'

'No doubt the result of him threatening to kill me during the last interview,' said Tom reflectively. 'He was probably under strict orders not to issue any threats this time.'

'As agreed, when his brief asked for bail, I dropped into the conversation how we were well-advanced pursuing other lines of enquiry which could result in additional charges being brought against his client. It was then that I also mentioned how we had a full statement from the man who had approached Mary.'

'And?' said Tom.

'Again, no response from Grace, although his brief did become a bit flustered and glanced a couple of times at him. But I might have been looking for something which wasn't there.'

'Well, at least we've given them something else to think about,' said Tom.

Tom eventually made his way up to the fifth floor. As was becoming the norm now, Jenny was waiting for him with a message.

'Don't tell me,' replied Tom, after she had mentioned the message, 'DCS Small wants me to call him back as soon as possible.'

'No, sir. It wasn't him this time. It was Commander Jenkins. He asked if you could call him back when you got the opportunity. He seems very nice.'

'Yes, I'm sure he is,' he replied. 'Anything else?'

'Nothing urgent. Well, apart from the reports. I'm afraid the pile seems to be getting higher each day,' she added, a bit defensively.

'Don't worry,' he said. 'Anything really urgent will, no doubt, work its way to the top.'

Tom began to walk towards his office. But, before he got there, Jenny suddenly said, 'Could I have a word with you, sir?'

'Of course. Why don't you come in?'

Tom could tell, simply by the tone of her voice, that this was unlikely to be good news. When they were both seated Tom asked, 'What is it you want to discuss with me? You haven't decided to leave, have you?'

'No,' she replied reassuringly, and then she added doubt when she immediately continued, 'Well, not really.'

279

'Why don't you just tell me?' said Tom quietly, sensing her sudden nervousness.

'It concerns David.' She immediately corrected herself. 'Sorry, I meant DS Milner.'

He could see she was struggling to get the right words out and so he thought he should help her. 'Is it that you two have been seeing each other and you're now worried that he might be leaving to work in Brighton?'

There was a sense of both surprise and relief in her voice when she answered. 'That's right. How did you know? Did DS Milner tell you?'

'I really don't mind if you call him by his Christian name, you know. Well, at least when it's just the two of us, that is. But, no, he didn't tell me. DS Milner tells me very little about his private life. I sort of worked it out for myself. It wasn't that difficult.'

This appeared to calm her nerves and when she next spoke it was with a light laugh. 'And we thought we were being really discreet.' She then became a bit more serious. 'He's been offered the Brighton job but is now unsure whether or not to take it.'

'Because of you, I assume.'

'Partly,' she replied, slightly blushing. 'But also because of you.'

'Me?' asked Tom.

'I don't know whether you know, but he has great respect for you. He feels a lot of loyalty towards you.'

Tom was suddenly genuinely moved. He'd suspected that might be the case but, somehow, it felt different when it was said, on his behalf, by someone else.

'Just so you know,' he said, 'I have great respect for him as well. But please don't tell him that I said that.'

Jenny laughed, albeit nervously, and then said, 'What do you think he should do, sir?'

It was a question he had been asking himself ever since Milner had mentioned the possibility of his leaving. 'For what it's worth, my strong advice,' he answered, 'although it's probably not that much practical use, is always to go with your instincts.'

As he said this he wondered whether or not he would be brave enough to follow his own advice.

280

Chapter 67

'That's a quite tremendous result,' said an enthusiastic Commander Jenkins. 'At the very least, between us and the Spanish, we should be able to make a good case for confiscating his assets.'

After his conversation with Jenny, Tom had returned Commander Jenkins' call. Understandably, Commander Jenkins had been eager to know the outcome of his discussions with Johnny Taylor and had asked Tom to come over, the following morning, to headquarters, to brief him and DCS Small personally. Tom had then spent his evening at home, reviewing all of the information he had gathered relating to the death of Susan Chambers and then writing a summary report which, chronologically, laid out the series of events that had got him to this point. He had finished by making an additional copy of his report.

Not surprisingly, given that the following day was likely to be the most important day of his career, he hadn't slept that well. As he lay in bed he repeatedly, in his head, went through all of the available evidence, as well as playing out all of the possible scenarios and the different approaches they might require. Despite his restless night, when he did wake, surprisingly, he immediately felt invigorated, no doubt helped by the upsurge in adrenaline flowing through his veins. Before his meeting with Commander Jenkins, however, he had had to make a slight detour to meet up with someone else.

'Thank you, sir. Let's hope so,' Tom replied. 'But, without you persuading the Commissioner, it wouldn't have happened.'

'I think you are being characteristically overly modest, DCI Stone. Don't you agree, DCS Small?'

'I do, sir,' DCS Small replied. 'DCI Stone is well-known for his modesty.'

Tom had arrived exactly on time for the meeting with

Commander Jenkins. He hadn't wanted to get there early and have time for doubts to start forming in his mind. Now, momentarily fazed, he wondered if this was meant as a genuine compliment or another of DCS Small's attempts at sarcasm.

Fortunately Commander Jenkins didn't give him any more time to dwell on this. 'Are you sure Taylor will stick with his testimony?'

'I don't see why not. Once he started talking it was clear just how much he wanted some form of revenge against Grace. I know that I shouldn't have, but I almost started to feel sorry for Taylor,' explained Tom.

DCS Small looked at his watch. 'If you'll excuse me, I'm afraid I have another meeting to go to.' He offered his hand to Tom, who took it. 'Well done again, and you won't forget to let me have your full report on this, will you?'

Tom was suddenly unsure as to whether or not this meant that their meeting was over and his own presence was no longer required. But, if that was the implication, then he had no intention of complying with it.

'I'll just finish my coffee, sir,' he said, 'if that's okay.' This bought him just enough time for DCS Small to leave the room. When he had gone, Tom continued. 'Actually, sir, there is one other matter which I would like to discuss with you, if you have the time.'

'I've got somewhere else to go shortly, but I'm sure I can spare a few minutes,' Commander Jenkins replied helpfully. 'Now, what is it you would like to discuss?'

Tom took a deep breath before answering. 'I'd like to speak with you about the Susan Chambers murder case.' He was looking for some sort of reaction from Commander Jenkins as he spoke. He couldn't be certain, but he thought he detected the merest narrowing of his eyes when he mentioned her name.

'And what, specifically, is it you would like to discuss with me? I would have thought that this would be something you ought to discuss with DCS Small.'

'Normally I would, sir, but given the potential sensitivity of the issue, I thought it only right that I should raise my concerns with you first.'

'Concerns?' repeated Commander Jenkins, his eyes now firmly fixed on Tom. 'What concerns?'

'Well, the main one being that I know that the man who was accused and subsequently found guilty of her murder couldn't possibly have done it.'

'And on what basis are you making this assertion?'

'I have evidence to prove it,' he replied, 'but I'll come to that later.'

Just then, there was a knock on his door and Commander Jenkins' PA entered. 'Sir, just to remind you that your meeting with the Assistant Commissioner starts in five minutes.'

'Please pass on my apologies and tell him that I have been unavoidably delayed,' he said calmly and politely, before adding, 'and hold all of my calls.'

'Yes, sir,' she replied, her slightly puzzled expression suggesting that this was far from normal.

After she had left, Tom said, 'Could I ask if you knew the deceased personally?'

For the first time, Commander Jenkins' usual equanimity appeared to disappear.

'With respect, Detective Chief Inspector Stone, why would I know her personally? She was a prostitute, wasn't she? Or are you insinuating something?'

'Not at all, sir. I just wondered whether you knew a bit more about her, that's all.'

'I knew *of* her. But that was because I usually do take an interest when someone is murdered. I am a police officer, after all,' he answered, albeit in a tone which suggested an increasing concern as to where their conversation was heading.

'I'm sure that's true, sir, but I wouldn't have thought your interest extended to being copied in on all of the case files and reports. Or are you saying that you read every single report relating to every single murder which takes place in London?'

'How dare you speak to me like that?' he demanded, now almost shouting. 'I suggest you stop right now. I don't know what you are trying to prove with this nonsense, but you are in serious danger of receiving a disciplinary charge. I was told that you were a bit of a loose cannon. I should have heeded the warning. You also seem to have forgotten that I'm your superior officer.'

But Tom had no intention of stopping. He was fully committed and well past the point of no return. He now had to trust his experience and instincts.

'So, sir, and just for the record, are you saying that you have never personally met Susan Chambers?'

'For the record? Who do you think you are to come here and question me like this? I won't stand for it.' Commander Jenkins was now in serious danger of losing all self-control. 'Get out!' he shouted. 'You haven't heard the last of this, Detective Chief Inspector Stone.'

'If that's what you want, sir, I'll go, but, before I do, I would like to leave this with you.'

Tom reached into his pocket and took out the Polaroid photograph which he had found inside Susan Chambers' folded birth certificate. 'I believe that person there,' he said, pointing to the young man on the right of the photograph, 'is you, sir, and that the other man in the photograph is Charles Cope, who is currently a government minister. I don't know the name of the young woman sitting on your knee, but I do know the name of the lady sitting on his knee. She's Susan Chambers.'

Chapter 68

Commander Jenkins picked up the photograph and examined it and, when he spoke again, had regained his composure. 'Are you suggesting that, somehow, I—' he began, and then he corrected himself, pointing at the two men in the photograph: '*we* are responsible for her death?'

'What I'm suggesting, sir, is that Susan Chambers was murdered primarily, but probably not solely, because of this photograph. I don't know who murdered her. I do know, though, why she was murdered, and that evidence was changed, or removed, resulting in an innocent man being wrongly convicted of her murder. That man, Jimmy Griffiths, was later killed by another prison inmate at a time when he should not even have been in prison.'

Commander Jenkins continued to look at the photograph. Eventually he said, 'Who else knows about all of this?'

'So far, sir, just you and me.'

Tom thought he detected the slightest hint of relief in his facial expression, and certainly Commander Jenkins was calm and composed when he next spoke. 'You mentioned other evidence. What evidence is that?'

So Tom told him how the note he'd inadvertently received, announcing Jimmy Griffiths' death, had initially grabbed his interest. It was, though, the reference to Pete Duffy's witness statement, and its absence from the file, which had really puzzled him. He also mentioned some of the other unexplained anomalies relating to the case: for example, the lack of Griffiths' fingerprints on the drawers and cupboards, suggesting that they had been emptied by someone else. From then on it was just a case of following up on all of the leads. Nothing particularly exceptional, just good old-fashioned police work, helped along the way by the odd bit of luck.

CCTV footage proved that Griffiths could not have murdered Susan Chambers as he was with Dale Thompson, in

Perivale, at the time of her death. So, if not Griffiths, the key questions then were 'who?' and 'why?' As is so often the case, it was the answer to the second question which provided the clue to answering the first one.

'How did you know it was me in the photograph?' asked Commander Jenkins, for the first time admitting it was him.

'When I first saw the photograph I knew something was familiar, but couldn't work out what it was. So I had the photograph blown up, and then I spotted it. It was your ring, sir.' He nodded in the direction of Commander Jenkins' right hand, where, on his little finger, he was wearing a ring with a jet-black stone. 'I remember noticing it as you shook my hand, when you first offered me the position of Acting Superintendent. The other man in the photograph is wearing an identical ring. It's quite distinctive. A black onyx stone set in a gold clasp and gold ring. It also has the inscription *Natus est ducere* on it. My Latin is a bit rusty, but I believe it means "born to serve".'

'Actually,' Commander Jenkins said, 'the correct translation is "born to lead".'

Tom, ignoring his correction, continued. 'But, of course, you and Mr Cope are not the only people who wear the ring, are you? I did some research, and it seems quite a few of your Oxford University contemporaries also wear the ring. Quite a select group, actually. Did wearing the ring mean that you had gained entry into some sort of secret sect? Or does it represent a code of honour, or trust, or was it simply meant to symbolise all of your destinies?' Before Commander Jenkins could answer, Tom added, 'Virtually all of you now hold high positions in what some people might call "the Establishment".'

'I suppose that's the benefit of a good education,' he said.

'With respect, sir, it doesn't seem very intelligent now,' Tom replied. 'If it was just down to some sort of youthful exuberance then I could possibly understand that, but this is more than that, isn't it?'

Tom, not giving Commander Jenkins the opportunity to respond, carried on, although this time with increased emotion in his voice. 'I think that the word is *hubris*, isn't it? An assumption on all of your parts that, simply due to your privileged backgrounds, you somehow have a right not just to lead but also, when it suits you, to be above the law. That's the part which I am struggling to understand and accept.'

Commander Jenkins, having waited until Tom had finished his little outburst, said in a surprisingly calm tone, 'I wouldn't expect you to understand,' before attempting to provide his own explanation. 'Yes, we were all very fortunate to be born into varying degrees of privilege. But that is hardly our fault. Instead, we saw it as our duty to use that privilege for the benefit of our country. That was, and remains, our overriding objective and, if it meant occasionally having to do things which some people might find unacceptable, then that was the price we were willing to pay.'

Tom, slightly regretting his earlier emotional outburst, was determined to stick to the facts. 'Then there's the question of Susan's baby,' he said.

'What baby?' asked Commander Jenkins, sounding genuinely surprised.

'Susan gave birth to a son, Peter, in February 1986. If you are interested I have a copy of his birth certificate. Peter was taken into care, shortly after he was born, as it was judged that Susan couldn't look after him. I don't know who the father is, but it's not beyond the bounds of possibility that you or some of your "born to lead" friends might. Anyway, DNA analysis would soon confirm who the father might be.'

Commander Jenkins remained silent for a while before he next spoke. 'So, what do you propose to do with your evidence?'

'That really depends upon you, sir. My inclination is to go public with all of this. I am, though, willing to hear what you have to say first. If you don't have anything to say, then I'll take that as a sign that you are happy for me to go public.'

Commander Jenkins looked directly at Tom, and, with a steely stare, simply said, 'You do know that this will ruin you, don't you? Let's see if your previous fifteen minutes of fame save you then. You are completely out of your depth with this. As you quite rightly say, I have some powerful friends. Do you think they are going to stand aside and let you, someone who is well-known for his paranoia, destroy the lives and careers of people who are doing their damndest to protect our country? For your information, Charles Cope,' he said, pointing to the other man in the photograph, 'is currently involved in an operation which directly affects the security of this country. Are you really willing to set that against the death of a drug-using prostitute?'

'You seem to have forgotten that Jimmy Griffiths also died as a result of this.'

'Don't get on your righteous high horse with me,' he answered, his anger suddenly rising. 'This is the real world. My strong advice to you, Detective Chief Inspector Stone, is to forget all about this and concentrate on what you know best: putting away people like James Grace.'

Tom was determined to get as much information as possible from him and so, ignoring his threat, calmly said, 'Why did Susan have to die? Surely one middle-aged woman with a record of drug use and drug dealing, as well as prostitution, was no threat to you. Particularly, as you say, with such a powerful group of friends.'

Commander Jenkins' earlier anger had, once again, disappeared and he was calm when he answered. 'She was trying to blackmail Charles. Admittedly, not very sophisticated blackmail, but effective enough to, potentially, inflict major damage. I don't know whether you are aware, but this country is currently fighting a war. Not a conventional war, but a war nonetheless, and Charles is at the forefront of that war. She must have recognised him when he was on television. He received a letter from her demanding money. She claimed she had a photograph showing them together. I didn't even know someone took that photograph until you showed it to me.' He paused. 'We had a strict rule. No photographs,' he added ruefully. 'Although it was a long time ago, a future government minister consorting with a known prostitute would not have looked good, even in these supposedly more enlightened times.' He continued, 'She also hinted that she knew something else about him, which could be even more damaging for him. Anyway, it was then he contacted me and ... well, let's just say a mutual friend, and asked us if we could handle it.'

'So she was given money but then came back for more. Was that it?' asked Tom.

'As all blackmailers do. My strong advice was to ignore her. Let's face it, there was enough going on in her life to totally discredit her and portray her as some sort of fantasist. It might have been a bit uncomfortable, for a while, but politicians have survived worse. But that wasn't the consensus view. Someone – and I genuinely don't know who – broke into her house to see if they could find the photograph. Unfortunately, she returned unexpectedly and disturbed him. He tried to get out but she came at him and so he tried to push her away. She fell and must have banged her head, and that was how she ended up dead. A short while later I took a call from a friend and he asked if there was anything I could do.'

'You mean to cover up the crime?' asked Tom rhetorically. 'So you decided to remove important witness statements from the file and allow an innocent man to be charged instead. Is that it?'

'I've explained already how the alternative was totally unacceptable,' replied Commander Jenkins. 'With Superintendent Peters no longer around – thanks to your efforts – all we had to do was to remove anything which might distract the investigation from Griffiths.'

'But no one legislated for a typical police bureaucratic cock-up, did they?' said Tom. 'If Superintendent Peters' name had been removed from the distribution list then none of this would have come to the surface and I wouldn't be here today.'

'What's done is done,' replied Commander Jenkins, before adding, 'and, anyway, I'm not sure it has come to the surface yet. All we can do now is try and control what happens in the future.'

'And what is that future, sir?' asked Tom, slightly unnerved by Commander Jenkins' slightly phlegmatic tone.

'That rather depends on you, Detective Chief Inspector Stone,' he replied, before repeating his answer, just in case Tom hadn't got the message. 'That rather depends on you.'

Chapter 69

After his meeting with Commander Jenkins, Tom had first returned to meet the same person he'd met earlier in the day. Derek Johnson was an old colleague of his and they had worked together a few times during their respective careers. Although Derek was a civvy, he had assisted the police on many occasions and was considered by one and all to be a bit of a telecommunications genius. It had been Derek who had, that morning, provided Tom with the small recording device which he'd placed just inside his jacket. Derek had known, from long experience, not to ask why he needed it, whilst Tom, of course, was not about to tell him. He'd returned to see Derek again because he wanted him to make a copy of the recording.

Afterwards he'd returned to the station and placed one of the tapes in his original file and the other one with the file copy he had made the previous night. This second file he now put into an oversized envelope and secured with brown tape. He sat back, took a sip of his coffee, and wondered how all of this would end. One thing he knew for certain was that he would never again be offered the opportunity of promotion by Commander Jenkins. More immediately, however, he was just about to have another difficult meeting. Almost on cue, his intercom buzzer sounded.

'DS Milner is here now, sir,' said Jenny.

'Ask him to come straight in,' he answered.

'You wanted to see me, sir,' said Milner, as he entered Tom's office.

'Yes, come in and take a seat.'

Tom thought he saw a slightly puzzled expression fleetingly appear on Milner's face.

'Is it about the Grace case, sir?' asked Milner, still slightly taken aback by DCI Stone's unusual degree of civility. 'Everything is in hand there.'

'Not this time,' he replied. 'There's something else I'd like you to do for me. It's partly professional and partly personal.'

'What is it, sir?' asked a now-intrigued Milner.

Tom stood up and walked towards his desk. He picked up the large envelope and placed it on the table, in front of Milner.

'Let me first make it clear that I will perfectly understand if you decide that you don't want to get involved.' He then added, almost as an afterthought, 'And, frankly, I wouldn't blame you if you did.' He continued, 'I've been working on another case over the past few weeks, and the background to the case, everything I've found out, the evidence I've accumulated and the people involved are all contained in this envelope. I have the original. This is a copy and I'd like you to keep hold of it as a contingency.'

'Contingency, sir?' repeated Milner. 'Are you saying in case something happens to you?'

'Yes, I suppose I am,' answered Tom, just a little too nonchalantly for Milner's liking, given what he had just been told. 'Not that I'm expecting any such thing to happen, of course, but you never know.'

'Are you able to tell me what it's all about?' asked Milner, not unreasonably.

'Please don't take this personally, but I'd rather not. It's better if you know as little as possible, then, if the worst comes to the worst, you can truthfully say that I simply asked you to look after something.'

'Sir,' said Milner, now clearly very concerned. 'What is it you specifically want me to do with it if ... well, if anything does happen to you?'

Tom handed Milner a small piece of paper. 'This is the name of an MP. I don't know him personally, but I understand he is not afraid to take on vested interests. I would like you to send it to him. You don't need to say it was from you. All you have to do is make sure he gets it.'

Milner looked at the name written down. 'Are you sure you don't need any help? You know that I'm more than happy to help.'

'I know you are, Milner, but not this time. Anyway, you've now got Jenny to think about.'

Milner blushed slightly. 'Yes, she told me that you knew

about us. Incidentally, when did you suspect? We thought we'd hidden it really well.'

'Milner. It's virtually impossible to keep any office romance secret. Let's just say there were small, tell-tale signs. Anyway, I'm pleased for you. For both of you, actually. Jenny seems to be a very nice young lady.'

This seemed to ease the earlier tension. 'Thank you, sir. It's early days but we both seem to like each other.'

'Enough to turn down the Brighton job?' he asked.

'I've already done that, sir. Jenny mentioned your little chat, and your advice about trusting my instincts. Even though my head was telling me to accept it, something deep inside was saying the opposite. Anyway, I'm afraid that you are stuck with me for a while longer yet.'

Tom, for a fleeting moment, was tempted to shake Milner's hand but resisted the impulse. Instead he picked up the envelope. 'So, what do you want to do?'

Milner took the envelope from Tom. 'Of course I'll do it, sir. Anyway, I'm sure I'll be handing it back to you soon.'

Chapter 70

Tom was now back at home. Commander Jenkins had asked if he could hold off taking any action for twenty-four hours. This, he said, would give him time to consult with his colleagues. Whilst this went against Tom's better judgement, especially as he realised there was potentially an inherent danger in any delay, he had reluctantly agreed to his request. Up to the moment when he'd been confronted with the evidence, Commander Jenkins had treated Tom with nothing but courtesy and respect on every occasion they had met. Nonetheless, sitting at his kitchen table, Tom couldn't help thinking that agreeing had, perhaps, been a mistake. Anyway, he'd done it and so, now, only time would tell if he'd made the correct decision.

He was just thinking about phoning Mary when his mobile started to ring. Wondering if there was some form of telepathy between the two of them, he picked it up. It wasn't Mary.

'This is Commander Jenkins,' the now-recognisable voice said. 'I'd like to meet with you as soon as possible.'

'How soon?' asked Tom, now trying to regain his focus.

'Tonight, ideally, but not at the station. How about we meet at your house?'

There was a silence as Tom considered the implications of what he was asking for. It was not surprising that he wanted to meet again. After all, that had been the purpose of the delay. Equally, the speed and urgency of the meeting should not have surprised him, given the seriousness of Tom's allegations. Nonetheless, he couldn't help feeling slightly uneasy about the request.

'Yes, if that's what you want,' he replied. 'When are you proposing to be here?'

'I'll be with you in less than an hour,' he replied curtly, bringing an end to their conversation.

There was not a lot Tom could do, in terms of preparation,

before Commander Jenkins arrived, other than to, once again, mentally review all of the evidence he had accumulated. He suspected, though, that the situation had now moved beyond the allegations stage.

It was just under an hour later when his doorbell rang and, when he opened the door, there were two men standing outside. Alongside Commander Jenkins was another man, of similar age, who Tom instantly recognised.

'May we come in?' asked Commander Jenkins.

Tom didn't reply. He simply turned around and led them into the kitchen. With all three standing, the kitchen suddenly seemed very small.

It was Commander Jenkins who spoke again. 'Let me introduce Charles Cope.'

Tom could see that Charles Cope was wearing a gold ring, which also featured the black onyx stone. He'd found over the years that, in such situations, attack definitely was the best form of defence. 'You'll excuse me if I don't offer you anything to drink.'

Before he could continue, Cope suddenly spoke. 'Yes, I think we all know why we are here. Let me be frank with you, Detective Chief Inspector Stone. Even though the photograph which you seem to have acquired was taken thirty years ago, when I was still at university, its publication will still cause me, and the government, considerable embarrassment. Whether that will be sufficient for me to have to resign, or be sacked, I really don't know, although my political enemies, I'm sure, will use it to try and effect one of those options. You might not believe me but, under normal circumstances, I would be willing to accept it. In politics, the saying "you live by the sword, die by the sword" is extremely apt. But these are far from normal circumstances. This country is facing an existential threat. My main role in government is to ensure that none of these threats are converted into action. It wouldn't be too melodramatic to say that the team I have been leading over the past few years has prevented numerous terrorist attacks that would have resulted, potentially, in thousands of UK citizens being murdered. You, Detective Chief Inspector Stone, have it in your hands to decide whether or not that work continues.'

'But it's not just about one photograph, is it?' Tom replied.

'It's about two people being murdered, one directly and the other indirectly, as a result of this photograph. It's about framing an innocent man and,' he said, now looking directly at Commander Jenkins, 'it's also about a very senior police officer tampering with evidence to cover up all of those crimes, in order to protect a senior government minister. Somehow, those actions don't sit comfortably with the values you are espousing.'

There was a brief silence and then Commander Jenkins spoke. 'Sometimes we have to make difficult decisions in the interests of the bigger national picture. On this occasion, it was unfortunate that two people died, but,' he added, 'the alternative would be far, far worse. Next time terrorists murder innocent Brits, perhaps you might like to think about this.'

Tom, declining to respond to Commander Jenkins' homily, instead continued to focus his attention on Charles Cope. 'And then there's Susan's son, Peter. I don't know, Mr Cope, if Peter is your son, but I suspect there's a good chance that he is.'

'My son?' he repeated with genuine surprise.

'Didn't you know that you might have a son?' asked Tom. 'Susan gave birth on the fifteenth of February, 1986. Not long after his birth he was placed into care.'

Cope looked at Commander Jenkins. 'Did you know about this?'

'It's mere speculation on Stone's part, that's all,' he answered dismissively.

But Cope didn't seem quite so dismissive. 'How do you know he's my son?'

'As I said, I don't for certain,' said Tom. 'But there's one way to find out. DNA analysis will confirm it, one way or another.'

Another period of silence followed before Cope responded. 'Do you know where he is?'

'I do,' replied Tom.

'I thought she'd had an abortion,' he suddenly said. 'My father had given her money to have one. Perhaps she just kept the money.'

Commander Jenkins suddenly interjected. 'Charles, let's stay focused on the issue at hand.' He turned towards Tom and said, 'We understand the difficult position you have now found yourself in. In many ways, it's a credit to the force that you were able to work this out simply because of one missing statement. I am, therefore, willing to make you an offer, but only if you agree to certain conditions. I'm giving you the opportunity to take early retirement at a time of your choosing. If you agree to this, your retirement and pension package will be based on the salary of a full superintendent. Of course, in return, we would need you to hand over all of the information you have collected. We would also ask you to sign a declaration confirming that you will never speak about anything connected with these events again.'

'It's interesting, sir, that only yesterday, you described me as a loose cannon, whereas today I seem to have become a credit to the force.'

For a moment there was a real danger that Commander Jenkins would lose his self-control. Perhaps realising this, Charles Cope stepped in. 'Occasionally we all say things, in the heat of the moment, which we later regret. I know I certainly have. Anyway, please consider what Commander Jenkins has suggested.'

'And what if I don't agree?' Tom asked.

'I'm afraid matters will then be taken out of my hands,' Cope answered in a subdued tone.

Chapter 71

It was the following evening and Tom was on his way home. He'd spent most of the day in his office at the station, working through the ever-increasing pile of reports that had accumulated over the course of the past week. Under normal circumstances this wasn't a task he would have looked forward to. But these were not normal circumstances, and so, in his need to take his mind off the events of the previous night, he had actually been grateful that they were still there waiting for his attention.

He had also met with Milner and DC Bennett in order to review all of the notes and evidence relating to the murder of Bogdan Inanescu and the subsequent arrests of Terry Birkett, Brendan Grace and James Grace. Over the past day or so the case against James Grace had, if anything, got stronger as new evidence emerged. The fraud team had already carried out an interim investigation into James Grace's business interests and were confident that, even with the evidence they currently had, there was more than enough to secure a conviction. Dave Clare's UK border team had also been busy preparing their own case against Grace. In addition, the Spanish crime and fraud authorities had now begun to look very closely into all of Grace's business and private affairs during his time there. Given the information that Johnny Taylor had provided them with, it was almost certain that their investigation would be equally successful. If James Grace's objective had been to develop some sort of family dynasty based upon the proceeds of crime, then Tom was now sure that it was all about to come crashing down.

Afterwards, when they were alone, Milner, unsurprisingly after their previous discussion concerning the envelope Tom had given him, had asked if Tom was okay. Although he didn't actually mention the envelope they both knew to what he was referring.

For a moment Tom had been tempted to tell Milner the full story and especially about last night's visit from Commander Jenkins and Charles Cope. Normally, he had little difficulty in keeping things to himself. He had never been the type of person who had to share all of his inner thoughts and feelings with other people, and he was conscious of the fact that this was a large part of the problem he had always had when it came to personal relationships. No doubt a psychologist would tell him that this was hardwired into his personality or due to some long-forgotten childhood incident. Whatever the reason, he had long come to terms with it and was unlikely to start changing his behaviour now. For some reason, though, this time, he did feel that he would have liked to share all of his concerns with someone else. Perhaps it was the increasing stress he was now feeling and he simply wanted to unburden himself of some of it by sharing it with another person. Mary, of course, would be the most obvious person, but she had not been around and, anyway, his logic for not confiding in her was that a problem shared might turn out to be a problem doubled. The other possibility was Milner, and that was why he had considered telling him the full story. That, though, he knew, would not be fair on Milner. Tom had, to some extent, already involved him by giving him the envelope containing the copy of his report, but that had been a calculated and pragmatic risk. Anything else could multiply that risk significantly. So Tom would continue to keep all of it to himself, even though the time was fast approaching when he would have to do something more proactive with all of the evidence he had now gathered.

In the meantime, at least he had Mary's return to look forward to. He had received a text from her, earlier in the day, to say she should be home sometime in the late afternoon and, this evening, would then come over to his place to see him. Although he knew that it had been the correct decision for her to stay with her son whilst Grace was making his threats, he had, nonetheless, missed her and the week, but especially the nights, had seemed very long.

He hadn't been home long when his mobile rang. Once again, hoping that it might be Mary, he picked it up in some anticipation but, again like previously, he was disappointed to see that it wasn't her. His surprise, however, soon matched his disappointment when he recognised who it was.

'I hope you don't mind me calling,' said Charles Cope. 'I know that yesterday's meeting was very difficult, but I wanted to speak with you privately about one of the things we discussed.'

Tom suspected he knew what that was, and Cope soon confirmed this. 'It's concerning the baby that Susan had. I've been thinking about this ever since you mentioned it. How sure are you that the baby was mine?'

'When I told you yesterday, I didn't know for sure. But, after what you said about paying for an abortion, I now think that there's a very strong likelihood that you are the father.'

'That's what I thought, as well,' he answered, albeit in a fairly subdued tone.

'Peter was born on the fifteenth of February, 1986,' explained Tom. 'If, as you say, she was pregnant when your father gave her money, then it would have been impossible for her to have the abortion, get pregnant again and then give birth just a short while later. Of course, it all depends on how many months she was pregnant when she received the money. I guess only you and your father know that.'

'Actually, only me,' he replied. 'My father died about ten years ago.' There was a very brief pause before he continued. 'I've checked the dates and, theoretically, at least, I could be the father.'

'DNA would confirm that one way or another,' suggested Tom. 'Although that, of course, would depend on Peter agreeing to his own test. He might not want to do that. After all, thirty years is a long time.'

'Yes, I understand that,' he replied, before adding, 'Would you be willing to provide me with his contact details?'

Tom hadn't expected this and was momentarily drawn between keeping this purely professional and, potentially, helping a father and son to be reunited. But only momentarily.

'I'm not sure that would be a wise decision, given the serious nature of everything we discussed yesterday. Anyway, I'm sure you have the resources to find that out for yourself.'

'Yes, I can see your point,' he answered. 'Thank you anyway for your help, and I hope that things work out well for you.'

As Tom reflected on their conversation he suddenly found it quite strange how he had begun to feel almost sorry for Cope. Here was a man who, at the very least, was complicit in the death of an innocent person and its subsequent cover-up. Yet, despite this, he couldn't help feeling some sympathy for him. Perhaps it was because their conversation had reminded him of his relationship – or the lack of any relationship – with his own son, Paul.

Chapter 72

A short while later his doorbell rang. He opened the door. It was Mary.

He moved towards her and kissed her. He immediately realised that his pleasure at seeing her again was not reflected in her embrace. He also spotted that she didn't have her usual overnight bag.

'Is everything okay?' he asked, suddenly concerned.

'Can I come in?' she asked.

'Of course you can come in,' he answered, slightly crossly. 'What is it?'

'Let's go inside,' she said.

In silence they walked through into the kitchen.

'Tom. This is not easy for me to say and, believe me, I have thought of nothing else for the past few days, but I think we should stop seeing one another,' she said, in an almost matter-of-fact manner. It was only when Tom noticed how she was trying hard to control her emotions that he suspected that it wasn't quite as it had appeared.

'Has something happened?' he asked, still trying to comprehend what she had just said. 'Have you found someone else?'

She suddenly began to laugh, although it was more a laugh of contempt.

'Why is it that men always assume that there must be someone else involved? Of course there is no one else. I love you. You know I do, but I can't go on living like this.' She began to sob.

'Sorry,' said Tom, starting to move towards her.

'Don't,' she said, holding out her right palm.

'What can I do?' asked Tom, now upset himself to see her crying.

'I think it's too late,' she answered, after she had stopped crying. 'Being away this week has allowed me to think about our relationship. I can't see a future for us together, Tom. I really can't. Your work will always be between us. I'm not blaming you. The job you do is always going to put pressure on any relationship. I knew that when we met ... well, I thought I knew. But this last couple of weeks has shown me just how much pressure. We can't plan to do anything together with any certainty. On top of all of that I worry about you all of the time. I know that I shouldn't, but I can't help it. This business with Grace was the tipping point.' She began to sob again, quietly.

Tom moved towards her again, but this time he wasn't about to be pushed away. As he held her close he could feel her rhythmic sobs pulsing throughout her body. After a while, he gently pulled away from her and, taking hold of her hands, said, 'What if I retire from the force? Then we can spend as much time together as we want.'

She looked at him. 'But you don't really want that, do you? After a few months you'll start to get bored and blame me. I don't want our relationship to end in bitterness and blame.'

'But you would rather it ended like this, would you?' he asked. 'Even though we both still love each other.'

'I don't know. I'm not sure what I want any more,' she answered. 'I think it's best if I go now.' She pulled away from him and walked towards the front door. 'I hope you know how much I love you,' she said before walking towards her car.

Tom was numb and spent the next hour trying to remember everything that Mary had said, looking for any gesture, or words, which would still give him hope. His spirits were raised when the doorbell rang again and he got to his feet, hoping desperately that Mary had decided to return. He opened the door, but it was not Mary. Instead it was a man who immediately pointed a gun at Tom and shot him.

Lightning Source UK Ltd.
Milton Keynes UK
UKOW04f1533150615

253529UK00001B/9/P